cus

THE POISONED STREAM

Contents

Corrupt are they, and have done
abominable iniquity: there is
none that doeth good.

Psalms, 53, i

The Speakers

EMILIO BOSSI   31, *reporter*

AURELIO MORELLI   58, *murderer*

FRANCESCO VANETTI   23, *Press photographer*

CARLO VANETTI   54, *magazine proprietor*

ANTONIO ZEMPACH   36, *attorney*

CHRISTA SONNTAG   26, *call-girl*

OSKAR ENZIAN   59, *butcher*

ITALO CANONICA   62, *C.I.D. Superintendent*

CHAPTER

1

The Youth-killer

Emilio Bossi, 31, *reporter*

I could have hanged him on Sunday but I didn't want to spoil his Sabbath.

Instead of going to Morelli's execution I called on Vanetti, uninvited.

I'd never seen the inside of his house before. Vanetti thinks it's infra dig. to mix with his reporters socially. He keeps his distance. His villa in Parioli keeps its distance too. There are ancestral portraits in the drawing-room. Not his ancestors, of course.

It was early still, but Vanetti already had his high-buttoned black suit on, like a superannuated priest. Stiff white collar. Celluloid sans celibacy, deviousness with dignity.

I said, "I've got the man who murdered Hertha Enzian."

He almost fell off his Renaissance chair. It may have been a baroque chair. Anyway, it looked uncomfortable.

"How did you find him?" he asked.

"Reporter's luck," I said.

Vanetti rates good luck a virtue and bad luck a crime. In his book an unlucky reporter ought to be fired on the spot. I really wanted to say: it was luck, *basta*, but I went into details all the same.

My sister Fiorella, twenty, had been at a 'happening' two weeks earlier. They were demolishing a house in the Via Cesare Beccaria. The owner of the house had turned it over to the hippies instead of the bulldozers. Fiorella plays the hippie at my expense. They tore the place to bits in two minutes flat: a happening, Q.E.D. While it was in progress an elderly gentleman attached himself to her, a monkey-gland hippie. He offered

11

to take her home in a taxi. On the way he tried to strangle her. Didn't even give her time to say no. Pretty stupid of him, really, with the driver sitting in front. She told me all about it next day.

Vanetti said, "Well?"

"Fiorella's description," I said. "About sixty, lean, glasses, intellectual-looking. It was the eyebrows, mainly. Bushy eyebrows meeting in a line above the bridge of his nose, like the peak of a baseball cap, only made of hair. Just the way they described the suspect to me at the scene of the crime. He introduced himself to Fiorella. I was a bit pessimistic at first because murderers don't usually give their real names. The name tallied: Aurelio Morelli, author."

"Never heard of him," Vanetti said, as if he knew every author in existence. He only reads the authors he publishes.

Hertha Enzian had told the Contessa that "a writer" was after her, an old man, and an assistant in the shoe-shop on the corner of Via Sicilia remembered seeing someone with "a bird's nest" over his eyes. A completely motiveless murder, like the attack on Fiorella.

"Evidence," said Vanetti.

Evidence? I wasn't there when the Enzian girl was strangled. I could have photographed Morelli and flashed his picture around, but that would have alerted the police. Why should I do their job for them? They were sure it was a pimp at first. It always has to be a pimp when a call-girl gets murdered. There are too many sophisticated criminals and too many unsophisticated policemen. Now they're gunning for a film-producer because there are plenty of elderly film-producers. Elderly pimps are at a premium.

Vanetti said, "Of course you're going to turn him in."

He knew full well I wasn't there just to parade my principles. A man of principle would have waited until Monday. You can accuse Vanetti of anything except an inability to catch on fast. He wanted to hear my plan straight from the horse's mouth.

He had misgivings, though. He sat there under one of his ancestral portraits and had a moral bilious attack.

Vanetti employs other people to do the dirty work. Immorality costs money. "I could go to any number of magazines," I said.

"You couldn't," he said.

I named a fee, a thoroughly immoral one. You get fired for

bad luck. Good luck has to be rewarded. "A percentage of the world rights as well, of course," I said.

"What if they arrest him first?" said Vanetti.

"Not to worry," I said. "No reason why you shouldn't commission an author to write his memoirs."

"You commission him," he said.

"You're paying," I said. "We'll go fifty-fifty on the film rights." It was an erotic pleasure to haggle with Vanetti.

"Sixty-forty," he said. "I'll foot the expenses."

"As soon as we get our hands on the manuscript we'll turn him in," I said.

"You turn him in," said Vanetti. He went to school with Pontius Pilate.

"If the police confiscate the memoirs too soon we won't know what's in them," I said. "We'll be absolutely amazed."

"Absolutely," said Vanetti.

We argued terms for a while longer. And expenses. Vanetti always economizes in the wrong place.

He showed me out like a Father Superior seeing a visitor off the precincts. He never even gets up from his desk at the office. I don't know which impressed him more—that I'd found the murderer or that I wanted a percentage.

Three P.M. Monday I drove to Morelli's. It was raining. Perfect atmosphere. Almost too perfect, like the sort of cheap reporting where everything fits.

Morelli lives on the outskirts of town. One of those super housing estates built by the Duce. They already look as old as Pompeii. The marble bell-plate was the only luxurious thing about the house, like a showy tombstone in a poverty-stricken Sicilian village. *Dott. Aurelio Morelli.* A university graduate, no less. Perfect qualifications for a call-girl killer.

I'd been watching him for a fortnight, but I was surprised even so. Born on the 8th of August, 1909. A Leo. We might make something out of the astrological angle. I checked, being keen on accuracy. Fiorella put him at sixty, but that was understandable. At a happening anyone over twenty looks like sixty. He doesn't strike you as somebody with a yen to kill call-girls. Emaciated elegance. You can never tell whether an intellectual is starving his way up the ladder of success or down. Greying temples, lofty brow, beaky nose, rimless glasses like twin monocles. The eyebrows merged into a single line which sliced across his head. A bar sinister.

"Emilio Bossi, representing *Quest' Ora,*" I said.

"I don't read magazines," he said.

That was stupid. There were at least six *Playboys* lying on his table—vintage numbers, but breasts never depreciate. Morelli wasn't the man to miss a pair of tits if he could help it.

Two rooms. Garden furniture in the living-room, mainly bamboo. Even a deck-chair with green, white, and red stripes, comfort with patriotism. Against the wall an outsize aquarium full of tiny little fish gobbling water.

"Signor Morelli," I said politely, "I'm here because we know you murdered Hertha Enzian."

"I know no one of that name," he said.

He deserved to be strung up just for that. I was reminded of the railway murderer who when arrested said, "It can't be me, I didn't have a ticket." The papers have been featuring Hertha Enzian every day for the past two months. Even Vietnam runs a poor second to her. An innocent man says, "I haven't murdered anybody"; he doesn't get down to cases. Plenty of people knew the Enzian girl. She was a walking 'phone-book. Only one man murdered her.

"I resent this intrusion," he said, a bit late in the day.

"I'm not from the police," I said. "I'm Santa Claus in disguise."

I didn't explain the bit about Santa Claus straight away. I had to convince him that he was hooked.

I'm all for candour. Even a lie sounds like the truth when you're candid. That's the best thing about candour.

I started with Fiorella, candid as all get out. Criminals are unlucky, hence superstitious. If a bus drives off under their nose it reminds them that their luck could be even worse. I wanted Morelli to feel he'd been unlucky.

The more detailed a lie the more it sounds like the truth. "I photographed you outside the Cinema Royale last Wednesday," I said. He really had been there, seeing *Blow-up.* "Hertha's neighbours recognized you. You ought to have your eyebrows shaved." I gave him some more friendly advice, like next time wear rubber gloves. "I grant you the homicide squad are on the wrong track," I said, all sweetness and light, "but it's their duty to follow up any information received. I only need to say 'Aurelio Morelli' and they'll check your prints. You weren't very careful, even the opposition would admit that. The odds against two people having the same fingerprints are sixty-four thousand million to one. You squeezed nice and hard, Dottore."

He tried to hide his hands, like a child with inky fingers. Small hands, but quite muscular. He comes of peasant stock, at least on his mother's side. His mother is eighty. I'll interview her in due course.

"Why don't you denounce me?" he asked. "Were everyone in this sodomitical society of ours to neglect his civic duty . . ."

I don't know what sodomitical means. Something to do with buggery, I suppose. He talked affectedly, like a lot of authors who are scared to speak differently from the way they write. "Don't try and teach me my civic duty," I said.

"I have no money," he said.

"I'm not a blackmailer, I'm Santa Claus," I reminded him. "You're going to write your memoirs for *Quest' Ora*. Every last detail. I'll give you a hand."

He said, "Once my memoirs are down on paper you'll denounce me."

"Think straight," I said. "If we denounce you we'll be admitting that we've neglected our civic duty. You'll get a ticket to anywhere you like."

"What about Interpol?" he said.

I was a bit surprised that he caved in so quickly. Maybe he thought he had nothing to lose, or that he could deny it all later. Or maybe he was the sort of man who murders with confession in mind.

"Not every country has an extradition treaty with Italy," I said. "Anyway, they'd have to find you first. You can get your nose bobbed. Think of all the Nazi war criminals they've never found."

That comforted him, but he said, "If you publish my memoirs people will know that you had prior knowledge."

"We didn't buy them until you were over the hills and far away," I said.

"The neighbours will go to the police," he said. "They'll tell them that you photographed me."

"I fixed that," I lied. "You're an expensive investment."

15

THE POISONED STREAM

He was standing by the window, looking out.

I thought him the least likeable murderer I'd ever handled. He didn't look sadistic or sick. More like a professor of anatomy who prefers vivisection. Intellectual arrogance survives everything, even a strangled call-girl. I got the impression he was counting raindrops. My mistake. He swung round and said, "Three million."

I don't know what made me save money for Vanetti, but I said, "Two million plus expenses. You'll have to go to the country so you can work in peace. There are too many policemen wandering round Rome."

"What about my nose?" he said.

"Book it to expenses," I said.

"My memoirs will be worthless without a name," he said. "All anonymous newspaper stories are fictitious."

The man was getting above himself. As soon as people start writing their memoirs they feel like fellow-journalists.

"Your name won't be mentioned," I said. "You underestimate the public. The public don't need names, they've got an unerring instinct for the truth." I borrowed that from Vanetti. "The only people who might be interested in knowing that Aurelio Morelli is the murderer are the dailies. Our readers want to learn things. They'll want to know why you murdered the Enzian girl. For instance, you might be insane."

"Only murderers are normal," he said.

"The more psychology the better," I said. "*Quest' Ora, the Magazine for the Discerning Reader.* You probably hated your mother."

"I love my mother," he said.

"Never mind," I said, "our readers will want to know what sort of person you are, how you got to know the Enzian girl, what sort of person she was. People are wondering why Christa Sonntag didn't hear anything—the girl next door. Don't skimp details. We can always cut anything unsuitable for juveniles."

"No part of my manuscript will be changed," he said. "Not even Feltrinelli would dare to delete a single line of mine."

That proved he was a writer. First, none of them wants to cut a line, then they cut whole chapters. Virginity only lasts till it reaches the typesetters.

"We're planning on fifteen instalments of roughly eighteen

16

pages each," I said. "You're welcome to use up four instalments on the murder. Thirty characters per line, thirty lines per page. We're paying you like Hemingway."

"I write by hand," he said huffily.

He was standing beside the aquarium now, gloating over his fish like the old Prince of Monaco.

"I shall take my aquarium with me," he said.

Why not? As camouflage. Who ever heard of a murderer travelling with an aquarium? *The fish went too* will make a nice subheading.

"Your gutter-press style is utterly beyond me," he said. "I was awarded my doctorate for a thesis on ostracism."

"Ostracism schmostracism," I said. "Just write whatever comes into your head."

I was quite flattered by the gutter-press bit. He must have read some of my stories. I've never read anything of his. You're always one up on an author if you haven't read any of his stuff.

"When do I get my two million?" he asked, looking lecherous for the first time.

"Three equal instalments," I said.

"Fare and expenses?" he said.

"Nose as well," I said, generously.

That settled it.

"I shall take my aquarium," he repeated.

The fish were delighted. They seem quite fond of him.

Aurelio Morelli, 58, *murderer*

I cannot, in all conscience, pretend that my desires are fulfilled, my mental processes stimulated, or my creative impulses kindled by the place of residence selected for me by the young reporter who calls himself Emilio Bossi, the place where I am destined to spend weeks or even months of exile—and oh, how sinister a rôle was ever played by exile in the ancient world, as, for instance, in the cases of Alcibiades, Coriolanus, Aristides, and Themistocles; whether it be that men shrank from passing sentence of death in a simple and dignified fashion, or that they deemed enforced separation from hearth and home to be more lethal than the death penalty!

THE POISONED STREAM

The place is known as Foce Verde, 'green estuary', a designation which suits it to the extent that the Fosso Mascarello discharges its waters into the Mediterranean at this point—though the word 'discharges' does not aptly describe the manner in which the docile little stream debouches into the bosom of the deep, diffidently, as though wearied by long journeying and bereft of the desire to flow farther. As to colour, the eye can discern no vestige of greenness here, or, at most, a green which seems ashamed of its natural gradations. Beyond the bridge across the aforesaid Fosso Mascarello, the broad expanse of sandy shore which borders the small town is dotted with scrub-clad hummocks so closely attuned to the prevailing colour of the sand that shore and vegetation combine to give an impression of apathy, neglect, and shabby *tristesse*. This impression persists despite the gaily-painted bathing-huts which present their zebra-striped posteriors to the main road leading southward, and which now, in any case, it being early October, stand there deserted and forlorn. They are eloquent of the pleasures of the poor, of their flight from diurnal routine, of their short-lived *repos*—for the weekend escapism of the lower middle class seems to me still more jejune than the reality of its workaday existence. Not a single plot of open or unencumbered ground can be seen beside the slightly elevated asphalt road which runs along and above the beach. It is as if houses, villas, apartments, cafés, and shops had thronged seaward, only to be arrested by the road at whose margin they now stand, like beggars denied access to a paradise of uncertain charms.

Albeit that closer acquaintance may enable me to discover a more clement, appealing, or even gladsome prospect, I cannot but doubt it: the omens are unfavourable indeed, for no sooner had I crossed the bridge than I found my attention drawn at once to a motley band of fishermen, insidious fellows who were lying in wait for their innocent prey with a murderous armoury of rod and net. As if that were not enough, the windows of my hotel overlook a stony recreation ground, situated betwixt road and beach but at road-level, where of an evening the local youngsters indulge in a game known as basketball; and when I look out—as I cannot refrain from doing on occasion—I become witness to an irritating and idiotic form of contest in which—in accordance, I presume, with the law of the dangling basket—all

18

the most muscular and overgrown louts of the township participate. Night sees the strident proclamation on the façade of my
hotel—*Pizzeria, Bar, Ristorante, spezialità marinari sempre vive*
—illuminated in green neon letters, and, since my curtains are
anything but opaque, I often awake to find myself lapped in
eerie radiance. Unhappily, the establishment is among those
which boast of being 'open all year round'—and justly so, since
the dining-room, which is adorned with marine murals of the
most execrable kind, serves the leading lights of Foce Verde as a
nightly rendezvous for card-play, gossip, and political chit-chat.
My one solace amid all this uncongeniality is, I suppose, that my
aquarium has withstood the journey relatively unscathed: with
the sad exception of two sea-horses and my beloved *Giganto-
cypris agassizii*, which have evaded exile, I am still accompanied
by my aquatic friends.

I now perceive something more than mere coincidence in the
fact that my thesis, a notable work, should have been devoted to
the subject of ostracism: even as a student of tender years I was
outraged by a plebeian juridical process whereby six thousand
votes—or potsherds, to be more precise—sufficed to banish an
unpopular figure, however innocent, from his native land for
ten years, twenty years, or even life. Taking my ease on the hotel
terrace, I am involuntarily reminded of the noble Themistocles,
who, impaired in mind and body, sojourned on the alien shores
of Persia until released from his torments by the envenomed bull's
blood with which he so understandably engineered his own
demise.

I had no choice. Even though the so-called proof flaunted in
my face by Bossi—a stocky young man not unreminiscent of a
Neapolitan boxer, with a tiny inquisitive nose and hair of a
repulsive sandy hue—amounts to no more than circumstantial
evidence, the quality of the rope that hangs one is of minor
importance: once in bureaucratic hands, that which is termed
circumstantial very soon becomes alchemized into evidence of
the most incriminating kind. Lifelong penal servitude or even
confinement in an asylum would have been my lot—possibly the
latter, since everyone has heard of lawyers who recommend their
clients to feign madness, and there are judges in plenty whose
eagerness to appear progressive and humane prompts them to
pilot an accused man into the haven of insanity.

THE POISONED STREAM

Not that I overrated my chances, nor do I even now. By no means! In the popular fairy-tale *Hansel and Gretel*, which was recorded in writing by the Brothers Grimm but undoubtedly originated in the mind of a sadistic psychopath, the evil witch plies her youthful captives with nourishing tidbits, just as, in general, it is the human custom to lavish especial care on the fattening of beasts for slaughter. Ah yes, Signor Bossi and his unseen employer plan to drive me to the slaughter-house; first, because an account bearing the name of so distinguished an author possesses far more appeal than a purely anonymous story, and, secondly, because the citizen's sense of duty springs to life and craves its sordid pound of flesh as soon as he has lined his pockets sufficiently. Meanwhile, I derive comfort from the 'happy ending' of the grisly fairy-tale, in which righteousness emerges triumphant. I too have secured a respite: *Le temps est un grand maître; il règle bien les choses*. In comparative leisure I can now prepare to steal a march on the evil witch who, with a cunning smirk, feeds me tidbits in my cage. I must further concede that the prospect of committing my recollections to paper—needless to say, not all that I write is destined for the flimsy periodical known as *Quest' Ora*—inspires me with a certain gratification, first, because I am at last able to plead my own cause, and, secondly, because few things are more pleasurable than the remembrance of past achievements: *Forsan et haec olim meminisse iuvabit*.

Past achievements, I said, and I used the plural by design, for the sandy-haired Neapolitan pugilist is not by any means as shrewd as he believes himself to be: Hertha Enzian, the endearing Viennese girl, was not the first or only victim of my righteous indignation. Four years ago, on the eighth day of August, 1963, to be exact, I released the schoolgirl Lucia Chiesa from a worthless and depraved existence. Two years later, on the 8th of August, 1965, I did the same for Vera Pisenti, a peasant-girl. The fact that neither case aroused much attention, and that both were submerged in a morass of local news, is symptomatic of the hierarchical hypocrisy of our society: no claim to general interest is exercised by a high-school student, still less by a girl from the provinces, whereas a lady with a white telephone and tiled bath-room may rest assured of plebeian sympathy. Being of a more democratic temper, I can discern no essential difference between my actions, which ignorance of motive might encourage some people to describe as crimes: the value of human life, in which I cherish at least a subsumptive belief, is unrelated to white telephones.

But I must curb my reveries. True, I shall delineate the gentle deaths of Lucia, Vera, and Hertha with my usual scrupulous attention to detail, heedless of the crude requirements of the baneful magazine, but as ransom I have promised the evil witch an autobiography—the equivalent, in a man of letters, of selling his soul. And, even though I do not intend to begin with the trite phrase "I was born on . . .", I must, I suppose, hark back to the day on which I resolved to stand forth as the avenger of my misjudged, maltreated, and misbegotten generation—as a latter-day Count of Monte Cristo, *pour ainsi dire.*

I feel no guilt, none whatsoever. The whole juridical system— Roman Law, the Code Napoléon, the American Blue Laws, and the rest of the legal scrapheap—reposes on the absurd hypothesis that a murderer should be punished for committing this act or that, whereas he ought in reality to be commended for the acts which he has refrained from committing. Every day, in our every waking moment—not to mention the dreams that haunt our slumbers—we are all of us minded to commit murder, whether it be that a friend betrays us, that a man in a public conveyance appropriates our rightful seat, that a faster driver ruthlessly overtakes us, that a mistress deceives us, that an exasperating queue forms ahead of us in the post-office, that a better conversationalist reduces us to abject silence, that a rival puts our achievements in the shade, or even that a waiter impudently adds the year of his birth to our bill. I know hundreds of young men and women who have deserved death at my hand. Only my humanitarian principles, soft-heartedness, and, possibly, in the case of the men, lack of opportunity and a certain dread of physical violence, impelled me to exercise merciful restraint.

But to return to my autobiography, and the point in time when I first became aware of the feelings which uncomprehending criminologists have categorized as homicidal tendencies.

Of the seven books which I published between the twenty-seventh and forty-fifth years of my life, only the novel *Thou art Alcibiades* found favour with the public at large, yet the critics dealt most appreciatively with one and all, and my modest resources—I am noted for my austere way of life—ultimately permitted me to devote myself at leisure to my *magnum opus*, the novel *Signora Angelotti*. For more than three years I laboured to produce a book which not even my innate modesty dissuades me from comparing with the masterpieces of Dostoievsky. By a quirk of fate—or was it that?—I was summoned to my publisher's office on the very day that marked the fiftieth anniversary of my birth, an uncommonly hot and humid August day which taxed my nervous system to the utmost.

The fact that Signor Bernasconi did not greet me in person impressed me not only as a gross impropriety but also as an evil portent of what lay in store. I was further disheartened by the manner of the secretary who brusquely waved me into a chair in the outer office. This creature, the personal assistant—how personal it was not hard to guess—of Paolo Canova, a young editorial director hitherto unknown to me, not only kept me waiting for a good half-hour, but did so without deigning to glance in my direction, being wholly engrossed in daubing her finger-nails with some species of noxious red fluid. Secretaries are a pestilential evil in that their demeanour, gestures—indeed, tone of voice—constitute a magnified reflection of their employers' moods; but they are doubly irksome when chosen, as in this day and age, less for their ability than for their length of leg, suppleness of hip, and amplitude of breast.

Passons! I at last found myself seated opposite a young man of not more than thirty, a bland-featured individual whose hair hugged his head in a smooth fringe across the brow, but hung in ringlets on his neck. He puffed incessantly at his pipe, wafting an aroma of scorched leather into my face. Had he simply returned, nay, for all I cared, furiously hurled back the manuscript which lay before him in such a tattered, dog-eared bundle—alas for the loving care which I always lavish on my recorded *pensées*! —I might yet—who knows?—have spent a tolerable birthday. Fate decreed otherwise. My inquisitor, cropped in front and hirsute behind, explained with all the inexorable arrogance of youth that "my kind" of literature was "obsolete"; my linguistic resources were "antiquated", devoid of originality, and—"as I myself must surely admit"—totally irrelevant to a novelty-seeking era; my problems were meaningless to the younger reader and possessed only academic interest, though even this was doubtful, since "nobody builds Renaissance churches these days"; I was not only dumb on the subject of sex for six hundred pages, but deaf to the thunder of the modern age and incapable of interpreting it; my heroine, Signora Angelotti, did not get "laid" until—he thumbed through the manuscript—page four hundred and eleven, and then only by her husband; consequently, her grand passion seemed sentimental and ludicrous; like the legendary Rip van Winkle, I had obviously lost touch with the world and did not know what to make of it; finally, so far from being exhorted to fresh endeavours, I was advised to lay aside my literary aspirations, look around for another form of livelihood, possibly a teaching post, resign myself with good grace to the idea that time had passed me by, and yield the stage on which I had played such a "creditable" rôle to other, younger men. In other words, he bade me expire gracefully in a grave of my own digging.

This, however, occurred on the 8th of August, 1959, my fiftieth birthday, in itself a catastrophe which few self-respecting men would survive were not death the sole alternative—death, unloved only because its attainment entails the act of dying.

Having thus taken leave of Signor Canova with the fruit of three years' unremitting toil beneath my arm, I sat down outside the Café Doney in the Via Vittorio Veneto, intending to review my life over a modest glass of grappa. However, what I saw to my horror was not my own life but a visual demonstration of precisely what I had just been told by the complacent manikin with the bland visage.

Evening had descended on the Borghese Gardens, luring the youth of Rome into the streets. Young men in tight trousers strutted to and fro in front of me like ballet dancers who flaunt their testicles or emphasize their genitalia by factitious means. Watching them, I should indeed have been devoid of imagination had I not been reminded of the phallus-parades to which, so rumour hath it, the Tsarina used to summon her guards officers. Great and, in my estimation, unwarranted merriment reigned among the young people; and I thought of my own youth, which had lacked such gaiety, not because the youthful soul was deficient in the ingredients of happiness, but because no morsel of bread, still less a jingling coin, was ever there for the taking, because strictness and discipline imposed iron restraint upon us, because men had yet to devise the atom-bomb whose smoking mushroom, far from threatening humanity as some would have us believe, hovers above it like a tutelary hand which wards off the beginnings of evil, because all are aware that it signifies the *ne plus ultra* of destruction. Voyeurs frequenting the bordellos of Marseilles in olden days would have paid a pretty sum to witness the scene which unfolded before my newly-alerted gaze: the nudity of girls whose *décolletage* barely concealed their nipples, the rampant, upswept hair, reminiscent of fingers groping in lust, the lewd giggling, the moist, inviting eyes, the undulating hips, the shameless embraces, the whole prelude to coition, the whole animal performance in which the street-corner becomes a bed.

In view of subsequent events, to have committed such thoughts to paper would seem—and here I cannot repress a chuckle—to point along the prescribed, predictable, cliché-strewn path which leads to the sex-murder. Ladies and gentlemen, you have a great surprise in store! Even then, on my fiftieth birthday, it became clear to me that if anything turned me into a murderer it would not be my diminishing libido—my 'waning powers', to employ a euphemism favoured by hawkers of patent aphrodisiacs. No, it was the challenge which I read in those youthful eyes, and to which I alone, in this twentieth century of impotence, had been ordained to respond in a befitting manner. Their gaze contained no hint of respect for an ageing man— not even pity for a loss sustained. To them I was not an ageing man who had lost his youth but an old man who had never been young. They could see, all too clearly, that I had never indulged in or enjoyed their freedom, their licentiousness, their brazen candour, their anarchic *joie de vivre*, their bestial emancipation— never comported myself like a urine-sniffing, copulating mongrel of the streets. In none of those pairs of eyes could I read the question: "Who are you?" My identity was immaterial to them; as immaterial, indeed, as are the character, talent, beauty, ugliness, virtues, and vices—even the erstwhile gender—of the dead and gone. They paraded past me as if I were a corpse which someone had neglected to bury; as if I were a ghost, they even omitted to do me the honour of toppling me into the grave with a kick or two.

I looked round in quest of potential allies, and then, as I perceived my coevals and seniors of both sexes—Italian film people, American tourists, ageing men on pleasure bent, rich but wretched libertines beyond number—I was seized with despairing rage. I had sought allies, and I was encompassed by traitors. There they sat, overawed, with a half-admiring, half-timorous smirk on their lips. Some of them were ashamed of their age, others proud of their executioners; some quailed before the stares of the homunculi whom they themselves had conjured from the alembic, while others, abrim with wonder and envy, feasted their eyes on that which had escaped them by reason of their own cowardice; some withered and grew old while others were seduced into ludicrous mimicry.

This, I imagine, was the moment when there awoke in me the decision to kill, a decision which the forensic psychiatrist would never comprehend because he and his kind wallow in the slough of sexuality, whereas they ought more properly—at least in so far as the murderer Aurelio Morelli is concerned—to lift their gaze to the exalted heights of social revolution. Millions forfeited their lives in the Russian Revolution, in the Spanish, Finnish, and Indonesian massacres, yet all these revolutions, counter-revolutions, rebellions, and uprisings dwindle into insignificance when set beside the indispensable revolt of old age against its menacing adversaries. Were each man over forty—for one cannot, in truth, begin too soon—to dispatch three young people to eternity, we should successfully avert a dictatorship compared with which the dictatorships of Hitler, Stalin, Mussolini, and Mao Tse-tung seem but the merest bagatelle.

To assert that I formed a definite plan or pursued my ideas to their logical conclusion on that sultry evening in August would, however, be to incriminate myself unnecessarily and lend gratuitous support to a charge of premeditated murder. Another four years and the most outrageous provocation had to intervene before the girl named Lucia Chiesa received her quietus at my hands.

Francesco Vanetti, 23,
Press photographer

My father is Carlo Vanetti, it's bad enough Carlo Vanetti being my father, I'd rather have a different father, or better still no father at all, if I hadn't had a father I wouldn't have been a sperm, a seed, or I'd have been a wild oat, if I'd been a wild oat I'd have given a woman pleasure, all I gave my mother was pain, or perhaps I didn't, my mother doesn't feel pain, if she did feel pain she'd have killed my father, which would make me the son of a murderess, I'd have no father and love my mother, a murderess.

I am Francesco Vanetti, maybe somebody who isn't Francesco Vanetti would like to be Francesco Vanetti, but then he wouldn't know that Francesco Vanetti isn't ME, that I'm not ME. I'm a Press photographer with my father's magazines, my father owns a lot of magazines, eight or eleven of them, he publishes a financial journal full of fake balance sheets, and a housewives' magazine full of fake recipes, and a children's comic full of Mickey Mouse and Superman, and an illustrated weekly for fools, and a political review for the insane. I'm a Press photographer with the magazine *Quest' Ora* because the worst a Press photographer can do is waste film, I have an eye not a brain, no, I don't have an eye, the camera has an eye, nobody minds if I do waste film because films are allowed for in the fake balance sheet. When I'm not wasting film I fake my own balance sheet by writing poems, nobody sees my poems, nobody sees poets' poems, poets lie together in a mass grave, there's no monument to the unknown poet, poets are put to bed with a shovel.

They don't give me 'big assignments' at *Quest' Ora*, that's what my father calls them, he thinks I'm hurt because I don't get big assignments, he doesn't realize I couldn't care less about big assignments, my father thinks it's impossible to survive without ambition, my father is bursting with ambition, he's got ambition on the lung and a bloodstream clotted with ambition, he'll die of ambitio-thrombosis one day, I get along fine without ambition only no one realizes it, no ambition no thrombosis.

Now I've been given the assignment, not because my father

believes in ME, he believes in Francesco Vanetti, his SON, he doesn't have another son, just a daughter, it riles him that his daughter isn't a son because he can only give this assignment to his SON, his son's name is Vanetti, so he can give him a great big stinking assignment, his SON won't split on him because his name is Francesco Vanetti.

They've sent me to Foce Verde, that's where Aurelio Morelli is, Morelli's a murderer, he mustn't ever find out I'm in Foce Verde, I have to lie low like a sniper, a camera-guerrilla shooting film, he mustn't notice, the photographs are for later on, when my father denounces him, when he's locked up, he will be locked up, for life.

I drive to Foce Verde, along the coast or inland, I take the Alfa Romeo, my own Alfa Romeo, they pay me as if they believe in me, as if they give me big assignments, I'm the son, the S-O-N, and my car has one-sixty-seven h.p. under the bonnet, I'm happy in my car, it does two hundred kilometres an hour, when I'm in my car I'm not Francesco Vanetti, wherever I am ME is not, anyone who is Francesco Vanetti must be somewhere, and ME is nowhere.

I drive to Foce Verde and keep watch, but Morelli doesn't come out of his hotel, the murderer doesn't come out of his hotel, so I walk up and down, up and down, from the bridge to the hotel, from the hotel to the bridge, up and down. There is a bar by the bridge, there isn't a bar by the bridge, there's a bar at the end of the spit of land by the bridge, I go there and sit in the sun, a frozen-pat-of-butter sun, it's autumn, down below the children are fishing and catching nothing, I order Coca-Cola but they only have Pepsi-Cola, Negroes drink Pepsi-Cola, I drink Pepsi-Cola. The children never catch anything, the proprietor says, the sea-water isn't contaminated but the waters of the Fosso Mascarello or the Fiume Astura are, I can't remember which, contaminated by the nuclear power station which lies beyond Foce Verde, the proprietor points it out to me, it's a secret, a white secret six storeys high, it hasn't any windows, it's a blind nuclear power station, a big blind giant. I drink up my Pepsi-Cola and start walking towards the blind nuclear power station, towards the secret. I come across some barbed wire and a notice-board reading *Divieto di eseguire fotografie e rilievi anche a vista* Art.250–250 o. L.P., anybody taking photographs or films will be locked up pursuant to para so-and-so, I lie down in the grass with my cameras, I carry a camera shop round my neck, and it's cold and the grass is damp. If a carabiniere comes I'll be arrested and my cameras confiscated and I'll be a Communist spy, I'd spy for Mao except that Mao wouldn't trust me with a big assignment, no one would believe I was spying for Quest' Ora, they'd think I was spying against NATO, I'd tell them my name and they'd call my father, they'd develop the films and find nothing, not even the murderer, my father would play dumb, maybe he really is spying for Mao, he'd say.

No carabiniere comes, I lie in the grass, thinking, and ME decides to go to the police and denounce Aurelio Morelli, Dottore Aurelio Morelli, murderer and author, he strangled Hertha Enzian on the 8th of August, 1967, in the house on the corner of Via Veneto and Via Sicilia, second floor, flat twenty-one, and I know that I won't go, that I won't denounce Morelli. ME is determined to go, but I don't have any legs, I never did have any legs or they were amputated and I never get anywhere. I wait for the police so I don't have to go to the police, I'll tell the policeman I'm not a spy, I'm Francesco Vanetti, son of Carlo Vanetti, the murderer's accomplice, the murderer is skulking in the Hotel Palma, dredging his memory for Quest' Ora. No policeman comes, I lie in the grass beside the canal, they built a canal, water flows from the sea to the nuclear power station, clean water, salt water, water flows from the power station into the river, dirty water, the children can't catch fish because the fish have had it. The canal stinks, mist decapitates the blind giant, the grass is damp and my arse is wet, the cameras lie on my belly like wreaths on a coffin, the cameras don't get wet, only my arse gets wet.

I walk back to the hotel, that is, I put one leg in front of the other, why do I put one leg in front of the other, I watch my feet, I observe my shoes, why does one do naturally what comes naturally, no one thinks about that, no one thinks at all. My Alfa is outside the hotel, my Alfa is red and lying in ambush. I drop my cameras on the seat, the murderer comes out of the hotel. On a balustrade in front of the hotel stand six figures, stone Lilliputians, emperors and generals, all tiny, maybe a few gods too, but I don't have time to worry about the Lilliputians, the murderer is talking to a waitress with nuclear breasts, he doesn't look round, he isn't afraid, the murderer isn't suspicious, he's had his eyebrows shaved, I could photograph him, it's too dark to photograph him. Next time.

There won't be a next time. ME decides to denounce the murderer. I climb into my car, I do what comes naturally, I climb into my car, naturally with a tight arse, I drive to Rome. I'm not in any hurry, the police stay open all night, I drive along the coast, most of the hotels are shut up, most of the houses are shut up, waiting for next summer, waiting for Rome to get summer sickness and spew over them again. I'm pleased with myself, I do feel pleased with myself sometimes, the longer the route the better, ME is driving, I don't know that I'll never reach my destination.

Outside police headquarters I sit in the car and think of Sofia, brain-cripple sits in the car, Sofia laughs at everything I do, she laughs and gets angry, she despises me because I'm Francesco Vanetti, son of Carlo Vanetti, Sofia has electron microscope eyes, Sofia puts me under the microscope, she despises me because I'm not convincing, it's true, I'm not convincing. I notice I haven't switched off, I don't want to denounce Morelli, ME wants to denounce him, I don't. I don't have anything against Morelli, he must know why he killed the Enzian girl, they found her money untouched, two hundred and forty-two thousand lire, maybe she made fun of him because his cock was too soft, that's how he looks, like someone whose cock's too soft, he must have had his reasons, maybe she only came to Rome to get herself killed. I will denounce my father, but it's too soon for that, he'll say he's never heard of Aurelio Morelli and Morelli will back him up, memoirs he'll say, I don't know anything about any memoirs, anyone who writes memoirs must have a bad reason. If I denounce Morelli now people will ask why, and I'll have to say I want to protect society from a murderer, I don't want to protect society from a murderer, society murders children, why not call-girls, I'm not protecting a call-girl from a murder-society, I'm not protecting society from call-girls and murderers, they'll end up by giving me a life-saving medal, a dog-tag, the sort of thing they pin on good swimmers, I don't want any medal, I don't want to save anyone.

The engine is still ticking over, an Alfa never cuts out, I put my foot down, I drive like the devil, I cut corners, I want to catch my father while he's still at the office. It's dark, the neon signs devour the buildings, the buildings are ember-red, Coca-Cola has burnt humanity, humanity is immolated by Pirelli, I drive like the devil. On Tuesdays and Fridays my father stays at the office till eleven, he tells my mother till one, he's just a small-time cheat, he only cheats her out of two hours.

He's alone, worse luck. I tell him what I think of the whole sordid business, count me out, says ME. He refuses to get rattled, he thinks he can still twist me round his little finger, he praises my moral sense, he tells me how proud I make him of me, his son. I say nothing, I don't hate him when I see him, I only hate the people I don't see, when I see them my brain is as empty as a hollow drum. ME tells him how I planned to denounce Morelli. He starts talking about ingratitude, he only begot me so that someone would be grateful to him, he squirted his semen so it would sprout into gratitude, he always bribed me, when I was in my cradle he bribed me with a silver rattle, then with an anti-diphtheria injection, then with an Alfa Romeo. The murderer will get his just deserts, he says, it doesn't matter when life imprisonment begins as long as it's l-i-f-e i-m-p-r-i-s-o-n-m-e-n-t, hence the photographs, you are the eye of the law, my boy, the camera of justice, the memoirs are meant as an object-lesson, to parents, to children, Morelli must be a psychopath or he wouldn't have left the two hundred and forty-two thousand lying there, and if Quest' Ora hadn't latched on to it first Lui e Lei would have snapped it up like a shot, they're bringing out Claretta Petacci's memoirs now, "The Duce as a Lover", Quest' Ora got there too late or we might have been able to dispense with Morelli. I mustn't be discouraged by my failure, he says, success or failure is the only criterion he knows, we stand at the window, the lights are burning in the machine-room, tycoons dream by neon. I'm not getting any younger, he says, one day you'll bear the burden of responsibility, that's another bribe, he doesn't realize I'd sooner be eighteen or eight or thirteen, I don't want a son, sons are corruptible, sons lurk in ambush.

I drive home, Mama is still up, she'll still be up at two when he gets back from the Sacchi woman, freshly washed and lipstick-free. She asks what's new at the office, and I say, nothing new, just more fighting on the Jordan border, Papa's annoyed about Petacci, even if they did hang her upside down the least she might have done was not leave any papers behind, not for *Lui e Lei*, anyway. Mama doesn't understand, she asks did I see Papa and I tell her he's bound to be on the job till one, first up last to bed she says, and I say yes, first up last to bed. I head for my room and trip over the tidiness of it, they always tidy up when I'm out, I have to mess it up again, I mess it up again and sit down at my desk and start on a new poem, *Opus XXIII*, one more for the mass grave.

Carlo Vanetti, 54, *magazine proprietor*

I drove to Claretta's. My talk with Francesco had agitated me, not that I showed it. I have to be on my guard. Francesco is a weakling, and I suffer from the strong man's fear of weaklings. He had his first dose of gonorrhoea at fifteen, his first car at seventeen, his first moral hang-over at eighteen. When he was twenty he became a Communist. I've spoilt him. *One spoils those for whom one has no time.* Francesco has every conceivable failing and Beatrice has none, apart from her membership of the female sex. It makes me shudder to think that I shall have to bear the burden of responsibility far into old age. Beatrice will marry and Francesco will never be competent to assume responsibility for the family firm. He simply cannot grasp the importance of my publications.

My publications combat boredom, humanity's worst scourge. Boredom prompts men to betray their brothers, commit crimes, beget children who are strangers to them. There is an exact correlation between affluence and boredom—rich children have too many toys. The poor suffer from boredom too. The rich, who look after them, even begrudge them the fun of a revolution. The tax-payer glued to his television set has an answer for everything, like the Protestant catechism. In the old days, a man with an inferiority complex wondered what was the matter with him. Now, he knows he has an inferiority complex. Who doesn't? Disease is to the mind as the nose is to the face. It is boring to have a nose, but anyone who is bothered by his nose can get rid of it as easily as a cold. Our society dispenses recipes like a slot-machine. Insert a coin at the top and a recipe shoots out at the bottom. Now that everything can be seen, nothing can be

31

*imagined. Imagination traipses around like a beggar. My maga-
zines are charitable—they drop a coin in the beggar's cup. I rack
my brains constantly for ways of rescuing people from their
boredom. Men of genius build roads for men of talent to travel
on. I'm a road-builder. It isn't easy, though. You can't amuse
people with travellers' tales any longer—they'll buy themselves
an air ticket instead of a magazine. You can't amuse them with
scandal—scandals are impossible in a totally permissive society.
The adventurers of yesterday are the commuters of today. A
strip-tease act would only be amusing if the girl peeled off her
skin as well as her clothes. People have lost interest in the future,
too—they have enough toys as it is. Because nobody will earn a
lira more, feel less jealous or grow a month younger if we conquer
the moon, space-travel bores people. When an astronaut returns
from outer space, he isn't asked what he saw there but how old
his wife is. The series on the six astronauts was our biggest flop
in years—circulation slumped by twenty thousand. We had to
pay all six of them even though the sixth instalment never
appeared. The series might still have been a success if the astronauts had written about their fear of being cuckolded up there—
after all, an astronaut can hardly catch his wife in flagrante; she
always knows where he is. Utopias aren't for sale. Children are
only interesting if they have no future. Identification—that's
my maxim and I haven't done badly out of it. Wars are interesting because people get killed in them or the authorities introduce
rationing. Murderers are interesting because no one is immune
to them. Prostitutes are interesting because no one is immune to
them either. Politics have no appeal except when associated with
war, murder, disease or prostitution. Unfortunately, the raw
material is available to everyone. Even Lui e Lei serve up war,
murder, disease and prostitution, though not in the correct proportions. It won't be long before erotic techniques are taught in
school, thereby destroying the demand for everything but perversion. I'm a moral man—I won't touch perversion. I have to
operate with the raw material available. However, once people
have watched a murderer on television, seen pictures of him in
the dailies and illustrateds, and heard him on the radio, he
becomes boring. Bored people get perverted ideas and may even
turn into murderers themselves. Boredom can't be cured by
entertainment because entertainment is the acme of boredom.*

THE YOUTH-KILLER

It's easier to bribe two monkeys not to copulate in their cage than to stop people from behaving like pigs in return for bread and circuses. You have to enthral the reader, not entertain him. As I always tell my editorial staff, the secret is exclusiveness. My predecessors had it easy—they invented false news items. Only the inventor of a false news item can publish or deny it. These days, every report is double-checked. Another thing I've drummed into my editors: an exclusive report must be authentic as well. You must manufacture the truth, not concoct lies. The murderer isn't exclusive but his memoirs are. They aren't immoral—they're manufactured truth. Generals know precisely what they're doing when they make sure their troops are never at a loose end. Anyone who gives bored people something to do promotes morality. I fight boredom, the source of all evil. Ergo, I promote morality.

Unfortunately, the permissible hobbles along some way behind the acceptable. Interesting things are always dangerous—war, murder, disease and prostitution, for example. I would never have touched the Morelli story if *Lui e Lei* hadn't run off with Claretta Petacci's papers. The Petacci memoirs are nauseating, by the way—I've told Beroglio to write a piece on them in *Positivismo.* Mussolini was the only man who recognized Italy's historic mission. He defeated Haile Selassie and drained the Ligurian marshes. If only he had not become involved with Hitler! The publication of his bedroom secrets could undermine people's respect for a great patriot.

On the way to Claretta—her name worries me a little; I bear a certain resemblance to the Duce, and am as superstitious as he was—on the fond and familiar way to my beloved, I thought of Francesco's reproaches and of the mischief he could make. Thoughts of that kind do not contribute to my potency. At my age a man ought to concentrate on love even before enjoying it. Francesco's reproaches! He preens himself on his uncompromising attitude. *Wars, law-suits, and matrimonial squabbles are simply and solely resolved by compromise, therefore compromise must be moral. Yet the word 'compromising' is used almost exclusively in a pejorative sense, which is quite as illogical as it would be to employ 'promising' in the same way.* We soon learnt how to compromise when I was young. Thanks to Italy's wartime defeat and my own commercial success, Francesco has grown up in a

33

society in which no one recognizes the need for compromise. He's happy enough to lord it in his Alfa Romeo, but it was his father's compromises that paid for the car. As soon as he sits down in it, he turns his nose up.

Morelli is a compromise, I admit. I never delude myself. Last month *Quest' Ora* sold one million sixty thousand copies. *Lui e Lei* has a guaranteed circulation of one million three hundred thousand. If we drop sixty thousand we dip below the million mark and lose between eleven and nineteen per cent of our advertisers. As for those new reduced advertising rates! I mustn't even think of them, least of all on the way to Claretta. On the other hand, if we start running *I murdered Hertha Enzian* in the Christmas number, which people always read in an exalted frame of mind, we ought, with a bit of luck and the right promotional build-up, and unless Vietnam wrecks all our calculations, to outstrip *Lui e Lei* by Easter at latest. They can't have much up their sleeve or they wouldn't be spinning out the Petacci story the way they are: there was no copulation at all in the sixteenth instalment. My spies tell me that *Lui e Lei* plan to launch the memoirs of the lawyer who claims to have uncovered the Kennedy plot at Christmas, but politics twice in a row is quite wrong, even when the link-up is sex in one case and assassination in the other. Besides, I regard Kennedy as old hat.

Claretta reads me like a book. She said I was looking worried— she noticed my "dachshund wrinkles", as she calls them. We drank a glass of champagne and went to bed. I love Claretta's gloriously down-to-earth approach. None of those long-winded conversations which Luisa insisted on before every manifestation of passion. We lingered in bed for a long time afterwards—I get up fairly quickly as a general rule and we go and talk in the sitting-room: it isn't advisable to hurry out into the cold night air straight from a warm bed. She turned the radio on low and I told her about Morelli.

"I hope you haven't put anything in writing," she remarked.

Her solicitude warmed my heart. "Would I sign a contract with a murderer?" I replied.

"Is he under contract to anyone?" she asked, gently caressing the hairs on my chest.

"Yes, Bossi," I told her, "and Bossi has a contract with me. There's nothing about Morelli in the contract between me and

Bossi, of course. Bossi is simply selling me the exclusive rights of the *Enzian Story*."

She got up and fetched some cigarettes. Claretta is an impressive erotic spectacle, both before and afterwards.

"What's to stop Bossi selling the Morelli memoirs to *Lui e Lei* or *Familiarità?*" she inquired.

"Bossi knows that I'd denounce him without a moment's hesitation," I said.

I pulled the quilt over my belly and Claretta stretched out beside me. She loves lying with her head at the bottom of the bed and tickling my nose with her toes. She never gets cold. She turned forty a few weeks ago, but she doesn't look a day over thirty-five.

"I can't stand that man Bossi," she observed. She knows him because he patronizes her florist's shop. "I don't think he likes you," she pursued. "You know me, I'm a good judge of human nature. What about film rights?"

Claretta is a grand creature. She had proved, yet again, that our relations are not exclusively sexual in character.

The film rights are giving me a headache. We could sell the Morelli story to Hollywood for three hundred thousand dollars without any trouble at all. The Italian film people certainly wouldn't give more than five million lire, quite apart from the fact that their heads are stuffed with *nouvelle vague* claptrap. However, there obviously can't be a *Morelli Story* without an *Enzian Story*. The female lead belongs to the Enzian girl, after all. The Americans aren't fastidious as a rule but they're very punctilious in legal matters. They won't pay a sou without the Enzian family's authorization. Legal action by the family could ruin an entire film company.

Claretta is a lawyer *manqué*. She was only giving vent to the misgivings which my legal adviser ought to have voiced when I hinted that we were planning an *Enzian Story*. "You must make sure of the personality rights," she said, putting a lighted cigarette in my mouth—a favourite habit of hers. "If I were you I'd send your lawyer to Vienna to see the girl's family."

"I thought of that," I said. "However, I'd prefer to send Dr Zempach from Zürich. I don't know him personally, but our business relations have been excellent. His mother comes from the Tessin, apparently, and he speaks fluent Italian."

"I should be careful with a Swiss," Claretta exhorted. "They tend to be very proper, at least outwardly."

"I'm not asking him to do anything improper," I retorted. "You surely don't imagine that I'd let Zempach in on the Morelli business? He'll buy the dead girl's life from her family for *Quest' Ora*, that's all. It's lucky she wasn't a German. The Germans have got American ideas. An Austrian family ought to be satisfied with three hundred and fifty thousand lire—in other words, twenty thousand Austrian schillings."

It was nearly one when I girded myself for departure. I generally say I must go at half-past twelve and allow myself to be coaxed into staying another half-hour.

Claretta is a sensible woman except in two respects. She would dearly love to be seen with me in public. *Women are far fonder than men of putting their possessions, or putative possessions, on display*. Here, however, she comes up against a brick wall, because I owe it not only to my public image but also to my wife and children to lead an irreproachable private life. This time she violated the second tabu at ten to one—just as I was donning my socks.

"I'm going to sell the shop," she announced. "There's a prospective buyer coming from Florence tomorrow."

"I don't understand you," I said, as usual. "It's a flourishing business in every sense."

She made a moue and stressed, as usual, that she would not be a burden to me. "I'll hang on to the house," she said.

"You intend to live over someone else's flower shop?" I countered, pulling on my trousers.

"I'm not sentimental," she retorted.

How can I make her understand that it isn't the money which worries me? I'm generous, and she's comfortably off. Time is the only thing I'm mean with, not money. I'm in the thick of a competitive war—a life-or-death struggle, you might say. The new printing works cost a fortune to put up, our advertising policy requires constant supervision, and I'd still like to build up *Positivismo*. *Positivismo* is the runt of the litter. For the time being, it exists on the profits made by *Quest' Ora*—I still can't fulfil my dream of a political daily. In this sort of situation a mistress with a regular job is the perfect answer—Luisa was chief secretary at a paper factory. You can't afford to run a woman who thinks about you before lunch.

I always have such dismal thoughts on the long journey home. Maria is a good wife and a loving mother. We've simply grown apart, as they say. The poor dear has never got over the change of life. *Being familiar with every facet of human nature, I understand her better than she understands me. Nature plays cruel tricks on women: it robs them of their former grounds for complaint and inflicts new sufferings of which they cannot complain; it humiliates them and transports them, all unwitting, to a frontier where they are brutally stripped as though their intention was to smuggle something more sinister than the tattered remains of their youth.* My kind of personality develops continuously, whereas Maria has come to a full stop. Her idea of heaven is to sit at home every evening and stick photographs of our last holiday trip—how I detest those holiday trips!—into her album. She can hardly wait to get her hands on the latest issue of *Quest' Ora*, and she even reads *Lui e Lei* in secret. A man like me, condemned to live with a woman who reads *Quest' Ora!* Is it my fault if I possess such unflagging energy and show no signs of age? On the contrary, I've grown younger in recent years— I can prove it statistically. Four years ago things had reached the stage where I slept with Maria once a week at most, usually on Saturday—although my father, God rest his soul, continued to perform his marital duties daily after every siesta, between 2 and 3 P.M., until he was carried off by a stroke at the age of sixty-nine. I now visit Claretta twice a week after stop-press time on Tuesdays and Fridays. I often feel exhausted, but half an hour later we're in bed. The last time I took Claretta with me on a business trip—foreign trips are different, of course—I made love to her twice a night three nights in succession, a grand total of six times in one week. I'm growing younger, the figures prove it. Nobody appreciates that.

Tomorrow I'll ring Zempach.

Dr Antonio Zempach, 36, *attorney*

Yvette drove me to Kloten to catch the 'plane for Vienna. She wasn't her usual self. Thin-lipped and untalkative. A flower with its petals folded against the rain. I used to call it piquancy when I was courting her. I courted her for ages. It was attractive to me then. It could change. Things sometimes do, if you wait. Piquant wines, sour wines—only the connoisseur can distinguish between them. It isn't piquancy any longer, it's bitterness. Too soon, after only two years.

She waved until the 'plane was out of sight.

The stewardess brought the regulation thin coffee and hygienic sandwiches. A pretty girl. From Thun, she said. Stewardesses go for me. I've got the bachelor look in spite of my wedding ring. That's the first thing stewardesses look at, even before they see if your seat-belt's fastened. I generally flirt with them. No ulterior motive—Yvette's my ulterior motive. I said thank you like a Swiss who wants to sleep. I didn't want to sleep, I didn't want to flirt. I was plain angry.

I can't believe Yvette will rat on me at the first opportunity. Her father: You're a fully qualified lawyer. By all means take it on if you must, but not in the firm's name. The usual tone of voice, half schoolmaster, half elder statesman. We laugh at it usually, Yvette and I. Atavistic emotions come crawling from between stones, like lizards. The patriarch and his daughter. Yvette thought you could rebel without revolution. What will the neighbours say? We don't have any neighbours—the garden's too big and the firs are too tall. On the Dolder everyone has invisible neighbours behind the firs.

Yvette: You don't buy dead daughters from their fathers. I, sharply: Some fathers sell their daughters alive. Faust is quite all right, Yvette thinks, but Mephisto. . . . You can't have dealings with a man who owns Quest' Ora, she says. Really, why not? I've already had dealings with him, on behalf of the firm. He buys antiques which turn out to be reproductions. Yes, she says, but then he's in the right. I thought even murderers were allowed defence counsel, say I. I know this cosy little country of ours has more millionaires than murderers, but that's pure coincidence. Dr von Helis was enormously impressed by my book, Criminality and the Press. A genuine contribution to legal literature, my boy. You can have my daughter. Very kind, but Lohengrin's wedding march isn't a hymn to the firm of Dr von Helis. Learn to swim like a good boy but don't get your feet wet. Bathing allowed, swimming prohibited.

The stewardess cleared away the coffee things. Didn't you like it? Not today. She came from Thun, she assured me proudly.

THE YOUTH-KILLER

Flies to Bombay and stays in Thun. My father died in the Galapagos Islands—fell out of a tree while photographing an owl.
Perhaps I'll fall out of a tree too. If so, let's hope I do it in the
Galapagos and not in the garden, on the Dolder. Yvette: You're
ambitious. I must look that up in the dictionary some time, there
are too many meanings. Taking over Dr von Helis's firm is a
good ambition, consenting to act for Vanetti is a bad ambition.

Personality rights are personality rights, a legal concept.
Personality rights are vested in parents, call-girls' parents not
excepted. You can keep them or sell them—that's one of their
essential features. Even the Swiss are talking about the murder
in Rome. Our newspapers supply crime reports complete with
moral indignation, like a gift wrapper. In French Switzerland
they don't call a child-rapist a child-rapist, they call him *un triste
sire*. It was shocking to murder Hertha Enzian but even more
shocking that she was a call-girl. Child-rapists are sad gentlemen
and call-girls don't exist, not in the cosy little world between the
Bahnhofstrasse and the Dolder. Safe, smug, and cosy. We have
licensing hours for sin: time, gentlemen, please!

It was foggy. The 'plane circled over Schwechat. The girl from
Thun smiled soothingly, fog-proof, accident-immune. No smoking, of course. Most air disasters occur on landing.

It may turn out to be quite straightforward. Oskar Enzian,
butcher, of No. 8 Joseph-Kainz-Gasse, Vienna 17, accepts twenty
thousand schillings for his dead daughter, Vanetti says thank
you, sends a cheque, Yvette and I have lunch in the grillroom of
the Baur au Lac, drive down to Ascona for the week-end. Yvette
says: An Italian Chichikov who trades in dead souls like something out of Gogol. *Criminality and the Press* ... I doubt if
Dr von Helis ever read my book. A reputable publisher and two
editions, that was good enough. You can have my daughter. He
probably mistook the book for a thesis. I can understand his
interest in criminality, but the Press? I'd like to meet Vanetti.
My interest is more than just academic—Edizioni Vanetti don't
devote themselves entirely to call-girls. Yvette used to listen for
hours while I read to her from *Pitaval*. Far worse cases, but we
were only engaged then. There's something very elegant about
antiques, even fake ones. Yvette: You don't know what you're
letting yourself in for. All right, as long as I'm safely perched in
the tree.

We landed without incident.

I dropped my bag at the hotel and called Yvette. Good flight, a bit foggy. She'd been waiting at home for me to call.

Joseph-Kainz-Gasse, in the rather disreputable suburban quarter known as Hernals. If Kainz had guessed what a miserable suburban street was going to be named after him by a grateful posterity he'd have gone on playing Hamlet till he was a hundred. Metropolitan grey: virtually unknown at home in Switzerland, where even the cities are towns. Grubby children, a small boy chasing a mangy dog. The shop—*Oskar Enzian, Sausage and Cured Meats*—was closed. It had just gone six. The peeling shop-front was adorned with two painted gentians, a not over-subtle allusion to the owner's name. An embellishment like the oranges they stick in the mouths of New Year sucking-pigs. The house smelt of the scraps from a not quite clean butcher's shop, a sour smell. Anyone who left there for the Via Veneto couldn't fail to appreciate the change of scene.

The butcher had been warned of my arrival by an express letter from *Quest' Ora*. He showed me into the living-room. Shades of H. G. Wells's time machine. Instead of going forward in time I had been wafted into the past. Best regards from the nineteenth century. The only contemporary touch was the television set, which sprawled in the middle of the room like a St Bernard on a hearth-rug. Everything else was straight pre-1900, the red plush sofa with brass lions' heads, the old German sideboard with columns and knobs, the ornate china, the plump leather chairs, the pale-blue saints' pictures, and the hand-sewn tapestry cushions showing cats playing with balls of wool.

The butcher surprised me. Hertha Enzian had been twenty-three, but he was verging on sixty—bony, almost starved-looking, with a tapering head, sparse hair, and pallid skin. Discounting the square-trimmed moustache, he bore a ludicrous resemblance to Hexi, the fox-terrier bitch that lay at his feet watching television throughout our conversation. The sound had been turned down when I arrived but the picture continued to flicker away, madly. Sometimes we took our cue from Hexi and stared at the screen. Hexi's 'papa' surprised me, but Frau Enzian lived up to my expectations. A lady of considerable girth, taller than average, younger than her husband, with a brisk manner and eyes like two dark and shiny buttons. She tried, not always successfully, to peer over the top of her bosom at the floor—in other words, to catch a glimpse of the wheezing fox-terrier at her husband's feet. Papa Enzian made desperate efforts to speak educated German. Foreign words stitched on like sequins, platitudes polished like the silver salver on the sideboard. I got on better with Frau Enzian's broad Viennese. He spoke diffidently and often, she little and to the point.

"About our poor Hertha . . ." said Frau Enzian, gazing at the tinted photograph above her husband's tapering head. A family group: father, mother, three children, a boy and two girls. I recognized Hertha immediately. Fifteen at most, in a little white dress with a pink sash, in the centre. The focal point, even then. She looked as if she might have gone far. Old photos always make people who die young look as if they might have gone far —crashed pilots or call-girls, it doesn't matter who.

"Yes, about poor Hertha," I said.

"They'll never find the murderer, those Italians," said Papa Enzian. "You're Swiss, of course." He sounded half apologetic, half admiring.

"And the magazine wants to help find him," said Frau Enzian.

"Among other things," I said cautiously.

To my surprise, both of them were exceptionally well-informed about their rights. Papa Enzian talked like a used-car dealer who never buys a car without running it down first. "It's like this, Herr Dr Zempach," he said, "I don't like this business one little bit. My name's been dragged through the muck too long as it is. Like a bolt from the blue, it was. We thought Hertha was a dancer with a touring company. Now it seems she was a call-girl." He pronounced it 'kull-geerl' like a German who has only seen the word in writing. "If the magazine starts on about her too. . . ."

"She was a good girl, Hertha," Frau Enzian said, sorrowfully eyeing the fox-terrier. "Who'd have thought it?"

"One can't know these things in advance," I said profoundly. The dailies were almost bound to go on plugging the tragic case, which was why it would be better if Hertha's life was viewed through the loving eyes of her family.

"Quite, quite," said Papa Enzian, "but you don't know the Viennese, Herr Dr Zempach. The remarks I have to put up with all day long, and my son too—he works in the shop as well. . ."

"Mizzi, our other daughter, is happily married to a police superintendent," Frau Enzian broke in, "Police Superintendent Bauer of the Excise Division."

"You wouldn't credit how many customers have stayed away," Papa Enzian said with emphasis. "Even old customers, and if Hertha's name goes on appearing week after week. . . ."

"Hardly anyone in Vienna reads *Quest' Ora*," I objected.

"The gentleman that wrote to us . . ." said Papa Enzian.

"A gentleman by the name of Vanetti," amplified Frau Enzian.

"He talked about world rights," said Papa Enzian. He didn't look at me as he spoke, but stared fixedly at the television screen, on which outlaws were blazing away silently at an equally silent stage-coach as it rolled across the prairie.

World rights, I thought. No flies on the inhabitants of Joseph-Kainz-Gasse, Vienna 17. However, I wanted to get the money question settled. *Quest' Ora* was prepared to pay twenty thousand schillings, I said, provided that Herr Enzian waived all legal claims. A further ten thousand would be payable in return for full details of his daughter's adolescence: a reporter from the magazine, probably Signor Bossi, would visit Vienna for research purposes. Pictures of the girl, family snapshots, and even the photographs which *Quest' Ora* planned to take on the spot would be paid for separately.

Frau Enzian bustled out of the room before her husband could utter a word. She returned with a green velvet jewel-case—a rich harvest for the Italian Chichikov. Frau Enzian had tears in her eyes, fat tears, the fat tears of a fat woman. They plopped on to some touching Confirmation photographs of Hertha, lily in hand. Bikini-clad holiday snaps, head and shoulders craning. A shot taken in the Prater. Little Hertha—none other, Frau Enzian assured me—riding a merry-go-round horse. Photographs of a school outing—"she always did well in class, Hertha did"—of a boozy New Year's Eve party, of skiing in the Vienna Woods. Finally, picture-postcards—"she was good about writing, I'll say that"—from Rome, Venice, Capri.

Papa Enzian took no part in this excursion into the dear dead days. Either he was scared of being overcome by emotion or he wanted to watch the Wild West chase even if he couldn't hear the thunder of hoofs. I only tore myself away from Frau Enzian's treasure-chest when he said, "I'm afraid it's out of the question, Herr Doktor." I gathered that Papa Enzian was thinking in terms of hundreds of thousands of schillings, not tens of thousands. Big money. Even Dr von Helis might have pricked up his ears.

It wasn't as cheeky as it sounded, actually. A German film company, as yet unnamed, had already mentioned a figure in that price-range. That the company likewise laid claim to the world rights, literary rights included, Papa Enzian described as "only natural".

"These few pictures are all we've got left of our poor little girl," lamented Frau Enzian, shutting the box with a crisp click. That was it. No hundreds of thousands, no pictures. "They haven't even sent us her bits and pieces of clothes and jewellery," she added.

"That's the Italians for you, Herr Doktor," remarked her husband. "They've hung on to the cash too—two hundred and forty-two thousand lire."

I trod carefully. I couldn't promise him the sort of money he had in mind. Yvette: You see, you shouldn't have got involved. I didn't intend to go home empty-handed. When you can't buy something you take an option on it. I feigned polite but unmistakable disbelief in the existence of a film offer, and was informed that its source was a Herr Hermann Vorneweg, acting on behalf of Kronos Films of Berlin.

"Herr Vorneweg is very set on the idea," the butcher told me.

"Hertha would never have wanted people to haggle over her," said Frau Enzian.

"Ten thousand schillings and you bind yourself to us for three days," I said. "If you agree terms with Herr Vorneweg after that we get the money back. If you settle with us we deduct it from the final payment."

Papa Enzian patted his dog. Maybe I'm not a good judge of character. Yvette always says—in the nicest way, of course—that to learn about people you have to be suspicious. At any rate, I got the impression that Enzian wasn't used to taking decisions without consulting his wife. Bristling moustache but timid underneath. I devoted my attention to an oleograph of the *Madonna del Granduca* and left them to whisper together.

I found an ally in Frau Enzian, probably because I'd looked

suitably impressed by the photographs. Her husband declared his readiness to take ten thousand schillings for a three-day option. Borrowing a rather crumpled letterheading, *Oskar Enzian, Sausage and Cured Meats, Vienna XVII,* I drafted a brief document to which the butcher appended an ornate signature. A graphologist would have identified whole strings of sausages in his squiggles and flourishes. Then I counted out ten pale-blue thousand-schilling notes on the table.

Frau Enzian escorted me into the hall, where the aroma of sausage and cured meats mingled with that of some chubby apples laid out on top of an elongated clothes cupboard. She assured me that her sole concern was to act the way Hertha would have wanted her to. A bit ambiguous, in the circumstances. Meanwhile, back in the living-room, Papa Enzian had restored the long-lost sound, but a news-reader seemed to have taken over from the daredevil horsemen. Fighting was still going on in Vietnam.

Christa Sonntag, 26, *call-girl*

The Englishman had only just gone when Canonica turned up. He's becoming a real nuisance, that man.

The Englishman is a proper pig—at least, I think so. He rings me once a month from the Hassler. Must be quite well-heeled. I always know what to expect. He arrives at my flat on the dot of three. Marches in as if he's just come from a funeral, carrying a doctor's bag—one of those things that hinge in the middle. "Well, my dear, how about it?" he says—nothing more. I understand English *perfettamente*, of course. I wear a nightie with nothing on underneath. I take it off and lie down on the couch, nude. "Where's my smock?" he says. I keep it hanging in the bathroom, a white doctor's smock. He brought it the first time he came. He puts it on and carries the bathroom stool in. Then he sits down by my feet, puts his horn-rimmed glasses on, and opens his little bag. I stick my feet on his lap and he starts to pedicure me. No, honestly, he does a perfect job—nail-scissors, cuticle-scissors, orange-sticks, the lot. He takes five minutes to select an instrument sometimes. It's enough to drive you crazy. He never looks up or says a word. Never touches me, either, not above the knee anyway. It takes about forty-five minutes. Then he gives a little moan, packs up his stuff neatly, and hangs the smock on the hook in the bathroom. "Thank you," he says, very gentlemanly, but he doesn't bother with the 'my dear' this time. Puts twenty thousand lire on the table, gives a bow, and drifts out. It may be easy money but he's a pig just the same.

Then Canonica arrived.

I like him quite a lot, really—that's to say, I find him *simpàtico*. You shouldn't go by first impressions. He's a teeny little man, like a lemon with teeth. I'd love to introduce him to the idiots who flock to those James Bond films. They say Canonica's got two university degrees. He's deputy chief of the homicide squad. He's sixty-two—he told me so himself. Any criminal could snap him like a twig in two seconds flat. Sometimes I feel I ought to take him under my wing. Not in a sexy way, of course.

He's got to know me since Hertha died. *I've grown accustomed to her face*, as it says in the song. Very imaginative, Canonica is. He thinks I know something about the murder because Hertha lived next door and we were friends, or supposed to be.

If I've told him once I've told him a hundred times, honestly I have. Hertha popped her head in at half-past four on the 8th of August. I'd just woken up from my beauty-sleep. "Got any grappa?" she asked. She meant a whole bottle, of course. Hertha was a great one for borrowing things and never returning them. Needless to say, I gave her a bottle out of the goodness of my heart. "You're a doll," she said. That was the last I heard of her—"You're a doll"—until that scream at five past six.

It's true I didn't make a point of that to the police. "I was fast asleep until you lot came banging at the door," I told them. Silly of me, really. That's why Canonica keeps badgering me. In the first place, though, it wasn't a 'death cry'. Hertha often yelped, so how was I to know? Secondly, I was scared, and thirdly, I didn't want to get involved. It's easier to get into a mess than out of one. A fine thing, if I went to the police at this stage and said, "Yes, I heard her scream". I didn't see anything, just sat on my bed and trembled like a leaf until the police hammered on the door in that rude way. Anyone would think they didn't know what a door-bell's for. The caretaker woman saw the murderer. Lilio the shoe-shop assistant did too, probably, but they're pillars of society, of course. The police couldn't care less about them.

Canonica's got it into his head that I was friendly with Hertha because we were both "night-moths from the North", her from Vienna and me from Munich. That's what it said in *Gente*, in black and white. Big deal! A call-girl is just a call-girl to the police—outsiders haven't got a clue about these things. I own two mink coats, a dark one and a light one, but Hertha didn't even have a pony-skin. I've also got a house with its own garden, just outside Anzio, but that's strictly my business. I don't put on airs, honestly I don't, but Hertha never got anywhere because there are call-girls and call-girls. I wasn't a friend of hers, either, because in our profession failure is as catching as a head-cold. She didn't enjoy her work, and the customers knew it. It isn't all caviare and champagne, this job. Take that Englishman—he was on the eighth toe when he left off. Most men aren't so bad, though, even if they do behave like trained monkeys in bed. You feel sorry for them, really. I give everyone a fair crack of the whip because I'm an understanding soul. They wouldn't come here if they were happy at home. A man has to feel at home somewhere. That's why they come back for more. I don't set store by casual customers, otherwise I'd be walking the streets back home in Munich. I believe in a small turnover and big profits, which means I can do what I like with my spare time. The girls who complain they don't 'feel' anything let themselves be milked by pimps. If you don't 'feel' anything you might as well get married. I could have one husband for every day of the week if I wanted—I don't need any pimp. The whole thing's psychological, basically. If a girl's got a bad conscience she passes her money on to a pimp. I haven't got a bad conscience, and if I fancy sleeping with somebody who doesn't have any cash he can take it as a compliment. It's an honour, free, gratis, and for nothing, otherwise I'd be like my customers. I gave Hertha a real talking to, but it all went in one ear and out the other because she got off on the wrong foot. She thought you started out as a fully-fledged call-girl. Whenever someone 'phoned up and said he was in films and wanted her to do some screen tests she thought she was Sophia Loren—and there are more film producers wandering about in the Via Veneto than there are cameras in the whole wide world. I walked the streets back home,

I admit. You have to learn every profession from the bottom up; the streets are a stepping-stone. A flat in the Via Sicilia isn't a stepping-stone, it's the top of the tree. Except perhaps for a house near Anzio. I may buy the plot next door as well. Then I can sit in the garden in the evenings and listen to the murmur of the sea. I like the murmur of the sea better than anything. Anybody who doesn't get a kick out of it deserves to be pitied. Like Hertha. I used to take her along to parties to begin with, but she acted like a kid on Christmas Eve. I don't go to parties for fun. My idea of fun is to stay in bed and read a good book. You mustn't be overawed by your own profession or you never make the grade. Hertha used to hand out smiles at parties. I made myself hoarse, telling her that parties were where you handed out your 'phone number. I get quite weepy sometimes when I think of her, but she was a silly little bitch for all that; God rest her.

Anyway, in came Canonica, sniffing. One thing I'll grant him, he plays fair. He isn't one of those bogies who are all over you one minute and down on you like a ton of bricks the next. There are plenty of those around. Canonica isn't friendly or unfriendly, just businesslike. He doesn't make promises, and he doesn't threaten to have you deported. He's educated, too. A university graduate. The more educated a man is, the easier you can talk to him. It's the same with women. Vosti, the housekeeper, she looks me up and down as if I was a pickpocket, poor bitch, whereas a real lady would accept me as a member of society. I don't have any false illusions about Canonica, honestly. A man of blemished character doesn't become a policeman. But Canonica has a couple of hundred bogies under him, so why does he have to go to all this trouble himself? That's what I can't understand. He's so cussed it's beginning to get me down. You have to know when to call it a day. Enough's as good as a feast.

"It smells good in here," he said. "What are you cooking?"

"Spaghetti," I told him.

"Show me," he said.

We went into the kitchen. His eyes came out on stalks. I don't suppose he'd ever seen a kitchen like it, not on his pay. It's got everything, even if I do say it myself. There's an ice-box complete with deep-freeze, a washing-machine, a dish-washer, an eye-level grill, a Mixmaster, a pop-up toaster, an electric

47

vegetable-slicer, a waffle-iron, and an electric stove with a see-through door. Nothing built in, of course. It's all going to *Pace*—that's what I call my house at Anzio. I've already ordered the name-plate.

"Not bad for a start," said Canonica.

"What do you mean, for a start?" I said.

"Try *Spaghetti alla tellina* some time," he said, and rattled off the recipe. Shell your mussels and cook well. A little onion browned in butter. A big heap of parsley, finely chopped, and a dollop of tomato purée. Pepper and herbs to taste. Stir the mussels well in with the spaghetti and put plenty of butter and Parmesan on top while they're still hot in the pan. "You ought to write it down," he said.

"I'll show you how we do hock of veal in Munich," I said.

"It's the same as *ossobuco*," he said. The nerve of the man!

We went back into the lounge.

"What's new, Contessa?" he said. It's a sort of silly habit they've got into down the Via Veneto, calling me the Countess on account of my elegant manners.

"Nothing," I said.

Canonica never beats about the bush. "Has anyone asked you about the murder since we last saw each other?"

"Who hasn't?" I said, without a word of a lie. "I don't seem to have a friend left who isn't itching to hear the morbid details."

"You've got a sense of humour," he said, like the gentleman he is. "I'm not talking about your friends," he said. "Has any outsider asked about the Enzian girl? Anyone who only came for that reason?"

"Ah," I said, "you mean criminals get an urge to revisit the scene of the crime?" I went all cold as I said it, down my back.

"No," he said. "I didn't mean that."

"Only reporters," I said.

"Reporters?" he said. "Still?"

I'm all for telling the truth when it doesn't cost me anything. "Little Bossi from *Quest' Ora*," I said. "He's almost as big a pest as you are."

"Did he offer you money?" asked Canonica.

"The police are the only people I speak to free of charge," I said. That wasn't a lie either.

"What did he offer you money for?" he insisted.

"For nothing," I said. "He wanted to pay me not to speak to any other reporters. The same goes for film people. Believe that and you'll believe anything."

Canonica was all excited, I don't know why. "Let's do a deal, Contessa," he said. "I can't pay you anything but I could be useful to you. Tell Bossi what you like, and tell me what he wants to know." He laughed, as well as he could with that lemon-face of his. "If you help me," he said, "I'll let you have all my best recipes."

"O.K.," I said.

Before he went he made me swear a sacred oath that I wouldn't breathe a word about our arrangement to Bossi. Well, why not? It's a good thing to keep in with the police when you can. Besides, I feel really sorry for Canonica sometimes.

At sixty-two he'd probably prefer to sit in the garden and listen to the murmur of the sea. Perhaps his wife's dead, or he never had one, or she ran off with someone else. I don't know why, but I feel sorry for men who do their own cooking.

Oskar Enzian, 59, *butcher*

I went along to the Social Club Tuesday evening. If you win you have to put something in the kitty. Me, I lost all the time. Didn't have such bad cards, couldn't keep my mind on them, that's all. Paula came and sat with me a couple of times. "Penny for your thoughts, Herr Enzian," she said—she always calls me "Herr Enzian" in front of the others. I gave her bum a squeeze when she brought my beer, meaning, there's life in the old dog yet. I haven't been with her once since Hertha died. Don't fancy it at the moment, somehow. Paula ought to understand that.

I had four halves, which was just what the doctor ordered. Three don't do a thing for me, and five knock me sideways. Four blow the cobwebs away, help me to see things I wouldn't see otherwise. I had a good hard think on the way home.

The fact is, I've got to make up my mind. I prefer Vorneweg, myself. In the first place, he's a German. Reminds me of Major Schumpeter, my C.O. in the War. I got on with him like a house on fire. The Swiss are a crafty lot. No ideals, the Swiss, always on the make. I took a dislike to that Zempach the minute he walked in, him with his natty suit and la-di-da manners. Good-looking and knows it, like one of those tennis stars on TV. He spoke smarmy, too, like a Yid, but then the Yids have a finger in everything, worse luck. "What's your boss's name?" I asked Vorneweg. "Kohn," he said. I didn't blame him for sounding shifty. I knew there was something fishy about Kronos Films from the start—they probably changed the name from Kohn. The trouble is, I'm bound to be wrong whatever I do. If I settle with Vorneweg the Yids get the rights. If I settle with Zempach the Wops get them. They're getting above themselves, too, these days, the Wops. It's all this foreign labour. Well, as a famous man once said, you pays your money and you takes your choice. It's a terrible thing, really, what Hertha did to me.

Paula's right, I ought to lay off the cards for a bit, but I couldn't stick not going down the Club every Tuesday. It's the only spot of leave I get. The Club's my one bit of light relief, that and Paula. It's hell at home. The way Franziska tells it, you'd think the whole thing was my fault. She always did put the blame on me. I ought to have kicked over the traces years ago, that's what Paula keeps telling me. Now it's too late. Not that Franziska's a bad sort. She's been a pretty good wife to me, done her bit in the shop and that. It was fair enough while I still had my health—no argument about who wore the trousers then. I'm not getting any younger, either. Butchering isn't really my line any more, which is why I specialize in sausage and cured meats. It got too much for me, lugging carcases around, and I can't stomach the sight of blood all over the shop. Mind you, I did build up the business, no-one can say I didn't. Quadrupled the turnover since my father died, I have, and a man who can do that is entitled to a bit of respect from his wife and kids. I handled the Swiss pretty well, too—even Franziska couldn't deny that—just as if I was master in my own home. She started on at me again, though, right away. Said it was all because I'd spoilt the child. Hertha was the apple of my eye, I grant you. She was too good for this world, that's what I always say, but Franziska turns a deaf ear. Hertha looked like an angel, and now she is one, even if she was a call-girl. I can't help remembering the way we used to go for walks together, her and me. We went walking in Neuwaldegg, and did trips up the Kahlenberg. She used to hold my hand. "Buy me a soda-pop, Papa?" she'd say, and it was all I could do not to buy her a whole crate of the stuff. She only had to look at me with those big blue eyes of hers—like angel's eyes, they were. We always went to the Prater by ourselves, just the two of us. We'd watch the Punch and Judy show and go for rides on the scenic railway. It doesn't bear thinking of now. Another thing, we've still got all her dolls. I must have bought her a dozen at least, even though trade was rotten just after the War. I can't look at those dolls without piping a tear—it's terrible, how easy I cry. My father was just the same. He used to blub at the drop of a hat, and he was the strongest man in the whole of Hernals. I used to be as strong as an ox myself. Been going downhill these past ten years, though, ever since I had that lung trouble.

Anyway, I thought it all over as I walked home down the High Street. The weather was a right bastard—drizzling, it was, and cold enough to freeze the balls off a brass monkey—but I had to have a think, and I can't get any thinking done at home, not with Franziska yapping the whole time and Hans making Communist speeches. He picks it up at night school—they turn out proper little Reds at night school. I ought to have a son like old Hödelmoser, but it's no good, you can't choose your own flesh and blood.

It pays to be honest with yourself, that's what I always say. I came over all queer, walking down the High Street, and I don't care who knows it. Even the street-lamps made me jump, and once I stopped and looked round because I heard footsteps behind me. I'd only had four halves, too.

Mind you, it doesn't really matter who I sell the rights to, Vorneweg or the Swiss. Things have gone pretty good so far, if you don't count Mizzi. That Mizzi and her police superintendent! He ought to be a priest, not a policeman, the way he rushes off to church every morning. Franziska calls him St Boniface. He's a bloody hypocrite, that man, no two ways about it. Didn't address a word to me at the wedding, but he was happy enough to let me foot the bill. Insisted on getting married at that posh church and invited twenty-five guests to the Social Club afterwards, all on me. Well, I mean to say, even a butcher has his pride. I bet he doesn't say "Give us this day our daily bread" when he gets down on his knees, the toffee-nosed bastard, I bet he says, "Give me my promotion to chief superintendent".

Mizzi's been having to visit us on the sly ever since this business
with Hertha came up. "Look," I said, "if your husband's
ashamed..." "It's only because of his promotion," she said.
Franziska took her part, but then women don't have any self-
respect. If the story comes out in the magazines or the films that
bloody flatfoot will divorce Mizzi like a shot—he isn't all that
Catholic—and who'll be to blame? Yours truly, of course.

Mizzi's superintendent can get stuffed, that's what I told myself as I passed the tram shed. I stopped right beside the shed—
they go on shunting till all hours—and stood there gawping like
a kid of eight. "Win anything, Herr Enzian?" one of the conductors called out—they all know me down at the shed. It did
me good to hear a friendly voice, and no mistake.

I'm not bothered about Mizzi or the shop—trade's been picking up, to tell the truth, because folk are so inquisitive. No, it's
because of the Jew-boy in Taborstrasse and Pollack's villa in
Braungasse. They can't nick me for faking that questionnaire
right after the war, Dr Habichl says, it's too long ago. "Don't
give it another thought, Herr Enzian," that's what he told me.
Well, how was I to know the Jew-boy would hit his head on the
kerb when he fell over? He must have had a weak skull, that's
all. Dr Habichl would get me off in two ticks, he says so himself,
but first they'd remand me for questioning, and I wouldn't survive that, what with the disgrace and my health.

I could always turn them both down, of course, Vorneweg and
the Swiss. The idea hit me just as I was passing the tobacconist's,
quite close to my home, if you can call it that. Brought me up
short, it did, but I soon put it out of my head. I'm a focus of
attention—that's what they called me in the *Kronen-Zeitung*—
so it's no good. Added to that, the barney with Franziska would
just about finish me. "Trust a fool like you to chuck good money
away," she'd say, and I couldn't deny it. We've slaved our
guts out long enough, that's a fact. I could buy the cobbler's
next door—old Hintermayer is on his uppers anyway. I could
fix up the butchery again, too, give Hans something to do. Idle-
ness is the root of all evil, to coin a phrase. As it is, he lounges
around the shop half the day. He'd soon show me a bit of respect
if I branched out. Added to that, we need a new TV set. Colour
TV's on the way. A new couch, that's another thing we need.
I've got taste, you see—I know our furniture looks out of date.

Made me feel proper embarrassed, having that Swiss there. Christmas is just around the corner, too. Mizzi wouldn't say no if I bought her a fur—a short one, of course—you can bet your sweet life on that, Superintendent. I don't want anything for myself. I never did want much, nobody can say different, but a family man's got to think of the future. That's what Hertha did. She was the only one with any family feeling. You can't expect a healthy girl of twenty-three to make a will, but she always sent her cast-offs to Mizzi. They were as good as new, not that anyone gives it a thought now. I can see her plain as can be, blue eyes and all. Like an angel's, they were. I couldn't do it to her, not turn down the money she left us.

I'm scared, no two ways about it, but I'm not going to be done in the eye, not by the Yids, and not by the Wops either. Franziska gave me hell because I told the Swiss about Vorneweg, but it would have come out anyway. Murder will out, as the saying goes. You can't sell the same rights twice over, it isn't fair. Vorneweg won't go any higher. "Berlin won't pay any more," he said. The magazine people would, but they want the film rights as well. Franziska's got a point, I can't just sling the Wops' money down the drain. Always have two strings to your bow, that's my motto. I've always been in favour of compromise, but then what choice have I got? If I say no to the Yid he'll start nosing around, sure as fate, and newspaper writers can be just as much of a headache when they've got it in for you. The two sides ought to come to some arrangement, that'd be the simplest thing.

It was bright of me to walk home with those four beers inside me. I even took a turn outside the house, and that was where I got the brightest idea of the lot, outside the house. Dr Habichl! He joined the Party too, long before the Anschluss. Nowadays, when they haul these so-called war criminals into court, Dr Habichl gets them off. A stitch in time saves nine, as they say. I don't have to keep anything from Dr Habichl—broad-minded, he is, even about that business in Taborstrasse. It wasn't intentional, I can swear to that. Dr Habichl will make me a special price all right. We both belonged to the Party, and he's a member of the Club, same as me. He'll find some way of bringing the two sides together without turning me into what they call a focus of attention. I can't wait to see Franziska's face when they wheel in that new couch Christmas Eve.

Italo Canonica, 62,
C.I.D. Superintendent

Friday, 27th October. Questioned Lilio Negri again, twenty-eight, shoe-shop assistant. To recapitulate: the building has two entrances, one in the Via Sicilia, one in the Via Vittorio Veneto. The shoe-shop stands on the corner. The Via Veneto entrance is situated between the florist's and the shoe-shop. In the courtyard behind, the *Night-Club*. Not open until 9 P.M., so the murderer didn't come from there. May have visited it on other occasions, though. Logically, he would have left the building by the Via Veneto exit, but Negri is certain (?) that he saw him in the Via Sicilia. Confirms my impression that the man was an amateur. A professional criminal would have lost himself in the evening crowds in the Via Veneto. It always pays to recap. At 4.30 P.M., the Enzian girl cadged a bottle of grappa from the Contessa. She was obviously expecting a visitor. Bottle found unopened. The housekeeper/caretaker Ada Vosti, sixty-four, heard a scream at 6.5 P.M., as she was cleaning the third-floor landing. Says the scream came "from downstairs", but cannot specify which floor. Decided, after two or three minutes (?), to go downstairs herself. Met the man in the dark suit on the first floor. He didn't use the lift. Description fits the one given by Negri. About sixty, height roughly six foot one, slim build, greying hair, prominent nose, glasses, unusually heavy eyebrows. A "proper gentleman". Vosti asked him if he'd heard anything. Didn't reply, simply shook his head. Crime must have been committed between 4.30 and 6.5. However, I'm inclined to think that the murderer was only with Enzian for a short time, from 5.30 at the earliest. Grappa must have been his favourite tipple, because Enzian had seven other kinds of drink in her flat. Unopened bottle probably means he went to work quickly. The deceased was wearing a nightdress but had a slip underneath—white lace. Suspender belt, right suspender undone—could be coincidence. No signs of a struggle, no sexual intercourse. Minimal resistance, victim taken completely unawares. Corpse was lying face upward on the couch, so the murderer probably bent over her. Lipstick smudged, possibly by the murderer's hand. Prelude to intercourse? Two hundred and forty-two thousand lire discovered among articles of clothing in the bedroom cupboard encourage the assumption that motive was not theft. Would not like to commit myself on that point. All suspects' alibis have now been checked—completely watertight. Fingerprints: no trace in Records. I never thought the murderer was one of her regular 'visitors'. Street pick-up equally unlikely, in my opinion. Grappa. More likely to be a platonic friend, quite common among such girls. Estimates of age given by Vosti and Negri suggest that he was a 'soul-mate' of some social standing. Genuine or fake film-producer? My recap hasn't yielded much. Time is not on my side.

Saturday, 28th October. Glanced through yesterday's entry and was brought up short by the last sentence. I meant, of course, that the passage of time makes any case harder to solve. As they stand, the words are too revealing. I'm tempted to cross them out because they betray my dread of time. If I'd retired two years ago, as regulations permitted, I could now be sitting outside the Café Doney reading the story in the papers. Except that I'd probably be dead. Retirement is the outer office of death, and I've always hated outer offices. I nearly decided not to join the service because the Super who was dealing with my application kept me waiting in his outer office for two hours. Waiting is the worst of all humiliations, waiting for death not excluded. I'm starting to philosophize again, even though I realize that my theories don't add up to a philosophy. I wanted to write books on philosophy, and all I do is keep a diary. "You, as an LL.D. . ." people say, when I'm really a D.Phil. It's no wonder I haven't gone further—criminals have always interested me more than crime. They call me "the Professor" at headquarters, but I don't know if it's meant as a compliment. They probably think I'm a garrulous old man! Why did I get my teeth into the Enzian case when one of my younger officers could have handled it just as well? It's too late for a serious philosophical work, but I can still play the game of detection. The murderer stands to get life imprisonment, I stand to get lifelong peace and quiet. Not that I ever dreamed of heading Homicide. I'm a born number two. Types like me do exist—men who have more talent and less personality than their superiors. They promoted an older man over my head when I was forty and a younger man when I was fifty-eight. I was the wrong age at every stage of my life. Character is like a solo voice which, however lovely in itself,

sounds discordant if it doesn't match the orchestra. The character one possessed as a twenty-year-old is no use at thirty, and a
thirty-year-old's character in a man of fifty verges on the disreputable. At sixty one dresses up, at seventy one dons the veil—
few people realize that character, too, has its nakedness. It's no
less disreputable for an old man to pursue his own character than
it is for him to chase after young girls. . . . But I'm digressing
again, when all I wanted to say was that I had too little ambition
at forty and too much at sixty. My character hasn't adapted
itself to my age. I shall retire as a number two. Inactivity won't
kill me—that's a fallacy—but I won't bow out on a defeat. He's
a hard worker, *il professore*, they claim, but they're wrong. We're
all lazy at heart. It's just that some people like to finish what
they've started. I shall write the last chapter of the *Enzian Story*
myself, not leave it to young Signor Bossi.

. . . Had another chat with the Contessa today. Munich girl,
twenty-six, full figure, white skin, freckles, genuine red-head.
Former street-walker, but has a certain natural elegance. Three
years in Rome. Even though she lied to me—of course she heard
the scream, may also have seen the murderer—I have a soft spot
for her. Bossi, a repulsive young man but the smartest crime
reporter in Rome, seems to have some very definite ideas about
the murder. Sonntag suddenly (?) remembered that Enzian had
mentioned a 'writer' who was 'chasing' her. Sonntag alleges
that Bossi's only interest is in this 'writer'. When I asked her
why she had never mentioned the writer to me she said she'd
forgotten, which may be true in view of Enzian's turnover—we
found a hundred and thirteen addresses in her notebook. No
'writer', incidentally. The Contessa claims it was Bossi who first
reminded her of the 'writer'. If true (?) this suggests that Bossi is
confirming an existing suspicion rather than searching for a new
lead.

Sunday, 29th October. Lunch at Alfredo's. It was his turn
again. On Sunday the 15th I was at Flaminio's, last Sunday at
Pia's. I think I must be the most successful father in the world.
If it's true that children are the immortality of the common man,
I'm immortal three times over. I've done little enough to deserve
it. A detective who believes in hereditary factors ought to retire
on the spot. My only contribution was to leave the children's
upbringing entirely to Adele, and Pia was twenty-two by the

time she died. Even so, I don't seem to have spoiled anything—not to spoil anything is the crowning glory of mediocrity, it seems to me. Sunday with Alfredo, Bianca, and the three grandchildren was as enjoyable as ever. The new house in the Via Capo d'Africa is charming, with a view of the Colosseum above the roof-tops. Bianca cooks beautifully—we had *spaghetti bolognese, bollito misto,* and *zabaione.* It's not enough to be lucky in one's children; daughters- and sons-in-law are just as important. As I was leaving Bianca whispered that there would always be a spare room for me in her new house. What more could an old man want than a three-roomed flat—one room in the home of each of his children! Needless to say, I shall never take her up on the offer. On the contrary, I advised the children years ago against issuing mutual invitations on Sundays. As long as each of them only sees me once in three weeks I retain my popularity. I certainly retain my popularity with the grandchildren—having a grandfather who's deputy chief of the Homicide Squad means more to them than if I were going to leave an Onassis-sized fortune behind. Even I enjoy playing detectives with them. A toy car is still more glamorous than the most expensive Ferrari—imagination packs more punch than two hundred horse-power. When I play detectives with the children I make believe I really am a detective. It was like that in my young days. I played the detective long after I actually was one. People stop playing at their profession in the end. It's sad.

Wednesday, 1st November. Visited the cemetery. The tenth All Saints' Day since Adele's death. Nothing had changed.

Thursday, 2nd November. Bought myself a *History of Cooking.* Excellent. Am always discovering something new—for instance, that dishes have a class-system of their own. In the fourth century A.D. (!) Emperor Gratianus issued a decree which forbade people of 'low degree' to eat 'noble' dishes on pain of death. It appears that several such offenders were publicly executed. Augustine also mentions that the consumption by plebeians of delicacies reserved for the upper classes was a 'mortal sin'. Lucky I was born in the twentieth century.

Friday, 3rd November. Bossi came to my office. Asked if *Quest' Ora* could have any photographs so far withheld. I wouldn't entertain it, of course. "The case is dead anyway," Bossi said. "Then why do you want to revive it?" I asked. "We plan to run the whole story again," he said, "as a deterrent. I've recruited some first-class collaborators." He avoided my eye as he spoke—Bossi is incapable of looking anyone in the eye. "What's your version?" I said. He opined that the murderer must be a prominent figure who was being blackmailed by Enzian. I can't shake off the feeling that he knows more than he admits. He'd hardly dare lead the police up the garden path. All the same, prominent covers a pretty wide field.

. . . At bottom, Bossi and his breed are simply representatives of the photogenic age. I think of that every time I'm forced to release the more repellent type of police photograph. The more murdered girls appear in print, the more girls are murdered. Deterrents have been glamourized by mass reproduction. Since the incredible happens, it has to be proved; circumstantial evidence, which is never more than a pointer, will not suffice. All senses are dominated by the eye. Man actively wants to remain illiterate: forced to read and write, he substitutes vision for education and experience. The peasant who visualizes God as an old man with a white beard possesses more imagination than the educated man who only believes what he can see. That much, however, he does believe in—unreservedly. Optics are the juju of the modern illiterate. Politicians gauge their popularity by the number of times their photograph appears in print, like the jealous gods who used to check how many idols had been erected in their honour; authors scurry from lecture to lecture because visibility is the only passport to credibility; painters exhibit themselves rather than their pictures. People think physics is the science of the age; in reality, anatomy is. The visible has lost its terrors, the invisible is—at best—unbelievable. God ought to use the tabloids to improve his image.

. . . Couldn't write any more, had to prepare supper. Made it easy for myself—*spaghetti alla carbonara*. Just with ham and bacon. Mushrooms are too heavy at night.

. . . I'm probably being unfair to Bossi. I could never have become a philosopher because I don't believe in the certainty of the uncertain. The empiricists? As a young man I felt drawn to Mill, Bacon, and Locke—until I asked myself what experience really was. Is experience a known quantity? It's far from certain that the Bossis are creating a need; they may only be satisfying it. Men have always feared loneliness, but as long as mountain

58

villages remained inaccessible by road, as long as it was impossible to 'dial' the remotest towns, as long as the 'big wide world' was not channelled into the living-room, they took it for granted. Loneliness is the delusion that others are not lonely. Robinson Crusoe could endure loneliness because he did not miss television. The individual is lonelier in the world of mass communication than Crusoe on his desert island; he sees and hears everything, but nobody sees or listens to him. I can't help thinking of the road casualties I saw during my police cadetship—people who heard and saw everything but couldn't even tell you where it hurt. A world full of casualties—injured, perhaps fatally, but prone to the delusion that the Bossis can save them from their loneliness. All the Bossis do is supply remote villages with consignments of prefabricated soul. Man doesn't wonder who he is; he thinks he can recognize himself in others, even though the others wear the same cloak of invisibility as he does. There are souls of every size, for every purpose, at every price; you only need drape them on a coat-hanger. Slip into your prefabricated soul. . . . No made-to-measure soul could fit more snugly. You don't have to look for your own patterns—they're hanging on the rail too, identical in cut and material, varying only in size. How can people identify themselves when they don't even know whose soul they've slipped into? I'm no exception, of course. I chatter about others to avoid thinking about myself. I've no right to be angry with the Bossis of this world. They didn't invent the ready-made soul, they merely supply it in bulk to the department stores.

Saturday, 4th November. A possible ray of light. I again questioned the owner of the night-club at the rear of the premises. Enrico Gasparoni, forty-two, Sicilian, three convictions for pimping. He went into his shell at once, told me his place was closed at the time of the murder. "Do you take me for a fool?" I said. My question was, what did he know about Enzian's customers? Enzian thought she was "too good" for his night-club, he replied. She always treated his hostesses "like dirt". I told him we had established that Enzian occasionally visited his place for a drink. Two days prior to the murder she had been there with an elderly man whom nobody could describe—gloom being synonymous with chic nowadays, you need a guide-dog in that bar. "But you have admitted that you heard scraps of conversation while you were standing at the bar," I said. "What did you hear? Tell me again." He did so with reluctance, obviously afraid that I was trying to make him contradict himself. He repeated a few nebulous remarks, then mentioned that the man had said something like: "I shall write a novel about you". "Just a minute," I said, "you're on record as stating that the man said, 'You belong in a novel.'" "It's the same thing," said Gasparoni. Perhaps it is, but since the Contessa talked about a 'writer' I'm not so sure any more. Could it really have been a man who was planning a novel about a call-girl?

. . . Tomorrow, Sunday lunch at Flaminio's. He's the least well-to-do of the three, really, in spite of his exceptional talents. If I get down to the stove this evening I can take Flaminio and Elisa a cheese-cake *alla Canonica* tomorrow.

CHAPTER

2

The Hagglers

Aurelio Morelli

Bossi, the Neapolitan pugilist, informed me during the most recent of his distasteful visits that investigations into the Enzian case are being conducted by a certain Canonica, Christian name Italo. I must confess to an irresistible urge to laugh at this intelligence. Although the maladroit little gnome of a man has never yet been privileged to shake me by the hand, I myself have had an opportunity to scrutinize him at leisure, since funerals lend themselves admirably to covert observation.

I have always looked upon funerals as a diversion of the most exalted kind, nay, an aesthetic delight, especially when the deceased happens to be a young person. The longer a man lives the more knowledge, achievement, and experience go down into the grave with him, and the more futile his trials and tribulations prove to be; whereas the young person who has achieved nothing has nothing to lose. One ought by rights to assume, in the case of the latter, that he has made a timely escape from earthly affliction. How right the handsome Lord Byron was when he declared in *Don Juan*—the context is more than coincidental —that "'Whom the gods love dies young' was said of yore"; a shallow poet, he did not deem it necessary to substantiate his assertion, yet the reason is plain for all to see: only those who die young escape the mordant carcinoma of senescence, whose causes can never be ascertained because the child kicking in its cradle is already infected with the deadly poison.

Not wishing to digress, however, I shall content myself with remarking that I have always appreciated funerals to the full: the heathen pomp with which even the poor are buried, the timeless ceremonial, the eulogistic tributes bestowed even upon those to whom one has shortly beforehand denied a crust of bread or a hospital bed, the unintentional element of comedy in faces pregnant with sympathy and commiseration, the host of supernumeraries who scurry from one funeral to the next, the 'last' respects which are, in most cases, the first. Suffice it to say that Signor Canonica and I were both present at a funeral held more than four years ago, in August of the year 1963, he in an official capacity, I for pleasure and propriety's sake.

I need not add that it is Lucia Chiesa's funeral to which I allude, though even this allusion is an anticipation of events. However, since Signor Bossi has, with due promptitude, delivered the first instalment of my fee—six hundred and sixty-six thousand six hundred and sixty-six lire, to be exact—the worthy *Quest' Ora* shall not want for the murder of Lucia Chiesa; the less so because, as soon as Signor Bossi has received my first draft, I propose to insist that my emoluments be increased: only the murder of Hertha Enzian was included in our bargain, and no court on earth could compel me to cast the cases of Chiesa and Pisenti into the scales of journalistic success free of charge, as a premium, bonus, gratuity, or other form of unrewarded supplement.

By the close of 1962 my financial resources were exhausted. Thanks to its superabundance of literary merit, my novel *Signora Angelotti* had been rejected on all hands, so that my only recourse would have been to my aged mother, who still administers her small farm with vigour but scant material success. Ever since my illegitimate birth—my father's identity is unknown to me, but he must have been an admirable fellow; I could never have inherited such outstanding gifts from my estimable but primitive mother, and it is said that children born out of wedlock have a peculiar and almost invariable tendency to take after those that beget them—in short, ever since my natural birth, my good mother has endured more than enough ills on my account for me long to entertain the notion of becoming a charge on her modest exchequer. Even though my profound erudition has ever been an annoying impediment to my artistic self-expression—because the artist can strive for untrammelled originality only if he is blind to the inescapable influence of the past—I yet recalled, in my hour of need, that I was the possessor of considerable academic qualifications. The season of end-of-term examinations being close at hand—an ordeal viewed with greater foreboding by parents than by their irresponsible offspring—a small advertisement in *Il Messagero* sufficed to obtain me some private pupils.

Praise be to destiny; praise be, in equal measure, to my self-esteem. So far from introducing myself as the author of *Thou art Alcibiades* and other masterpieces of like stature, I hid behind the specious anonymity of the unremarkable name which fate had fortunately bestowed on me: a common-or-garden tutor, I, a coach and crammer, a schoolmasterly saviour of dim-witted pupils—nothing more. In addition, I do not flatter myself that Signora Chiesa, the mother of my Lucia, spared me a second thought, for she was a thoughtless person, this widow of a small but prosperous manufacturer of the most bizarre articles, to wit, lavatory seats—provocatively delightful to look at but just as provocatively frivolous in her approach to life. Interested only in baubles, finery, and cosmetics, she was a butterfly of a woman whose failure to abort her child was, I suspect, attributable to negligence alone.

Although in her early forties, Signora Chiesa comported herself as if she were not a day older than her seventeen-year-old daughter, who she insisted should address her by her Christian name—Luigia, if my memory serves me aright. Mother and daughter exchanged clothes from time to time, the mother borrowing from the daughter more frequently than the daughter from the mother; they both read the same abstruse books, and both disfigured their apartment with the same abstract pictures; a detestable blare of music assailed my ears whenever I crossed the threshold, and I was more than once greeted by the spectacle of Signora Chiesa lolling on the carpet amid a litter of gramophone records which surrounded her like ludicrous X-ray photographs of a mindless age. If the young people of today have no other excuse, they can at least cite in their defence that it is extraordinarily difficult for someone to rival those who emulate him, copy those who imitate him, respect those who admire him. Seventeen-year-olds who behave as if they were seven are unerringly and instinctively reacting against the childish conduct of the adult world; now that age encroaches upon youth, the latter seeks refuge in the no-man's-land of Peter Pan, the little boy who never grew up.

Not that my seventeen-year-old pupil Lucia Chiesa behaved like a girl of seven—the situation was by no means as simple as that. Her few interests and mode of conduct, code of behaviour and sense of values, were infantile to the point of imbecility; her frivolity, lack of scruple, inattention, and incorrigible rudeness poured scorn on any attempt to educate her; yet physically she was far in advance of her years, knew how to exploit her bodily charms in the fullest and most provocative degree, and could manipulate the erotic keyboard with all the dexterity of a virtuoso. While I was endeavouring by the sweat of my brow—fruitlessly, I might add—to enlighten her on the difference between *ablativus absolutus* and *ablativus mensurae*, I was reminded of a story which I had heard in my childhood, and which had greatly stirred my senses. Situated in the vicinity of my birthplace was a mental institution for patients of the female sex. An escaped madwoman from this establishment copulated her way through the surrounding villages, indeed, fornicated wildly not only with every peasant-lad in the district but also with an entire company of infantrymen stationed close by—not a 'bodyless woman' of the sort that used in former times to be a traditional attraction at annual fairs, but, on the contrary, a lascivious body devoid of head and brain. On the pretext that she found it more 'comfortable', Lucia used to receive me in skin-tight slacks and 'pullovers'—a sensual term, borrowed from the English, which suggests a mutually caressing relationship between material and body. There were occasions when I would discover her seated before her toilette mirror, lightly clad, nor did she hesitate to dress her ungirt hair in my presence, plying her comb with bored and monotonous movements for half an hour on end, just as if I were not there; and in the warm season of the year she found it quite natural to expose her bare knees and thighs to my bashful gaze—indeed, to manifest her respect for me with a bow which revealed the nudity or, worse still, semi-nudity, of her breasts. The Madwoman of Viterbo, as we called her, may have acted *sine dolo*, without guile, but the same could not under any circumstances have been said of my brainless pupil, just as all that is cited in support of its slovenly style of dress by the shameless youth of today—emancipation, convenience, naturalness, revolt against outmoded conventions, war against hypocrisy—itself amounts to nought but pharisaical humbug; to what end would these creatures comport and conduct themselves like women of the street if not to kindle the male libido, titillate it, and fan it to a white heat?

Evidence, you say? There is plenty and to spare, ladies and gentlemen of the jury, both of a general and of a personal nature. How simple it was in our parents' day, when mothers or domestics ranged themselves outside the gates of well-run educational establishments at midday, and when pupils dismissed from class made their virtuous way homeward, singly or in pairs! Not so today! Even now, as I draw aside my curtain and bestow my reluctant attention upon the soul-destroying tussles on the so-called basket-ball pitch, my thoughts turn involuntarily to the muscle-bloated, muscle-flaunting youths who loiter at school gates, eager to bear the brazen little whores off to their beds of lust. If the *taupou*, or virgin queen of a Samoan village, fails to bleed on her wedding-night she is struck dead, be it only that she has omitted to provide herself with a suitable supply of chicken's blood; and so it is that, in civilizations which aspire to be worthy of the name, people uphold at least that semblance of morality without which morality would be condemned to death, whereas with us no queen can be chosen by the *virgines* because no such electors exist.

But there is no need of such indirect evidence, for I now come to the root of the matter.

It was my practice to take Lucia's exercise-books, together with any essays she might from time to time have written at my behest, back to my house, there to correct them with the utmost care. The more the summer nights laid their hot and heavy hand on Rome—I was preparing Lucia for a supplementary examination in the autumn—the more frequently it happened that, as I opened the blue exercise-book, my attention was drawn to a peculiar rustling sound: incredible as it may seem, the infamous girl had actually secreted her fragrant undergarments between the pages! When, all unwitting, I turned the pages in order to correct an essay on the campaigns of Septimius Severus, my ear caught the rustle of brassière, petticoat, knickers—indeed, the shameless creature so far forgot herself on one occasion as to insert pubic hairs between the pages, after the manner of pressed flowers. As for her writing, not only did the wretched girl transform every jutting 'l' into a penis, every pendant 'g' into a scrotum, but even a blind man could have discerned, in the slender loop of her small 'e', the oval shape of a vagina. Small wonder, therefore, if I was so overcome by righteous indignation that I not infrequently spilled red ink over the odd page or an entire exercise-book; small wonder if I unintentionally, or on occasion intentionally, perpetrated a minor bloodbath and was next day compelled to explain—shamefacedly, for I am incapable of lying—that I had lost the school-books in question. Why, you ask, did I not take brassière, petticoat, and knickers back with me to the accursed Chiesa abode and cast them upon it like the rain of fire that engulfed Sodom and Gomorrah? Some piece of deviltry was involved here—I dare say that without hesitation— for, whenever I went to bestow school- and exercise-books in my briefcase next morning, the wicked *dessous* were gone; even if I kept vigil, slept, as the saying goes, with one eye open, or laid traps of the utmost subtlety, the *corpora delicti* continued to disappear just the same.

Be patient, dear readers! I come now to the 8th of August, the fifty-fourth anniversary of my birth.

To the question whether it was a premeditated act, conscience would permit me to respond only by posing the counter-question: what do you seriously understand by premeditation? An imbecile and malevolent juridical system has promoted emotional disequilibrium to the status of an idol, quite as if the irrational act, the unbridled outburst of fury, the moment of uncontrolled rage, the headlong plunge across the frontier of the subconscious—in other words, the unpremeditated murder—were symptomatic of a higher moral sense, and more to be condoned than the well-considered act which in general, as in my particular case, has its origin in an unbroken concatenation of humiliating and ultimately intolerable insults. Was it my intention to murder Lucia Chiesa? In the legal sense of premeditation, not at all, for I had stifled the urge to kill which had awoken in me on that humid day in August 1959, outside the Café Doney, throughout four long years of total abstinence. If it had been premeditation, why Lucia Chiesa and no one else, why that enchanting little creature with the wide-set almond-shaped eyes, saucy little nose, graceful figure, disproportionately large but shapely breasts, firm yet silky thighs—ah, a certain feeling of compassion steals over me at the remembrance! I had neither more nor less intention of helping her into a better world than I had in regard to any of her contemporaries. I acted on impulse, if you will, but the impulse had germinated within me for a full month.

It was in July—on the 18th of July, to be precise—that Lucia confided the secret of her pregnancy to me. For the second time, so she informed me, her period, curse, monthlies, or menstrual bleeding, had failed to materialize, and there was no doubting her unhappy condition. She further told me that she felt 'disinclined' to inform her mother—yes, that was the word she used; no mention of shame and disgrace, no fear of being driven from her home, no intimation that she might drown herself— just a 'disinclination' to discuss the necessary steps with her mother. I asked her what had 'inclined' her to discuss such an abominable subject with me. She perched on the arm of my chair, dangled her legs in my lap, stroked my cheeks with practised fingers, and, with her hair playing about my ears, apprised me in tender terms of her great affection for me, of her faith in my judgment, of her confidence in my readiness to help. I did not venture to utter any outraged inquiry about her perfidious partner in crime, but this proved unnecessary—indeed, I should only have made myself an object of ridicule, for Lucia voluntarily and without ceremony began to tell me of him, nor was there any talk of a perfidious partner in crime. For more than half a year, she said, as though speaking of some merry prank, she had been conducting an affair with a young man, only twenty-six years old but already married and the father of a "dear little boy"—I quote her actual words. The prolific youth could not afford a second and this time illegitimate child, nor, "worse luck", did he possess sufficient funds to remunerate one of Rome's numerous abortionists. And so, she continued, brushing my chest with her right knee and stroking my temples lightly with her fingers—and so, with a heavy heart, she had resolved to enlist the aid of a "fatherly friend", beseech him to look around for a suitable medicine-man, and solicit the loan—"half ought to be enough"—of a certain sum if need arose.

It would have been an 'unpremeditated act' of the sort beloved by courts of law if I had strangled Lucia Chiesa there and then. God alone knows how bitterly I have since regretted my failure so to do, for I should have spared myself much of what I had to endure in subsequent weeks—much of what beads my brow with perspiration even now, when I conjure it up. My promise of assistance—I could swear on oath that I never, even for a single moment, seriously entertained the idea of complicity in so criminal an assault on a burgeoning human life—emboldened Lucia to make the most scandalous admissions. Even today—in fact more so than ever before, in the neon-green solitude of Foce Verde—I am fearful lest the remembrance of Lucia Chiesa's lewd revelations should drive me to frenzy. She spared me nothing, from an account of her first night with the young criminal in a girl-friend's hospitable bedroom, to their orgiastic embraces in the warm sand of Ostia, to their obscene fumblings in the criminal's car—indeed, she had the effrontery to tell me, by way of excuse, that "nothing would have happened" if only she had troubled to retire to the back of the car and avail herself of a bottle of effervescent mineral water. I can almost hear the sibilant hiss of the opened bottle which she habitually introduced into her person once the act was consummated—precisely where, it is not hard to guess. But what was my rôle in this witches' sabbath of immorality? That of the "fatherly friend", of course, of a man whose fifty-four years put him beyond the pale of good and evil, of the eunuch and harem attendant, probably emasculated in his childhood and thus devoid of sexual memories, of the mere neuter who is handed a candle and told to light the lovers to bed. Or was it worse still? I am tempted to assume so, for the Bacchantic confession was accompanied by blandishments beyond number, almost as if the penitent had entered her priest's confessional half-naked or entirely unclothed. She probably imagined that she could, with impunity, display herself to an ageing man of fifty-four autumns in the flimsiest of négligées, waft her hot breath into his ears, gaze meaningfully into his eyes; that he would be immune to such blandishments, or, better still, grateful for a few brief moments of tingling but unconsummated excitement.

She did not go unpunished. On the pretext of conducting her, after the advent of darkness, to a physician who would release her from her spiritual burden, I arranged an evening assignation in the Borghese Gardens, not far from the Giardino Zoologico, which is deserted at that hour, having first requested Signora Chiesa to meet me, barely an hour later, for an urgent discussion of her daughter's educational problems. It was—and I say this with a certain pride—the perfect crime, the crime whose existence is denied by legal authorities only because their experience is confined to murder and rape, murder in the furtherance of theft, *crimes passionnels*, and other clumsy acts. A man is as strong as his adversaries permit him to be. Crime does not pay, but only in so far as the perpetrator is a criminal.

I had long since exacted a promise from Lucia, a sacred oath to the effect that she would not so much as breathe a word about me to her lover. Although I had good reason to believe that she would keep her promise, I was nonetheless compelled to put my trust in what the strategist would call a calculated risk. Choosing a name at random from the medical section of the classified telephone directory, I gave her the address of a doctor and instructed her to enjoin her paragon of a married man and paterfamilias to wait for her outside the doctor's surgery, ready to escort her inconspicuously home as soon as the illicit operation was accomplished. I further instructed her to arrive at our rendezvous armed with a small bag containing a nightgown, hand-towels, a change of underclothes, and a few toilet articles. With that the scene was laid, the stage set, the performance at liberty to commence.

The night was favourable to my enterprise. No rain having fallen for a considerable period, the ground was hard and unsuited to the recording of footprints. A starless sky, so eternal that the phrase 'eternal city' seemed a blasphemous and puerile mockery, reared its purple vault above Rome; the gardens of Cardinal Scipio Borghese were pervaded by a warm fragrance like that which rose from the perfumed baths of pampered Roman ladies in days of old; like stalwart Negro slaves, the trees seemed to stand guard against the brazen clamour of the surrounding city. It was a happy omen that Nature had bedecked herself so festively in honour of my birthday, for my choice of occasion was not, of course, fortuitous: revered by none, forgotten by all, lost to the world, and unprovided with birthday gifts, I proposed to confer the most princely of gifts upon myself.

The question with which Lucia approached me—namely, why I should have desired her to meet me at that particular spot—did not take me unawares; indeed, I had been expecting it. By way of reply, I told her that her tutor was not quite as elderly as she might imagine, nor was the lean and haggard pedagogue by any means as spent and unfeeling as he might appear; it was true that my youth was a thing of the past and that it was long since I had yearned to nibble at forbidden fruits, but she, yes, she—did she not suspect it?—had rekindled in me the alluring memory of past delights and made me painfully aware of what I had lost. I was resolved not to cut Lucia off in the flower of her youth without granting her the final boon of compassion, for nothing can be more cruel than a meaningless death, and nothing more atrocious than the confrontation between an incomprehensible demise and those who stand condemned without appeal. It would indeed have been cruel, merciless, and brutal to deny Lucia Chiesa the gift of knowledge. I enumerated her every transgression, rather in the manner of a father confessor who, before granting absolution, vicariously confesses the sins of his erring penitent. All this I did without once raising my voice. I was not a prey to excitement, as any ignorant and hidebound criminologist would instantly conclude, nor did I forget that one cry of alarm on the part of my victim—victim, what a banal term!—might imperil my entire project. As it happened, so far from taking fright, Lucia actually—to her eternal shame, let it be said—mistook my accusations for a hymn to her youth, a tribute to her beauty, coquetry, and sex: we are grown so old, my friends, that youth no longer even fears us! Impervious to the true meaning of my words, and impatiently swinging her suitcase to and fro like a schoolchild's satchel, the little whore demanded to know my pleasure—and would, I am convinced, have yielded herself to me there on the warm and fragrant greensward of the Borghese Gardens for the mere price of an abortion. For my part, I proceeded to enact a comedy, which, had I been able to present it on the stage, would have been assured of thunderous applause—a comedy or parody, call it what you will. I burlesqued myself as seen through her eyes: a love-sick dotard, a ludicrous romantic of the *dernier siècle*, a sentimental old ass, a senile lecher who demanded no more than a kiss and the opportunity to hold her, just once, in his arms. Satisfied that the old man could have no serious designs upon her, and positively eager to get the inescapable moment of embarrassment behind her, practised in all the arts of love but cold to the core, my vile sacrificial lamb stood on tiptoe with all the repulsive self-assurance of an innocent child, pursed her lips, and docilely offered them to me to kiss.

I did not touch her with my hands, I can swear to that despite anything the pathologists, those moronic diagnosticians of decay, may assert to the contrary. I know not to this day how it came about that she sank to my feet, clasped my knees, gurgled, and expired. Death by strangulation was the term employed by the following day's journals, whose banner headlines spoke of the "Zoo Strangler". They ought rather to have spoken of death by poison, for there is no doubt in my mind that I poisoned Lucia Chiesa with a kiss. Protruding from the poison-rings of the Borgias, so we are told by the chroniclers of a more colourful age, were golden serpents whose sharp little tongues had but to puncture a man's skin to send him into his death-throes. Why, then, should I lack the ability of the golden serpent? Why should not some higher authority have endowed me, the avenger of my dishonoured generation, with superhuman powers?

It only remains for me to stress, with all the force at my command, that Lucia's execution afforded me no sensual pleasure. There was no question whatsoever of erection, orgasm, or perverted sexual gratification: I felt no more than any revolutionary and anarchist might feel while valiantly eliminating an archetypal foe.

No lust-intoxicated sex-maniac would have acted with the serenity, prudence, and deliberation which characterized my own remarkable behaviour. Hardly had I subjected the lifeless body to thorough examination than I betook myself on winged feet to the near-by Café de Paris, where Signora Chiesa was waiting to discuss her daughter's future with me. Since the time at which death had intervened would be established with relative, but only relative, precision next morning, I could boast a positively flawless alibi: at the putative time of the murder, I was in the company of Lucia's mother.

All the more doubt attached, by contrast, to the alibi of the young man who was bound, in the nature of things, to attract the attentions of the myrmidons of the law. The undergarments in the little suitcase on which Lucia's hands had tightened so convulsively, the comparatively large sum which she had with her—these and many other things provided even the unimaginative members of the Homicide Squad with food for thought. The fact of her incipient pregnancy was quickly ascertained, and the finger of suspicion pointed straight at the young man who, being married, the father of a "dear little boy", and penniless to boot, was as perfectly provided with a motive for murder as I was deficient in the same. Since the impudent youth had been waiting outside the doctor's house in a remote street, doing his utmost—and with good reason—to escape notice, he was unable to give an account of his whereabouts at the crucial time. Not a soul believed his tale about the rendezvous because—I cannot refrain from laughing, even now—chance came to my aid in the most convenient way. Although I had deliberately chosen the locality—that is to say, a doctor's house in a remote suburban quarter—I devoted no thought to the doctor himself, deeming it to be immaterial whether he was an obstetrician, gynaecologist, or general practitioner. Strange to relate, it was only from statements made by the suspected murderer that I learned that, when looking through the classified directory, my eye had chanced to light on an ophthalmic surgeon! As one can see, fate devises the most amusing jests. In addition to the crime itself, the father of Lucia's unborn child stood indicted of crass stupidity: having concocted the tale of the abortion—or, rather, of his weary vigil outside the quack's house—he should scarcely have given the address of an oculist or eye specialist. It was not he who had 'laid on' the good doctor, he stammered, but an unknown friend of Lucia's. The police could only shake their heads at this introduction of a mysterious 'third party', and not even the most incompetent detective could have failed to ask why the prospective father—or abdicator of paternity—had not at once departed when he realized that the doctor in question was a glorified purveyor of spectacles. Moreover, the intention to procure an abortion on his beloved—a rash admission made for the sake of an alibi—incriminated the 'murderer' still further, the majority of defendants being convicted less for proven offences than for their moral turpitude. I thus came within a hair's breadth of ridding the world of a second youthful transgressor, at least for a considerable term, yet I am glad that it did not turn out so, and that he was released because of 'insufficient evidence': not only would my all too sensitive conscience have been overburdened by the lifelong incarceration of an unknown, but, like every good revolutionary, I balk at imposing sentences which I do not carry out in person.

To repeat, I made a point of attending the funeral, which took place on one of those warm but rainy August days more typical of Rome than is generally supposed by visitors from northern climes. With characteristic modesty I remained in the background, and although the ceremony owed its very instigation to me, yielded pride of place to members of the immediate family, friends, and relations. Some two hundred persons thronged the grave; flowers and garlands, garlanded speeches, and flowery words proliferated; the Homicide Squad appeared in full array, presumably on watch for the murderer; and I, as I stood there beneath my open umbrella—what more solitary sight than a lone man beneath an umbrella?—wondered involuntarily whether, apart from my worthy mother, a single living soul would have troubled to escort me to my own last resting-place. Finally—and incidentally—Lucia's youthful classmates were also present in full force.

Carlo Vanetti

Zempach did his best, but his best isn't good enough. Enzian is being stubborn. I instructed Zempach to remain in Vienna and invite Hermann Vorneweg to Rome. Nothing ever gets done properly unless you do it yourself.

I asked Vorneweg to lunch at my office. He looks like a St Bernard whose little barrel contains arsenic instead of brandy. Also, he wears brown crêpe-soled shoes with a blue suit. Elegance which stops short at the knees is not elegance. One should be wary of such people.

I have my own technique with Germans. They think caviare and champagne are chic, especially in the morning. *German men despise us, German women like sleeping with us. Being a psychologist, I recognize the existence of a close relationship between those two facts. Now that our immigrant workers are sleeping with German women, the Germans despise us twice as much. Beware, treacherous St Bernard—I am a historian as well as a psychologist! Young men like Bossi and my son Francesco dismiss me as a tradesman, but I base my business dealings on a knowledge of history and human nature. The Germans are revenging themselves on our workers because we took their immigrant workers, the gladiators, and threw them to the lions.*

Two thousand years too late! Unable to conquer us by force of arms, the Germans run us down in their long-distance coaches. They lock their cars as soon as they cross the Italian border in case someone robs them of a pound of oranges. In Germany they get their cars stolen. Such is the difference between culture and civilization.

I have never felt prouder of my bargaining tactics than in Vorneweg's case. I was determined not to get embroiled in an auction. Kronos Films are prepared to pop three hundred thousand Austrian schillings into Papa Enzian's gaping mouth—possibly more. I'd sooner risk a libel action than follow suit. However, that wasn't the main snag. All I had to offer in exchange for the Enzian girl's life-story was her murderer. On the other hand, I couldn't very well say to Vorneweg, Look, you've got the victim and we've got the murderer—let's swap. He could lay the late lamented Hertha on the line, whereas Morelli was a far more awkward proposition. After I had assured him of my discretion, I said:

"How will your story end? I mean, are you planning to identify the murderer?"

"That's up to the script-writers," he replied vaguely.

"Didn't you say you were budgeting for a five-million-mark production?" I asked. He nodded proudly. "So you invest five million marks, more than a million dollars, and as soon as you finish shooting they arrest the murderer. Let's say your script-writers put their money on a business tycoon who's being black-mailed by a call-girl, whereas in reality it turns out to be the Enzian girl's brother. Know what you can do with your film then?" I laughed. "Celluloid burns beautifully."

"Do you know who the murderer is?" he asked, just as I intended him to.

"Not a business tycoon, anyway," I replied. "Nor her brother."

That was a bull's-eye. No admission that I knew the murderer's identity, coupled with a hint that I did know after all. However, it doesn't do to underestimate the Germans. Vorneweg guessed that I was steering for some kind of compromise, and tried to reinforce his bargaining-position. He helped himself to another tablespoonful of caviare and said:

"We'll simply leave the murderer's identity in the air."

"Fine," I retorted, "so long as he isn't arrested."

"Anything goes in a class production," he parried.

"That depends," I said, and leant back in my chair. I make a point of doing that before I start lecturing. "I may not be a film-maker, but I do know the ropes," I went on. "Look, my friend, we're both in show business. You can't entertain people by dishing up reality. The entertainments industry falls into two sections." My pet theory. Curiously enough, it annoys Beatrice as well as Francesco. Intellectuals can't bear to be rumbled. "You can either flee from reality into abstraction," I continued, "that's intellectual show business—or flee from reality into illusion—that's mass-media show business."

"What are you driving at?" Vorneweg asked, being a German. His inability to understand me was making him sweat.

"You could produce a *nouvelle vague* film," I said, "but not for five million." *Abstraction is cheap, illusions are expensive, but the St Bernard would never have grasped that.* "Nobody knows that better than you do," I pursued, "otherwise you wouldn't be badgering Herr Enzian for his approval. In the case of a *nouvelle vague* film your script-writers would invent a symbolic call-girl and the director would fit her out with two heads." I leant forward as people do in serialized novels when they want to indicate that a punch-line is coming. "You plan to use the girl's real name. Well, I don't blame you, considering the priceless publicity we've given it—Press, television, radio, and so on. However, semi-realism is a crime against racial purity—if you'll pardon the expression." I used it on purpose, of course. After all, Vorneweg is a German. "So," I said, "first you press fifty thousand crisp D Marks into the Viennese butcher's hot and sweaty hand for the privilege of using his name, and then you leave the murderer's identity vague. You can't cast anyone as an unidentified murderer—no star would wear it." I laughed.

"You do know who the murderer is, then," said Vorneweg.

I feigned astonishment. "What makes you think so?"

I wish Francesco had been there to hear me, though he probably wouldn't have learnt anything. Beatrice would, but my children are the wrong gender. She'll marry her ski-instructor, that ruddy-cheeked Don Juan of the Dolomites who has snow instead of brains and, like all snowmen, melts away to a broomstick when the season ends. It's tragic to have a daughter who's only intellectual in the summer.

The secret of skilful negotiation is to provoke the replies you want to hear. Vorneweg replied that I wouldn't be competing for the rights myself if I didn't know how the story "turned out"; that I couldn't have hoped to sell the *Enzian Story* to the films from the outset without knowing "something more"; that, finally, I wouldn't have invited him to Rome unless *Quest' Ora* had something to offer.

"There aren't any flies on you," I said brusquely, then continued, with the suggestion of a wink, "I can't supply you with the murderer, of course, but I can offer you a script-writer who'll describe him for you, explain his motives, and give an account of the crime. You can always put your own people to work on it afterwards." *I know more about films than Herr Vorneweg suspects. Films are rewritten even before they're written.*

"What if the murderer gets arrested in the meantime?" Vorneweg retorted, applying himself with gusto to my Louis Roederer Brut Rosé 1959. *I only mention that because our serialized novels always give brand-names in full. Champagne no longer impresses by itself—the brand-name is essential. Hermann Vorneweg is just the sort of magazine-reader to be impressed by a brand-name.*

"Should the murderer fail to fit the description supplied by *Quest' Ora*," I replied, "we will refund you the script-writer's fee in full."

"I don't remember agreeing to pay your script-writer's fee, Signor Vanetti," the German said craftily.

"I'm a born gambler," I replied with a smile. "If our description of the murderer doesn't fit we pay you an indemnity of fifty thousand D Marks—a nice fat contractual penalty. You retain all rights, of course."

Vorneweg's eyes narrowed. "And what do you get out of it if your murderer is the right one?" he asked.

"My principle," I said genially, "is to agree terms which are favourable to both parties. I suggest you acquire the world rights from Herr Enzian for any sum that suits you. You relinquish the Press rights for Italy and the rest of the world to us, free of charge. You also pay the script-writer appointed by us. We get a thirty-three and a third per cent share in the net proceeds of your film, and if you resell the material—to America, for instance—you pass on fifty per cent of the purchase price."

Vorneweg laughed. It was a pretty inexpert performance. "You keep telling me what we're expected to do," he declared.

"You did ask me," I reminded him. "We're guaranteeing you the real murderer. That's our contribution, and that ought to be enough for anyone."

"You forget we're supplying you with the victim," countered the German.

"I hadn't forgotten," I said, ready for that too. "The victim is a pure luxury."

Vorneweg eyed me with astonishment.

I was on top now. All that remained to be said was the unvarnished truth. Truth is the best ploy of all, that's my maxim. Nothing better than safeguarding your own interests without cheating the opposition.

"Hertha Enzian is a public figure," I enlightened him, "like Churchill or the Holy Father. Every Italian periodical, including our competitor *Lui e Lei*—which has a much smaller circulation —has devoted whole columns to Hertha Enzian."

"I'm surprised you're so interested, then," Vorneweg cut in sarcastically.

I leant back, not by accident. "We're both in the same boat, Herr Vorneweg," I said. "We don't want any old story. My office has enough material—it's at your disposal, by the way, free, gratis, and for nothing—for us to start running an *Enzian Story* tomorrow. However, our slogan is *Quest' Ora, the Magazine for the Discerning Reader*, and we take it seriously. *Noblesse oblige*, my dear sir. We require full and authentic details of the girl's past life, details which only her family can supply. I won't disguise from you, either, that a sales slogan like 'Sole authorized biography' would be worth something to us. We have our reputation to consider, too. No litigation, that's my motto. The only successful litigation is the kind that never takes place." Affable as my tone had been, I now concluded—leaning forward —on an unmistakably emphatic note: "What we're acquiring from you is a luxury. What you're buying from us is a necessity."

I'm sure this did the trick, for—as I never tire of telling my reporters—truth has a ring of its own. Morelli will be in durance vile before the film is completed or my name isn't Carlo Vanetti. I'm saving Kronos Films from disaster.

Vorneweg announced that he would have to go over my proposals in detail with his boss, Herr Armin Kohn of Berlin. I took the opportunity to bid him a cordial farewell. You have to know when to make a move.

Needless to say, this isn't the last of the matter. Herr Vorneweg will consume at least one more tin of caviare and many a bottle of Louis Roederer Brut Rosé 1959 on my premises. It doesn't pay to stint expenses. The gentlemen in Berlin will demand a stiffer penalty clause and haggle about my share in any future American rights. I, in so far as my interests allow, will give way gracefully. I won't cut the Germans in on my receipts, though: better to allow someone the run of your bedroom than let him examine your books.

Being essentially a philosopher rather than an entrepreneur, I am reminded by such negotiations of the wartime comedian who had the effrontery to suggest that every belligerent Power should bomb its own cities, thereby achieving the same results at less expense. Both parties in a business deal know that everyone demands the maximum in order to obtain the minimum. It would be more respectable, more economical of time and money, if they reached an acceptable compromise straight away, but who ever heard of an honest broker?

I am especially proud of my script-writer idea, though that will be another hard row to hoe. It was positively paternal of me to think of Bossi as I did, because Bossi has been trying to sell his stuff to the films for years. *Every journalist fancies himself as a script-writer. Once a script-writer, he wants to direct.* I couldn't have foreseen that Kronos would cross things up when I agreed terms with Bossi. If I only get thirty-three-and-a-third myself—fifty per cent at most—I can't very well relinquish forty per cent of my modest share to him. The Germans will pay him well at my sole instigation, so it's only right and fair if he reduces his claims on me to twenty per cent. I shall offer him ten.

After such an exhausting day it did me good to attend an excellent performance of *Tosca* by the visiting San Carlo Opera Company and relax—as far as possible, that is, because the ability to relax is not one of my strong points. I pity any poor devil who has to bear my sort of responsibilities unaided.

THE HAGGLERS

I was so jumpy before the lights went down that even Maria spotted it. Claretta—it was 'her' Tuesday—never misses a guest performance, and I had kept quiet about my prospective visit to the opera with Maria. Foolish of Claretta to push me into a lie, but her common sense doesn't extend to the subject of my wife. *Why can't women understand that a double life implies two separate lives? Mistresses absolutely refuse to grasp the fact that a man has a right to his marital existence. Luisa was just the same. No wife finds it surprising that her husband sleeps with his mistress, but every mistress wants to monopolize her lover's bed. This is unfair. A mistress yearns to be part of what she calls a man's 'life', yet she begrudges his lawful wedded wife the smallest share of his love-life. She wants to hear him say that his wife is frigid or unfaithful or physically repulsive. How humiliating for the mistress, who in that case only exists faute de mieux! Mistresses profit by polygamy and demand monogamy. The result? Instead of being accomplices, they become dupes. Most men fear their mistresses more than their wives, and end by defending the latter against the former. The tolerant mistress has yet to be invented.*

Sitting in our box, I studied Maria in profile, and came once again to the conclusion that she is a wholly presentable figure—at least, away from her domestic stamping-ground. Shapely, with a still imposing *décolletage*, a pretty little nose, and unswept jet-black hair, she is one of those women who prompt people to say that they must have been "very lovely once upon a time". Women of her type are like temples which only claim admiration when ruined. *Casanova, whom I have read in the original unabridged edition, knew less about women than people suppose. "The absent are always wrong" does not refer to love; absent women are almost always right.* Maria may not suit me as a person but she fits my rôle in society like a glove. The wife of a leading magazine proprietor has to look the part, especially in our country, where even the ludicrous *apertura a sinistra* has failed to make a dint in Catholic tradition. People envy me far too much as it is, so it would be intolerable if they begrudged me my wife as well. Men, the people who ultimately matter, do not begrudge me Maria, but women begrudge Maria me. Looking at a married couple, one wonders involuntarily whether the husband is deceiving the wife or vice versa: with Maria, unlike

Claretta, anyone can tell that I do the deceiving. All things considered, Maria is the ideal matrimonial partner.

Although I pride myself on an above-average appreciation of music—the fact that my Beat-fan son would dispute this leaves me cold—I was unable to concentrate on the opera. In any case, the enjoyment of Puccini's music stimulates thoughts of other things.

The moral aspect of the Morelli case is a constant headache— not the legal repercussions, which I have insured against, but the need to preserve my self-respect. My secret dream is to sell off all my publications except *Positivismo* and fight the good fight. *There is no allergy worse than the itch induced by an inability to tolerate injustice.* My needs are few—a three-roomed flat would be quite enough for me. Beatrice will marry, and Francesco can see how he fares on his own. Unfortunately, *Positivismo* wouldn't survive three months without *Quest' Ora.* People think I'm only interested in amassing money. In reality, the Morelli business weighs heavily on my mind.

While Scarpia was singing: "*I cannot leer nor ogle nor coo like any turtle-dove,*" I suddenly recalled the story about the French State television service. State television! Two climbers— Germans, I think they were—had sought refuge on a rocky ledge below the Dru peak in the Mont Blanc massif and were hovering between life and death—nearer death than life, in fact. I can picture the scene vividly, even though I have always held all forms of sport to be a gross abuse of the human body—hence my excellent physical condition. There they stood or sat on a foot-wide ledge of rock with the wind whistling about their ears, stomachs aching for food, and tongues cleaving to the roofs of their mouths. Rescuers from Chamonix reached the exhausted mountaineers, who by then resembled living icicles, at 5 A.M.— *Paris Match* sold us the exclusive pictures. You can't beat *Match* when it comes to on-the-spot pictures. Rescued and rescuers were to be lifted off by helicopter, but a television station, which was financing the rescue operation, said no—no rescue without tele-vision, we're footing the bill, so we say when. It was still too dark for them, that was the trouble. The climbers' relatives wrung their hands, and the crowds at the foot of Mont Blanc grew restive, but they waited until the clouds had dispersed and the helicopters could approach from the right camera-angle in sunny photogenic weather. The other story is that the French newspapers only launched their attack on the 'irresponsible' climbers because the conquerors of the Dru had refused to sell their first-hand story to a big Paris daily.

Maria whispered to me, anxious to know what I was thinking about. She probably thought I was preoccupied with some strip-tease girl, whereas I was really intent on my conscience. I'm glad I thought about Mont Blanc. A man who works at my sort of pressure seldom gets a chance to think. *One of the tragedies of life is that he who works doesn't think and he who thinks doesn't work.* There is something sublime about grand opera.

The French State television service has no more reason to feel ashamed than I. *The human craving for information is a primeval instinct. Children soon succumb to it, some by lifting their dolls' skirts, others by slitting their bellies open. This is both naughty and virtuous, for who would call the thirst for knowledge a vice? We cannot stipulate what man, in this proud age of omniscience, should want to know. All he wants to know is everything. Why, since he is shown astronauts floating around in outer space, shouldn't he want to see his fellow-men scrabbling at a rock-face? Why shouldn't he want to know whether a sex-maniac had an orgasm when he murdered his victim? The world is a doll's house with the front open. Nothing is more out-moded than privacy. I turn on the television set, and what happens? Two women struggle through the Vietnamese jungle before my very eyes or a child drops dead at my elbow. However, since more than one camera is operating, I have the added advantage that I can also see the soldier who shoots the child. I can be in Paris or Bombay, at a world fair or in a court-room, at a theatre or an execution—and at the same time I can be drinking beer or stuffing my hand down a girl's cleavage. Doggedly, I amass knowledge. "L'appétit vient en mangeant", so it's only natural that I should want to know more and more. Am I to take up a lone stand against this trend? I wouldn't even if I could, because I'm a moralist. Doesn't more knowledge make for better human beings? Doesn't he who knows more serve a higher form of morality? Take pornography, for instance. Yesterday porno-graphy had to be dressed up in a hypocritical little chastity-belt of scientific jargon; today they show a modern Swedish sex film; tomorrow, the Arabs who used to hawk filthy post-*

*cards round the streets of Paris will be out of a job. The sight of
two people copulating will only arouse interest if their cardio-
grams are shown as well. Cardiogram changes during ejaculation
are relatively unfamiliar, whereas any fool knows what an
orgasm is. It was left to the scientific age to make man human.
Ergo, anyone who refuses to satisfy man's need for knowledge is
automatically thrusting him back into the animal state. The two
climbers might have plunged to their death between 5 and 8 A.M.,
but would it not have been worse to plunge millions of television
viewers into the abyss of ignorance? Again, how could climbers
for whom brave men risked their lives and the State television
service furnished helicopters have been allowed to keep their
experience to themselves?* Aurelio Morelli may continue to enjoy
freedom for a few weeks longer than he deserves, but our series
of articles will supply millions of people—they will be millions,
much to the annoyance of *Lui e Lei*—with the freedom of knowledge.

Tosca was singing her great aria: "*Love and music, these I
have lived for*". I could at last devote myself to the music—in
fact I was in such good spirits that Maria suggested having a bite
together at Passetto's. I shall get Beroglio to write an article in
Positivismo on "The Moral Obligations of the Mass Media".

Emilio Bossi

I had to take Francesco along because of the pictures.

We didn't drive there in his red Alfa. We took my Fiat instead. Not bad, either.

I hadn't seen Francesco for days. That meant I had to brief
him on the way. "Morelli's mother is seventy-nine plus," I said.
"We'll tell her her son is in line for the Nobel Prize."

"She won't know what the Nobel Prize is," said Francesco.

"A cash prize," I said. "Don't worry, she'll understand that."

"I won't say a word to her," said Francesco.

"Just take pictures," I said.

"Why don't we wait till they arrest Morelli?" he asked.

"She may be dead by then," I said.

I don't like working with Francesco even if he does take pretty
good pictures. He trails his conscience around like a ball and

chain. Now he's grown a beard he looks like a camera-toting Christ. People over thirty don't go for that sort of thing.

"Do you still see Fiorella?" I asked, to get him off the subject of old Mother Morelli.

"Of course," he said. "Tell me, is she really your sister?"

"So my mother says," I said.

"Fiorella's a human being," he said.

"I have to earn a living," I said. "I don't have time to be a human being. Joined any good demonstrations lately?"

"I don't know about good," he said. "We demonstrated against the war in Vietnam."

"Everything's O.K., then," I said.

"You're not human," he said.

"We're going to photograph the room where Morelli was born," I said. "*The Cradle that Rocked a Murderer*. Let's hope she's still got the cradle. Use a zoom lens."

"I don't need any advice from you," said Francesco.

"Do as I say," I said. "That way you won't get your conscience dirty. How many pictures of Morelli have you taken?"

"Not enough for my father," said Francesco. "He wants more close-ups. Morelli always goes walking near the atomic-energy place. It's forbidden to take photographs in the grounds."

The boy needs his head examined. Why didn't he say so before? That's all we need, Morelli held on an espionage rap. The proverbial banana-skin. It would be typical of them to arrest the spy but let the murderer run loose.

"What does he do in the grounds?" I asked.

"Hauls dead fish out of the water," said Francesco.

"What does he do with them?" I asked.

"Buries them," said Francesco.

Francesco didn't find this odd. Fiorella wouldn't find it odd either. Fiorella ought to marry Francesco. I'd take over the publishing house, Vanetti and I would look after the two kids, the two kids would demonstrate against the war in Vietnam and bury dead fish. Happy ending.

"I'm planning to denounce Morelli and help him escape," said Francesco.

"One or the other," I said.

"No," he said, "I want to spoil your game without sending Morelli to the gallows."

"We don't operate the death penalty," I said.

We drove inland towards Viterbo. The sky looked like an ice-hockey rink after Moscow versus Quebec. I said as much to Francesco, but he doesn't appreciate these things. He writes in secret and lets everybody know. Fiorella says he's a great poet. I'd be a great poet too if my father was Carlo Vanetti, but he isn't. He's an engine-driver. That's to say, he was. He's dead now.

"It's a rotten business," said Francesco.

"What?" I asked.

"Pumping Morelli's mother," he said.

"Nothing compared to Vietnam," I said.

We drove through Viterbo. I know the place like the back of my hand, but I still feel mellowed by the sight of all those walls and fountains and cloisters. I told Francesco that every year on the 3rd of September eighty *facchini* carry a huge illuminated contraption down the Via S. Rosa in honour of the saint. No other lights are permitted inside the town. He said "Crap" and stared straight ahead. I know what crap is myself, especially the crap served up by the Holy Roman Catholic Church. Except that fourteenth-century crap is antique. Francesco ought to know that. He may look like Jesus Christ, but he's beyond redemption.

We reached Montefiascone about midday. I didn't want to ask for old Mother Morelli in the village in case the police made inquiries later. As usual, I was in luck. I learnt my luck from Vanetti. The second farmhouse I stopped at belonged to Signora Morelli.

It was a pretty dismal set-up. A decrepit stone house standing at the sunless end of a vineyard. Two or three cats suffering from mouse-deficiency and a few clucking candidates for Sunday lunch. The place might have had something to offer if it really had been the birthplace of a future Nobel Prize winner. It was too much in character for the birthplace of a murderer.

"Start shooting," I told Francesco. "They may set the dogs on us." You never know; earlier on, when I was less lucky, my pants were a mass of holes.

Signora Morelli was just clearing away the midday meal—only soup and bread. An old man was helping her. The place stank of cats. A cat which had kittened the night before was lying in a basket.

"Signora Morelli," I said, "we're from *Quest' Ora.*"

She stared at me blankly, though her eyes were the only sign of life in her face. She must have been quite tall once, almost as tall as her son, but now she rattled around inside her skin like a mendicant friar in bishop's robes. I'd visualized her with glasses like a pair of monocles. She didn't wear glasses. She might have been described as a well-preserved eighty-year-old, if it hadn't been for the senile mouth, which was tiny and almost toothless. Wrinkles converged on the lips from all sides like streams trickling into a lake.

"*Quest' Ora*," the man shouted in her ear, "you know, the magazine."

She nodded.

"Your son Aurelio," I yelled. "They're giving him a Nobel Prize. That's a big prize they give to famous writers."

"Aurelio?" she said. "I haven't heard from Aurelio for twenty years."

"Two years," said the man.

I decided it would be simpler to speak to the man. "Signor Morelli is famous now," I said. "That's why we want to find out something about his childhood."

"They want to know something about Aurelio's childhood," bellowed the old man.

"I'm sure he was a good child," I said.

"He was good at book-learning," said the old man. I put him at seventy-two or three. He didn't consider it necessary to transmit my implied question over his personal loud-hailer. "The priest sent him to school," he said. "He studied all the time, never did a day's work."

Francesco stood propped against the door-frame, doing nothing. He was getting on my nerves.

"How come Signor Morelli never married?" I asked.

The old man said scornfully, "The girls didn't fancy him. His head was stuffed with books."

I asked, "Have you been here long?"

"Always," he said.

He looked at Signora Morelli tenderly, like a vineyard playboy. I wondered why the two of them had never married. Signora Morelli is technically a spinster—I checked that in the civil register.

"You're talking nonsense," said the old woman.

She didn't mean anything specific. She'd probably got into the habit of repeating the sentence at regular intervals.

"Has Signor Morelli ever supported his mother?" I asked.

"You'll have to speak up," said the old man. He was hard of hearing himself.

"Has Signor Morelli ever sent his mother money?" I asked again.

"Once at Christmas," said the old man. "Once at Christmas, out of the blue."

"Has she supported him?" I said.

"She sends him some wine every year," the old man said disapprovingly. "He was here two years back, in summer. For eight weeks. Then he disappeared again. He didn't even say thank-you."

"You're talking nonsense," said Signora Morelli. I think she heard him that time, because he bellowed the way deaf people do.

The stench of cat was unbearable. Francesco drooped against the door-post like a damsel about to swoon.

"Signor Morelli is going to be very famous," I said loudly. Which was true. "Was he born here in this house?"

"In this room," replied the old woman.

I tipped Francesco the wink, but he didn't budge.

"Do you still have Signor Morelli's cradle?" I asked.

The bucolic boy-friend shook his head.

"Would Signora Morelli have any pictures of him, childhood photographs or snapshots of him as a young man?" I asked. Childhood photographs of murderers are important. No one can believe they looked like children when they were children.

"He wants to know if you've got any pictures of Aurelio," yelled the mummified gigolo.

The old girl smiled but said nothing.

"She's got a whole drawerful," the old man murmured spitefully. He sounded jealous. "I'll give them to you later."

"I'll make it worth your while," I said—quietly, because I was getting a bit chary of Signora Morelli's deafness. Just as quietly, I asked, "Has nothing ever been heard of Signor Morelli's father?"

Francesco cleared his throat.

"He was a sailor," the old man replied, even more spitefully. "He must be an admiral by now."

"My friend would like to take a photograph of Signora Morelli," I said.

The man bent his mouth to the woman's ear. "The gentleman wants to take a photograph of you," he bellowed, pointing at Francesco's camera. "It won't cost anything."

She was sitting on the bench at the half-cleared table with her hands in her lap. My grandmother used to sit like that, hands folded and fingers slightly splayed as if they were scared of touching each other. She shook her head.

"Maybe you can persuade her," I said, with an I'll-make-it-worth-your-while look. In the first place we needed the pictures, and in the second place Francesco would have been overjoyed if we'd had to leave empty-handed.

The old woman beckoned her boy-friend over with a spidery forefinger and whispered in his ear. I only caught the odd word.

The old man straightened up and said, "She won't be photographed like this. But if you'll wait. . . She wants to change."

"We aren't in any hurry," I said.

"The gentlemen aren't in any hurry," bellowed the old man.

Signora Morelli got up with surprising agility, glanced at the kittens in the basket, said, "The little ones were born in the night," and went out.

Silence fell. Then the old man crept to the door and flung it open. "She peeps through the keyhole sometimes," he said. He opened the bottom drawer of the dresser and took out a bundle wrapped in a brightly-coloured handkerchief. He undid the knot and laid the photographs out on the table.

There were eight photographs of Morelli. Four of them—the most important, naturally—were pretty faded. Mounted in grey folders with the photographer's florid signature in the bottom right corner. Not easy to reproduce, but retouchers can do marvels. *The Murderer at his Christening, in the Arms of his Ill-fated Mother. The Murderer in his Sailor-suit, Aged Six.* Another one of the murderer in a sailor-suit, probably in honour of his noble father. We can't publish both. The art director will have to pick the better of the two. *The Murderer at his Confirmation, Aged Thirteen.*

"I'm going to be sick," said Francesco.

I thought: not before you've taken your pictures, my old

Vietcong. A lad who doesn't get sick on protest marches ought to be able to stand a couple of childhood photos and a spot of cat-shit.

The future *dottore* was easily recognizable in the Confirmation picture. Two others showed him in an old-fashioned swimsuit, chest covered, white skin, a drowned mariner with an erection. Must have sent them home while on holiday. One with glasses, one without, both usable. The seventh photo wasn't an original print but clipped from a publisher's blurb. I already had it. The eighth was first-class. An informal snap with his mother, probably on his last visit. I must find out more about it. *The Murderer with his Mother during a Recent Visit to his Birthplace. Note the Affectionate Pose, Head on one side, Arm round the Old Lady's Shoulders.*

"I'll send them back," I said.

"No need to," said the old man. "She never looks at them."

"Isn't she fond of him?" I asked.

"She doesn't want anything more to do with him, not since he disappeared two years ago," he said.

The door opened. I hardly recognized the old girl. She was wearing an Umbrian peasant dress made of heavy silk, grey-blue, with lace. Her sparse hair was covered by a little bonnet. All in all, she looked like something out of a book on regional costumes. She stood in the doorway, stiff as a poker, as if she had grown into her dress. She looked sixty, and every inch the *dottore's* mother. I hoped Francesco would get a good likeness.

"Shoot," I told him.

Francesco worked with flash because it was dark in there. The old woman never flinched once. Either she enjoyed being the centre of attention or her thoughts were elsewhere. I thought of Madame Tussaud's and felt happy that we'd found her alive and kicking.

"Go and stand next to Signora Morelli," I told the boy-friend.

"I'm to be photographed with you," the old man yelled fondly.

"You're talking nonsense," she said, and flatly refused to pose with her veteran Casanova.

I shoved a chair towards her. She sat down majestically, tweaked her bonnet into position, and gave Francesco a smile.

Francesco was behaving himself now. He photographed her from every angle, and moved in quite close. I held the flash. The old woman still didn't move, almost as if she was thinking: they're the last you'll have taken, so better be a good girl.

"Have you got any of your son's books?" I shouted into her ear.

"She's only got a Bible," said the old man.

I told him to fetch it. Luckily, it was quite a big Bible. I opened it and put it into her hands. I told Francesco to shoot it so people might be forgiven for thinking it was one of Morelli's books.

The old girl played along. The only time she dug her heels in was when I suggested photographing her outside the house. Francesco took at least two dozen shots of her. No use as a cover-picture, of course, because nobody over twenty qualifies for a Vanetti cover, but there could be a full-page studio portrait. We'll bring out at least three instalments of straight background material before we start on the memoirs. The public need warming up. If the memoirs are a success we can tack on another two instalments. Readers take a while to cool off.

The old man escorted us to our car.

"How much money will Aurelio get?" he asked. "From the prize. . ."

"A million or two," I said. It wasn't much of an exaggeration, even if I wasn't talking about the Nobel Prize.

The old man laughed till he wobbled.

I slipped a couple of bank-notes into his hand. He tried to back off, but pocketed them all the same. He waved us goodbye, even though it was dark by that time.

"I hope she dies before the story breaks," Francesco said on the way back.

"So do I," I said.

"You couldn't care less about the old woman," said Francesco.

"I care about the police," I said. "We'll have to say we were doing background research for a book by Morelli. That's what it says in the contract, anyway."

"She looked so sad," said Francesco, "almost as if she suspected something."

He had a point for once, but all I said was: "She didn't look sad at all. Just old."

Francesco silently nursed the cameras on his lap like a litter of embryo piccaninnies. Eventually he said: "You're covering for my father."

"That makes two of us," I said.

"I don't care," he said. "There's no difference between Morelli and my father. It's more important for my father to go to gaol than Morelli. Morelli only murdered a call-girl."

"Society would be within its rights if it put your father inside," I said. "It would serve you right."

Listening to him beefing was almost enough to give me a bad conscience myself. That's one of the reasons why I can't stand Francesco. I've worked like a black ever since I matriculated. I even worked before that, in summer, as a bell-hop. I've never married. My mother only gets a pittance and Fiorella's college fees are a drain on my pocket. Francesco writes poetry, drives an Alfa, plays the guitar, and plans to shop his father—and yet one look at him is enough to give me a bad conscience. The idlers look down on people like me. Smirking Buddhas who know it all. It's a grand illusion. Now that *dolce far niente* has been superseded by *amaro far niente* the bitter idlers aren't parasites any more, they're philosophers. Or rebels. That's why they don't smile when they play their guitars. They play guitar so as not to do anything else, allegedly, and if they smiled they'd be smiling for society. World-reform through laziness is the latest creed. Anybody who works for a living is barred from the club and banished to the Vanetti underworld. I sometimes feel tempted to apologize to Fiorella for soiling my hands with the money she needs for her studies. When I was fifteen I bought a bike on hire purchase. My father told me it was reprehensible to spend more than you earn. Now it's reprehensible to earn more than you spend. I can endure the disgrace of it, but why do I have a bad conscience? Probably because I work for my own benefit and the others idle for theirs. It doesn't make me a Vanetti, though, not by a long chalk.

"I wonder why Morelli pushed off so suddenly two years ago," I said. Francesco's silence was getting me down. It was a meaningful silence.

"Because he's crazy," said Francesco.

"Only murderers are normal—that's what he told me," I said.

"Maybe he's right," said Francesco.

We didn't speak again until we reached Rome. We never have anything to say to each other.

Francesco Vanetti

Bossi is an old man, he's thirty or thirty-one, he isn't an old man because he's thirty or thirty-one, he's an old man because he made me photograph old Mother Morelli, he made me photograph old Mother Morelli, my father told him to, Bossi is like the slave-drivers who are slaves themselves, slave-drivers who are slaves themselves are the worst of all, I prefer slave-drivers proper. Bossi is a bridge, a flesh-and-blood bridge, his feet are on the mainland and his head is on the island, he's a bridge and my father marches across him to me, my father marches across his belly to the island, thanks to Bossi I can't be alone, thanks to Bossi WE can't be alone, on the island. WE want to be alone on the island because anyone who comes to the island brings experience with him, his luggage is full of experience, all experience is dirty, anyone who has experienced anything exists, anyone who exists has escaped, anyone who escapes has sold himself, otherwise he wouldn't be alive, anyone who is alive is dirty. Soldiers blow up bridges so no-one can follow them, soldiers are sensible, they blow up bridges but the enemy rebuilds them, temporary bridges, the enemy follows them across the bridges, no bridges no enemy, no bridges no pursuit, no bridges no defeat, bridges are more treacherous than enemies, Bossi is a bridge, Bossi is a traitor.

I tell Fiorella: Your brother is a traitor, but I don't tell her about Morelli, I promised my father I wouldn't, Morelli is a family secret, I am Francesco Vanetti, I am a bridge. Fiorella says: My brother is a traitor, he's a traitor born and bred. Emilio admits his father was a Fascist, Emilio's father wore the Fascist emblem in his buttonhole, red, white, and green, national colours are poison, they ought to be put on prescription. Fiorella says Emilio despises his father because he was a Fascist with poison in his buttonhole, but he's a Fascist himself, because he bridges the gap. Who cares whether someone was a Fascist, who cares whether someone wore poison in his buttonhole, anyone with eyes saw the murder, anyone who saw anything is an accessary, anyone who discloses anything is an accessary, anyone who has been to the theatre or read a book or slept with a woman is an accessary, anyone who has experienced anything is an accessary.

We're in Bruno's flat, Bruno is my friend, Bruno could be my friend, Bruno is a Jew, Bruno's mother's second husband was a banker, the Nazis beat Bruno's father to death or gassed him, I don't know which, Bruno could be my friend but Bruno always takes the other side, I know he's one of US when the other side is on top but he won't see that the other side is always on top, it's the other side because it is on top. Bruno has his own flat, we organize a happening in Bruno's flat, the walls are white, we plaster the walls with all the things we like, tits from *Playboy* and spaghetti and banana-skins and Fidel Castro and half a Toulouse-Lautrec poster and the hair from a Christmas angel and bootlaces and a page from the Bible, we don't like the Bible, it's full of lies. We drink Coca-Cola, Fiorella gets drunk on Coca-Cola, she says: Let's go into the bedroom and lie on the bed, we go into the bedroom and lie on the bed, we start kissing, I put my hand up her skirt, it's cold outside and she's wearing tights, she says: I can always take them off, and I say: keep them on, I'm in love with Sofia.

We go back into the living-room, Sofia is there, she still has her coat on, she looks at me with contempt, she doesn't care if I have come out of the bedroom, she always looks at me with contempt because I'm Francesco Vanetti, son of Carlo Vanetti. Sofia is a history student, she knows all about history, she isn't beautiful, neither beautiful nor ugly, she has an ivory-yellow body. She doesn't sleep with me, if she slept with anyone else I'd kill her, she mustn't sleep with anyone else, I wouldn't forbid her to, just kill her, she never sleeps with anyone. Her father is a compositor in a printing works, luckily it isn't my father's printing works, he's a shop steward, they can't sack him, they'd like to sack him but he's a card-carrying Communist. Sofia looks at the happening; idiots, she says, she doesn't use lipstick on her mouth, she uses contempt instead, you're an idiot like all the rest, she says, your father and Bruno's mother would love that spaghetti on the wall. Fidel Castro's on the wall too, I say, Fidel Castro doesn't belong among banana-skins, she says, this place is a mouse-trap, she says, you are cheese-nibblers, flower-children are weeds, and spaghetti is the noose they hang Fidel Castro with.

The others carry on, Bruno plays the guitar, Ernesto is in the kitchen mixing flour and water, he plans to erect a monument in flour, Ludovico nails his scarf to the wall, he hates his scarf, he always has to wear a scarf, he's got chronic bronchitis, Sylvia goes into the bedroom with Alfredo. Why not take your coat off? I ask Sofia, because you're idiots, she says loudly, they're demonstrating against Vietnam outside the American Embassy and you drink Coca-Cola, just drink Coca-Cola, you idiots, every bottle of Coca-Cola means another bullet, they're shooting children in Vietnam, they're shooting Vietnamese children with Coca-Cola. No-one takes any notice of her, only me, Bruno has put the guitar away, Alfredo has found a child's shoe in the bedroom, he wants to nail it to the wall but it's a child's shoe which Bruno used to wear, I don't know why it should be so important, a child's shoe, trodden soft, baby-foot-warm, Bruno defends his child's shoe, he goes red in the face, he won't let Alfredo nail the shoe to the wall.

Ernesto comes out of the kitchen, my monument is finished, he says, look at my monument, Sofia takes no notice of me, she talks to Ernesto. You never missed a happening in the old days, says Ernesto—it's true, Sofia and I met at a happening—then set fire to a department store, says Sofia, only a fool sets fire to his own house, only idiots hold private happenings, if you don't get yourself clubbed by the police there's no point in demonstrating, the oldies hold happenings for their private enjoyment. It amuses me, says Ernesto, department stores don't amuse me, I'm a sculptor. You ought to shame the workers, says Sofia, I shame my father, my father's in the C.P., he's ashamed, I shame him, hippies and yippies are outmoded, provos beatniks and peaceniks are outmoded, guitars are outmoded, you prepared the ground I grant you, but carry on this way and the oldies will reap the benefits, stones aren't outmoded, barricades aren't outmoded, you can't strum your way to heaven.

Bruno defends his child's shoe, he's not very strong, I ought to defend Bruno, Bruno's a Jew, he's my friend, Sofia would laugh at me, it's too easy to defend Bruno, they're demonstrating outside the American Embassy, Renato plays the guitar, Alfredo is stronger than Bruno, he wrenches the shoe out of his hand, Ludovico passes him the hammer, the scarf is hanging there already, Alfredo nails the shoe to the wall. Idiots, says Sofia, I-d-i-o-t-s, anyone who doesn't want to come along to the Via Veneto needn't bother, they all say they want to come along. Come along, I say to Bruno but Bruno doesn't hear, his eyes are

full of tears, he stares at the child's shoe, ME could punch Alfredo
on the nose but I don't punch him on the nose, come along, I say
to Bruno, Bruno doesn't come, he stays behind, alone with the
child's shoe and the spaghetti and Fidel Castro.

I get scared in case Sofia takes another car, but Sofia goes
straight over to my Alfa and I roar off before anyone can squeeze
in between us. You drive like the devil, says Sofia, I drive like
two devils, I love you, I say, I love you too, she says, if I go to
bed with anyone I'll go to bed with you, she says, you don't need
to go to bed with me, I say, I love you.

The sky has put on a grey beard, the street is jet-pitch-black.
We've lost the other cars, we get stuck in a hellish traffic jam,
everyone toots like a madman, I toot like ten madmen, I look in
the rear mirror, the other cars aren't ours, Sofia says they aren't
coming, they're chicken, I say no, they aren't chicken, they can't
drive, that's all. A traffic policeman plants himself in front of me,
I see the red light anyway, I'm not colour-blind, ME says: I'll
flatten the man, ME would like to flatten law and order, authority
has to be flattened, but the light turns green, I don't need to
flatten authority. I park the car outside the Hotel Palazzo degli
Ambasciatori, right under the No Parking sign, they ought to
paint fasces on the signs, red, white, and green, the colours ought
to be on prescription, we mustn't get caught *in flagrante*, I say,
Sofia laughs, let's run before a policeman comes, I say, Sofia gives
me her hand, I squeeze her hand, we run.

We're not too late, the street is crammed with people, hundreds of heads are a single head, the Hydra only had nine heads,
the Hydra has nine hundred heads, WE have one body and nine
hundred heads, the police only have bodies, no head. We storm
the Embassy, we can't storm the Embassy, the Embassy is a
marble-smooth monster, a stone Moloch with glass eyes, they
defend it, the defenders defend the aggressor, I don't think of the
aggressor, I think of the defenders, I think of the slave-drivers
who are slaves themselves, I think of the bridges. Sofia links arms
with me, she has hard little breasts, ivory-yellow, I link arms
with a friend, he looks like me except that his beard is longer,
I put my head down like a bull taking a toreador on its horns, I
shall take the policeman on my horns, I am ME. It starts to rain,
a razor-blade rain, it's cold, I don't care, *Ten Days that Shook the
World* by John Reed, Vladimir Ulyanov and Rykov and Kry-

lenko and Dzhugashvili alias Stalin, one doesn't have to be a Stalinist, Stalin was a hippie himself, today could be the first of the ten days, November 6th, the rain douses the flames, the American flag stops burning. The walls give way, the cotton-wool walls of the aggressor-defenders give way, a steel helmet tumbles to the ground and rolls, steel helmets should be banned, steel helmets should be put on prescription, the steel helmet won't fit me, my friend puts the steel helmet on, laughter frisks about like a billy-goat, the glass eyes of the marble monsters are quite close, Sofia lets go of me, take this, she says, someone distributes stones, someone distributes stones like Easter eggs, I get a handful of stones, I throw my stones, I aim at the steel helmets, I aim at the glass eyes. A policeman grabs at me, I'll be arrested, I tell myself, my name is ME, that isn't a name, what's your real name, my name is Francesco Vanetti but I'm ME nevertheless, my father is Carlo Vanetti, call my father, he'll have a heart attack. I taste blood in my mouth, I feel nothing, I lick blood, my tongue tastes of blood, you're bleeding says Sofia and throws a stone, she holds the steel helmet in her hand, the steel helmet is full of stones, the Easter-egg basket is full of stones, I put my hand to my temple, my hand is full of blood, my hand isn't bleeding but my hand is full of blood, I can only see through one eye, you need a doctor says Sofia. She takes me by the arm, she clears a path for me, if she sleeps with anyone she'll sleep with me but she sleeps with no one. I see an ambulance on the corner of the Via Bissolati, no ambulance I say, we're back at the car already, I haven't got a ticket, no ticket today, the first day, *Ten Days that Shook the World*. You can't drive, says Sofia, I can drive, I say, you're needed here, I say. I climb behind the wheel, my head swims, MY head doesn't swim, ME sees crystal-clear, ME starts the car, ME switches on the windscreen-wipers, the windscreen is cloudy, my brain is cloudy, ME gets under way, I see Sofia in the rear-view mirror, Sofia is waving, she has a stone in her hand.

My mother is at home, Beatrice is at home, my father isn't at home. My mother screams, you've had an accident, she screams, I always told your father he shouldn't have given you that Alfa Romeo, I bought the Alfa Romeo myself, I say, I haven't been in an accident, I say. A doctor, a doctor, screams my mother, as though the doctor was standing on the chest of drawers, Beatrice goes to the 'phone, get off to bed, she says. The doctor lives round the corner, he doesn't take long, I've known him for a hundred years, put your tongue out he used to say, pressing my tongue down with a wooden spoon, say aaah like a good boy, a few days off school and green cough-mixture and *zabaione*, I've always hated *zabaione*. A superficial wound, nothing serious, he says, but it might have gone in your eye, he sews up the superficial wound, I don't say anything, I think of Sofia, the Leathernecks are killing little children, my mother shuts her eyes, serves you right, says Beatrice.

My mother shows the doctor out, she asks him if I'm going to die, as soon as she's outside she always asks the doctor if somebody's going to die, I lie on my bed, I lie in my room, I hate my bed, I hate my room, say aaah like a good boy. Beatrice sits down beside me, what's Vietnam got to do with you, that's what I'd like to know, she says, you wouldn't understand, I say. Papa will blow his top, she says, let him, I say. If they'd arrested you it would have been in all the papers, she says, it would have harmed *Positivismo* as well as *Quest' Ora* and *Positivismo* is liberal. You poor innocent, I say, *Positivismo* is bromide for the bourgeoisie, a narcotic for nervous garden gnomes, *Positivismo* ought to be put on prescription, *Positivismo* lives off *Quest' Ora* and *Quest' Ora* is a murder-rag, *Quest' Ora* lives off murderers. Hence Vietnam, I say, you wouldn't understand, I say, you're a bridge. I lie in bed, Francesco Vanetti's bed, the rain sings a lullaby, ME would have taken the ambulance, the ambulance would have taken me to hospital, the hospital would have asked my name, but I drove home to Mother and her children's doctor, rock-a-bye-baby. My head grows out of the pillows, I forget what I promised my father, ME forgets, I was at Morelli's mother's place, I say, Morelli won't get the Nobel Prize, he'll get life. You're delirious, says Beatrice, I'm not delirious, I say, I'll tell you something, I say, you probably think Papa tells you everything, you're Papa's pet, he's in love with you, that's why he hates your ski-instructor, but he doesn't tell you everything, he lies to you, he lies to everyone, he's an inverted slot-machine, you put lies in at the top, chewing-gum lies, and money comes out at the bottom. I tell Beatrice about Morelli, he goes walking in the grounds of atomic-energy establishments and buries dead fish, he writes up the murder of Hertha Enzian for *Quest' Ora*, I can't take any photos because the grounds are out of bounds, they're working for NATO, manufacturing death for Vietnam, I can only shoot the murderer's mother in close-up, with a zoom lens. Beatrice isn't shocked, she simply says, I hope no one finds out, they will find out, I say, because I'll tell them, I'll tell them I knew all along, I lay in ambush, I waited for the murderer who buries fish. My mother comes in, would you like something to eat, she asks, I don't need any *zabaione*, I say, we'd better tell Papa you had a car-crash, she says, he'll be terribly upset, he doesn't look well, he's worried, we mustn't upset him, she says. I want to be left alone, I say, I get Beatrice to fetch me a pencil and paper.

> *blood is not*
> *blood*
> *your blood is not*
> *my blood*
> *hangman's blood is not blood*
> *murderer's blood is not blood*
> *soldier's blood is not blood*
> *red water, rusty hydrants*
> *my blood is*
> *blood*
> *girls don't bleed*
> *blood-drained virgins*
> *dead virgins*
> *violated*
> *no murderer's blood, no victim's blood*
> *letters bleed*
> *red paper, rotary paper*
> *the murderer stays clean*
> *I get bloody*
> *my hand is bloody*
> *my hand is clean*
> *my blood*

Antonio Zempach

Vanetti asked me to stay on in Vienna for a few days. He had agreed terms with Kronos Films, the contract was on the way, and I was to attest it. Not unnaturally, because although the Kronos people could enter into a binding agreement with *Quest'*

Ora they couldn't sell what would not be theirs until they had agreed terms with Enzian.

Time started to drag, so Yvette decided to join me in Vienna. She'd never been there before. I moved into the Hotel Sacher—Edizioni Vanetti can afford it. I thought it would amuse Yvette. Lots of sentimental splendour, archdukes in gilt frames, memories of a cosy world which went bust, *Sacher-Torte*, antique value—after all, how much would the Venus di Milo be worth if it had two arms? I took a suite. It occurred to me later that I only did it to impress Yvette. Or because I wanted a writing-table of my own. Yvette makes a habit of commandeering hotel writing-tables and turning them into her own private beauty parlour. Our windows faced the back of the Opera, with the ballet school at eye-level. Children and demi-children, animated Degas, *pliés* and *battements* and *arabesques*.

I gave her a humorous description of Enzian. She didn't see the funny side, though we generally manage to laugh at far less comic figures. Her manner said: I came to Vienna because you're in Vienna, because it was too long to be away from you, I don't want to hear about your safe-cracking activities. Not to be able to say something to Yvette is like not being able to say anything to her, almost as if I had a mistress. I said, "People who poke fun at snobbery and indulge in it themselves are double-eyed snobs." She said, "I've got a nasty feeling, that's all. I'm afraid for you." It unsettles you when someone's afraid for you. You might fall out of a tree.

That afternoon I had to leave her to her own devices and drive out to see Dr Vinzenz Habichl. I didn't mention my own misgivings. Even I wasn't amused by what I'd found out about Dr Habichl. A specialist in the defence of war criminals—no other claim to fame. His address was the one slightly reassuring feature: only a few blocks from *Oskar Enzian, Sausage and Cured Meats*. Neighbourly relations?

A prosperous firm by all appearances, despite the suburban address. A suite of rooms, several juniors, a whole army of secretaries. I was taken in by the old-fashioned look of the place at first—the waiting-room with its lace mats and antimacassars, the dusty files, the roll-topped desks, the secretaries like refugees from a home for maiden ladies—but the Pickwickian solidity was a subtle form of camouflage, a retreat into the nineteenth century designed to evade questions about the twentieth. The genial boss had a camouflaged air too. Bushy mutton-chop whiskers à la Schubert, dove-grey patriarchal suit, watch-chain, long-winded phrases. There was a duelling scar on the pockmarked face. A sabre-cut had reduced the mouth by half and frozen the rest of it into a permanent smile of derision.

"The point at issue, my dear and esteemed colleague," said Dr Habichl, "does not relate to what appears in the contract between my client and Kronos Films. It relates to what does not appear in it." He went on to assure me that his "client"—he studiously avoided calling him anything else—was acting contrary to his "explicit advice", he himself being opposed to "any such contract". His client had waived all legal rights in favour of the film company, and thus of Quest' Ora. He had not, however, guaranteed his "collaboration", and separate agreements would have to be made in respect of "material".

"What do you understand by 'material'?" I asked.

Precisely what Quest' Ora seemed so anxious to obtain, he replied: details of the unfortunate girl's adolescence, of her route from the bosom of her respectable family to the gutters of the Via Veneto, of the temptations to which she was exposed. There were the photographs too, of course. The illustrated catalogue of a mail-order house.

"I see," I said. "So your client plans to sell his daughter's life twice over."

That was rash of me. After all, I was there in Vienna to buy Hertha Enzian's life-story, twice over if necessary. I fumed at Enzian, Habichl, Yvette, and myself. But for Yvette's opposition I would have reacted more shrewdly. You can't afford to tote your conscience around like one of those pocket-alarms. They always go off at the most inconvenient moment.

Much to my relief, Dr Habichl wagged his head and said that he shared my misgivings, that there was "a very real difference between waiving one's rights and abetting sensationalism". One of his black-clad minions brought in some coffee, and he poured out.

That left me holding the hot potato. After all, my only reason for sitting opposite him was a wish to buy what I had just described as unpurchasable. I retreated in good order.

"You advised your client not to sell," I said. "I would have advised my client not to buy, but it's too late for either party to withdraw. How much is Herr Enzian asking for the whole of his material?"

"Ah," sighed Dr Habichl, "that, my dear sir, is another delicate matter. We settled with Kronos Films for four hundred thousand schillings—without the necessity for any effort on my client's part. He has priced his personal collaboration at half that sum—to wit, two hundred thousand schillings."

I said, "We offered approximately fifty thousand schillings, inclusive of world and film rights."

"That was before the Kronos offer," said Dr Habichl.

The business was beginning to amuse me again. Evidently, dead call-girls appreciated in value. As with investments so with immortality—even, it seemed, when the immortal was a prostitute. I said I would transmit the offer to Rome.

Vanetti had asked me to await Vorneweg's return, so I was free to show Yvette the city.

We used to have a musical clock at home, a Biedermeier clock in a glass case with all kinds of figures round it, gentlemen in frock-coats, curtsying ladies with hour-glass waists, children playing. They all worked. On one occasion the clock stopped before it had run down. The top-hats hovered in mid-air, the ladies never straightened up, the cavorting boy held his stick poised menacingly above a motionless hoop. I thought of that clock as we toured Vienna. The top-hats hover in mid-air, the ladies are congealed into curtsies, the hoops fail to roll. However, the Sleeping Beauty analogy would be inaccurate: here, even the saviour prince is sound asleep. In any other city I'd probably have had it out with Yvette, but the atmosphere was all wrong. Nobody has replaced his top-hat in Vienna for half a century. The clock has run down, rigor mortis for ever!

Yvette said little. She has her own view of the world—she doesn't need to look at it.

That evening Vorneweg called. I told him I was still awaiting the draft agreement from Rome. He thought we might "make contact" just the same. There are some expressions which grate on me—"make contact", for instance. I told him my wife was in Vienna. All the better, he said, and invited us to join him in a tour of the *Heurigen*, or inns which serve young wine.

Yvette had overheard the conversation—I couldn't keep it dark. Even though I put forward the most tempting propositions —*Rosenkavalier*, for instance, and a promise to pick her up after the performance—she announced that she wanted to meet my Chichikov. "I thought Vanetti was Chichikov," I said. "Vorneweg is the German version," she retorted.

I watched her put the finishing touches to herself. An orchid on a dung-heap, I thought. Obviously I was already under her influence. I hadn't thought of the whole business as a dung-heap until then, merely as an interesting case which lay outside the orbit of Dr von Helis. I'd sooner have gone alone. Was I scared that Vorneweg would let something slip? What was he supposed to let slip, anyway? Or was I afraid that Yvette wouldn't bother to hide her resentment? I'd always thought of Yvette as a good sport. Being a good sport is fine, she thinks, but her game is tennis, not Russian roulette.

It was fuggy inside the *Heurigenlokal*. They aren't ideal in winter, those places. The scent of lilac is part of their charm. Without it, all you get is the smell of wine and sweat. The atmosphere was so *gemütlich* that Yvette looked out of place in her pale violet gown. It didn't seem to bother her.

Hermann Vorneweg had all the refinement of a regimental sergeant-major commissioned in the field. I wouldn't have worried if Yvette hadn't gone out of her way to encourage him. She smiled as graciously as the Queen of England presiding over the annual servants' ball. Vorneweg instantly bought her a dozen roses from an itinerant flower-seller. Very gallant, except that he instantly forgot the gesture and groped in his pocket every time the *Blumen-Toni* appeared. By the second dozen he was expansive, by the third jovial, by the fourth stupefied. I hoped that his contact-making would confine itself to amorous advances—those I could handle. I was even prepared to show an interest in his films, but it was no good. As soon as you stub your toe someone treads on your foot. Before long he broached the subject of 'business'.

He got off to a comparatively innocuous start by calling my client an Italian bandit. Contact-making phraseology. He had no use for the Italians, a nation of traitors who had demonstrated their perfidy in two world wars. He knew what he was talking about, he had fought at Salerno, Anzio, and Casino, they'd have hurled the Yanks and Tommies into the sea if it hadn't been for the gutless Italians.... "Mussolini," he declared, "had the following slogan chalked up on all the walls: *The German soldier has astounded the world; the Italian soldier has astounded the German soldier.*" It was true, but not the way Mussolini meant, ha ha ha. I wouldn't know, being a Swiss. I told him I was a captain in the infantry. A ridiculous remark to make. We haven't fought any wars, after all. Vorneweg thought it was ridiculous too. The Swiss Navy, ha ha ha. Yvette ought to have gone to *Rosenkavalier* after all. I was in a jaw-punching mood, but I restrained myself. National pride is a substitute for self-respect— one shouldn't take it too far. After his third measure of wine and second bunch of roses, Vorneweg temporarily dried up.

My stock of conversational gambits still included the Russian campaign, which was good for a couple of hours at least, but I hadn't reckoned with Yvette. It gradually dawned on me why she hadn't gone to *Rosenkavalier.*

There must be more to his attitude than a prejudice against the Italians, she told our host. What did he really have against Vanetti?

"You'll find that out tomorrow, Dr Zempach," he said. "Your fine publisher friend has inveigled us—my firm, I mean—into making some almost incredible concessions."

"I haven't seen the contract yet," I said. "However, I'm quite sure nobody coerced you into accepting Signor Vanetti's conditions."

Vorneweg turned to Yvette. "He's a card, your husband! Look at him! Anyone would think he didn't realize what his client's got up his sleeve. I take my hat off to him—I'm a poker-player myself."

Yvette didn't look at me.

The musicians advanced on us. Any requests? I always feel as if I'm being quizzed: Well, and how many tunes do you know, little boy? No such inhibitions in Hermann Vorneweg's case. He ordered *Lili Marlene.* Why not? The Austrians have survived the *Kaiserjäger March,* the *Horst Wessel Song,* and the *Harry Lime Theme.* "Underneath the lamplight, by the barrack gate..." Even that was preferable to a 'business discussion' in front of Yvette. Herr Vorneweg raised his glass to Yvette with a jerky elbow-movement. The wine, which had earlier incurred his expert disapproval, he now described as "lovely". He didn't notice that we were only sipping at our lovely wine. "Know what Signor Vanetti would do if he had a grain of professional integrity?" he demanded. "He'd say: The murderer's name is such-and-such, he lives at such-and-such an address, carry on, help yourselves, we're partners."

"I think my wife is tired," I said.

"Oh, no," said Yvette, who can flake out at 9 P.M. when she's bored enough. "What does Herr Vorneweg mean exactly?" she asked me, all wide-eyed innocence.

"Take the casting problem," complained Vorneweg, removing a slip of paper from his wallet. "Late fifties," he read, "tall, lean, bespectacled, intellectual appearance. Chooses his words with care, speaks in a low voice. Could be an artist of some sort—musician, painter, or writer." He shrugged helplessly. "What can we do with a man like that? We were thinking either of a brutal killer or of an elegant one. Intellectual murderers aren't good box-office—never have been."

"Never," said Yvette.

I said, "Presumably that's the description on the warrant."

"Not a clue," replied Vorneweg. Then, tolerantly: "I'm not blaming Vanetti for that. He can't pick his murderers, after all. I don't expect miracles, but to make provisos and keep the killer to yourself is going a bit too far." With that he bought Yvette her third bunch of roses.

"It sounds as if Signor Vanetti has someone quite definite in mind," said Yvette.

My forehead prickled with sweat. *Tales from the Vienna Woods.* . . . This really was going a bit too far.

Vorneweg suddenly turned to me. Left arm round my shoulders, right hand belabouring his thigh: a paroxysm of mirth. I was one hell of a fellow, he spluttered, a Swiss Machiavelli. I had concealed even from my lady wife—"but then, you cuckoo-clock manufacturers don't allow your women to vote either, do you?"—that I knew the identity of Hertha Enzian's murderer. He could die laughing. Then, indulgently: "I quite understand, of course. You're a lawyer, and ethics is ethics, but you've got to admit it, Vanetti's a dirty swine. No reason why he shouldn't have taken me into his confidence." He went on to mention that he had been an officer, Panzer Grenadier Regiment

No. 351. "Vanetti's a swine, I tell you. After all, we are partners. No offence, my dear sir. Cheers."

Yvette finally looked at me, a lion-tamer's look. I was grateful to her. At least she realized that I was tempted to punch Vorneweg on the jaw. A little old man was celebrating his birthday at the next table. He kept on requesting *Two Black Steeds have I*, so often that he had a whole stableful by now. People had pricked up their ears at the name Enzian. I signalled to Yvette and she said, "I'm tired."

We bumped into the flower-seller on our way out. Hermann Vorneweg promptly acquired a fourth bunch of roses. I relieved Yvette of her rose-garden, which relieved me of the need to shake hands with Vorneweg at the cab-rank.

We hardly spoke in the car because of the driver. Yvette looked twenty. No I-told-you-so manner, no echoes of her father. There was no way out, of course, even if we went home next day. A gracious patriarchal stare from Dr von Helis: Glad to have you back, my boy, there's a rather complicated tax case you might like to handle. Thank you, Papa, it's good to be back on home ground. An increase in capital for the Kaiser Corporation? How thrilling! On the other hand, I could press on regardless. Who cares what that drunken film man said? Edizioni Vanetti are a multi-million-dollar concern. They publish an influential political review—*Positivismo*, I think it's called. Anyone can make a mistake, and I'm no exception, but it doesn't invalidate the cases I've won for Dr von Helis's firm.

Back at the hotel I said, "I'm packing it in. We'll head for home."

Yvette was removing her make-up. She looked fifteen now. "You're mad," she said. "Think of Papa. Don't let's give him the satisfaction."

I frowned. "But you were the one who . . ."

"That was before you committed yourself," she said.

I said, "Do you think our Panzer Grenadier was imagining things?"

"Probably," she replied.

That reassured me. If the alarm doesn't go off it means Yvette hasn't set it.

"The contract will be here tomorrow," I said. "Then we'll see. I can still say no."

She sat down on the bed and shook her head. "You can't throw in your hand. We must find out more. If it's true, you'll have to do something."

"What, for instance?"

She didn't know either. It had simply registered with her that I was half-way up the tree.

Christa Sonntag

I'll spend the rest of my life regretting that I ever went out of my way to be nice to the silly little thing, I know I will, but it's time to give the whole subject a rest. I've got other worries, really I have. They've locked my brother up, back home in Munich. Homosexual practices. He always did act unnatural. My mother was to blame, God rest her. It's a psychological thing. Some mothers spoil their sons rotten, which makes the little fellows scared to sail out into the storms of life—and love between the sexes is a stormy business. These professors spend too much time at their desks and too little sailing the seas of life, otherwise we'd know more about it all. When a boy clings to his mother's apron-strings, like Peter, you'd think he'd admire the opposite sex. But no, if there's one sort who don't fancy having anything to do with women, it's mothers' darlings like him. Either they just don't fancy the fair sex or they're scared stiff of them. Peter always fought like a tiger with my father, and yet it's men he's crazy about. I ought to have set him up in a hairdresser's, that's what my father wrote me. What am I supposed to do—support the economy out of the wages of sin? I'd have ulcers inside three months. I keep my father as it is, seeing he lost a leg because of Hitler. Now I'm told Peter would never have got into the papers, because you don't get into the papers on account of straight-forward homosexual practices. They picked on him because he was the brother of the call-girl who lived opposite Hertha Enzian. I ask you, could Peter help it if Hertha was murdered? That's what they call the curse of notoriety. Life's unfair, I know, but Peter would have been a queer come what may. Owning your own hairdressing salon doesn't stop you indulging in homosexual practices.

It goes on for ever, the Enzian case. Someone called Aldo

Fontana rang me up and said he'd met me at one of Howard Grainger's parties. Could be, I thought, because I always have to be on tap when Grainger throws a party for his business contacts. We've got a first-class working relationship, Grainger and me. The Americans are crazy about credit cards. It all started with the Diner's Club. Live now, pay later—that's their motto. When a business friend of Grainger's comes to me I don't ask for a *centesimo*, just do it for *amore*. Afterwards I send in my account to Grainger's office and he settles it *pronto*, but *pronto*. Just like the Diner's Club, as I said. With us in Europe, the credit system is still wet behind the ears.

Could I see him, the caller asked. We fixed an appointment for six o'clock. Naturally, I called Grainger's office right away. I mean, you have to check on a person's credit rating. No, said Johnny Malone—he handles the entertainment side for Grainger —never heard of any Signor Fontana. I got the shivers when he said that, because it doesn't take much to make me nervous since the Hertha business. I 'phoned Françoise—that's a French colleague of mine—and asked her to call me about seven. I popped my little automatic in the drawer of my bedside table, too. Safety first. I kept all my clothes on, what's more, like a knight in armour.

Fontana arrived on time. I almost fell off my chair—that's to say I stood rooted to the spot, by the door. Clients like him are few and far between. Not a day over twenty-five and pretty as a picture—he looked like Alain Delon, honestly he did. There's something wrong here, I said to myself. I smelt trouble a mile off. He could have had any teenager he fancied, and as for respectable married women, you could have bought yourself an oil-field in Texas out of his earnings.

My mind worked like lightning. It does—that's my strong point. There were two possibilities. Either he was a queer who wanted to be cured, which I don't go in for on principle, because firstly I'm not in the Red Cross and secondly I can't help thinking of my brother Peter, which cramps my style; or he was a sadist. That wasn't *probabile*, because everyone knows that sadists are stingy. Whipping they like, but they don't like shelling out. It's a psychological fact. Paying hurts, and the Marquis de Sade fans—I bought some of his stuff, but he's a drag— prefer hurting other people. On the other hand, he might be a masochist. That was the likeliest bet. The bottom would drop out of our business if it wasn't for masochists. A man doesn't think twice about thrashing his wife or some other female, but he's too shy to hand them a whip and tell them to do it to him—it's part of his nature. If he wants a thrashing he buys it on the open market. It's a double pleasure, firstly because he gets thrashed and secondly because he has to pay—and that hurts too. With his own wife or society ladies all he gets is a thrashing, which is only half the fun.

As I was calculating the odds like a computer, the fourth and fifth alternatives flashed through my mind. Either he was a young hopeful who'd heard rumours of Grainger's account with me and didn't know his credit rating would be checked. Or he was a sex-maniac.

My instinct never lies. He wasn't a sex-maniac, that boy, but he wasn't an ordinary client either. We drank one of my world-famous Martinis—eight to one, eight parts gin to one of the same, I say, by way of a joke. Then he asked, discreetly, what it would cost. He thinks I'll do it at cost price for the sake of his bonny blue eyes, I said to myself. He's come to the wrong place if he does, firstly because it isn't my job to tickle men's vanity and secondly because I'd sooner give some poor old codger a treat than get done in the eye by a baby-faced brat. That's the way I'm made. I told him sixty thousand without batting an eyelid. Then he really took me by surprise. "A hundred thousand," he said, reaching in his pocket. "Later, sonny-boy," I said sternly. It dawned on me, quick as a flash, that this was the first time he'd been to a top-class call-girl. You have to draw the line between prostitutes and the upper crust. A *contessa* doesn't ask for cash in advance. It's all part of the credit system.

That boy looked like a god when he stripped off. Hips like a ballet dancer and shoulders like a boxer, skin like a white Negro, and as for equipment—a moon-probe, word of honour. Nothing perverted about that one. *Pagliacci* wasn't a patch on his pre-liminary performance, and he wasn't in a hurry, either, like most clients. Inconsiderate, they are, especially the Italians, who never have much in the way of self-control. I didn't have to put on any kind of act—not that I lost my head. My woman's intuition kept telling me there was something wrong with the whole set-up.

As soon as he was dressed he put a pile of ten-thousand lira notes on my Empire-style table. I saw them lying there when I came out of the bathroom. I didn't count them, of course. I can spot a swindle right away—I'm like a croupier from that point of view, which is why I never get bilked. He polished off my Martini, straight ice-water, and then he came out with it. His manner changed abruptly, as they say in novels. The point was, he told me, that *Lui e Lei* wanted to pay me half a million lire to write my memoirs. "You won't have to write a word," he said, "we'll take it all down on tape. I'll handle the writing end." He addressed me formally, which isn't the done thing after mutual satisfaction.

"Ah," I said, quick as a flash, "you're one of Bossi's competitors." I called him *tu* in a sneery voice.

He didn't try to deny it. *Quest' Ora* had an exclusive story about the Enzian girl, he said. "We plan to kill it stone dead," he said. "We'll have to be quick, though. They're launching it in their Christmas number. They think they've found the murderer. Either that or they've invented one."

The whole thing stank to me, but I said, "I don't know anything about the murder."

"You don't need to," he said. He was calling me *tu* now. "We'll publish the story under the title *Hertha Enzian told me the Truth*."

"The truth about what?" I asked.

"About men," he said. "Her sex-life."

"Hertha never told me anything," I said. "Only respectable women talk about their sex-lives." I made that sound sneery too.

"Alternatively, we could call it *Death and Dolce Vita*," he said. "That's not your worry. You just lend us your name. And some pictures."

"What pictures?" I asked.

I didn't know what to do for the best, honestly I didn't. In the first place he'd gone to my knees—that's a sign of appreciation, feeling it in my knees afterwards—and in the second place you can't turn down five hundred thousand lire just like that. Another five hundred thousand and I could buy that seaside plot, where you can hear the murmur of the waves.

"All the pictures you can dig up," he said. "Family snapshots."

"Why should I have any family snapshots of Hertha?" I said. It was stupid of him.

"Of you, of course," he said. "You're just as interesting. The murderer may have knocked at the wrong door."

"*Mille grazie*," I said.

"We'll photograph you too," he said. "No need to hide anything, I assure you. You couldn't wish for better publicity. By rights, you should be paying us."

"Anything else you'd like?" I asked, sharp as a knife. I was cold with rage by this time. As if I was a filter cigarette that needed advertising! I know me. I can be awfully cutting when I go cold with rage. I'm easy-going by nature, but when I go cold with rage I forget all about my higher education.

He didn't notice. He might be a god in bed but he was pretty much of a sod anywhere else. "You'll have to bring the murder into it, of course," he said. "You must voice some kind of suspicion. We want a definite and exclusive lead."

I was fed up with the word exclusive, I'd heard it so often. I played dumb, though, which doesn't come easy to me.

"You undertake not to say another word to *Quest' Ora* or any other home or foreign publication," the boy said. "We'll put you under contract. You can hang on to the hundred thousand."

"What hundred thousand?" I said, all trusting.

I honestly don't know what would have happened if he'd acted decently. Money talks, even if they do call it the root of all evil. I'm no saint, granted, but if anyone takes me for a ride it has to be a Rolls-Royce or nothing.

I couldn't believe my ears, and God knows I've heard a thing or two in my time. He didn't mean I could keep the money because I'd sacrificed my precious time on the altar of love. Not a bit of it. He meant it as an advance. He honestly thought I'd take another four hundred thousand and leave it at that. Well, he hadn't reckoned on me being a capitalist, thanks to my higher education. The insult I might have swallowed, seeing the way he'd gone to my knees, but he was trying to cheat his employers into the bargain. They'd meant me to have the hundred thousand as an unearned bonus, and the youngster thought he could help himself to a cut off the joint at the firm's expense.

Well, I said to myself, you've got another think coming. I mean, another girl might have done business with him or acted vulgar, one of the two. Not me—I know how to behave, even if I wasn't born a *contessa*. No fuss, no fireworks. I cut that youngster down to size until you could have flushed the pieces down the pan. "Kindly relieve me of your presence," I said, all restrained, "otherwise I'll wrap my Empire vase round your earhole. Compared to you, Bossi is Sir Laurence Olivier in person. *Lui e Lei* won't get a peep out of me, even if it means committing suicide for the sake of *Quest' Ora*." He started stammering something, but I wouldn't listen and marched him off the premises in double-quick time.

I felt a bit sorry afterwards, what with the five hundred thousand and the seaside plot. It started me thinking. A film producer I used to know told me he reckoned to make money even if he was plugging a flop. Me being a good pupil, I 'phoned Canonica.

He came to see me about nine that evening. You can't help admiring the way that man works. A university graduate, and every flatfoot in Rome stands to attention at the sight of him. He carries so much weight he could even get me a permanent resident's permit, but he's not stuck up. He always comes in person.

"Dottore," I said, because that's what I call him now we've established diplomatic relations, so to speak, "Dottore," I said, "I promised to tell you all I could about Hertha."

Then I told him about Fontana's visit and the offer. I left out the sexy bits because it isn't fair to get an old man worked up, also because it makes a good impression if you only do things for the best reasons. "Being so honest has cost me half a million lire," I said.

"How much did Bossi give you?" he asked.

"Two hundred thousand," I said, which was true.

"Ask him for another three," he said. A decent old stick, Canonica is. "Did Fontana really tell you that *Quest' Ora* is getting ready to dish up the murderer for Christmas?"

I raised my right hand.

"Listen, my girl," he said. "You could do me a big favour. Tell Bossi you're planning to shake the dust of Rome off your heels."

"Nothing could be further from my thoughts," I said. "I'm an adopted Roman."

"I know," he said approvingly. "Just pretend otherwise. Tell

Bossi you want to move because you feel creepy with the murderer running around loose. If you can work in a few unkind remarks about police inefficiency, so much the better."

"What's the object of the exercise?" I asked, not committing myself. I mean, I don't get mixed up with the police unless I know what they're after, Canonica or no Canonica.

"I have complete confidence in you, Contessa," said Canonica. "It isn't beyond the bounds of possibility that *Quest' Ora* is following a definite lead. Bossi won't tell you the whole truth, but anything is better than nothing. Since he's anxious to keep you here in Rome, he may tell you something about the murderer. You're much in demand since the Enzian girl's death. I hope it isn't going to your head."

He came to a full stop in front of the door between the living-room and the bedroom. I'd been scared for a long time that he was going to notice the mirror on the door. It's one of those mirrors that looks like a mirror but when you press a button you can look through it and see what goes on in the bedroom.

"That's prohibited, you know," Canonica said, quite friendly.

"How did you guess?" I asked.

"We know them," he said. "The police use them too."

"Well," I said. "Business is business."

I think regulations like that are stupid. I mean, it's hypocrisy, really. People who don't even know what's normal lay down the law about what's perverted. There are experts on garbage collection, but they never call in experts on sex. Take Françoise's fat Dutchman, for instance—one of her best clients. I have to help her out when he's in Rome. Françoise puts her most fabulous gown on—you could almost mistake it for a Dior—and I dress up as a parlour-maid. We lay the table with silver before he arrives. Sterling silver—the Dutchman made her a present of it. Then he comes in, strips off, and stretches out on the table, nude, with his tummy facing downwards. That's to say, he lies on a silver tray. He's meant to be roast pork, you see. Pretty true to life, too, though I only mention that in passing. Françoise sits down at the table in her evening dress, sterling silver at the ready. I stand there, playing the parlour-maid. "What portion would Madame care for?" I ask. She says: a leg, or an ear, or the head. Then I carve him—only in fun, of course. All I really serve her with is the garnishing, because the Dutchman is surrounded by salad and potatoes and *petits pois*, you see. Sometimes he grunts, which isn't true to life because he's supposed to be roast pork, and who ever heard roast pork grunt? Well, there's a perversion for you. If the authorities heard about it you can bet they'd pass a law forbidding people to serve up nude Dutchmen on silver trays. That would be unfair, though, because the Dutchman gets a kick out of it, nobody gets hurt, and Françoise and I get paid and invest the money, which boosts the economy and supports the lira. But then, what do you expect from people who are so narrow-minded that they ban mirrors which the police use too, and not for fun? I always say an orgy is what more than two people are forbidden to do. Everything else becomes legal as soon as more than two people do it, so why not that too? It isn't fair.

"I'd be glad to take it down just to please you," I told Canonica. "I never use it anyway. It's for beginners."

"I'm only thinking of my colleagues," said Canonica. "The day may come when I need you as a prosecution witness, my girl, and when that day comes you'll have to be like Caesar's wife."

I'd like to help Canonica, but I'm not sure I fancy the prosecution witness idea. I mean, it's easier to get into something than out of it.

Aurelio Morelli

Most writers strive, successfully, in so far as the better among them are concerned, to preface their commencement of the action proper by creating an atmosphere in which events can unfold naturally, with an almost ineluctable logic and inevitability. This expertise, which should not be confounded with legerdemain, is quite as valid as it is inane and fallacious to suppose that, were the writer incognizant of his story's end, he would, like the still unwitting reader, be surprised by it. The writer is a vigilant god who is never surprised, let alone deluded, who does not co-experience what takes place, as our younger authors would have us believe, but who reviews and retrospectively reports, summarizes and expounds upon, that which has long since come to pass beneath his omnipresent gaze. The architect,

an artist of inferior rank, builds upward by pedantically setting
stone upon stone, whereas the writer, godlike in this respect too,
builds downward: to a roof which hovers in mid-air—a miracle
indeed—he appends course upon course of stone. The experienced novelist who creates a gloomy atmosphere does so because
he knows very well that, although 'bolt from the blue' may
possess some value as a pretty turn of phrase, no one has yet
witnessed any such natural phenomenon in real life. The heavens
grow dark ere lightning strikes and clouds disperse ere the sun
can shine: the writer, to whom past and future are one, darkens
the sky before the advent of lightning and disperses the clouds
before he sets out to describe a sunny day.

No mere chance dictates this line of thought. Were I writing
a novel, I should have to 'buttress' and 'underpin' the surprising,
happy—indeed, blessed—event which occurred this twelfth day
of November, a memorable date and truly deserving of note: in
retrospect, I should claim to have sensed, even in the morning
hours, the premonitory breath of spring which winged its way
to me that winter's afternoon.

Nothing could be farther from the truth. I was in fact compelled, that Sunday morning, to endure a visit from the Neapolitan pugilist—and an exceedingly distasteful visit it turned
out to be.

While I remained seated at the window, engrossed in the
Roman elegies of Catullus, poems which betray the influence of
Callimachus and Hipponax but far surpass their Greek exemplars,
my tormentor skimmed through the first quarter of such notes
as I had prepared for publication in his bodeful magazine.

The initial effect was precisely what might have been described as a resounding success. The information that I had not
only, with gentle authority, prevented the harlot Hertha Enzian
from further pursuing her ignominious profession but delivered
the young persons known as Lucia Chiesa and Vera Pisenti from
the grave sickness of youth, both for their own benefit and for
the common weal, filled Signor Bossi with lively amusement—
nay, more, with an unrestrained delight which I could not fail
to observe. He laughed uproariously in the unseemly manner of
young people who have never enjoyed the benefits of a careful
upbringing, smote the table so that my aquarium trembled,
babbled about his instinct, his "nose", his "sixth sense" or

"lucky streak", and, finally, declared his readiness to couple my demand to his unseen employer for an additional fee of six hundred thousand lire—three hundred thousand each in respect of Lucia and Vera—with a favourable recommendation of his own. Shortly thereafter, however, he voiced some criticisms of so preposterous a nature that I was forced to debate very seriously whether it might not be better, more advisable, and more consonant with my dignity, integrity, and probity—synonymous concepts, I may add—to surrender myself to the authorities and, in a spirit of proud resignation, submit to confinement in gaol or asylum.

The first point, though by no means the worst, was that the impudent young puppy had the gall to raise stylistic objections: in its present form, he said, the manuscript was unusable, could serve only as raw material, and would have—perish the thought! —to be "rewritten" by an expert hand—to wit, his own. What alterations and improvements could I possibly have made? Everything progressed far too slowly, declared my shameless censor: long before the public had reached the first murder it would have turned, yawning, to some other magazine. On the other hand, the events on the edge of the Giardino Zoologico were not related in sufficient detail: at least one whole instalment—eighteen pages of thirty lines, each of thirty characters—would have to be devoted to the deed alone, because praise belonged only to the author who could report events in such a way that the reader felt himself to be "on the spot". And what, pray, I objected, about modern literature, whose exponents are quite unconcerned with subject-matter, greet any form of plot with a snort of suspicion, exclude the unprivileged reader from all sense of participation, lay him low with a veritable barrage of boredom, and generally behave like the surgeon who proceeds to operate only when anaesthesia is complete? My tormentor's sole response was to inquire what I thought I was talking about. I must surely realize —"if not, the sooner the better, because rewriting takes time and we plan to launch you in the Christmas number"—that there were only two sorts of readers: those who had no desire to read, and consequently bought books by modern authors, and those who could not read, and consequently bought illustrated magazines. Intelligible writing had to be readily comprehensible in order to preclude any hint of literary pretension; difficult writing had to be unintelligible in order to preclude any suspicion of banality: even I had to admit that it was hopelessly old-fashioned to make intelligible writing difficult and difficult writing intelligible.

So far from being content with this bout of literary flagellation, he imparted other and far less savoury advice. All passages in my work which related to motivation—in other words, to my revolutionary beliefs and my heroic battle against the pestilence called youth—would be "cut" without more ado, first, because it would be impossible to "sell" so unfashionable a murderer for fifteen to twenty weeks, and, secondly, because Quest' Ora had indented for a sex-maniac and could not accept the revolutionary that had been delivered in his stead.

Pure imbecility, one would suppose. Was I really to believe that a murderer who had sent three vivacious young creatures to kingdom come for his own pleasure, morbid satisfaction, and foul sensual gratification would excite greater public sympathy than a rebel who dared to cast a scaly eye at the youth of today? Most certainly I was, said Signor Bossi—and I must confess that he convinced me entirely, though otherwise than he intended.

The tremulous fear of youth, the blind respect which it enjoys, the senile admiration with which it has infected us, the hypocritical voguishness with which we surround it—all this stems from the most convincing and, thus, the worst of motives. Our worthy parents were no more than doing their duty and fulfilling the proper functions of education when they prevented us from clambering on a roof or falling off the same, when they taught us that it was unbecoming to pick our noses, when they caused us—on pain of worldly and other-worldly punishment—to respect the Ten Commandments. Then it was, in my childhood, that a new branch of knowledge was proclaimed from the Sinai of science: calling itself psychoanalysis, this presumptuous brand of mass-erudition claimed to lead us into the tangled undergrowth of the childish mind. The new science not only made much of the sensitivity of the budding psyche but undertook to prove that the decision whether a man was to be robust or frail, hardy or susceptible, well- or ill-disposed, whether he was to become a potent lover or an impotent libertine, a benefactor, green-eyed monster, pioneer or murderer, indeed—what hubris! —whether he was to be happy or unhappy, was taken in the cradle or during the early years of childhood. Debauched by this theory, mankind lit bonfires to celebrate the downfall of God: and, in truth, it was the parents who, filled with vain exultation, preened themselves on their superhuman, god-replacing *omnipotentia*, and quaffed their new-found power in heady draughts. Emulating Prometheus, they now believed that they could not only procreate children but mould them completely; overcome by the sick libido of responsibility—ah, that devilish word!—the foolish creatures aspired to be architects and sculptors of the future, shapers of destiny, shields and bucklers against mishap, mischance, and misfortune. Disenchantment was soon to declare itself. Because the sad new science was unable to equip parents and elders, the new formative deity, with a capacity for divine prescience which would match their intoxicating power; because they could not know, guess, or even sense what effects would be produced by their amateurish manipulation of the childish mind and their dogged experiments with living and undeniably explosive material, they, the parents and elders, soon put aside the Danaean gift of power, plummeted from superhuman authority to utter impotence, and rendered themselves powerless by their own act. Confusion was complete. Thus it was that parents no longer knew whether children should be forbidden to pick their noses, positively encouraged in such misbehaviour, or at least suffered to pick away merrily for their spiritual welfare's sake. Small wonder that ill-bred children should have grown into ill-bred adolescents. The sensitive dynamite was tampered with no more. Unlike the parents of Hansel and Gretel, the besom-maker and his wife, we no longer sought our lost children, no longer cried for them in the dark forest; instead, we left them to their own devices, content to leave them alone and be alone ourselves. But what did the abandoned Hansel do? So far from yearning for and aspiring to the home where his kin had forgotten or tried to forget him, where his beloved parents were enjoying themselves hugely without him, he took up his abode with the witch. It was not, however, a permanent domicile, for the witch grew tired of feeding her voracious guest. Left alone in the forest, he transformed himself into a forest creature. The modern Hansel's name is Tarzan. Well, Tarzan has now returned home: long-haired, unmannerly, club-wielding, carnivorous, sexually inquisitive, devoid of moral sense, subject only to the law of the jungle, and grimly resolved to wreak frightful vengeance upon his fugitive parents. Were it not so—and my reluctant daily perusal of the gutter Press convinces me that it is—there would be a difference in conduct between the young people of East and West, North and South, of white, black, or yellow continents, between rich and poor, between those who live without coercion in an affluent society and those to whom such privileges are denied. Nothing could be farther from the truth, however, for Tarzan is in no wise and on no account concerned for the future or even for himself: his sole concern is for the murder of his parents, for sanguinary revenge. The forest creature asserts, in so far as he is at all capable of self-expression, that he is revenging himself because he was forbidden to pick his nose—revolt against authority is the term he uses—whereas in reality he is revenging himself because his parents and elders, unable to ensure his spiritual welfare, failed even to impose a ban on nose-picking. What precautions do the imperilled parents take against their prodigal son? None, I say—none whatsoever. They bury their heads in the sand, fondly equating lack of vision with invisibility; or fraudulently allege that they planned and willed it so, that descent into chaos is really synonymous with progress, that they can discern their beloved Hansel beneath the Tarzan-like exterior; or don a leopard-skin and run bleating through the countryside under the erroneous impression that such mimicry will render them unrecognizable, that Tarzan will either fail to notice them or mistake them for his own kind, and thus that they will escape the joyful St Bartholomew's Eve massacre of the young; or fall on their knees and surrender to the illusion that they are evading the blows from Tarzan's club by investing their ill-bred offspring with the resplendent attributes of a vigorous and wholly admirable youth who aspires to better things. All are massacred notwithstanding. Thus it is that a missionary of my kind, who because it is too late to bear the cross bears the sword instead, finds himself in a position of the direst solitude and isolation; that the charge is stricken from his indictment; that he is degraded into an eccentric buffoon; that his status as a harmless sex-maniac earns him two million lire—or, as I hope, two million six hundred thousand plus fares and expenses—whereas the rebel against the forest-creatures attracts far less 'popular sympathy' than the sex-maniac, and is so repugnant that he cannot be purveyed to the resigned, stupefied, and self-lacerating masses.

Why, then, did I permit my youthful executioner to pop my manuscript between the dead reptilian jaws of his crocodile-skin briefcase? The answer—a humiliating one, I know—is that even supermen are men. On the very eve of that day I had taken the first hesitant but crucial steps towards preparing for my Bolivian exile. The artful Signor Bossi noticed nothing. Rubbing his hands with glee, he could hardly wait to inform his faceless employer not only of my humiliation but also of my suicidal confessions, which, though anonymous, will inevitably point to Aurelio Morelli. Would I have exposed myself thus foolishly had I not known of the intention to use my half-forgotten but still distinguished name? Had I not cherished the deliberate resolve, on receipt of the second instalment and my hard-earned additional bonus of six hundred thousand lire, to abscond before delivering the final chapters and—to employ the vernacular phrase—make myself scarce?

The noonday hour, which I spent in the dining-room of my hotel after the departure of my tormentor, gave equally little promise of the good—nay, the supremely wonderful—thing that lay in store for me.

Among the abominations peculiar to this eating-place is its claim to 'specialize' in fish dishes. The proprietor, a portly individual whose ear-lobes resemble two hamburger steaks, has had the effrontery to surmount the entrance of his establishment with the proclamation *Spezialità marinari sempre vive*. Not only is this a barefaced lie, because any child knows that such specialities cannot be served in the living state, but, to pile Pelion on Ossa, the shameless advertisement further represents a neon-illuminated threat to murder, because it implies naught else but that live 'specialities' are summarily slaughtered at the customer's behest.

My affection for my aquatic friends is of the simplest and most natural kind, they being the only living creatures which in no way resemble man, the waste-product and detritus of Creation, whose Author created him last of all and, as it were, left-handed: they have no need of air—indeed, lose consciousness if exposed to its dubious delights; they breathe with gills in place of lungs, possess neither arms nor legs, dispense with the abomination called hair, boast, instead, the most scintillating scales and armour, express the healthiest of instincts without indulging in wanton display, are inarticulate and therefore pester no one with superfluous information, lay eggs without previously performing the ridiculous sexual act, play no hypocritical maternal rôle but leave it to the watery element to fructify their eggs, do not, with a few inglorious exceptions, maintain an attitude inimical to man, as wild beasts do, nor yet an opportunist one, as of household pets, but chastise him with casual and well-merited disdain. They are superior beings indeed, as the Holy Writ itself implies: *"And all flesh died that moved upon the earth, both of fowl, and of cattle, and of beast, and of every creeping thing that creepeth upon the earth, and every man."* The Lord's anathema struck down *"all in whose nostrils was the breath of life"*, yet we are not told, for instance, that Noah had to rescue two trout or halibut in his ark. They, of course, would have been in their element when the Flood came. Little wonder, therefore, that man, sensing the mysterious aloofness and divinely privileged status of fish, should assail them with all the barbarity at his command. The ordinary huntsman does incur a measure of personal risk: many objects of his pursuit he confronts in open combat; in order to slay others he scales crag and mountain by the sweat of his brow. He, at least, is an honest murderer. The fisherman, by contrast, preens himself on his gift of contemplation, his peaceable and patient disposition, his mild and philosophical nature. The huntsman pays his adversaries the compliment of using the same murderous implements with which he slaughters other men; the fisherman uses rod and line, harmless-looking implements yet very like a dangling gallows with bait attached—in other words, a snare and deception of the most malicious kind. Traitress that she is, Dame Language has borrowed some of her most objectionable metaphors from the fisherman's vocabulary—"hook, line, and sinker", "fishing in troubled waters", "making a haul", "netting a profit", "green about the gills", "a good catch", "cry stinking fish"—yet respect for the murderous angler persists undiminished.

The hotel dining-room, whose pale-blue frescoes naturally depict fishermen at their despicable trade, and whose walls display a magnificent victim of the fisherman's lust to kill, *Carcharias glaucus*, twenty feet long and inaccurately labelled a man-eating shark, possesses a scrubbed unpleasantness all its own. However, my malaise that Sunday was intensified not only by the sight of fish-devouring cannibals from near and far, but also, to make matters worse, by the presence of Foce Verde's basket-ball club, whose members had convened for a ceremonial jamboree.

Am I doing them an injustice, these young people? Such was the question I asked myself, not for the first time, and, not for the first time, I myself supplied the answer: no, a thousand times no! What inspired the young waitress, a pretty creature with the bovine eyes of a Hera and the enormous, no less uptilted breasts of a Rubens Venus, who waits on me daily and to whom I dispense the most lavish tips, *mancè* or *pourboires*, to keep me waiting a good half-hour for my vegetables while serving the boisterous rabble of plebeian sportsmen and casual customers with coquettishly simpering zeal? The answer, alas, was all too plain. They were potential candidates for bed, one and all, those competitive anglers with ball and basket—potential and potent, the common root is not without significance. As long as young males felt, simulated, or were forcibly encouraged to show respect towards the elderly, even the older man possessed some attraction for womankind, whether as a preceptor of youth or as a member of a privileged caste. Now that sex has acceded to absolute power, however, everyone flatters the sexual potentates—another significant cognate. We have abdicated our privileges in favour of youth—knowledge, understanding, freedom, amatory finesse, and financial independence—without bargaining for lasting potency in return. We were heedless of the inevitable consequences when we lewdly promoted sex, or, more accurately, the sexual attributes of the female, to be the bugbear of our age: the penis, vanquisher of glorified femininity, became our tyrant and dictator. What was that tableful of muscular exhibitionists, bone-headed, bawling, and bumptious, what were those botched blueprints of adults-to-be, what was that festive board, if not an asparagus-field of male genitalia, and what was the waitress Grazia if not a peasant-girl roaming that field in search of the finest stems? *Genesis* refers to sex but not to youthful sex: no one, no student of the Bible, sociologist or psychologist, has yet been struck by the fact that Adam and Eve came into the world as adults. We, however, have isolated sex, and isolated sex is young; we have isolated it as one isolates bacteria, and thus find ourselves in the midst of a thriving asparagus- and bacteria-plantation.

Although the winter's afternoon was leaden and bleak, I hastened to flee the inhospitable hostel, and set off on the constitutional which is so essential to my physical well-being.

No part of Nature being alien to me, I have grown accustomed to the bleakness of Foce Verde. I walked, as ever, along the deserted bathing-beach, paused on the bridge over the Fosso Mascarello, and engrossed myself—still without presentiment, that I can swear—in the spectacle of the castle-like mansion which stands on a tongue of land to the left of the bridge. The sea, grey and restless as a prowling wolf, leapt repeatedly at the flanks of the mansion, in which—clear evidence of habitation—some precipitate hand had lit a scattering of lights. I strode briskly past the wire fence which encloses the uniform huts of the army encampment on the farther side of the bridge, situated there because the atomic pile doubtless has need of military protection. The interminable fields on the right, still scorched by the sun but already tanned with age like the face of an American Indian, are also enclosed by shoulder-high fences, but only—in accordance with the somewhat casual disposition of my race—on three sides: at the point where the Fiume Astura flows past the nuclear power station and into the sea one can, by following the course of the stream, approach the solitary work of man and devil without more ado. The building forms, as it were, the apex of an isosceles triangle, two sides of which are constituted by the rivers Mascarello and Astura and the third by the coast road. The power station takes water from the Fosso Mascarello, as everyone knows, and discharges radioactive water into the Fiume Astura, the little stream which has become the grave of so many innocent fish. As often as my time permits I stroll along the banks of the Fiume Astura, defying all prohibitive notices and brazen admonitions to the contrary, in order to do my duty and pay my last respects to those who have been foully slain by poisoners.

Thus it was on this occasion too. The sky, so grey that it appeared cloudless, resembled the domed glass roof of a grimy railway station, and a raw wind blowing from the sea whipped the wintry waters of the Fiume Astura into eddies. Producing from my overcoat pocket the rubber gloves which I had, be it noted, procured for this sole purpose and no other, I knelt by the edge of the stream in order to rob its chill waters of the corpse of a luckless little fish which was drifting down from the nuclear power station in an unnatural, horizontally inclined position.

At that moment I was startled by a voice—startled, I say, for I refuse to employ the literary conjuring trick which, by anticipating a favourable outcome, transmutes alarm and surprise into a promising omen. And yet I could, with good and sufficient reason, have spoken of a fairy-tale apparition, of an apparition from a fairy-tale—an inverted fairy-tale, admittedly, for it was not the ugly toad that accosted the blonde princess, but rather the blonde princess who addressed herself to the ugly toad. The young creature who had approached me with such noiseless tread was perhaps nineteen years old, yet ageless, as I at once realized: with her long hair falling to and playing about her shoulders, her artless dark-blue eyes, her dainty nose and full-lipped, almost rectangular mouth, she had, beyond any shadow of a doubt, stepped from between the pages of a book of fairy-tales, and this certainty persisted despite the eggshell-yellow trench-coat buttoned high on the slender neck and tightly belted about the hips.

"What are you doing?" inquired the apparition; yet, so far from sounding condemnatory or inquisitorial, the question carried a note of genuine interest, a touch of childish curiosity, and, so it seemed to me, a hint of admiration for my charitable resolve. Although shy by nature and averse to any invasion of my privacy, I rose with a smile and, as if under some sweet compulsion, gave her an account of my actions which, to my surprise, went far beyond the bounds prescribed by simple courtesy. "Are you a scientist?" asked the girl. "Are you something to do with the reactor?" "Certainly not," I replied. "The reactor, as you call it, commits foul murder on these unhappy creatures. I do not presume to call myself a scientist, merely a human being who catches dead fish and buries them in a meet and fitting manner."

Not being the fool for which the Neapolitan pugilist takes me, I recognize with crystalline clarity that the only humane form of fishing—to wit, the recovery and interment of dead fish—cannot be regarded as an every-day occupation. All the more jubilantly did I hail the propitious hour of my encounter with a soul-mate, for the supernal apparition expressed no surprise whatsoever, neither by word nor gesture. "How nice to think someone worries about the poor little fish!" said the girl. Turning to the mist-enshrouded colossus, she added, "That awful power station—how we hate it!" "We," she said, and I found it hard to suppress a pang of jealousy until I realized, as I did almost instantly, that the suspect plural must be a reference to her worthy parents or relatives. "Shall I show you where I bury the fish?" I asked, overcoming my timidity, and—lo!—the fairy followed me, without the slightest misgiving, to the spot where I had marked the atomic victims' burial-place with a stone of peculiar shape—a natural tombstone. Difficult as it had been to conceal my joyous excitement from the first moment onward, only years of iron self-discipline prevented me from crying aloud with exultation when she asked if she might be of assistance to me, if I would "permit" her—yes, that was the word she used—to share in and contribute to my sad and reverent endeavours.

On the way back to the bridge she confessed that, although she had known nothing of the power station's murderous and poisonous properties, she now found it wholly logical and self-evident, having been "enlightened"—yes, "enlightened"—by me, that nuclear fission and all its concomitants served no purpose other than to defile the pure, violate the natural, profane the invisible, kill the living, and transform the green estuary into a grey egress.

Early evening had descended on Foce Verde by the time we reached the bridge. The first lights were twinkling in the quay-side taverns, a merciful twilight shrouded the ugliness of the beach in fantastic shadows, and even the wolfish baying of the waves sounded more like the reassuring clamour of the distant village-dogs that barked me to sleep in my childhood. There we stood on the bridge, side by side, man and woman, as solitary as Adam and Eve, and just as steeped in paradisial illusions.

Without waiting for the question whose discreet formulation had been taxing my brain for some considerable time, and obviously at pains to relieve me of such embarrassment, the celestial being in the trench-coat informed me that it was obliged to depart the very next day, "unfortunately", since "we only spend the week-ends at our house"—and here it pointed to the castle-like edifice on the promontory. How could I have been in any doubt that I had encountered a high-born damsel of days gone by—indeed, that the mansion's sole purpose in rising from the sea, with its thick walls, heavy gates, battlements and gables, was to safeguard this latter-day prodigy? My pulses raced at the thought that, although I could not set eyes on my fairy princess for another whole week, I should certainly see her when the week was up. Then, as I hesitantly and with pleasing diffidence inquired if we should meet there on the bridge next Sunday, ready to dedicate the dead fish to eternal peace, I murmured my name and finally introduced myself. The end of the miracle, at least for seven interminable days? But no, there was more to come. "Aurelio Morelli?" the girl said, her voice trembling with humility. "Not *the* Aurelio Morelli, who wrote *Thou art Alcibiades?*" Oh, what a blessed thrill ran through me at the sound of my own desecrated name, what new resonance it gained in such an innocent and lovely mouth, how suddenly the title of my forgotten work seemed to blossom—nay, it was as if it had acquired meaning and significance for the very first time!

After promising that she would appear punctually at two next Sunday, before the light failed, the girl extended her hand—a fleeting, virginal gesture—and almost bashfully told me her name.

Agnese! Agnese, like the Signora Angelotti of my spurned but splendid, maltreated but immortal novel! Having written the book, I am now destined to live its every page.

Oskar Enzian

I didn't half get a turn when Hans said there was a Herr Pospischil on the telephone. I'd just cut Frau Steinmetz a quarter of *Krakauer*—she always likes it in one piece. "Wrap it," I told Hans, sharpish.

"Well, how goes it, old pal?" Pospischil asked. I recognized his voice straight off.

"All right," I replied, on the cautious side.

"I know," said Pospischil.

"Why ask, then?" I snapped.

"I've got to speak to you," said Pospischil.

I knew what the score was. Made me feel proper sick, it did, because I hadn't seen Pospischil since 'forty-four. Old pal—after twenty-three years! He said he'd be happy to call on me, but I soon put a stop to that idea. Pospischil isn't going to darken my portals if I can help it.

So then he said, "In that case you'll have to call on me. At my offices."

Have to, he said! I never was what you'd call strong-minded, he knew that perfectly well, the dirty dog. Anyway, what was all that about offices? He used to be a junior book-keeper at Gerngross's when we were in the Brownshirts. Didn't have an office in those days, just one room, kitchen, and toilet.

"Who's Pospischil?" Franziska asked when I was out front again, in the shop.

"Nobody important," I said. "Another sponger, that's all." We've been bombarded with hard-luck stories ever since the papers said they were going to make a film of Hertha's life. Any-one'd think I'd won the pools.

I took a cab that afternoon. I was pushed for time because it's harder to get ten minutes' break from Franziska than squeezing a forty-eight-hour pass out of a bloody-minded sergeant-major. Cabs are a luxury, but I can't resist giving my arse a treat. No-body's perfect. It makes you feel like a toff, riding in a cab, because it isn't the regular thing and you don't have to drive yourself. You get driven in a train, too. Owner-drivers are the only ones who think they're God's gift to the world. Besides, I needed cheering up because I was feeling so queer. Everything seems to be getting on top of me just lately. Sometimes I feel as if the walls were going to fall in on me—and the sky, come to that. It's nothing to do with my lungs, either.

I drove to the address I'd been given in Hamburger Strasse. The house is in Margarethen, beside the Vienna Canal but past the Naschmarkt.

I wasn't wrong. There was a film I'd seen on TV a few days back, and this reminded me of it. Two fellows robbed a bank—in America, of course—but the police only got one of them. The other lived to regret it. Turned into a respectable citizen, too, even if he did come from Texas. Got himself a wife and four children and a gas-station and all. Well, one evening when he went out into the garden he heard a rustling sound in the bushes, and who do you think it was, lurking there? His old mate! He came and lurked in the bushes every night from then on, all scars and five-o'clock shadow, which suited him because he was a right villain the same as he'd always been. He was after a half-share in the gas-station, of course. The first man, the respectable one, started losing sleep because there isn't a softer pillow than a clear conscience and he didn't have one. I don't know how the film ended, worse luck. I got into an argument with Hans about his sarcastic remarks. I hope everything turned out for the best, though, because you couldn't help liking the garage-owner and crime doesn't pay.

It's all because of Hans. If I played Lotto the way my mother used to, I'd bet on ninety-nine. Ninety-nine means a bad dream. Hans wants to marry Hermine. He's known her since she was a baby. Hermi's a decent enough girl, I'll say that for her. She works for Wiesinger's, the livestock people, but she's got her sights set a bit higher than that. Neat little thing she is, too. It's just that she hasn't got a schilling to her name. They can't live with us if they marry. Our accommodation's limited, so Hans sleeps on the couch. They can't rent from Hermi's parents because they're dead, and Hermi lodges with her aunt. They can't live there, either, even though her aunt's deaf. If I get the money, I told Hans yesterday, you can get yourself a flat. Living-room, kitchen, toilet—the lot. It just slipped out, but I never go back on my promises. A man's word is his bond. Franziska tore me off a proper strip afterwards, of course, but I was only doing right by the family. When I see Hans standing there in his white smock, slicing the fat off a leg of pork, it brings a lump into my throat, honest it does. I used to look like that myself once, and if I'd only married Paula everything'd be different. Well, you can't start from scratch again yourself, but you've got to do right by your children if you're a decent type of parent. The only reason Hans is a high-brow and a Red is because he sleeps on the couch. Give those lads a living-room, kitchen, and toilet and a bed of their own and they shit on world revolution inside two minutes. What Franziska can't get into her head is that I've had an itch to become a grandfather since Hertha's death. I expect it's because Hertha never had any children and Mizzi doesn't seem able. Ten to one it's her policeman's fault, because nobody ever made a child with holy water. But if Hermi has a little girl she's to be christened Hertha—Hans has got to promise me that. I'll lay odds it'll be a girl with sky-blue eyes the same as Hertha's. Hans proper fell on my neck, he did. I can't remember the last time he gave me a hug. Pospischil can lurk in the bushes till he drops, for all I care.

Outside the entrance I saw straight off why Pospischil had talked about his "offices". There was a posh-looking name-plate which said: *Joseph Pospischil, legally certified expert and adviser on taxation problems.* I ran my hand over the plate to see if it was engraved. It was, in gold letters. The wording made me feel better. Nobody who's legally certified can afford to get mixed up in anything crooked. He wants to offer his services as a tax consultant, I said to myself, feeling easier in my mind. I'll need a tax consultant anyway, when I'm lousy rich.

Pospischil's worn well, I'll say that much for him. Only two or three years younger than me, and still a fine figure of a man. Got a back like a ramrod, even if he has lost his hair. Bald as an egg, he is.

All that talk about offices was eyewash, but then Pospischil always was a line-shooter. All he had was a one-room office, and his wife was in bed next door. He said she was poorly and we'd have to keep our voices down. He wasn't married in the old days.

Then he got down to brass tacks, as they say. I was a rich man now—that was the long and the short of it. Hold hard, I said, don't believe everything you read in the papers, all that glitters isn't gold. But he only sniggered at that, dead sinister. Pospischil always did laugh like a horse, and that's sinister, because horses haven't got souls like us, and it's a bad sign when they laugh. He started on about Taborstrasse right away.

"We cleaned up Taborstrasse because we were ordered to— you know that as well as I do," I said. "The Jew-boy put up a fight. His skull was too thin, that's all. It must be some kind of a racial defect."

All that racial stuff is over and done with, Pospischil said. People don't look at things objectively these days. The Jews won the War, he said, and that put paid to objectivity.

Fair enough, but what's that got to do with me? I steer clear of politics myself, I don't even belong to the Austrian People's Party, because if you join a party one day you find yourself in dead bother the next. Politics are a public menace, like drunken driving.

"I was promoted, even," I told him, but I didn't let on it was

129

because of Pollack's villa. Pospischil wasn't there, thank God. He'd been sent to Russia by that time.

"No need to justify yourself to me," Pospischil said, but he went straight on to mention that the Jew-boy had some relatives. He must have made inquiries, the foxy bastard. "Stern was his name," he said. "Isak Stern, known as Fritz." Jews were still allowed to use Aryan names in those days. Now they're allowed to again because people aren't objective any more.

"Nobody can prove anything against me," I told him, straight. "I'm friendly with Dr Habichl. We belong to the same club."

That didn't cut any ice with Pospischil. "I never got in touch while you didn't have anything yourself," he said, all gracious, "You've got to admit that."

"I'm admitting nothing," I snapped. I was hot under the collar by this time, and my veins had swelled up, which happens pretty often since my lung-trouble. "You're trying to blackmail me," I told him—said it to his face, I did. "You're a legally certified blackmailer, that's what you are."

I wasn't going to give in without a fight. Franziska knows all about the Jew-boy, but whenever I call Hans a Red he comes that sins-of-the-father stuff, and he doesn't know a thing, except that I was in the Party. I never knew anything about the concentration camps, and I never set foot in Taborstrasse again. Mizzi doesn't know anything either. Pospischil didn't reckon on dealing with a family man who had a will of iron.

"All right, have it your way," he said. "You can lead a horse to water but you can't make it drink. I only wanted to be helpful."

Weighing things up, I decided that if I turned him down flat the family would get to hear about it, sure as fate. On the other hand, if I slipped him a little small change I might be able to weather the storm. No point in pushing your luck when you're in the shit, so I said:

"How much do you want, you legally certified bastard?"

"Pipe down," he replied. "My wife's ill." He looked towards the door as he said that, all affectionate. He can't be making much from his consultancy business. Next time he spoke his voice had gone all soft: "We've had some rare old times together, Oskar. . . ."

"You can say that again, Peppi," I said.

"Well, then," he said, pouncing on me. "You hand over twenty-five per cent of your income—only the extra income, of course, from Hertha. I don't want a slice of your shop. I shouldn't have to tell you that—we've known each other long enough."

He shouldn't have said that. Attack's the best method of defence, that's my motto, even if Franziska does take me for a fool.

"You didn't get in touch because you were in clink," I told him, straight. "It even said so in the *Kronen-Zeitung*."

He might be a tax expert, but that floored him. He turned white as a sheet. Pospischil always did have unhealthy colouring —cheesy, sort of—even when we first met in the Brownshirts. He stared out at the canal with those watery eyes of his, and then he came out with it like a judge summing up. Yes, he had spent seven years inside. Nine years, they'd given him, but he got two years remission, and they counted the time he'd spent on remand. "Dr Habichl defended me," he said, making sure I got the point. But that was quite different, he said, because he wasn't with the Brownshirts any longer. The Jews he shot, he shot as a soldier, in compliance with orders. In Poland, what's more. It made all the difference if somebody had paid his debt to society, he said. He was a free man, and he could look anyone in the eye. That was because we lived in a democracy. His new status as a legally certified expert and adviser on taxation problems proved it. "Besides," he ended up, all pompous, "you don't seem to be very conversant with the statute-book. Reproaching someone with an offence for which he has already atoned renders a person liable to a fine or imprisonment."

"I'm not reproaching you with anything," I said. "You were only doing your duty, same as me, but there's no reason why I should stand for blackmail. That's in the statute-book too."

"Some people have all the luck," he said. "My hair never grew again after those seven years inside—you can see for yourself. That's all the thanks I got from a grateful Fatherland. You always were a lucky dog."

"Somebody murdered my daughter," I said. "My favourite, Hertha was."

"My wife's got cancer," he said.

Then he went out. I got up and walked to the window and looked out at the canal. He's a poor bugger for all that, I thought.

It doesn't take much to soften me up. Too soft-hearted for my own good, I am, like my father. There was one rotten little file on Pospischil's desk, and his typewriter must have dated from the year dot. That's the same as if I only had one salami and no bacon-slicer. His wife's got cancer and nothing to do all day except stare out at the canal. You don't need to have cancer to feel low, with that outside the window. If he'd only tried to touch me for the money I might have given in, what with being soft-hearted and never spending much on myself. We were both young once, and a man can't forget these things. He used to have red hair, Pospischil did, like a cartload of carrots.

"I'll tell you something," Pospischil said, when he'd come in again and eased the door to behind him. "If you become a millionaire the tax inspectors'll skin you alive."

"The tax inspectors can get knotted," I said, not too convinced. People are always saying that, but no tax inspector ever got knotted yet.

"Don't you believe it," Pospischil sneered. "They'll go through your books with a fine tooth-comb, and that includes the ones from your butcher's shop. You may not even get away with a simple demand for income tax. After all, it's a sort of inheritance."

He had a point there, but I didn't let him see I thought so.

"Listen, Oskar," he said, "I tell you what we'll do. You pay me twenty-five per cent and I'll take on your tax problems free of charge. Mother Austria won't get a groschen, I guarantee you."

"How are you going to manage that?" I asked.

"Leave it to me," Pospischil replied. "We'll claim so many expenses the inspectors won't know if it's Christmas or Ramadan. In the first place no one can check how much the negotiations cost you, and in the second place you have to keep up appearances. After all, the fact that you're Hertha's father makes you a public figure."

"You're right there," I said, because I saw what he meant. This business about keeping up appearances, for instance. Franziska's gone and bought herself a new dress, and it's only right and proper that the State should foot the bill.

"I'll save you forty per cent minimum," Pospischil bragged. "You'll still be making fifteen per cent over the odds."

A man's got to be able to make up his mind, I always say. That's Hans's weakness, not being able to make up his mind. You can't even rely on him to decide how much liver-sausage we ought to make.

I said, "There are plenty of tax consultants as sharp as you, but you can have my business for old times' sake. I'll pay you fifteen per cent of my film income."

"There'll be income from other sources," Pospischil said.

"You don't know you're born," I told him. "I've got lung trouble but the national insurance people couldn't care less because I'm self-employed. My eldest daughter isn't too well placed either. As for Hans—that's my son—he's got to get married because his girl-friend's expecting." I jumped the gun a bit there, but still. "I've got to help him out or he'll turn into a Red."

"My wife's got stomach cancer," Pospischil repeated.

"You wouldn't want my Hans to turn into a Red on your account," I said.

That made Pospischil stop and think. I spotted it straight away, being observant. "I'll meet you half-way, Oskar," he said. "Fifteen per cent from all sources of income."

"Fifteen from the film," I said, firm as a rock. "Ten from the rest."

"Shake," said Pospischil. "Don't try to diddle me, though, because being your tax consultant makes me responsible for your declaration form."

"What if you try blackmailing me again?" I came back at him, remembering that film on TV.

"I've agreed to advise you on your tax problems in full cognizance of your previous history," Pospischil replied. "And kindly don't sign any contracts without consulting me. For instance, it would be better from the tax angle if the film company employed you as an adviser. Sign a contract without a tax consultant and you'll never get rich."

It was only then he started talking about Hertha. How a girl from a respectable Viennese family could have gone off the rails like that in the first place, and how the least she might have done was take a professional name, and how he wasn't surprised at Hans, young people being what they were these days, and why the Wops had hung on to Hertha's money, and whether my contracts contained safeguards against them catching the murderer in the meantime, because even the Italian police catch a murderer occasionally. He knows a thing or two, Pospischil does, there's no denying it.

Of course, I made a point of asking about his wife. Not a hope of saving her, he told me, lowering his voice, and all because the bloody doctors caught on too late.

I started talking about the old days, firstly because I wanted to steer him off a painful subject, and secondly because we'd been through a lot together. Added to that, I was thinking of Pollack's villa. Karli Krahl was the only one who knew about it, probably, and I'd been itching to find out if he was still in the land of the living. It's a menace, conscience is, even if Pollack did exploit the German people. I couldn't afford to give up another fifteen per cent, not at any price, and Karli Krahl wouldn't be as easy to deal with as Pospischil. He always was a dirty swine, Karli was. I felt a bit safer when Pospischil told me he was supposed to have been killed in Russia. Well, never speak ill of the dead, as a famous man once said. It's sad to think how many of the lads have gone. Franzi Huber—the one who was always cracking jokes—he bought it way back in France. Toni Sommer didn't take long to die a hero's death either. Berti Rammer left his bones somewhere in Italy, and as for Gustav Emmich, the baby of the company, he got strung up by the Russians in Hungary. "Heini Pittner's the only one I bump into from time to time," Pospischil said. "He still chases the girls." We laughed at that, because old Heini always was one for chasing girls. He's lucky with women, we always used to say—he fancies the lot.

"Give my best to your family," Pospischil said as I was leaving. "I hope I'll have the pleasure of meeting your lady wife before long."

It fair gave me the creeps to hear him say that, because God help me if Pospischil goes and lets the cat out of the bag. About his percentage, I mean. It isn't in a woman's nature to forgive and forget, that's a fact.

I thought I'd give him a gentle nudge. "It's all to do with tax, mind," I said.

"It is anyway," Pospischil replied, taking the hint. "You won't lose by it, believe me. Tax consultants' fees are a deductible expense."

I didn't feel too happy, all the same, walking along the Vienna

Canal and across the Naschmarkt. The Naschmarkt looks pretty sad when it's empty, with lettuce-leaves scattered all over the paving-stones, where they don't belong. A man with a conscience can't afford to have a past, and vice versa. On the other hand, having a tax consultant is important. A common butcher I may be, but I didn't let Pospischil do me in the eye. Except that ten or fifteen per cent is a fair old whack whichever way you look at it. I can't go back on Hans's flat because that would be like chucking my parental authority out of the window. Hertha always had a soft spot for Hermi, too. They used to play sand-castles on the Gänsehäufl when they were kiddies. What I always say to myself is, Oskar, it isn't your money, it's Hertha's, and you can only dispose of it the way Hertha would have wanted. She'd have bought Hans a flat right enough, but then she didn't know about Pospischil. I wouldn't have a snowball's chance in hell of convincing Franziska that a tax consultant costs ten or fifteen per cent. "You easy-going idiot," she'd say, "anybody can diddle you." I can hear her saying it now. That's typical feminine logic for you. All women think the same about their husbands, but they can't be right because it would mean all men are idiots, which they aren't. Dr Habichl's going to cost me a packet too, God help me. Nothing in life is free except death, and even that costs you your life. All the same, I'm not such a fool as Franziska thinks. It struck me, as I was wading through the lettuce-leaves, that I might be able to persuade the Swiss to slip me at least half of it under the counter. What the tax-man doesn't see Pospischil won't grieve for. When you come down to it, my Hertha didn't die under tragic circumstances just to line the pockets of Messrs Habichl and Pospischil, let alone the tax inspectors.

I took a tram from the Sezession, which showed the business had got under my skin after all. I wouldn't have rolled up in a cab because of Franziska and the neighbours, but I didn't have the heart to take one anyway.

Italo Canonica

Monday, 13th November. Discovered a good recipe for *Tonno chioggiola.* Take four slices of tunny-fish, two finely chopped onions, four diced tomatoes, one clove of garlic, a glass of white wine, some chopped parsley, one pound of peas, salt, pepper, four tablespoonfuls of oil, and six ounces of butter. Rub the fish well with the crushed garlic, then pepper and salt it. Lightly simmer the onion, parsley, and tomato in hot oil, add the wine and fish and some stock, and allow to braise. Important: lid on! Meanwhile, simmer the peas with parsley and butter in a little water and serve with the tunny-fish.

Tuesday, 14th November. My hunch that Bossi is one step ahead of us grows stronger. Rang Christa Sonntag at midday and invited her to supper at my flat. It's against regulations, but I don't care. I doubt if they would take disciplinary proceedings against me at my age. I don't want to show myself at the Contessa's too often, and I'm anxious to gain her confidence. She arrived punctually at half-past seven, wearing a smart fur-coat but hardly any make-up. Mother-of-pearl lipstick seems to be all the rage. Young women nowadays look as if they had jaundice. At least Christa Sonntag smiles. The mannequins and photographic models one sees in fashion magazines either look deathly sad or grimly defiant, like strikers on the way to a rally. It's probably rather shrewd: they mutely invite the customer to buy a smile as well as an evening dress. I could see the surprise on Sonntag's face. She hadn't expected a policeman to have such a nice three-roomed flat. She handed me an envelope almost before she was inside the hall. It flashed through my mind that it might be the murderer's name, but it turned out to be a neatly typewritten recipe for hock of veal, Munich-fashion. "Just to show you it's nothing like *ossobuco*," she said. I showed off my library a little. Two thousand-odd volumes—the hall and living-room are lined with them. Over two hundred cookery books in five languages. I made sure she didn't notice my *Dekameron bayerischer Küche*, which contains an excellent recipe for hock of veal. I didn't want to hurt her feelings. I'd laid the table with my best china and antique silver to make her feel that I looked on her as a personal friend. She didn't misconstrue my motives: she has the sort of unerring instinct which women of better class often lack. I didn't want to waste any time in the kitchen, so there was only *Vitello tonnato alla casa*, five kinds of cheese, a *zabaione*, and two half-bottles of white and red wine. "Let's hope it's a success or I'll have to do away with myself," I said, and told her the story of the chef who committed hara kiri. This was the Duc de Condé's chef, who discovered too late that there wasn't enough roast meat to go round at a *rendez-vous de chasse* and skewered himself with a sword on the spot. I deliberately waited until coffee-time before broaching the subject of my call. "You're a genius," she said. "Threatening to leave Rome did the trick. Bossi says I needn't worry about the murderer. He's safely tucked away in Spain, writing his memoirs for *Quest' Ora*. When I looked shocked, and asked him why he didn't turn the murderer in, he only laughed and said, 'Poor old Canonica can find him himself'. The man's well guarded anyway, he says, and when the time comes *Quest' Ora* will serve him up on a silver platter. He says it'll make the bogies look twice as silly as they do already." The Contessa apologized for the expression, even though she had only been quoting Bossi. Bossi wouldn't say more, she told me, and she had been afraid that further probing would arouse his suspicions. Did she believe that Bossi had been telling the truth? I asked. She was convinced of it, she replied, because he had drunk a fair amount earlier on and ended by apparently regretting his outspokenness. "He's as vain as a peacock," she said, not without a certain worldly wisdom, "and vain men can't keep secrets." She begged me not to interrogate Bossi because he would deny the story. I promised her not to question him until it became absolutely unavoidable. Bossi would feign ignorance, and I would lose a source of information in Christa Sonntag. Above all, it would go against the grain to follow Bossi's trail instead of the murderer's. I have to reckon with the newspapers, which would claim to have deputized for an incompetent police force. Nowadays, newspapers track down murderers, dispense medical advice to the sick, the obese, and menopausal women, instruct the public in legal procedure and tax avoidance, and attend to the sexual enlightenment of children, whom they have taken out of their parents' hands.

It was ten o'clock by this time, so I offered—the only polite expedient—to escort Christa Sonntag home. However, she found it so 'cosy' in my flat that I didn't have the heart to turn her out. The rain was falling in such torrents outside my little windows that it even blotted out the lights in the Piazza Navona. She asked me if I didn't feel "awfully lonely", a question to which I responded with a cautious negative—although I'm sure it was harmlessly intended. I talked about my children and grandchildren and showed her a few photographs. The pictures of Adele had already caught her eye. I told her that I was going to keep my retirement a secret from the grandchildren because it was easier for a criminal to admit to his grandchildren that he had been caught in the act than for a detective to confess that he had stopped catching criminals. She confided that she was worried about her brother, and asked my advice about purchasing a piece of land. Tact forbade me to ask if she too was contemplating retirement. I made absolutely no reference to her profession, although in recent years—and more especially since the murder of Hertha Enzian—I have made a careful study of the call-girl phenomenon. She eventually raised the subject of Enzian of her own accord, and I learned a number of things which may prove useful. It was nearly midnight when she insisted on my calling her a taxi—because of her fur coat, she said. It was still raining. I don't regret having flouted police regulations.

Wednesday, 15th November. Not that I really admit it to myself, I am sometimes worried by the prospect of what to do when I retire. Read and cook? Hobbies are like bank loans: the only time you can count on them is when you don't need them. As my retirement date draws nearer, so I feel increasingly tempted by the idea of committing my recollections to paper—without any ambition to publish, of course. Four or five years ago I shouldn't have dared to admit such an intention. Memoirs are the false teeth of the toothless. Most people write their memoirs not because they have something to say but as a form of occupational therapy for the unemployed. But today as I was walking home—the rain had washed Rome clean and the Piazza Navona shone like a ballroom floor—I was overwhelmed for the first time by an irresistible urge to record what I have experienced, learned, and thought. It may have had something to do with the Contessa's visit. We live in the call-girl era. Everyone thinks he knows about call-girls, and almost no one does. The great hetaerae of the ancient world learned the art of love so as to exploit it in politics. Both Aspasia and Phryne pursued political aims. They were the forerunners of the suffragettes, except that they operated through a partner instead of a party. The mistresses of the French kings were just as politically- or, failing that, socially-minded. Married off to dim-witted old courtiers at the monarch's behest, they continued to wield influence long after their beauty had faded and their physical charms were a mere memory. No less shrewd were the mistresses of the late nineteenth century. The mistress was not a wife, but neither was she a whore. She often gave her lover more enduring loyalty than his wife did, and he provided for her in his will—monogamy in the afternoon. Even the most rudimentary form of prostitution was respectable in comparison with the call-girl's trade. I think this stems from a difference in objective. The Marquise de Montespan aspired to become a duchess, the cocotte to become the wife of an industrial tycoon, the prostitute to become a provincial landlady. All of them lived with a second way of life in view. Only the call-girl uses the money she acquires in order to remain a call-girl—the "end of the line", as Christa Sonntag puts it. On the other hand, the vendors of love are less responsible for this than the consumers. The immediate predecessor of the call-girl, the cocotte, made the same sort of demands on a man as his wife: she claimed time as well as money, jewellery, and clothes. This is my explanation—the research has been useful to my work—of why call-girls deal predominantly with married men. The married man has a family in addition to his profession. Consequently, he has just enough time for a telephone call and a mistress between conferences. At the same time, in contrast to the prostitute, the call-girl has become a status symbol. The aristocrats of affluence reach for the telephone as they would for a caviare-spoon. They 'treat themselves' to a call-girl, whose main criterion of quality is price. When fashion dictates the collecting of Impressionists the price of paintings rises concomitantly with the reputation of those who collect them. Like Impressionists, call-girls are subject to imitation. I recently came across the following sentence in a book by the British psychologist G. M. Carstairs: *Public morality has become a desert abounding in the ruins of shattered conventions.* I jotted down in the margin: *Convention—or hypocrisy, if you like—is the ugly sister of morality, but the beautiful sister cannot exist without her ugly counterpart.* Carstairs goes on: *Concepts such as integrity and even common decency sound old-fashioned, but nothing, absolutely nothing, has taken their place.* My comment: So *much immorality has occurred in a moral world that people assume they have no choice but to throw out the clean baby with the dirty bath-water.* Theories? The Press believes that I am seeking the murderer in the land of the pimp, the so-called 'milieu'. Nobody in the 'milieu' had any reason to strangle Hertha Enzian. She was killed by a man who had lost his way in the wilderness.

Thursday, 16th November. At 10.15 I was informed that I had a visitor, Roberto Pisenti from Lubriano, north of Viterbo. A bucolic figure of medium height, sturdily built but diffident in manner, like most hill-farmers. Unmistakable Lazio accent. I recalled the Pisenti case straight away, even though it was two years old and I hadn't worked on it myself. A peasant-girl named Vera Pisenti had been found strangled in a barn on her father's farm. No trace of the assailant. Hesitantly, with a flood of apologies, Pisenti stated his business. He had turned the matter over in his mind for weeks, and now his conscience had brought him to Rome. A confession, I thought—though only a poor judge of human nature would have taken my visitor for a murderer. "This girl," he said at last, "this Hertha Enzian—she had a father too, according to the papers, even if she was a bad girl. Not like my Vera." "What do you know about Hertha Enzian?" I asked. "Nothing," he said stoutly, "except that the things they're saying about the murderer seem to fit the wretch who murdered my Vera." "What, for instance?" I asked. I wasn't too impressed, in the first place because we had checked on every unsolved murder in recent years, and, secondly, because prostitute-murders are almost invariably committed by 'prostitute-murderers'. Bruce Graeme's *Passion, Murder and Mystery* (1927) and the Wilson-Pitman *Encyclopedia of Murder* (1961) both have something to say on the subject. Nevertheless, I had to concede the layman's contention that the two murders had certain features in common: murder by strangulation with the bare hands, apparent lack of motive, absence of intent to rob (?), no rape, no sign of indecent assault, probably not the work of a professional criminal but traces obliterated with extreme care, probably not the impulsive act of a madman (?), nor, finally, a sex-killing in the commonly accepted sense. My visitor shuffled to and fro in his chair and started to mumble something about "superstition", without, however, giving any further indication of what he meant. Eventually he came out with it: had it not struck the gentlemen of the police that "this creature", Hertha

Enzian, was murdered on the 8th of August, two years to the day after the murder of his daughter? This, he felt, must signify something. I pledged him to secrecy, and promised that I would take the matter up. It preoccupied me for the rest of the day. If the newspapers latch on to the similarity between the dates there'll be no holding them. I can see the headlines now. "The August Murderer still at large" will make a nice change after the "Fairground Murderer", the "Lover's Lane Murderer", and the "Midnight Murderer".

. . . Rang Primavesi at his flat. He was on leave, so failed to contact him all day. Ordered him to report to me tomorrow. Have decided not to mention the Pisenti case to the Chief—there's time. The relationship between Giannini and me is businesslike with an undertone of hostility. I don't think it's my fault. Giannini can't forgive me because he was promoted over my head. It's easier to forgive a man who's injured you than a man you've injured. Giannini feels he has to apologize because he's sitting in my chair. He jumps up whenever I enter his office, then stands or wanders around until I leave the room. He's nearly twenty years younger than I am, and incorrigibly ambitious, an excellent detective but narrow-minded and chary of experience. Like most men of his generation, he's convinced that everything must be modern in a modern world, and that experience is merely a collection of dusty anecdotes. It is a mental cliché to believe that we were just as hostile to the older generation in our youth. Adults of different generations vary, so why shouldn't the same apply to the youth of different generations? We too felt the itch for independence, but even if we didn't take our elders' advice we were at least anxious to eavesdrop on their experience, and if necessary steal or expropriate it. Giannini's age-group, not to mention the younger generation, fears our experience like an infectious disease, and cherishes its own mistakes as if they were virtues. It annoys me that Giannini and I have a common aversion to intellectuals. We can spend a solid half-hour talking as if we understood one another, when all the time I know that our understanding is based on a misunderstanding. He confuses cultivated men with intellectuals and hates them for their progressive attitude, whereas I repudiate intellectuals for their reactionary arrogance. Giannini is short-sighted. Although the entire credit for solving the Enzian case would go to him, he would prefer me to retire on a defeat. I don't think I shall do him that favour.

... Two A.M. Couldn't sleep, so got up with the idea of skimming through my diaries. Have a dreadful suspicion about the deputy chief of the Homicide Squad, Dr Italo Canonica. About four years before the murder of Hertha Enzian a schoolgirl named Lucia Chiesa was strangled in the Borghese Gardens. We have been re-examining the case, but the exact date of the murder escapes me. It was some time in midsummer. Could it have been the 8th of August? I can't find any indication in my diary. Till tomorrow morning!

Friday, 17th November. How incredibly stupid of me! Am I going senile? Should I have quit the force two years ago at the very latest? Lucia Chiesa was murdered on the 8th of August, 1963.

... To take things in turn: first the Pisenti case. I asked for a report from Dario Primavesi, who headed the inquiry. A dry stick, Primavesi, sceptical and unimaginative but superbly trained, doggedly determined, and absolutely devoted to me. We compared the two cases with astonishing results. The murder of Vera Pisenti took place at her father's farm, not far from Viterbo, on the 8th of August, 1965, during or after a country wedding celebration attended by approximately eighty people. Primavesi's inquiries unusually difficult. Almost every male wedding guest equally suspect, presence of outsiders not excluded. Primavesi gives a less glowing picture of the murdered girl's morals than her father did. At twenty, she had already had relations with at least seven men. Primavesi traced them all, but all were patently (?) innocent. He investigated along *Cavallerìa rusticana* lines on the assumption that the motive was jealousy. Most statements implied otherwise. A country call-girl? No recorded allusion to any man with even the vaguest resemblance to the Via Sicilia murderer. This signifies little. Vera Pisenti left the inn where the wedding-night dance was being held between 10.15 and 10.40. From there to the barn on her father's farm would have taken her six minutes at most, using her bicycle. A rendezvous? Quite possible that the murderer was not among the guests. No footprints, no fingerprints of note. The state of the body—fully clothed but with the skirt over the head—quite similar (?) to Enzian's. I ordered a re-examination of the Pisenti case. No one apart from Primavesi knows that I am taking up the Chiesa case as well—the man we arrested, though probably guilty, was released for lack of evidence. Giannini would think I was mad. I can hear him say in that dry voice of his: "We're detectives, not astrologers". He'd be right, too, probably. The similarity of date may be a coincidence. A damned strange coincidence if it is.

Saturday, 18th November. Confined to bed for two or three days by a bout of tonsillitis. Feeling a bit feverish, but glad that this annoying inflammation of the throat has struck me down at the week-end, now I'm sure I'm on the right track. Got the doctor to give me a penicillin injection, and hope to be able to resume work by Tuesday at the latest. Have asked Primavesi to call tomorrow. Meanwhile, I read and brood in bed.

... Breadcrumbed sliced cucumber—it really exists. The recipe appears in the *Grand Dictionnaire de Cuisine* by Dumas *père*. The author of the *Three Musketeers* knew as much about *Filet de sole à la Orly* and *Dindon à la Cardinale* as he did about writing adventure novels. The recipe: carefully remove the rind of the cucumber and steep the slices in boiling water for a minute or so. Meanwhile, melt some butter in a casserole. Place the cucumber slices in the casserole, sprinkle with flour, fry, and pour a little water over them. Then season with salt and pepper, and braise. Add some chopped parsley, a little mace, and thicken with cream and egg-yolk. Allow to stand for a few minutes!

... Is there really a resemblance between our own age and some epoch in the past? I can hardly believe it. There can't be any resemblance because we have come to an entirely new realization, the Hiroshima-born realization of man's destructibility by man. Space-travel means nothing beside the message of Hiroshima: we knew man's capacity for achievement, but never even suspected his capacity for destruction. Hiroshima was an attempt to wrest God's last prerogative from him, the right of the Flood, the *ius ultimae noctis*. Instead of divine omnipotence, the omnipotence of man. I recently read of the panic unleashed by Halley's Comet in 1910. People fled to the mountains, fell on their knees and prayed. This, it seems to me, constitutes the difference between the comet and the atom-bomb. Divine punishment was credible, man's punishment of man is not. I'm not a particularly good Christian, but I do believe that our redundant God has played a trick on us. He has allowed mankind to usurp his power but not his prerogatives. He cannot be replaced as supreme judge, because unlike him man cannot exploit his omnipotence without self-annihilation. Despite the Flood, God remains God. Man is only a ship's captain who goes down with a vessel which he himself scuttles. Doesn't the malaise we complain about so sadly spring from the impotence of our omnipotence? Can the atom-bomb really cause still greater havoc than it has already? Can omnipotence be abused when omnipotence itself is an abuse? Incapable of living in the shadow of destruction, we live as if we had already been destroyed. All is permitted to those who dwell among ruins, even the general free-for-all of a Western saloon. The last night is already behind us. What surprises me, when I interrogate criminals, is not their crimes—which are nothing new—but their own surprise that the free-for-all does not extend to them. They may be justified. The asphalt jungle is more impassable than the primeval forests of our ancestors because it is choked with memories. I wonder how it came into being. I don't have an answer, simply a conjecture. Past and future are inhabited, but between them yawns the chasm of the present, like one of those Chiricos which are full of emptiness. People live on one side of the chasm as if the atom-bomb did not exist; on the other, as if it had already reduced everything to ashes. One man feels threatened by the past, another by the future, youth by age, age by youth, tradition by progress, progress by tradition. Nobody builds on an awareness of that which already exists, on the *objektiver Geist*, as Hegel termed it. We do not understand what we ourselves have created, and distrust of understanding produces a crisis of communication. Good governments are as discredited as bad ones because their power is uncanny; governmental power and mass mistrust grow at the same pace. Youth denies the validity of what existed yesterday; it behaves "progressively" without realizing that it really hates the progress which has engendered a hypertrophy of authority. Incongruously, while demonstrating against the past, it fetches down grandfather's bits and pieces from the attic. Fast cars with wax flowers on the bonnet. Anti-militarism and World War One uniforms. Space-suits and water-pistols. Old people like me don't want to know about the future—the potentialities of tomorrow make us shudder. We grew up in the conviction that everything was learnable, and now scarcely anything is understandable. We all betray the present for fear of becoming infected, the young with power, the old with bewilderment. Nobody lives in the no-man's-land or infinite vacuum known as the present. That's our tragedy, probably—that the present is the only human realm of human existence. It's a rendezvous, a place where the guard could be changed with a word of thanks to those going off watch and another to those who relieve them. No changing of the guard, though. The atom-bomb, which fell in the present, destroyed the only place where past and future might have met. One can see across a chasm—even join hands across it—but no-man's-land is a boundless wilderness. Nobody ever sees another soul.

Tuesday, 21st November. Glanced through yesterday's entry and couldn't help laughing. The garrulous old man seems to be equally interested in breaded cucumber and philosophy. There must be a connection. I suspect I know what it is, but am too short of time to go into it today. N.B.—cucumber and philosophy.

... Pia, Bianca, and Elisa have taken it in turns to cook for me these past three days. I feel fitter than ever, needless to say. Primavesi reports that Lucia Chiesa's mother has remarried and is away on a trip. I must speak to her without fail. Tomorrow: Lubriano!

CHAPTER

3

The Compromise

Antonio Zempach

We spent the week-end at Ascona with my mother and drove down to Rome on Monday.

I left the driving to Yvette. Watching her in profile, I thought: I love you. I often think that when I'm sitting beside her in the car. It dawns on me suddenly, almost painfully, but that's only because love born into one's consciousness is like childbirth—it doesn't pass without pangs. Perhaps it's simply that the car's so big and Yvette's so small. The car menaces her but she dominates it all the same. A child on a big horse. You think: My God, what a seat! But you can't help feeling nervous.

Of course, she reverted to the contract between *Quest' Ora* and Kronos Films.

"Why that man Bossi?" she said for the hundredth time. "Why should Vanetti insist that the murderer fits his idea of him?"

"I don't know," I said, also for the hundredth time.

"He wouldn't risk such a big penalty clause for nothing," she said.

"You're doing over a hundred and twenty," I said. I'm a terrible back-seat driver. "Perhaps Vanetti's a gambler. Perhaps he's using his imagination instead of chips."

"Or he knows who the murderer is," said Yvette.

I tried to talk about other things, like the weather and the new autostrada. It was raining fine skeins of sunshine and the road was almost deserted, especially beyond Brescia. Italy goes Italian south of Brescia. The dark trees are slightly darker, the light trees a little lighter, every avenue of pines seems to lead to a cemetery, and the cemeteries are hospitable spa terraces with

149

tombstones standing proxy for deck-chairs. The grand houses are shut up. Grandeur and desolation are synonymous in Italy. The big farmhouses are grand too, but they're only old, of course—rain-washed terracotta.

"We ought to take a holiday in November some day," said Yvette.

"We're on holiday now," I said.

She shook her head. "We're trailing a murderer."

That wasn't my idea at all. Vanetti had told me on the 'phone that it was "business"—nothing to do with the *Enzian Story*, or only "very indirectly". Why should I worry about the murderer? I was interested in establishing contact with Edizioni Vanetti. Dr von Helis: You will take over the firm in due course. That means inheriting deed-boxes. I didn't marry Yvette for the sake of the firm or her father's estate, even reckoned in deed-boxes. Edizioni Vanetti are a million-dollar concern, not always the height of propriety but well within the law. It occurred to me that I ought to have driven to Rome alone. You never know with Yvette—never know when her alarm-clock will go off.

We reached Rome late that afternoon. Rush-hour traffic. Another phrase I'm allergic to, especially when applied to Rome, where "rush-hour traffic" is a double insult. Traffic jams outside the Colosseum are tantamount to vandalism in a museum. The weather was mild, almost early autumnal, with white clouds floating in the evening sky like clumsy Chagall angels.

Yvette paraded her army of occupation on my writing-table—pots, jars, little bottles. I strolled out on to the balcony. An aerial view of the Spanish Steps. Like most Swiss I prefer Paris, like most Swiss I allow Rome to take me by storm.

Vanetti sent his car for us.

"I'm curious to see what he looks like," said Yvette—our pet game.

"Lean, care-worn, and ascetic," I said.

"Plump, wily, and jovial," she said.

I longed to get the next couple of hours behind me. Yvette is romantic and sceptical, I am realistic and naïve.

Vanetti was waiting for us outside the Osteria dell'Orso. She was right, more or less. Above medium height, thickset rather than plump, cunning little eyes but not malicious, hair of that typical Italian grey in which black strands linger on. He reminded me, in his dark suit, of the monk Amador in *Contes drolatiques*. My first impression: one of those Romans who base their right to easy-going cynicism on Rome's millennial past. We've seen it all before—no cause for concern.

I wondered why he had selected a restaurant with background music, smart but noisy. He probably wanted to meet me on safe tourist-trade ground. He had the careful manners of the self-made man who shrewdly avoids social pitfalls. I was ready to bet that he always wore a black tie because it obviated tasteless colour schemes. He ordered like a man who never takes a risk— you can't go far wrong with smoked salmon and steak, Chablis and Moulin à Vent. I saw him through Yvette's eyes: *Grattez le Russe et vous trouverez le snob*. He started to talk business over the *hors-d'œuvres*. Safe ground.

He'd summoned me to Rome, he said, because half a dozen foreign magazines were interested in the *Enzian Story*. He wanted to sell it through a holding company and was planning— with my "expert assistance"—to form a limited company in Liechtenstein. Naturally, ninety-eight per cent of the shares would be held by him and the remaining two per cent by me, "being a Swiss". They like that sort of thing in the tax-dodgers' paradise. He would sell the *Enzian Story* to the new company for a nominal sum, and the company would resell the story abroad.

The most natural thing in the world, Yvette—the firm of von Helis handles that kind of transaction every day, in spite of the genuine Hodlers on the walls. Illegality has a code of its own. You get punished for tax evasion if you're found out, yet the blithe ingenuity with which people defraud the State is a favourite topic of conversation in respectable drawing-rooms. Adultery is regarded as immoral, yet men discuss their escapades like commercial travellers swapping dirty jokes. Smugglers go to gaol if they're caught, but when conversation flags you can always pep it up with a few little smuggling anecdotes of your own.

I couldn't talk to Yvette, so I said, dutifully: "I do find it a trifle odd, though, founding a company on the life of a dead call-girl."

Vanetti took the comment in good part. Three pretty young American girls had sat down at the next table. He shifted his chair so that he could watch them. Then he told me that he planned to market other stories via the Liechtenstein holding company. Hundreds of thousand of dollars were involved, and he didn't see why he should let them vanish into the maw of the Italian exchequer.

I didn't either. Look, darling, a man's day consists of compromises—ask your father. Husbands tell their wives the results of their work in the evening, but they never mention the compromises that produced them. Women form a chivalrous picture of society at their mother's knee. You could make a fortune, buying men for what they're worth and selling them at their wives' valuation.

Yvette's violet-blue eyes turned bluer, a familiar symptom. She smiled. "Herr Vorneweg hinted that you know the murderer's identity." She speaks fluent Italian. No misunderstanding, no excuse. Another minute, and I would be saying: What my wife really means . . .

Vanetti looked amused. "Ah, the clumsy Teuton. He takes everything literally. You don't seriously imagine, Madame, that I would hesitate for a single moment . . ."

I would have been satisfied with that, not being Sherlock Holmes, but I knew what Yvette would say afterwards. I always try to avoid post mortems with Yvette.

I said: "The contract does imply . . ."

"That we have some idea of him," Vanetti cut in.

"How did you come by it?" asked the public prosecutor in the black lace dress.

I started to say: "What my wife really means . . ." but it was unnecessary. Vanetti didn't prevaricate. He was in his element, oblivious of the three pretty American girls, deaf to the music. "Our competitors," he began. Radio, television. John Kennedy's alleged assassin was gunned down in front of the television cameras and their audience of unseen millions. A celebrated case but not exceptional. A few months earlier the B.B.C. had presented some candidates for extinction in their *Man Alive* series, cancer victims, only half-alive, ha ha ha. No, that was wrong. There was a twenty-four-year-old, for instance, hugely optimistic, deriving a double ration of enjoyment from the last few months with his young wife—you could see it for yourself as you watched him strolling hand in hand with her across the fields, giving the impression that life is quite tolerable even with leukaemia. A real feast for the eyes of cancer sufferers, actual and potential.

"I don't follow you," I said dutifully. A half-truth.

"The newspaper is an anachronism in the television age," Vanetti said. "It can't get by on facts so it has to operate with imagination. There's no such thing as novelty—look at Kennedy. Newspapers can only comment on novelties or illustrate them, whichever. A sensation is more than news. Journalism suffers from a lack of credibility. Once upon a time the sceptic used to say: I only believe what I see. Now, seeing isn't good enough for him—what he sees has to move as well. The age of optics has been superseded by the age of movement. *Movimento, movimento!*" He flapped his hands like a bird taking off.

You see, Yvette, there's no point. He won't close down his magazines for your sake. The Enzian case isn't anything out of the ordinary, it just looks like that from the Dolder. We're still living in the age of optics, back in our snug little world. The steaks tasted magnificent, except that we ought to have said we liked ours warm as well as *bleu*.

"One section of the Press," Vanetti was saying, "tries to compete by dishing out high-level politics and esoteric culture—television is still at a disadvantage there. Another section tries to be one jump ahead of the police or the psychologist."

"As in the case of Hertha Enzian," said Yvette.

I was afraid Vanetti would lose his temper, but he had the patience of the devil. I could read his thoughts: If I want Zempach I'll have to win over his wife. He probably married into her father's firm.

"It's all a question of technique," he said. "A magazine like *Quest' Ora*, with its million-copy circulation and wide territorial coverage, has to be printed at least a week in advance of publication—sometimes ten days. We advertise fresh meat and deliver canned goods." He sighed at the inexorability of fate. "If Hertha Enzian's killer were arrested tonight, our readers wouldn't find a picture of him in our next issue—perhaps not even in the one after that. We'd be serving him up deep-frozen, and by that time everybody would have seen him being escorted out of his flat in handcuffs—on television."

"So you photograph him a fortnight before he's arrested," I said, remembering post mortems.

153

"We should have to know his identity first," said Vanetti. "We're taking a gamble."

Call it a day, darling, he can't come any cleaner than that. Cynicism was originated by the Cynics, who were a school of courageous philosophers, sceptical ascetics. If Vanetti was really covering for a murderer he'd say: I'm harbouring the killer to stop him being arrested for the benefit of television, *basta*.

"So what we read in the newspapers is fabricated sensationalism," said Yvette.

What my wife really means . . .

But Vanetti, still mildly paternal, pulled another rabbit out of the hat. A DC4 belonging to Aerolineas Argentinas had taken off from Buenos Aires not long before, destination Rio Gallegos. Some of the twenty-four passengers threatened the pilot with a revolver and forced him to change course for Port Stanley, the diminutive capital of the Falkland Islands. Although situated off the Argentine coast, the islands were proclaimed a Crown Colony of His Britannic Majesty in 1833. Under the leadership of an attractive blonde, the rebels tried to reconquer the archipelago for Argentina. Everything went off pretty smoothly but the invasion was a flop. "Well, not such a flop, actually," said Vanetti. "You see, the blonde wasn't Argentina's answer to Joan of Arc but an employee of *Panorama*, the Buenos Aires illustrated. The coloured cover with its headline: *Nuestras Malvinas, hoy!* had gone to press weeks before. Exclusive pictures of the highjacking, invasion, and abortive rebellion. We ourselves paid a small fortune for the Italian rights." He turned to me. "If you don't want to miss a revolution in the television age, *caro amico*, you have to start it yourself." To Yvette: "Madame, everything is far more complicated than you imagine. The revolution wasn't fabricated—it actually took place. *Panorama* was on the spot, that's all. The Press has become active. We have too much of everything, hence drug-addiction. Better sensationalism than heroin, don't you agree?"

He cast a surreptitious glance at the American girls' table, but two fat middle-aged couples had taken their place. Disappointed, he turned back and devoted himself exclusively to Yvette. He hoped we would stay on for a few days. He and I would be discussing the Liechtenstein transaction at his office next morning—could he send his car for her? An audience with the Pope?

That might be arranged. Ah no, she was probably a Protestant. Well, the Pope was semi-Protestant himself. John XXIII should have lived longer. John, Kennedy, Khruschev ... Things had looked fairly promising, but everyone has to go in the end. What a draught! English tourists, probably, with their love of open windows. *Cameriere!* The music wasn't what it used to be, either. There was a better band last year, Peruvians.

Honestly, Yvette, you can't expect me to say: Apropos of John XXIII, what do you know about the girl's murderer?

Vanetti escorted us back to the Hassler. I said a rather too cordial goodbye, like a man apologizing for his wife. Men are always apologizing for their wives. Wives don't understand that you speak differently *à deux* than *à trois*, and differently *à trois* than you do when you're addressing millions of people. That's the whole secret of the newspaper business, probably.

We sat up at the bar in the heated roof-garden. I thought: now for the post mortem; you ought to have said this, that or the other—but Yvette seemed to be in high spirits. She looked like the cat that swallowed the canary.

"He admitted the whole thing," she said.

"I must have misheard," I retorted.

"He was justifying himself in advance. He thought his description of the cancer victims' fair would convince me—walk up, walk up and see the exhibits, every one doomed to die! I expect he's already printing his coloured cover—*Nostro assassino, oggi!*"

"I'm only a mere man," I said, which is what men always say when they're doing something unmanly. "I never pass emotional judgements."

"Are you going to involve yourself in this Liechtenstein business?" she asked.

"No, of course not. However, there's nothing wrong with the company formation scheme as such."

There was nobody left on the terrace now. Below us, Rome slept with its eyes open. Yvette looked gravely beautiful. I would happily have sacrificed Vanetti for her, complete with the *Enzian Story* and Liechtenstein.

"You can't get out now," she said.

I looked at her quickly.

She said: "You must investigate."

I said: "I'm not Sherlock Holmes, my dear Watson. Besides, the *Corriere della Sera* says it's only a matter of days now."

Yvette was thinking: Now you can see why Antonio got mixed up in this, Papa. Of course he never intended to act for Vanetti. We only went to Rome to fix the murderer's accomplice. I'm proud of Antonio, aren't you proud of Antonio?

"We'll see," I said.

In the morning I had a long discussion with Vanetti. Offices, editorial premises, the new printing works—all very impressive, very soothing to the visitor's eye. I declined the two per cent and Vanetti agreed. He treated me with the usual you're-a-Swiss-of-course respect. Our clocks are accurate to the split-second, we don't make war, we speak three languages, we leave our bags unattended in front of railway stations. Nobody knows our only real virtue, which is not to take the foreigner's view of us at face value. We agreed terms. A substantial fee. You see, Dr von Helis, it wasn't such a bad idea after all. Dr von Helis: I'm happy for you, my boy. I: Vanetti remains my personal client.

I was on the point of leaving when a young man burst into the room without knocking. Check shirt open at the neck, violet jacket, cords, thick red socks, sandals. Thin face fringed with the inevitable beard like a black-bordered letter of condolence. A monument to the unknown demonstrator. "My son Francesco," said Vanetti, who hadn't mentioned his family once. They swapped technicalities which meant nothing to me—block-making, page-proofs, type-faces—but the room was suddenly charged with tension. I felt that I was included in the charmed circle, as though the tension was associated with me.

I asked Vanetti to order me a taxi. Francesco offered to drive me back to my hotel. Vanetti rejected the idea, suggested summoning his chauffeur, calling a taxi, driving me back to the hotel himself—a hectic, agitated flood of words that sounded like an attempt to stave off disaster. My alarm-clock à l'Yvette promptly started ringing. I accepted the son's offer. "What sort of car do you drive?" I asked. "An Alfa," he said.

He didn't utter a word on the way to the car-park. He got in and opened the door from the inside, looking grim. I wondered why he'd made the offer at all. He drove like an ambulance-driver who knows that his patient is dead but hurries just the same. In the thick of the turmoil in the Piazza del Popolo he said:

"Are you the Swiss lawyer who bought Hertha Enzian's life?"

"I negotiated with her father," I said.

"Is money that important?" he asked.

"Funny question," I said.

I didn't feel like conducting an ideological discussion—after all, the boy was in uniform. We have his sort at home in Switzerland, lounging around the Limmatquai, waiting for infuriated citizens and getting infuriated when the citizens show no signs of fury. They don't wash because they've no need to—they're clean, spiritually. Life is like pitch: don't touch it and you won't get dirty. A simple philosophy. Pity I can't borrow it, but I'm an old codger of thirty-six. Corrupt to the marrow.

"Why don't you report my father to the police?" asked young Vanetti.

I ought to have taken a taxi, or the firm's car, or let Vanetti senior drive me back.

"Why should I?" I asked.

"Let's hope you've squeezed plenty of money out of him," said Francesco Vanetti. "Those memoirs will make millions. You'll be well out of it by the time they appear. Happy Christmas."

"You're being mysterious," I said.

Not so mysterious, really. My aim was true but I couldn't bring myself to pull the trigger. I was up in the branches now, and scared of falling. You shouldn't climb trees if you're scared. My father wasn't scared and he fell just the same. But then, he was only trying to photograph an owl.

"Why shouldn't you make money?" said Francesco Vanetti. "Everyone makes money when a call-girl gets murdered."

He swore as another car almost grazed the Alfa's wing. All at once, he behaved as if his one thought was to escape the sheet-metal foes that threatened his property. His Adam's apple bobbed up and down.

"Do you work for *Quest' Ora?*" I asked.

"I'm a poet," he said. "A photopoet."

We were hemmed in by cars. Francesco Vanetti leaned on the horn even though he could clearly see the red light. He said:

"What if my father did tell you a pack of lies? You believed them."

Vanetti junior drove me home, Yvette. A nice young man, a

photopoet. Is that all? He asked me to report his father to the police. Did you ask him why? Because of some memoirs. What memoirs? I didn't ask.

"What memoirs?" I asked. And again: "Why should I report your father?"

"Since when do people report their accomplices?" he said.

I did my best, Yvette, really I did.

I said: "It would be nice to see you again. What about dinner this evening? My wife and I . . ."

"There's no point," he said.

He didn't move when I got out in front of the Hassler.

You don't have to fall out of a tree. You can stay put, but it virtually amounts to the same thing.

Aurelio Morelli

Not without diffidence—indeed, with a certain embarrassment—do I fulfil my obligation to recount the passing of Vera Pisenti, a peasant-girl who numbered twenty summers at her death, and was formerly resident in Lubriano. Ever since I was destined, here at the Calvary of my exile, to encounter Agnese, the adamantine walls of my *Weltanschauung* have been quaking and my pen has balked at its task, even though, on the other hand, I am tempted to construe this as a good omen: greatness belongs only to the writer whose pen does not invariably obey him.

Set down on paper, the circumstances under which Vera Pisenti passed away will be likely to impugn my purity of motive and arouse the preposterous suspicion that my punitive hand was guided by sexual aberration, erotic frenzy, or the lust to kill. Were the oath of a defendant admissible in his own defence—and why, in the case of a man of my intelligence, should it not be so in actuality?—I could swear that, although I planned to rid the world of a young and consequently dangerous creature on my fifty-sixth birthday, it was chance, in the very truest sense of the word, that played the girl Vera Pisenti into my hand: no feelings of lust or repugnance were involved. Finally, I owe it to the well-disposed reader to explain why, after the death of Lucia Chiesa, I allowed two years to elapse without paying my tribute to justice.

THE COMPROMISE

Of the *dramatis personae* who head the cast of William Shakespeare's play *Julius Caesar*, Marcus Brutus, Cassius, Casca, Trebonius, Ligarius, Decius Brutus, Metellus Cimber, and Cinna are represented as "conspirators against Julius Caesar", although the dramatist might with far greater justification have called them murderers or assassins. My celebrated fellow-author did not act unthinkingly, however, for high-minded conspiracy is rendered superior to common murder by two factors: the deliberate and painstaking premeditation of the act, and the direct or indirect participation of as many persons as possible. The more deliberate the killing, and the more numerous those who determine upon it, the less despicable their violation of the Commandments; but, if it be slaughter perpetrated by one multitude upon another, it is then appropriate to speak of an ideal state such as war or revolution.

I do not say all this *post festum*, lightly, thoughtlessly, or without compelling reason. As the lonely pioneer of my generation, as a courageous 'lone wolf', to use the half-admiring but singular expression, I had guided Lucia Chiesa towards a better existence—better, I said, because there is not even the vaguest intimation that the young and the old, death's spring and autumn harvest, do not, on attaining the Elysian Fields or Plutonian realms, become coeval, ageless, and timeless, so that divine justice clearly begins with the total elimination of the seasons. That I had allowed two years to pass without performing my duty was not attributable to fear, a vanished sense of mission, waning energy, or debilitating remorse, but to my desire to become a Brutus rather than a lone wolf. Revolutionary organization, *conspiratio*, social revolt against the Tyrant Youth, the despot Gaius Juventus Caesar—such was my design; I wished to show myself worthy of the gracious destiny that had permitted me to evade the myrmidons of the law by rallying my generation, however belatedly, to the cause of self-defence, to a revolt in the tradition of Spartacus, to a last struggle against the mighty monster—to quote Shakespeare:

> Why, man, he doth bestride the narrow world
> Like a Colossus; and we petty men
> Walk under his huge legs, and peep about
> To find ourselves dishonourable graves.

I failed wretchedly. There is no excuse—not, certainly, for those who denied me their comradeship-in-arms. It is not simply that young people wish to silence, dominate, and enslave us—which is why the evolutionary tendency by parents and elders towards emancipation, equality, the right to vote, and immunity from corporal punishment comes too late and is already superseded. No, on their own submission, they wish to be 'left alone' —though the only means of attaining such 'aloneness' is the cold-blooded slaughter of others. Do we perceive this? By no means! The old and middle-aged nurse a bad conscience in respect of the young, a generation devoid of conscience. Yet how morbid and how like a bloated liver is this conscience of ours! Although there has never been a single epoch in human history which managed without war; although even Heraclitus knew that "war is the father of all things, of all things king"; although the supreme justice of war is all that hinders death from carrying off the old and sick alone, thereby preventing the emergence of a frightful majority and mass population of inexperienced, intellectually under-developed, helpless, and irresponsible youngsters; although, on the other hand, everything which is called progress, and from which the young derive most benefit, owes its existence to past generations, and here again almost exclusively to old men; although it is precisely my tormented generation which has presented youth with the three surest deterrents against future wars: material prosperity, social advancement, and the atomic bomb—despite all this, the older generation feels guilty, and, far from smiting its foe on the head, smites its own breast instead. Clemenceau, the shrewd old tiger, knew that war was too grave a matter to be entrusted to generals, yet we, in our stupidity, assume that we can entrust the future to the young. We created the atomic bomb, mankind's first shield and buckler against extinction, but for fear that it may slip through our fingers we have confided it to the hands of boys; for fear that it may destroy the children's quarters, we have—to our eternal shame—left it ticking away in the nursery. The voice of reason is stilled. The slogan "Student Power" would acquire true meaning, like the revolutionary slogan "All Power to the Councils", only if youth, like the revolutionary council, were a positive or constant quantity. In reality, youth too is subject to Nature's laws: scarcely has it seized power than it ceases to be young, and, if we are to believe its philosophy, becomes corrupted by the process of senescence; under the specious pretence of fighting for a new generation of young people it merely fights for a 'new' older generation which supplants its predecessor.

I will not deny that for two years I lived in false hopes of becoming a latter-day Brutus, a collective as opposed to an individualistic murderer—in short, a leader. Rejected newspaper articles, essays returned unread, the head-wagging abuse of my few acquaintances, a reputation for pitiable eccentricity coupled with social ostracism and financial impoverishment—such were the only fruits of my campaign. And yet, being consistently honest with myself, I cannot even shoulder the reproach of having overestimated the intelligence of my fellow-men. The mortal foe, grown bold, has long put off his mask, can be recognized by the least sophisticated simpleton and encountered by the most unobservant pedestrian. When young girls wear skirts which scarce conceal their pubic hair and young men's tresses fall to their shoulders, what other explanation than that the brutalized creatures wish to expose their mothers' thicker legs and their fathers' less luxuriant heads to scorn and derision? When schools degenerate into brothels, and universities into training centres for promiscuity, what other explanation than that youth has set the tangled forest in motion, like Birnam Wood, because parents and elders are bound to lose themselves in that forest? When young writers use an idiom which conveys superficialities in incomprehensible form, what other explanation than that youth is trying to communicate in a secret language or juvenile gibberish so as to exclude the older generation? Unable to deny the shining improvement in their lot which we have granted them, the young drag it through the mire. What, they ask, is freedom from hunger in comparison with transcendental values; what is freedom from war when peace is the product of rational negotiation; what is order when it must be defended? Such are the transparent pretexts for parricide—yet transparent to whom? Not, at all events, to the self-abasing cattle known as the over-forties.

Disheartened, exhausted, and bereft of pecuniary resources by two years of wasted endeavour, I accordingly betook myself to my mother's small farmstead. It was late in June, my favourite month. June is the autumnal month of spring, more melancholy than September, which is the springtime of autumn. The countryside surrounding Montefiascone, my birthplace, had donned its wretched finery. My worthy mother had vacated her own room for the sake of her long-lost son, and, as I gazed down from my little window at the luxuriant vines below, I felt beguiled by the thought of turning my back on the world and devoting myself to rustic pursuits. I had come armed with a copy of Aratus' thousand-hexameter *Phaenomena*—in the original Greek, of course—because its *mélange* of poetry and astronomy had stirred me deeply from childhood onward: how wonderful to observe heavenly bodies which lavish their deceptive radiance upon us long after they themselves have been extinguished! In order to preserve my physical resiliency—I do not look my age, so I am assured—I made it my almost daily practice to borrow old Giovanni's rickety lady's bicycle and propel it at random through the welcoming countryside of my native region, pedalling as far as Viterbo or—a remote but long-favoured haunt of mine—the little town of Lubriano. It often happened that I did not leave my mother's house until dusk was falling: normally a sound sleeper, I had unaccountably been robbed of sleep in recent years, and so, the warm nights having induced in me a state of heightened sensibility, I yielded to the influence of Aratus and kept secret assignations with the moon and stars.

The closing days of July finally ushered in the events which it is my sad duty to relate—sad because they occurred under brutal compulsion, but joyous nonetheless: "*Thank God, I have done my duty*," as the noble Lord Nelson is reputed to have said while he lay dying. Thus it came about that, as I roamed the fields one moonlit night in late July, wheeling the bicycle beside me, my attention was drawn to a barn whose closed doors permitted a faint shaft of light to fall on to the dark ground. The barn undoubtedly belonged to a farm but stood some distance from the farmstead itself; it was nearly eleven o'clock, and the neighbouring farm buildings, obviously the domain of a prosperous farmer, were dark and silent, a fact which intensified my curiosity about the glimmer of light. The barn which I approached so noiselessly was a new building only two or three years old—hence, too, the electric light—but constructed with an eye to economy, because it consisted almost entirely of wood, and the planks were so carelessly put together that it was not difficult to peer into the interior through one of the numerous chinks.

Alas, how to describe the spectacle that assailed my chaste eyes without falling prey to obscenity—for it was the very obscenity of the thing which so cruelly offended my sense of decorum—indeed, inflicted such deep and lasting traumata that my nights at Foce Verde are still haunted by the horrific visions which pursue me to this day.

Peeping through a crack in the side-wall, I beheld—pardon me, dear reader!—the bestial tupping of a girl of barely eighteen or nineteen, as I then thought, by a yokel of equally immature years. Bestial tupping I said, and I selected both words with care. There was no vestige of even the most rustic or rudimentary love-play, nor, equally, of the untutored passion which might have been expected in two robust young peasants. The couple had dispensed with that prologue which alone can excuse the hideousness of the sexual act; which alone distinguishes man, supposedly a creature of superior stock, from rutting cattle: hardly had the youth entered the barn than he and his mate were locked in loathsome copulation. Did they lie in the straw, body against body; did they wrap their arms about one another in sweet communion; did they kiss with the youthful ardour of midsummer love; did hand grope for hand, skin brush skin, desire seek the mutuality of desire? Nothing of the sort. The girl must have been well prepared for her wretched assignation, for she wore no petticoat, knickers, or undergarment of any kind, her nakedness being concealed merely by a voluminous skirt. Turning her back on her lover, she threw the skirt over her head and presented the lustful hobbledehoy with the spectacle of two pink hemispheres, conducting this manœuvre—I could scarcely believe my eyes then, and can scarcely credit the recollection now—in an erect position; while the youth, prepared for such a performance, simply dropped his trousers, bent slightly at the knee, leant backward from the waist, and—like the horse, the dog, the goat, and other beasts—executed the thrusting motions of coitus.

In speaking of horses, dogs, and goats, I am conscious of the injustice I do to these and other members of the animal world. For is it not so—having grown up in the flatlands, I have observed it often enough—that the stallion clings to the mare in an affecting display of passion, forelegs clasping the body of its mate, and that the dog arches itself over the back of the bitch as if bent on folding its partner in an amorous embrace? It is appropriate to talk of physical union in such cases, whereas the only union in that barn near Lubriano was a coupling as of railway carriages: no form of embrace was discernible, and if the lowly but, as I could not help but remark, over-developed human stallion touched the voluptuous girl at all it was only that he fastened his rough hands on her hindquarters as if they were a ladder, balustrade, or railing.

I persevered at my observation post as if my feet had taken root, but I did so with painful reluctance—more properly, out of innate tolerance: I wished to satisfy myself that this act of concerted bestiality, which had begun without prologue, would at least end with an epilogue. But no—no preliminaries, no sequel; the youth simply hoisted his trousers as another would have wiped his mouth after enjoying a repast, the girl tugged her skirt into place as if straightening up after plucking flowers. The two then sat down together on a barrel of fertilizer and began to converse in the most unconstrained fashion—I could not catch what they were saying, but their laughter drifted to my ears, and I fancied that they were laughing because there must be at least something which differentiates a human couple from breeding-stock.

Who can wonder if my visits to Morpheus have become still more fitful since that momentous night? If my experience of the opposite sex is confined to a few happily abortive experiments in early youth, I mention it without any hint of shame, being solely filled with amusement by the absurd conclusions which psychiatrists, sexual pathologists, psychoanalysts, and other voyeurs would draw from the fact. My profound erudition enables me to review the whole spectrum of pertinent literature— from Geronimo Cardano's *Synesorium somniorum* in the sixteenth century to Magnus Hirschfeld's *Geschlechtsanomalien und Perversionen*, from Vespa's *I sogni dei neuro-psicopatici* in the nineteenth century, via Menninger's *Love against Hate*, to Sartre's *L'Être et le Néant*—without recognizing myself in them to any perceptible degree whatsoever. Not even the most dispassionate self-examination has disclosed the "homosexual component" to which Professor Freud attached such great importance, neither have I ever indulged in, nor even been compelled to suppress the stirrings of, any of the perversions discussed by the Marquis de Sade and the Austrian writer Sacher-Masoch. As to the observations of the more serious of these authors, whose concern is not to arouse a craving for perversions by descriptions of the same, none of them can apply to me for the simple reason that I have, unremittingly and from childhood onward, enjoyed a perfectly happy sex-life—with the single difference that I have never required a partner, neither male nor female.

When Sartre asserts that vice is "love of failure", all this proves is the superficiality of my Gallic *confrère*. No failure attaches to onanism, masturbation, self-abuse, or however else one chooses, depending on the extent of one's prejudices, to describe this classic form of love—even the Bible is guilty of misrepresentation, as Mark Twain indicates in *Some Observations on the Study of Onanism*, since Onan spilled his seed on the ground after the sexual act and can thus at best be regarded as the father of *coitus interruptus*—no failure, in short, attaches to discreet self-love, to an abhorrence of disrobing in public, to a reluctance to share one's most intimate secrets with others, to the proud renunciation of collective urges: rather, it is a last triumph over the humiliating loss of human independence. How greatly God must have despised the human beings created by Him, that He dared not confide the duty of procreation to them without rendering this natural function palatable by linking it with sensations of the basest sort. For his part, bribed and hoaxed with promises of pleasure, man was incapable of intellectually isolating the boon that had once been bestowed on him, and so he allowed himself to be seduced by the erroneous belief that the generation of such pleasure actually required the presence of a fellow-creature, of another man or woman—in short, of a partner. God, mistrusting His creature, abdicated. Instead of decreeing that the seed of man germinate in the soil and produce new men, just as the eggs of fish are fructified by the divine element water, He had Onan put to death, compelled man to void his sap into the empty pod of woman, and created an idol and second God, the vain phallus, which human beings thenceforward worshipped far more devoutly than their Lord and Creator. The whole hypocritical doctrine of love, the *ars amandi,* reposes on the truly grotesque notion that human beings ought to give each other pleasure and amusement by performing their procreative duty, whereas each can obtain an equal or greater measure of satisfaction in solitude. The more civilization progresses—that is, runs away from mankind—the greater the care lavished by those who could satisfy themselves on the satisfying of their partners. Books, newspapers, and periodicals—even those of the 'family' variety—publish the most paradoxical pieces of advice: for example, how to delay the moment of orgasm by harbouring dark thoughts during coition. No one knows for sure how best to please the other; almost everyone has forgotten that the simple manipulation of one's own body can, promptly and with absolute certainty, produce those sensations which even the most assiduous study of the art of love is incapable of guaranteeing. The Biblical death penalty has been abolished, the hellish punishments proclaimed by the Church frighten no one, and even the bogy-man of physical impairment has finally been exorcised, yet psychiatrists allege that the isolated sexual act leads to feelings of inferiority, to a loss of pride and self-respect.

It may be that I belong to the elect. Even if it is necessary to be a darling of the Muses before one possesses an imagination such as mine, there can be no doubt about the divine nature of the imaginative faculty. Who is the more richly endowed: he who accomplishes that which is not even denied to a billy-goat, or he whose four walls are furnished with all the beauties of this world, with countless orgiastic scenes drawn from the past, present, and future, with every known and unknown potentiality in the sexual domain? A *grand seigneur* in the truest sense, I can with a single gesture, be it even in the mean and mouldering bedroom of my wretched birthplace, conjure up the hetaerae of classical antiquity, the courtesans of the French monarchs, the much-wooed stars of the modern dream-factory, the willing or reluctant victims of the Marquis de Sade, the vernal excursions of the most charming rococo couples, or the costly pleasures of the contemporary playboy. I say this not only from a wish to correct fallacious notions but also in order to prove, even to the most obtuse of judges, that the murder of Vera Pisenti—if so it must be described by the linguistic pauper—was not committed in a transport of jealousy, sexual rivalry, or uncontrolled excitement. Truth to tell, I had long beguiled my sleepless nights by usurping the place of the over-zealous youth, savoured his pleasure to the full, possessed the girl's buxom body, and attained a state of blissful exhaustion.

I behaved like the revolutionary who keeps the iniquities of the prevailing system daily before his eyes in order to derive insurrectionary courage from what he sees. I had cherished the illusion that the virus of immorality lived out its worm's existence only in the fissures that thread the asphalt of the great cities. Home is where one's childhood memories are. In my youth, girls like Vera Pisenti did not live primarily under the aegis of their worthy parents: they were protected by rural isolation, by the Church, by their fear of earthly condemnation and divine damnation, by their own chastity. Ought I to have toured the villages like an itinerant preacher? I should have been laughed to scorn. Revolution begins where preaching ends.

I was drawn back again to the place of infamy. At nightfall I set off in the hope of catching the vile children in the act, or—who knows?—in the hope of satisfying myself that I had yielded to a hallucination. It had been no hallucination. Not only did I become the unseen witness of more such outrageous occurrences the very next night, but I was soon forced to acknowledge that the two young animals met every night at about the same hour and in the same spot, there to indulge their lust with unwearying regularity. Adding their probable ages together, I found that their years totalled less than mine, yet no variant, no deviation, of physical love was alien to them, nor could storm and tempest deter them from their sinful assignations. On two occasions, much to the astonishment of my good mother and the feeble-minded Giovanni, I was compelled to set off in the pouring rain; I returned to my quarters soaked to the skin, out of breath because I had flitted from tree to tree for fear of thunder and lightning, and plagued by a disagreeable head-cold.

Had not the anniversary of my birth been imminent, I should long since have carried out my well-weighed plan to dispatch the pair with a few revolver shots in the midst of their bestial antics. Knowing that Giovanni had hidden his old army pistol behind some bottles in the wine cellar, I was able, without attracting attention, to purloin it, free it of rust, clean it lovingly, and furnish it with fresh ammunition.

And here—for I too am human—I must admit to a weakness. The closer the 8th of August drew, the greater my cowardly misgivings became. I was still dogged by pusillanimous doubts on the very morning of my birthday. Ah, yes, I have to concede that had a birthday kiss from my mother awaited me as I descended the creaking stairs that morning, had Giovanni, her grubby paramour, so much as pressed my hand in greeting, had the monotony of soup been relieved by a cup of coffee and a morsel of cake, Vera Pisenti would still be alive today. But who thought to commemorate the 8th of August, upon which that unwelcome mortal Aurelio Morelli first saw—irony of ironies, I was about to say 'the light'!—the darkness of this world? My mother was as usual preoccupied with her evil-smelling cats, Giovanni was sucking up his breakfast soup with repulsive gusto: the day was without love, goodwill, or gift. I kept silence, and postponed my birthday celebration until the evening.

The air was sultry, the sky innocent of stars. Like a mistress awaiting her lover with limbs aglow, the fields lay in the grip of storm-fever. I avoided the township, which seemed more lively than usual because a celebration was in progress at an inn on the outskirts. I was apprehensive lest the girl—I did not then know her name, and only learned it later from the newspapers, which testifies on the one hand to the gloriously impersonal nature of my act, and on the other to the circumspection with which I set to work—in short, I was apprehensive lest the young couple, detained by the *festa*, would forgo their orgy. The light from my bicycle lamp fell on the narrow cart-track, from which I took good care not to stray, because only there would the impress of my shoes be lost among other footprints. I did not extinguish the lamp until I reached the immediate vicinity of the barn. To my dismay, I at once perceived that the building was in darkness. I could have turned back, but my infallible instinct bade me persevere at my post.

My patience was rewarded. Some minutes later the faint glimmer of a bicycle lamp hove into view: I sensed, for I could not see her, that the girl was approaching the scene of her oft-repeated crime from the direction of the township. Only when I had crept up to the barn was my supposition confirmed. The whore had entered the building and switched on the light, a single bulb dangling by a length of flex. She looked about her, surprised that her lover was not yet in attendance, and sat down on a rough-hewn bench—gingerly, for she was resplendent in a silk dress.

My patience, one of my not inconsiderable virtues, was tried to the utmost, and a certain disappointment overcame me, because I had a hundred times rehearsed how I would kill the copulating youngsters in mid-coition, leave them lying there in the most undignified state, and expose them to general contempt as an object lesson. When fifteen minutes had elapsed—a small eternity—and the girl, who had remained seated, was making obvious preparations to depart—she already had her hand on the light-switch—I decided, in superstitious dread of the approach of the midnight hour, and with it the expiry of my birthday, to enter the barn.

No flicker of alarm showed in the wanton creature's eyes at first. Scrutinizing her at close quarters for the first time, I could not help but reflect, wrily, that I was more conversant with her naked haunches than her physiognomy. From close to, Vera Pisenti looked somewhat older than I had thought. Twenty or twenty-one, with almost blue-black hair, pronounced cheek-bones, and a lascivious mouth, she was peculiarly alluring in appearance because her generous hips, plump, almost childish legs, and full breasts—coquettishly emphasized by the close-fitting, low-cut bodice—were in sharp contrast to the pallor and daintiness—indeed, refinement—of her face.

In response to the girl's request to state my name and business I replied that I, for my part, knew full well who she was and what she was doing: namely, waiting for the nightly visit of her lover with a view to—and here I employed an appropriately vulgar expression which the little whore would more readily comprehend—indulging in fornication. Not in order to titillate myself—keeping calm was my more immediate concern—but simply and solely as a means of displaying my omniscience, I inquired if her skirt, on whose colour and material I gallantly congratulated her in passing, concealed the usual absence of underclothes or knickers: mockingly, I suggested that her sweet-heart might have failed to put in an appearance on this occasion for fear of time-wasting formalities. Still undismayed, the girl began to hurl the most scatological abuse at me—indeed, called me a "dirty old man", promised that I would get a sound drubbing from her "fiancé", and finally asserted that the only reason why she had not called for help was that she could deal with a "snake" of my type with one hand tied behind her back. These threats constrained me to reach for my revolver, which, though determined not to waste a bullet on the creature, I trained upon her from a suitable distance.

The fearless heroine was instantly transformed into a quivering bundle of misery. She must have supposed that she was dealing with a madman, for she not only begged me to spare her wretched life, wringing her hands and eventually falling on her knees, but resorted to persuasion, to confused and incoherent promises of money, goods, and her own body, to apologies for her churlish remarks, and, when I so requested her, to admissions that she had led a whorish life.

I bade the girl go stand against one wall of the barn, whither I followed her, placing my feet carefully on the hay. I then ordered her to present her back to me, prompted partly by cool calculation and partly by humanitarian scruples: I intended to put away the pistol without her seeing, but I also wished to grant her the privilege of turning her back on her executioner. Recalling my dainty Lucia, I decided that the rustic sinner should partake of an equal measure of compassion. Although the girl's white neck gleamed alluringly above her provocative *décolletage*, I took my time and proceeded to deliver a well-rehearsed homily. With the eloquence of a Savonarola, with the sternness of a father retrieving and making amends for that which has been neglected by the fathers of this unfatherly world, I made it clear to the averted figure of my victim that, as the representative of a chastity-spurning, purity-besmirching younger generation which was bereft of morality and ignorant of decency, she would have to go the way of all foul flesh. She must atone for the expression "dirty old man", not because she had uttered it but because she had thought it, and because her thoughts were in no wise different to those of other little Jezebels who were fortunate enough to have escaped punishment thus far. Aware that it is always easier to die at the stake, I graciously allotted her the rôle of martyr by informing her that she deserved to be burned as a witch, and then, in substantiation of this, gave her a concise but cogent account of all that I had espied from my observation post. My memory proved to be flawless. Just as the competent public prosecutor leaves not a single item of incriminating evidence unmentioned, so I took care to touch upon every last detail: on Tuesday she had thrown her skirt over her head, on Thursday she had seen fit to bestride her lover in an outrageously un-feminine position, on Saturday she had managed, by dint of brazen manual fondling, to incite him to further excesses.

Although the sinful girl knew very well that I was standing behind her, weapon in hand, she lost her head and recommenced to hurl the most vulgar imprecations at me—indeed, began eventually to utter ill-considered cries for help. An executioner, not a murderer, I kept my wits about me and allowed the good Giovanni's noisy weapon to fall noiselessly into the hay. A wise decision! I should never have been able to forgive myself—in-deed, it would doubtless have engendered complexes or severe mental disorder—had I made use of so cowardly, impersonal, and unmanly a weapon as the revolver; moreover, the sight of blood has filled me with revulsion since my childhood. The girl's neck bore marks consistent with strangulation, so I read later, though the absence of medically ascertainable fingerprints was enough in itself to show that I did not act senselessly, intoxicated by lust. I did not strangle Vera Pisenti, gentlemen of the jury, for as I stood there behind the girl, looking down at my hands, a miraculous transformation took place, doubtless ordained by some higher authority: my slender but sinewy arms became transmuted before my very eyes into two strong cords. I had but to lay them gently about the girl's neck, had but to tighten the noose formed by my metamorphosed fingers, and—lo!—my spot-less hands showed as little trace of the deed as the rope that encircles the neck of a convicted felon. They were instruments of execution, nothing more—tools of justice, organs of death, prostheses of an avenging destiny.

Vera Pisenti slid to the ground, face downward. Unswayed by panic, I prepared her a soft bed in the hay which had served her as a mating-couch during her lifetime—how often, God alone knew. Even today, seated at my little desk in Foce Verde with my gaze averted from the ugly prospect of the basket-ball pitch, I cannot refrain from smiling at the lack of imagination displayed by the foolish detectives who suspected a sexual crime because the girl's skirt was lifted so as to cover her mottled face. I had indeed lifted the skirt with the revolver-barrel, but only to discover whether the vile creature had kept her tryst unclad on this occasion too—in fact, her pudenda were concealed by some loose knickers—and, above all, because it is a pious and traditional practice to cover the faces of the dead. The hay which might have retained my footprints I secreted beneath some untouched straw; the bunch of hay on which I trod when leaving the barn I took with me, so as to scatter it on my way home. My gaze fell once more upon the limbs which I had so often seen convulsed with ecstasy, but which would never again afford pleasure to any impudent young coxcomb; then, cleverly using the barrel of my revolver for a second time, I switched off the light. The township still rang with the whoops and yells of revellers, the storm had dispersed.

Next morning—I do not seek to disguise the fact—I was gripped by the first pangs of fear. I did what no criminal acting with forethought and deliberation would ever have done: even before tidings of Vera Pisenti's death reached Montefiascone, I restored Giovanni's pistol to its former place in the wine cellar and fled the unhappy scene of my birth, my mother's house. I do not know if the deaf woman and her cretinous inamorato connected my disappearance with the death of Vera Pisenti, but I am half tempted to believe so.

Emilio Bossi

Had to take the early 'plane to Vienna, seven-fifty. That meant finding Francesco. Canonica would have had an easier job finding Hertha Enzian's murderer.

I called home. "He's bound to be at a party," said Fiorella. "You're a great help," I said. There must be a couple of hundred parties in Rome every night. Fiorella gave me four addresses.

I couldn't postpone the trip to Vienna. Equally, I couldn't leave Francesco behind. Where the Enzian case is concerned, we're a team. I have to be back in Rome soon, anyway, to dig out material on the Chiesa and Pisenti cases. I haven't yet told Vanetti that our trout has turned out to be a shark. I'm already thinking in terms of fish, like Morelli. I haven't yet shown Vanetti the first part of the manuscript either, though he's already paid for the second. I told Morelli it was an advance in respect of Chiesa and Pisenti. You have to manœuvre. Vanetti would fly into a panic. He's happy to do business with a one-time murderer; a triple murderer has to be turned in. Morelli is my big chance to break into films. If he's arrested too soon the Berlin boys will use a hack writer instead—one of the old faithfuls. I certainly can't wait too long; Morelli's agitating for a wage-hike. Lucky I based my fee on the number of instalments. I'm reckoning on twelve for Enzian, six for Chiesa, and four for Pisenti, making twenty-two, which is seven extra. It's a big gamble, of course, but if I can present the police with a triple murderer I'm made. In the States they'd give me the Pulitzer Prize. We could do a follow-up series called *Where the Police Went Wrong—Famous Unsolved Cases*. Old hat, admittedly, but stick it on Morelli and it'll look new.

Drove to the Via Catalana first. The flat belonged to Angelo Caratti, a young film director of my acquaintance. He gave me a warm welcome. "So glad you could make it," he said. Anyone would have thought he'd invited me. "I'm looking for Francesco Vanetti," I said. "So am I," he said. That didn't get me far.

The party was so restrained I didn't have much hope of finding Francesco anyway. About forty people, including a couple of very beautiful women. Conversation was limited to a single topic: *Quaranta personaggi in cerca d'un film*. An ageing comeback candidate like a jeweller's shop on stilts twisted one of my blazer-buttons and said, "You must promise to photograph me properly—always from below." If they don't know you they automatically take you for a cameraman. A perfumed cinematic trade union congress—not Francesco's style at all. I promised a star rôle to a sweet-looking girl with very hairy armpits, got her telephone number, and beat it. Long hair under a girl's arms gives you a line on her lover's tastes, but you can always shave it off. "You'll never marry," says my mother, who has a vested interest in keeping me single. You have to sleep with a girl at least twice before you marry her, and I don't have time for such a long engagement. It dawned on me that Fiorella had given me a dud address.

I drove to the other side of town, Via dei Villini. Reporter's luck? One of Vanetti's pet phrases. You have to have a double ration of luck to find another reporter. I've got that too, no doubt about that.

The door was open, of course. The open door policy.

I knew I'd struck oil, even though I didn't find Francesco straight away.

The host was pretty old, around sixty. A Principe della Metta. Sat enthroned in a high-backed velvet arm-chair, desiccated as a piece of Dead Sea Scroll. Reminded of my grandfather, who was a conductor on a rack-railway in his younger days, a one-track mountaineer. Sometimes he'd put his uniform on for us—unbuttoned, of course, because it wouldn't meet over his paunch. The grandchildren used to sit at his feet and listen to him telling stories about fairies and rail disasters. The Prince sat there the same way, except that some of his grandchildren had beards and the others were half-naked. The girls, naturally. He wasn't telling any stories, he was drunk. He supplies his beloved grandchildren with liquor, hash, LSD, and anything else that's in fashion—it's hard to keep up. They supply him with youth, he gets drunk on that.

I knew no one and no one knew me, but that didn't matter. The others didn't seem to know each other either. Or they acted like it. Individualists never know each other—it's smarter not to. The flat was pretty big, but consisted entirely of little rooms, like a huge dovecot. I headed straight for one of the bedrooms. A girl in a trenchcoat was whipping a naked youth. That's to say, she didn't have a whip so she was using his braces. I said sorry, but the girl was very friendly, she laughed and asked if I wanted a whipping too. I said thanks and asked if anyone had seen Francesco Vanetti. The bare-bottomed youth said he wasn't an information bureau. The only really funny thing was the décor. Palazzo-type furniture in a modern flat makes me think of oversize toys in a doll's house. Shift the bed a little to one side when making it and the whole caboodle would have fallen out of the window. Over the bed hung an equestrian portrait of a della Metta with a falcon perched on his shoulder. If the braces-artiste kept up the good work the prince was liable to gallop out of his frame.

I went into the kitchen, which was packed with young people like a bus in rush-hour. The refrigerator door hung open, but there was nothing inside except a bottle of beer and a mink stole. I drank the beer and went back to the drawing-room.

The master of the house had fallen asleep. One of the hairdresser's nightmares fetched a basin from the bathroom, a plastic one full of water. Two or three nymphets carefully raised the sleeper's legs and deposited his feet in the water, complete with shoes. He continued to snore with his head lolling on one side. The hairdresser's nightmare snapped him with a Polaroid. I laughed, and was noticed for the first time, because nobody else did.

Never one to give up, I asked a nymphet if she'd seen Francesco Vanetti. "He's upstairs," she said. I should have thought of that before. There were a lot of people sitting on the stairs. The Prince had another flat on the third floor, presumably for guests.

I found Francesco straight away, but he acted as if he didn't recognize me. He was lying in the empty bath. I don't know if his lack of recognition was genuine. At an LSD party, a tee-totaller who prefers Scotch to LSD can't judge these things. I was sick as a dog after I smoked my first cigarette. Didn't smoke any more cigarettes for four years, but I used to light them and hold them crooked so my fingers turned a nice shade of brown. I estimate there are nine phoneys to every LSD fan.

I wondered whether to turn the shower on Francesco, but decided to give him half an hour to sober up. I had his bag and cameras in the car. I'd have had to rub him down after a shower, and I don't play nursemaid to drug-babies.

I wandered around. There were as many rooms upstairs as down. The Prince's ancestors must have been hard workers. A man was sitting on the drawing-room floor. Fortyish, horn-rimmed glasses. The sort that manages to look intellectual even on the pan. He had a writing-pad in his hand and was making notes.

"What's that you're writing?" I asked.

"Notes," he said, "can't you see?"

"What have you noted so far?" I asked.

"Udo suffers from a vagina complex," he replied.

"Who doesn't?" I said.

The Professor took a poor view of this. I took care not to laugh, remembering my disagreeable experience downstairs. When I was little I used to play the don't-laugh game with my cousins. We took it in turns to pull faces, and the one who kept a straight face longest won. Now I know why beards are all the rage. So you can't see when people are smiling. It gives them an unfair advantage in the don't-laugh game.

The aforesaid Udo was lounging in a leather arm-chair, drivelling about female sexual organs. Meanwhile a honey of a girl, a German with long legs, was sitting on the arm of his chair. She was bored and looked it. I never drivel when I've got a blonde like that within arm's reach. Maybe I'm abnormal. I wouldn't be surprised, with my pedigree—engine-drivers and rack-railway conductors.

Perhaps things are livelier in the bedroom, I thought, but there were only two couples lying on the damask counterpane. The two girls and one of the boys were sound asleep, like babies. The other boy, a fair-haired lad of about seventeen, was lying on his back making all kinds of undulating movements with his hands—dancing, sort of. Maybe he had a ballet complex. More original than the other thing.

On the way back to the bathroom, shower-bound, I was accosted by a delightful little creature. Just my type. I always make a bee-line for the anaemic ones. They're usually starved of body-warmth.

"You're not switched on," said the bloodless belle, running her fingers through my hair.

"Nor are you," I said.

"I don't fancy it tonight," she said, apologetically. "Do you feel like a trip?"

"I'd sooner have a sandwich," I said. I didn't mean it nastily. I was hungry.

"Don't you ever take a trip?" she asked.

"I'm on one now, worse luck," I said. "To Vienna."

"Who are you?" asked my undernourished interrogator.

"I'm from the narcotics squad," I said.

"Let's sit down," she said.

She put her hand on my knee. Presumably she was cold.

I was mad because Francesco was lying in the bath, and our 'plane was due to take off at 7.50 A.M., and it was getting late. Being a good Samaritan, I'd have been happy to cure the girl of LSD. Even if I couldn't do anything for her I wanted to do my journalistic duty. News is all and all is news, Vanetti says.

"Tell me," I said. "Do you swallow this stuff because it gives you a kick, or because you're bored, or because it's banned?"

"It isn't banned," she said. "You're a virgin."

"Sure," I said. "I'm still on snow."

"Cocaine is poison," she said earnestly, fixing me with her great big deep-frozen eyes. "Cocaine isn't the answer."

"Never was," I said.

"You see," she said. "Don't you ever ask yourself who you are?"

"Every day," I said. "Only after office hours, though."

"We're born with all the answers," she said. "Then we lose them like milk-teeth. Do you know what you want?"

"Yes," I replied, "I want to boost my salary, get Francesco out of the bath-tub, and go to bed with you."

She let go of my knee and started fiddling absent-mindedly with my shirt-buttons.

"You're a Superman," she said.

"Thanks," I said, taking it as a compliment.

She said Superman was a symbol of repression. "LSD liberates you from authority."

"I go my own way," I said stubbornly.

"You aren't creative," she said. "You help to foster the monolithic society. I'm searching for the meaning of life."

"You've got LSD," I consoled her. "Haven't you found it yet?"

The girl shook her head. She seemed in need of consolation. It struck me that I could have ejected the sleeping quartet from the bedroom. However, being pressed for time and a good Samaritan, I said: "You won't find the meaning of life in the catalogue. Take a look in the shop window and ferret around among the goods."

"You have to find your personality," she said, categorically.

"I thought LSD lost it for you," I said, heretically.

"It's the same thing," she said, didactically.

"I'll try to understand," I promised, because she was clawing at me pretty expressively by this time.

"You're poor," she said.

"Pretty poor," I said. "My father was an engine-driver. He had an accident. He crashed a red light."

"He was an individual," she said. "Individuals are colourblind."

"The crash killed eighteen," I said. There were only three dead, actually. It was a goods train.

"You float on the surface," she said. "Like fat."

Swallowing the insult, I said: "If I had a bit more time I'd plumb your depths."

"Give up earning money and you'd have more time," she said.

"I'd starve," I said, thinking of the sandwich.

"You could always steal," she suggested.

A sound idea. It occurred to me that it would be quite reasonable to steal from Vanetti, but what would I do if Vanetti discovered his individuality too and there wasn't anything left to steal? Two neat little advertising jingles popped into my head—

> Unless you're keen to dodge your E—
> Go take a dose of LSD

or,

> There's nothing like a whiff of pot
> To plumb the depths of what you've got

but they wouldn't pack any punch until the LSD-consumer embraced the consumer society. Give it time, I thought. I buttoned my shirt because there was no point, not in view of Francesco and the early 'plane.

"I've got to get Francesco out of that bath," I said, to explain my lack of chivalry.

"Francesco has a father," she said.

"It can't be helped," I said, though I could see what she meant.

"Francesco will never grasp the meaninglessness of everything," she said with genuine compassion.

"He does his best," I protested in Francesco's defence.

"He doesn't love," she said distractedly.

"His father?" I queried.

"He isn't allowed to love his father," she said.

I suggested that nobody can choose his father but she didn't reply—she probably thought I was incorrigible. So I went into the bathroom. Francesco was still asleep. He looked like a baby who'd grown a beard overnight.

"Come on," I said. "Wake up, we're off to Vienna."

"Where am I?" he asked.

"In the bath," I said.

That seemed to reassure him. He crawled out of the tub.

It was too late to take him home and too early for take-off. We drove to the airport. Not wanting any trouble with the Customs,

I suggested to Francesco that he might have a wash. He came back from the wash-room looking less like contraband. He didn't say a word, just propped his feet on my briefcase and slept till seven. I read the papers, feeling like a baby-sitter.

When he came to he asked me where I'd found him. "Della Metta's place," I said.

"Ah," he said.

"Why do you take the stuff?" I asked. "They say it makes you impotent."

"I don't want to procreate," he said.

I said, "What's potency got to do with procreation?"

He dropped his eyes and said, "I feel ashamed of myself."

"No need to feel ashamed on my account," I said. Confessions always disarm me. "Just confine your personality-quest to the weekends, that's all."

"I'm ashamed for Sofia's sake," he said. "LSD is a bourgeois invention. It aids the Establishment and undermines militancy."

"Naturally," I said. "No potency, no militancy."

"I'll never go there again," he said.

"Very sensible of you," I said.

"But I don't want to earn money either," he said.

"You've got enough money," I said.

"If I'd stayed in the bath," he said thoughtfully, "I wouldn't have to photograph this Enzian character."

"But you couldn't protest either," I said. "Not alone in the bath."

"You don't understand," he said. "If you come into contact with this society you get dirty. We must yank it up by the roots."

"What then?" I said.

"Types like you always ask that," he said. "You squash a bug because it's a bug. Not as part of a long-term plan."

I don't know why I bother with Francesco, but I said, "You remind me of the Americans. They forced us to put chlorine in our water when they liberated us and then became so sterile that even spaghetti played havoc with their digestion. In the old days people died of dirt, now they die of asepsis. You lot are so pure it's killing you."

He wasn't listening. It obviously upset him that I'd interrupted his trip in the bath-tub.

"LSD is good at first," he said. "It corrupts society."

"I thought society was already corrupt," I said.

"But the masses don't realize that," he said. "If society shows itself incapable of dealing with drug addiction among the young, it'll bring the truth home to everyone. The same goes for the police. We have to show that they're powerless."

"They're not as powerless as all that," I said.

"Exactly," he said. "We have to coerce them into brutality."

"Hard to do that from the bath," I said. I'd had a bellyful of Francesco.

"That's why LSD is only good at first," he said. "My place is at the barricades."

"You can man the barricades when we're back from Vienna," I said.

"You wouldn't understand," he said. "You're too old."

A fair enough rebuke, I thought. After all, I am thirty-one. "What are you griping about, actually?" I asked.

"About your question," he said. "Next thing you'll be telling me that the masses have never had it so good. First you oppressed them and now you're corrupting them."

I don't know who he meant by "you", but I said: "That's what I call progress."

I might have converted him—who knows? Luckily, our flight was called.

Francesco dozed off almost before we were inside the 'plane. I flirted with the stewardess, although she had splash-guards instead of buttocks. I can't stand air-hostesses. They all have an I-don't-accept-tips or an I-only-sleep-with-the-captain look. Why do they wiggle their splash-guards if they're so damned virginal? *Noli me impregnare.* Also, they spend their whole time educating you. Voluptuous schoolmistresses. No smoking; fasten your seat-belts, please. You have to follow them in crocodile like geese trailing a goose-girl. I hated marching in crocodile, even at school. Francesco slept all the way to Vienna.

In the hotel I made sure Francesco took a bath—a wet one, this time. He looked quite human after a shave and a change of clothes. I filled in the time with orange-juice, coffee, and a five-egg scramble. All on expenses. Everyone fights the Establishment in his own way.

The Vienna correspondent of *Quest' Ora* called for us. A Viennese, but speaks fluent Italian. His name is Matzleinsdorfer, and he looks like it. Too many Wienerschnitzels. Like all correspondents, he can't stand special correspondents poaching on his preserves. I couldn't have cared less; I needed an interpreter. He took us to see Enzian in his Volkswagen.

Enzian looked like a dead man on a Sunday outing. He introduced his son, who looked far less improbable. His wife went better with the liver-sausage and salami too. Business was booming. He led Matzleinsdorfer and me into his glass caboose and sat us down with our backs to the shop. It was far too cramped, like an airless refrigerator. There wouldn't have been room for Francesco, but he had work to do outside anyway.

Papa Enzian annoyed me from the start. We'd paid the man to sing but he only cheeped. Diplomatically, like a sausage-slicing U Thant.

"When did you last see your daughter?" I asked.

"Hertha?" he said.

"Who else?" I said.

"She paid us a visit four months after she moved to Rome," he said.

"Didn't anything strike you?" I asked.

"Like what?" asked Papa Enzian.

"Like she had a lot of money," I said.

"She said she was with a touring company," he replied.

"Touring companies move around," I said. "Also, dancers earn peanuts."

"I don't know anything about touring companies," he said. "The shop is all I've ever bothered about."

"She left school at fourteen," I said. "For good."

"She always was artistic," he said.

"Did she help in the shop?" I asked.

"Oh, no," he protested. "She was a delicate little thing."

"I'm told she made her début in Graz at seventeen," I said. "As a stripper."

"We thought she was studying languages," he said.

"In Graz?" I said.

He didn't answer.

The sausage-slicing U Thant was making a big mistake if he thought I hadn't done my homework. I said, "The police called

181

you over the coals because your daughter made false statements. About her age."

Papa Enzian smote his breast. "I fetched her back from Graz in person," he said.

Yes, from the Berlitz School, I thought, but I didn't say so. It's pointless rubbing people up the wrong way if you've got to work with them for days on end.

He became slightly more communicative. Told us something about an industrialist's son who was to blame for everything. Hertha had met him at a ball during Carnival. "He was a gentleman, mind you," he said, "I'll grant him that." The only trouble was, he'd given her a false outlook on life. "Sports cars and so on," he said. He pressed a button marked Folksy Aphorisms. "You see," he said, "life is like a ladder: climb too high and you get dizzy." I suppose Matzleinsdorfer translated correctly. It probably sounded just as corny in German.

"How would you describe your daughter's character?" I asked.

"She was an angel," he said.

"Even though she ran away from home four times while she was still under age," I said.

Enzian looked more and more wizened. I had the feeling he'd sooner have handed back the money.

He applied his mouth to my ear and said, "Young people have an itch for independence—the wife never understood that. She always came back of her own accord. To me, mark you. She was a dreamer, that's all. Spent her whole time reading magazines—you know how it is!"

Touché. Peering through the glass door, I saw that Francesco was photographing the shop, Frau Enzian, and Enzian junior. Enzian junior looked a bit reluctant, but Frau Enzian poised her knife above a king-size sausage at least six times for Francesco's benefit.

"Is it true you'll be writing the film script?" asked Enzian.

I nodded. He asked if he could discuss his "problem" with me.

"What problem?" I asked.

"Well, I'm supposed to be appearing in the film," he said. "That wasn't in the contract."

I pricked up my ears. "She did have a father," I said. "We can't turn her into a waif-and-stray."

"But it doesn't have any bearing on the murder," he said. "Surely you could leave out my name."

"We paid for your name," I reminded him.

"It's a respectable name . . ." he said. "Another thing: Herr Vorneweg wants me and the wife to come to Rome for the world première." The expression tripped off his tongue. "That wasn't allowed for in the contract either."

"I'm sure Kronos will refund your expenses," I ventured.

Papa Enzian appealed to me less and less. He was looking for an out—I could smell it a mile off with the nose Vanetti relies on so much.

The Rome trip was out of the question, he told me. "There's my poor wife for a start. She'd have to go through the whole thing over again, even if it was only an actress being murdered. The wife's different to me. When she looks at the screen she forgets it's only a film."

Mama Enzian came in carrying a bill. She smiled at me like a salami-Circe. I asked if we could come back next day, Sunday, hoping that she would be more talkative than her husband.

I was determined to find out a bit more about Papa Enzian.

"I inherited the shop from my father," he said. "My father was the best-known butcher in the whole of Hernals. You may not credit it, but he could carry half an ox on his shoulder. I used to be quite a muscle-man myself when I was young, but then I got lung trouble."

"In the War?" I asked.

"Not until afterwards," he said. His lips gaped like the shell of a putrid mussel.

"Were you in the Army?" I asked.

I have a pronounced aversion to soldiers, past, present, and future. Sometimes it works the other way round: if I take a dislike to someone he usually turns out to be an ex-hero. Films show you villainous Fascists and Nazis, but honest-to-God soldiers abound on both sides. Unfortunately, it was honest-to-God soldiers who put Resistance fighters up against the wall in Rome, Venice, and Intra.

"I didn't see any action," said Enzian. "I was exempted. On account of the meat supplies. I'll warrant it was the same with you in Italy."

Of course it was. I know what exempted means. "So you belonged to the Nazi Party," I said, admiringly.

"Only for a spell," he said, looking too thin to shoulder a rabbit, let alone half an ox. "Hertha was born in the War," he added hurriedly. "At the height of the rationing. The cold was the worst thing. Me and the wife used to go out into the woods every Sunday, looking for firewood."

He must have thought I was green. Before I started talking about him he wouldn't say a word about Hertha, and now he was spouting information like a sports commentator. How Hertha had bought herself a car on hire-purchase, and how the car was to blame for everything, because "one things leads to another". And so on. It was an open-and-shut case. Papa Enzian could be Martin Bormann in disguise for all I cared, but I wanted to know.

Meanwhile the sun had slunk out. It turned the hunks of Leberkäse into gold bars. We went out into the street and I arranged the Enzians under the fascia—two blue gentians above and three white ones below. All we needed was the sister who's married to a police superintendent. Every time Francesco clicked the shutter Papa Enzian ducked behind his wife and son. I put him in front of the other two like a goalkeeper in a team photograph.

Francesco behaved surprisingly well. He borrowed a doll's pram from a little girl who was goggling at us and wheeled it into the foreground, in front of the family group. It was the sheer quest for originality that made him do it, probably. *Quest' Ora's* answer to Fellini. After all, I won't actually have to caption it as the doll's pram that belonged to Hertha Enzian—the readers will supply the text themselves. Never underestimate your readers, Vanetti says.

Quite a crowd gathered. Fifteen or twenty people, men, women, and children. In Rome they run away from photographers, here everyone wants to be in the picture. The Viennese must be a pretty backward lot. Mama Enzian sunned herself, partly in the November sunshine and partly in the publicity. However, when we went back into the shop Papa Enzian said, "I hope the pictures don't come out in Austria. It isn't allowed for in the contract, you see."

He was wrong, but I didn't want to argue. With a sudden

flash of inspiration, Papa Enzian presented each of us with a home-made sausage as thick as a bazooka. An original form of bribe.

Carlo Vanetti

Francesco brought some excellent pictures back from Vienna. The boy is doing nicely. We can't all be geniuses, but he is my own flesh and blood.

My family is conspiring against me—trying to hoodwink me. As if I didn't know that Francesco takes part in demonstrations! Of course I know—the police keep me informed. I could spoil the boy's pleasure by voicing my approval, but I don't propose to cure him in such an unsubtle way.

These demonstrations are a blessing. Politics were quite un-saleable here after World War Two, hence "Positivismo's" stagnant circulation. It was a straightforward vehicle for adver-tising—and limited in scope at that, since it only appealed to one category of advertisers. Market research divides advertisers into two categories. Detergent manufacturers advertise because they want to sell detergents. Firms which sell computers can dispense with that type of advertising because housewives who buy a million-dollar computer on the strength of an advert are comparatively rare. Firms of the second category like to see their names in publications which are so grand that nobody reads them. If the mass interest in politics increases—which it always does when people get their heads bashed in—we shall be able to serve up politics successfully alongside war, disease, prostitution, and murder. Brassière-manufacturers will advertise in "Positiv-ismo" and shipping firms in "Quest' Ora". Russian and American plays monopolized the political stage after World War Two, playing alternately or concurrently. Milady Europe sat in her box and watched. I suspect that Russian and American plays will continue to hog the limelight for another hundred years, because any spectacular would be a flop without the atom bomb. However, there's a difference between applauding politely from the comfort of a box and kicking up a rumpus in the gods. A theatrical uproar can be far more interesting than a play by Miller, Rattigan, or Tennessee Williams, let alone Ionesco and

Beckett. It's a very neat arrangement: the Russians and Americans perform; we brawl. We don't figure in the programme, true, but we certainly liven up the gallery. That's why I'm all for demonstrations. The intellectuals made no contribution to popular entertainment for decades. Now they've stopped writing dull novels and deliver inflammatory speeches instead. They're becoming really newsworthy these days. I fought a lone battle against boredom, but now the intellectuals are fighting it too. They refer to boredom as unrest, but it all comes down to the same thing—with more class, of course. I've gained new allies. Anyone who has dedicated his life to the public, as I have, knows that the reservoir from which the Press fishes its personalities is not inexhaustible. In the 'forties we fished out film stars and millionairesses. Film stars are only suitable for family magazines now, and I couldn't sell an American heiress even to my Mickey Mouse readers. Next came the semi-aristocratic playboys and good-time girls. Today they're as old-fashioned as a wind-up gramophone or a silent movie. There's a definite slump even in the bare bosom market—not that bare bosoms won't make a comeback. Sex is like Russian 5% Bonds—it's always quoted, which is why I'm staking such a lot on Morelli. But it must be the right mixture, as I keep telling my young staff-men. If we can only dilute sex and crime with a dash of politics we'll have the perfect cocktail. We've had enough bosoms for the present; what we need is faces, and as young as possible. Old politicians aren't photogenic. That's why—although Francesco would never believe me—I'm on the side of youth. Gin is gin, but a dry Martini needs a dash of vermouth. Youth is like vermouth: too much of it spoils the Martini, too little allows the gin taste to come through too strongly. "Lui e Lei" haven't grasped that, by the grace of God. My family don't think far enough ahead. They imagine that it would be terribly embarrassing for me if Francesco were arrested at one of his protest jamborees. Nothing could be further from the truth. Gone are the days when a father liked to brag about his well-brought-up children. I've done my own market research on the subject. If Francesco got into trouble, twenty-five per cent of my readers would view me with sympathetic commiseration because they'd tell themselves how much "better" their own children are; another twenty-five per cent would feel for me because their sons are lucky to be at liberty at all; and the remaining fifty per cent—including the whole of the younger generation—would hail me as a tolerant father and sincere democrat because I'd failed to bring up my son properly. All forms of hypocrisy are alien to me: I'm making an honest endeavour not to give Francesco a proper upbringing. I am, as might be expected, a modern man and a modern father.

A feeling of discomfort crept over me during the editorial conference, which I always rule with a rod of iron. I submitted Francesco's pictures for inspection, and discussed the make-up of the Enzian Story. It was a monologue, as usual, because men of my calibre are doomed to coexist with mediocrity. I'm all for democracy, but a newspaper isn't a nation; it's an orchestra which can only perform under the baton of a single conductor. All my editorial staff secretly regard me as an old fool who's investing millions of lire in a worthless antique. I should point out, in fairness to them, that they aren't fully in the picture. To me the Enzian Story is only a working title for the Morelli Story. Belotti, who backed me from the start, wants to steer Quest' Ora straight for the deep waters of politics, which would play havoc with our women readers. The man who pleads on behalf of public opinion is a barrister without a brief. Ida de Gottardi, my senior fashion editor, interprets every fashion literally, from bikinis to intellectualism. A veritable Mother Courrèges is our Ida. Fashion is something which only provincials take literally. I do my intellectualizing in Positivismo. One of my pet sayings is: Be smart, stay dumb. Whenever I trot it out—in fun, of course—Ida is all for picking up her hat—very chic too, by the way—and quitting. Rusconi, a talented youngster, thinks we can beat Lui e Lei and Familiarità with pornography, but pornography is a dessert, not a main course. Personally, I am concentrating entirely on Morelli. One-sidedness is the strength of genius, versatility the weakness of talent. Morelli combines pathology, pornography, and pedantry. If we only have a little bit of luck and are able to serve up some politics—the fourth 'P'—in our Christmas number, the opposition will have no choice but to surrender unconditionally.

What disturbed me most about the conference was Bossi's passivity. He never could look anyone in the eye, true, but he is the sort of person who occasionally comes up with a bright idea.

This time he sat there like a bad conscience personified. Being aware that he doesn't have a conscience, I couldn't reconcile this with his knowledge of the facts. After the meeting he buttonholed me and requested an urgent interview in private. I assumed that it must be about an advance, and felt relieved. Bossi's salary is mortgaged until the year 2000. Although it was nearing ten o'clock, and I had intended to visit Claretta earlier than usual, I led him into my office straight away.

He looked studiously hangdog. Then he came out with it. "I still haven't managed to squeeze any manuscript out of Morelli," he said.

This was disastrous news.

Christmas is just round the corner and Bossi must adapt the MS. at all costs, because neither murderers nor intellectuals— still less intellectual murderers—know what the public needs. I shall have to edit the manuscript personally. We have a maximum of three weeks in which to prepare the Christmas number, even though we can print the multi-coloured cover in advance. One of Bellini's Madonnas. Morelli won't appear on the cover because of the Madonna. We'll use placards to publicize him.

Bossi was so agitated that I became still more agitated. His excuses sounded as if he had learnt them by rote. While he was effervescing and avoiding my eye, a terrible suspicion took shape in my mind. How do I know for certain that Aurelio Morelli is really the murderer? He may be a con-man who never murdered anyone in his life. Alternatively, he may simply be one of those writers who crave publicity at any price. Who knows what would have become of Jean Genet, Francesco's favourite author, if he hadn't identified himself as a homosexual deadbeat? Or is Morelli planning to blackmail us? I let Bossi talk me into paying the second instalment, so Morelli is now in possession of 1,333,333 lire 33 centesimi, possibly without having done a single stroke of honest work. Can it be that I have once more fallen prey to my own generosity? This criminal is in a position to keep the money and give himself up to the police. We couldn't lay a complaint against him under any circumstances. Or, worse still—ghastly though it is to contemplate—who's to say that Morelli and Bossi aren't in it together? Bossi may have hung on to part of the money—he's always in financial straits. For the first time in my life, I've bought a pig in a poke. I wouldn't even buy Moravia sight unseen.

I found it hard to restrain my indignation. I don't raise my voice readily, but I'm afraid they must have heard me in the machine-room.

"The MS. is an absolute winner," Bossi said eventually, trying to pacify me.

"How would you know?" I demanded imperiously.

"Morelli read it aloud to me," he replied. "All night long. It was the best night I've ever spent."

"What was so enjoyable about it?" I asked caustically.

"Signor Vanetti," Bossi said firmly, "it's a world sensation. Three times as big as we expected."

"Splendid!" I exclaimed. "Signor Morelli is writing a master-piece. At my expense and for his own delectation. Now hear this, Bossi," I said, in the icy tones of a judge advocate-general, "I'll give you precisely one week. If I don't have the bulk of that manuscript on my desk by today week, you'll have to take the consequences. I'll report the murderer to the police—you can depend on that. If he is the murderer at all."

"If he is!" exclaimed Bossi. "You won't find another one like him in the whole of the criminal records office."

"A murderer is a murderer," I retorted angrily, because Bossi's allusions to the magnificence of Morelli's clandestine homework irritated rather than soothed me. "Don't run away with the idea that I couldn't get back at you," I threatened. "I'll sue you for repayment of advances. I'll kill your film job stone dead."

This only increased my agitation, because I suddenly became aware of the full implications of a fraud on the part of Morelli, Bossi, or both. My contract with Kronos, the guarantees entered into, the indemnity claims. Heaven help me if Morelli turns out to be a common or garden author! After all, my good name is at stake.

I remained unpacified, even by Bossi's relatively logical assur-ance that he was quite as interested in the film prospects as I was myself. Having repeated my ultimatum, I left the building in a state of mental turmoil.

My disquiet increased still further on the way to Claretta. On the one hand, she is the only person I can bare my heart to, especially since Beatrice hurt me so dreadfully by getting engaged to her snowman. On the other, my visits to her are associated with certain obligations. *I sometimes think that older men should refrain from taking a mistress at all. In the case of a loving spouse who has already received the gift of his name, a man can buy himself out of his marital responsibilities. But how is he to bribe a loving mistress when forced to admit that he does not happen to be in the mood for physical love? If he gives her presents he humiliates her, quite apart from the humiliating expense of them; if he gives her none he loses her; if he gives her neither jewels nor love he might just as well remain faithful to his wife.*

A momentary wave of nausea overcame me in the downstairs hall. The side-door of the florist's shop gives on to the hall, and whenever I open the front door at night my nose is assailed by a sort of funeral smell. *Strange how flower-shops smell like blossoming meadows until closing-time, but take on the aroma of a cemetery immediately thereafter.* I have grown accustomed to the scent of decay—in fact I have even learned to like it because of its association with pleasures to come. This time I fled from it up two flights of stairs and arrived out of breath. *Age beckons when you begin to notice the absence of a lift.*

As misfortune would have it, Claretta greeted me wearing only a négligé through which peeped some extremely seductive lace underwear. She usually awaits me fully clothed, because the strip-tease, as we jokingly call it, is one of our most agreeable joint diversions. Misfortunes seldom come singly: I was unwise enough to decline chilled champagne in favour of cognac because I thought something was wrong with my digestion. Far from stimulating me, the cognac only intensified the pressure in my abdominal region.

Instead of following my usual practice, which is to preface any exchange of ideas by an exchange of intimacies, I at once began to tell Claretta about Bossi and my various tribulations. *Casanova advises ageing men to organize their trysts in such a way that any failure on their part may be ascribed to some distraction or other, whether adventitious or deliberately engineered.* However, if I hoped that my business worries would create a situation which barred the way to bed, I was grievously mistaken. Claretta, who generally sets great store by not being loved 'just for that', was in an amorous mood—hence the lace underwear. Instead of going into conclave with me, she offered to dispel my worries in another way.

En route for the bedroom, which lies at the end of a long, narrow passage, I was smitten with a slight attack of shivering. "Is the heating on?" I inquired.

"More than enough for me," Claretta replied coquettishly, and slipped off her négligé to prove it.

It is my habit on such occasions to remove the rest of her clothing myself. One of the principal reasons why I remain faithful to Claretta is that I become aroused by the very sight of her imposing figure—promptly, and without the need for any time-consuming trivialities. No such excitement made itself felt this time—indeed, something positively uncanny occurred. All at once I was overwhelmed by the funeral smell which I had noticed in the downstairs hall. However, since it was impossible for the smell of the flower-shop to have penetrated Claretta's spotless apartment, I had the sudden and terrifying impression that I was attending my own funeral. I seemed to see Claretta, who was pouting at me because I had left her to remove her suspender-belt unaided, through a heavy pall of mist. Being a man of iron will-power, and one who does not readily yield to his weaknesses, I bent down to undo my shoelaces. At that precise moment I felt a violent stab of pain in my left side, between the ribs, and the word 'coronary' leapt into my mind with inescapable menace.

The bane of education is that the educated man finds a historical parallel for every personal experience. It goes without saying that I instantly recalled the fate of Félix Faure, the French President who departed this life under equally compromising circumstances. However, since no situation could ever make me forget my duty to my family and my rôle in public life, I retied my shoelaces with a supreme effort, told Claretta that I had apparently poisoned myself with some oysters—why oysters should have occurred to me, I have no idea—and announced that I must leave without delay.

This was easier said than done. Claretta at once resumed her négligé—despite the shock, or perhaps because it had sharpened my senses in a grotesque and alarming way, I distinctly noticed that her sagging stockings made her look like Puss-in-Boots—

although I suspect that, subconsciously, she was most anxious that I should breathe my last in her illicit embrace. I had to employ all my gifts of persuasion before she would allow me to go. She then insisted on calling a taxi, which was out of the question, because I could hardly leave my car parked outside her flower-shop. Will-power being all, my condition had improved slightly, and I felt confident that I could reach the nearest taxi-rank. I finally convinced Claretta of the irrevocability of my decision, but had to squander precious minutes on excuses and explanations. I *reflected, with a twinge of bitterness, that mistresses are more jealous of their lovers' widows than of their wives.* Claretta's eyes betrayed her disillusionment with a man who wanted to die at home after years of pretending that his real home was with his mistress. She escorted me to the street door, and I promised—yet another of my innumerable promises! —to telephone her early next morning.

Although still suffering from a certain breathlessness which obliged me to open both windows of my coupé despite the chill night air, I felt perceptibly better. The proximity of home lent me unsuspected strength. I also told myself that, in view of the predicament into which the Morelli affair had led me, I simply couldn't afford to die. My mind dwelt with some tenderness not only on my wife and children but also on the fourteen hundred and fourteen wage-earners and salaried staff for whom I cherish such paternal feelings. That was unwise, of course, because the realization that Edizioni Vanetti rested squarely on a single pair of shoulders only intensified the fear which had constricted my heart. I drove fairly fast—perhaps irresponsibly so—no longer because I wanted to die in my own bed but because I now felt convinced that I was not destined to die at home.

The lights were on. Maria was waiting up for me as usual, despite the lateness of the hour. I said nothing about oysters—simply indicated my heart. Maria asked no questions. She is the type of woman who always fears the worst but never panics. "You've over-excited yourself," she declared firmly, and telephoned for the doctor.

Christa Sonntag

I never get bored because I'm a psychological sort of person. Take that party at Howard Grainger's, for instance. I'd have been bored stiff without a bit of psychology—until Bossi turned up, that is. Firstly because it was a drag anyway, and secondly because I'd already been to bed with five or six of the men there.

It was an 'entertainment', and that's always a drag. Howard Grainger is in the export-import business—on a big scale, of course. And how! He's got a villa in Parioli with all the frills, just like Versailles. I don't envy him, though. I prefer my own little house, because there you can hear the murmur of the sea. When Grainger's business friends come over from the States he offers them a slice of *dolce vita*. It's just the same as those German films about life in the backwoods, honestly it is. Whenever I see a film about my own part of the world, Bavaria, I know perfectly well it's all make-believe. For instance, the Bavarian Forest doesn't start right at the foot of the Frauenkirche, and you don't find many people yodelling all day, especially not in the better-class establishments. People like having the wool pulled over their eyes, though. That's why, when one of these American ex- or im-porters comes to Rome, especially when he leaves his ever-loving wife behind, he wants to know whether *Dolce Vita* was based on real life. Because it wasn't, we treat him to a performance which corresponds to what went on in the film. In other words, what was only make-believe in the film actually takes place after all, so you could make another film about that, and that one would be based on real life. *C'est la vie*, as they say in the best circles, in French. Anyway, when Howard Grainger does a repeat of the film for the benefit of the business world, I play a part which puts Anita Ekberg in the shade, honestly it does. That's why it really isn't a lie when Howard Grainger—or Johnny Malone, because he's in charge of entertainment—introduces me as a budding film star. Nobody believes it anyway.

Of course, only top-class girls get invited to Grainger's business dos—Françoise, Rita, Gretchen, me, and sometimes La Napolitana, though only in emergencies. I took Hertha along once, but that was a big mistake. As I said before, people like to

have the wool pulled over their eyes, and any girl who can't see
that doesn't need a crystal ball—she's got hard times ahead. All
the guests know I'm not averse to a commercial proposition, but
if I acted like a call-girl I might as well turn in my telephone
right away and save the rent. I mean, it's part of a man's nature.
A man would sooner sleep with the dear old Queen Mother of
Mozambique—if there is such a person; I never did study geo-
graphy—than pick up the prettiest girl in the Via Veneto. No
call-girl earns the price of a seaside villa at Anzio unless she acts
refined. A man likes to go back home to his family with something special to remember—like the Queen Mother of Mozambique, for instance—because that makes him different from the
rest of the *dolce vita* brigade. Married men put their little adven-
tures into store, so to speak. They hoard them up like canned
food in wartime and live on them for years, back in the family
fold.

Anyway, I sat there in Howard Grainger's bar, looking hard-
to-get—and not right up at the bar, either, because that's common. I ordered a lemon-juice, although I'm against vitamins on
principle. "Give me a *citron pressé*," I told the butler, because
certain expressions show people you know your way around.
For instance, I always say, "Very mild, mind you" when I order
smoked salmon, even though I couldn't care less, and with
caviare I always ask if it's grey, because that's the done thing.
I've never yet heard a waiter say the smoked salmon was salty or
the caviare black. You can tell if a client has class by the way he
sends white wine back because it's too warm, and red wine
because it isn't room temperature. The only ones who encourage
drinking in public are nightclub hostesses, and they're nothing
more than common prostitutes when it comes to alcohol consumption. Why should I lure Howard Grainger's guests into
drinking? Firstly I don't get a percentage, and secondly I've no
call to bump up his overheads. Besides, it's bad for the health.

From time to time one of the men came over and sat with me.
Françoise came and joined me too, because being in the same
class as me Françoise knows it's refined for two women to converse without male company. She talked about her poodle, which
was down with distemper.

Two of the characters sitting at the bar I knew better with no
clothes on. One of them—I think he's called Lynn, or something

similar—had been to my place quite a few times. I'm part of his
Rome itinerary, like St Peter's. He's the bashful type. Whenever
he visits me he says he dreamt about me back home in Pittsburgh
—it could be Philadelphia, I always get them mixed up—and
then, with a bit of encouragement, he tells me exactly what he
dreamt. The trouble is, he always wants to put it into practice
right away, although it's usually pretty complicated and we run
into the odd technical hitch sometimes. He's daft really, because
he could tell me straight out what he wants, and besides, nobody
dreams that vividly, not even children with the measles. But
then, he's shy, as I said. As for his colleague—I think they're
both in the car business—he's a simpler type altogether. He
doesn't waste so much of my precious time.

Anyway, I sat there doing psychological research, because the
night was young, and the men normally concentrate on business
until eleven. Especially when they know they can have it any
time they like.

I can't stop thinking about Hertha, probably because of
Canonica. I lead a risky sort of life myself, which is why I'm
planning to pack up in January 1972 at latest. That's because
men are sick, and not just the exceptions, either. Far from it.
Canonica's probably looking for a sex-maniac, but there are
plenty of sick men around without them necessarily being sex-
maniacs. Hertha may have got herself done in by one of them.
I must tell Canonica. I could become a police adviser when I
retire—as a sideline, of course, because I plan to concentrate on
the real-estate business. Firstly I need another source of income,
secondly it's profitable, and thirdly it's in my blood.

Normal men don't grow on trees, and that's a fact. A woman
goes to bed to enjoy herself. A man isn't looking for enjoyment
when he goes to bed—he's looking for confirmation of his virility.
Youngsters go to bed to prove they're already men, oldsters do it
to prove they're still men. Either way, their nerves suffer and so
does their enjoyment. Men are wrapped up in a certain part of
their body from the cradle to the grave. They think they're
unique, whereas experience proves the opposite. There isn't a
more overrated commodity than the male organ, not even filthy
lucre. A girl has to realize that, of course. I wouldn't be the
success I am if I didn't tell all my clients how fantastic they are.
I mean, it's far less of a strain to flatter a man than have to

perform on the hard floor or dress up in a gym slip. You get places if you admire a man's dimensions or praise his technique, and it doesn't cost you a thing. There are two sorts of men. One sort feel specially like it when they're worried about business, the other sort fancy it when they're racing up the ladder of success. The first sort want a shoulder to cry on and the second sort want eggs in their beer. I can spot both sorts a hundred miles off, because men are as transparent as a pair of nylon panties. There's no connection with love either way, but the poor monkeys don't realize that. Men live on their nerves when it comes to sex. You never find the same sort of team spirit between men as there is between Françoise and me, say, because even little boys compare tiddlers when they go to the loo. Big deal! Men are always competing with each other, and that includes bed. They're always mad about something, from the cradle to the grave, either because a girl says no to them, or because she says yes at the wrong time, or because they think they can't make her happy, or because they think someone else is making her happier. The worst of it is, they're usually mad at themselves, only they don't realize it. Proper nervous wrecks, men are. They need a nurse, really, not a call-girl. People seem to forget there aren't any female sex-murderers, and nobody ever gets killed even when a woman does use violence, which tends to happen in the better class of society. It isn't that women are gentler by nature. The real reason is that they're naturally superior to men, so they've no need to strangle them—none at all. Apart from that, women don't compete in the same way, and competition can lead to some pretty sharp practice. It needn't have been a madman who murdered Hertha—they're all a bit dangerous at heart.

My dreamer had sold enough cars. He left the bar and sat down beside me. The fool thought I was waiting for him. I mean, that proves a girl shouldn't exert herself—when they've sold enough cars they show up of their own accord. Satisfy your regular customers, that's my principle. I'm not interested in expanding.

"Hi, Ginger," he said—he thinks that's funny. "I've been dreaming about you again. How about that?"

"How about that?" I said, because I speak English *perfettamente*.

"I dreamt about you back in Detroit," he said. He doesn't come from Pittsburgh, or Philadelphia.

"Something nice, I hope," I replied in an airy-fairy tone.

Just then Bossi joined us. "How come you're here?" I asked, and introduced the two of them—that's to say, I introduced Bossi first, because the other man was older and I know the form. You don't often catch me making a social blunder. Bossi was far more surprised to see me there than the reverse, because Howard Grainger was an old friend of his, or so he said. He told Lynn— I think he's called Lynn, anyway, his name's Theodore—that Mr Grainger had given him a lift to Marrakech once in his private 'plane. Grainger had some business to attend to in Morocco, and Bossi wanted to travel back to Italy with the Italian ace-burglar they'd caught down there.

"How interesting!" said my dreamer. He was furious because he'd been itching to make a date with me.

I winked at Theodore—very discreetly, of course. After all, he is an old customer. Also, he's on Grainger's special list, which means unlimited credit. What's more, it's no good making men even more nervous than they are already.

Then Howard Grainger came over to us with a full glass of Scotch in his hand. He always has a full glass of Scotch in his hand, and he looks like the Man of Distinction in the whisky ads. He obviously wanted to impress Theodore, because he gave Bossi the sort of build-up they give a new brand of cigarettes—Rome's most celebrated crime reporter, and so on.

"Emilio comes from Viterbo," he said to my dreamer. "That's a small town north of Rome. He's on the track of a murderer at the moment. If I know anything about Emilio, it's going to be sensational." And he gave Bossi such a thump on the back his whisky glass nearly shot out of his hand.

"How interesting!" said my dreamer from Detroit.

"Who's been murdered this time?" I asked.

"Nobody," said Bossi. "Howard's joking. Nobody's been murdered."

"That isn't what you told me," Grainger said. "Some girl or other..." He looked pretty angry. I'd seen it before. Americans are good-natured on the whole, but they can get really nasty when someone makes them look silly. I know that perfectly well, because I've always taken an interest in the psychology of the different races.

"Don't believe all you read in the papers," said Bossi, doing everything except look Grainger in the eye. "I was only putting on an act. As a sort of excuse for arriving late." And with that he started talking at Theodore in English as though he planned to sell him *Quest' Ora* by midnight—and Bossi's English wouldn't even get him into an American Bar.

As for me, alarm-bells started ringing inside my head. I know Bossi as well as if I'd slept with him a hundred times. Nobody had been murdered in Viterbo or it would have been in the papers next morning, and why should Bossi be coy about that? It's something to do with Hertha, sure as fate, and Grainger simply misunderstood the bit about the girl. Alternatively, it's something to do with me. If Bossi wanted to lie he could have lied to my dreamer as well as Grainger. It was me he didn't want to say anything in front of, that's why he said he'd been lying. Being quick on the uptake, I think that proves it's something to do with Hertha. Besides, Bossi sheered off so quickly afterwards anyone would have thought I had the plague.

Theodore asked if I'd care to go and have a drink somewhere and I said yes, because firstly I don't approve of taking a client home straight away, and secondly it does a girl's reputation good to be seen in smart places.

In the taxi my dreamer told me he'd just pulled off a huge deal. He's the successful kind, the kind that wants eggs in his beer. While he was talking I spent the whole time wondering whether to ring Canonica right away. It goes against the grain to turn someone in. On the other hand, Bossi doesn't mean anything to me and Canonica's a gentleman—we've become really friendly since I visited his place. The money Bossi gives me doesn't belong to him—his motives are strictly commercial. What's more, my resident's permit runs out on the first of the first. One word from Canonica and they'll hand me a new one on a silver salver. Besides, it's my sacred duty to see that the murderer gets his just deserts. Hertha was a colleague, after all.

THE COMPROMISE

Francesco Vanetti

Beside the little bridge over the Fiume Astura is some undergrowth, I hide in the undergrowth, I lie in ambush in the
undergrowth, the undergrowth is under the notice which says
*Divieto di eseguire fotografie e cinematografie e rilievi anche a
vista Art.250–250 oL.P.*, I lie in ambush under the notice.

> Eye in the forest
> Glass eye in the forest
> My eye is made of glass
> Like the leopard's eye
> —Nursery—the
> Leopard sleeps on the bed,
> Harmless, fever-dream
> Measles.
> The beast is harmless,
> Toy leopard in the undergrowth,
> Its eye is lethal,
> Bloodthirsty, hunter-murderer
> Hunter-hunted
> He is a man.

I peer through the undergrowth, my camera peers through
the undergrowth, I have three eyes, the Cyclops only had one
eye, one eye in his forehead, I have an eye on my stomach, a
total of three eyes. Only one of my eyes is a retentive eye, the
artificial eye is a retentive eye, the eye on my stomach, what it
sees is captured for ever, eye-captivated, monochrome, poly-
chrome, any size, behind the artificial eye runs the film, interchangeable, unlimited production, the film is interchangeable,
the eye is interchangeable, wide-angle, telephoto, my eye is not
interchangeable, what my eye captures it doesn't retain, my
memories can't be stuck into an album, my mother sticks her
memories into an album, she has reliable memories, I have none.
My eye is worthless, every eye is worthless, eyes can't be exchanged, only exchangeable eyes would be worth something,
Sofia could see me through my eyes, I could see Sofia through
her eyes, I could give my father my eyes, he would see himself
in the mirror with my eyes, he would recognize himself with my

eyes, one is blind with one's own eyes, one's own eyes are worth-less, they ought to be mounted in a camera, like a lens, snapshots for the album.

The murderer is wearing rubber gloves, he ought to have worn rubber gloves when he strangled Hertha Enzian, he's wearing rubber gloves because the water is cold, the fish are cold, the dead fish are cold, the murderer loves dead fish, the murderer is terrified of dead fish. I snap the murderer, I shoot him, as the Americans say, the Americans are always shooting, from the stomach, from the hip, I fire my camera, I'm a wild beast with a hunting rifle, cowardly wild three-eyed beast, I don't pounce from the undergrowth, I don't tear anyone to pieces, I take photographs. It goes click-clack, I shoot, I change my eye, tele-photo lens, one-thirty-five, I bring the murderer closer, I pull him towards me, my eye couldn't bring anyone closer, everything remains remote from my eye, it's worthless, I shoot, click-clack.

A camera slips off my shoulder, the camera falls to the ground, unexpected noise, it goes thump, not click-clack, the murderer is up the slope at a single bound, he confronts me, he has a white face and white eyes, his over-long overcoat flaps round his legs, his legs flap, he reaches for my camera the way he reached for Hertha Enzian, he tries to strangle my camera. You photo-graphed me, he says.

I snatch the camera away, you're mad, I say. This is the first opportunity, this is the opportunity I've been waiting for, ME could tell him that I'm Francesco Vanetti, son of Carlo Vanetti, I'm photographing you for *Quest' Ora*, *Quest' Ora* is going to print photographs of you, my father is going to report you to the police, they'll arrest you, they'll lock you up for life, they'll give you l-i-f-e i-m-p-r-i-s-o-n-m-e-n-t. ME could tell him that the *Enzian Story* is starting in the Christmas number, we already have the butcher, we already have the dead girl, from the police, get out of here quick, before Christmas, *Stille Nacht, Heilige Nacht*, they'll put you in the Crib on Christmas Eve, maybe they'll hang you from the tree, *Buon Natale*. My father's ill, he's ill in hospital, coronary thrombosis, ambitio-thrombosis, I can't denounce my father, they'd transfer him to a prison hospi-tal in handcuffs, the murderer is escaping, my father is dying, he's dead, I can't denounce him.

You're mad, I say, who are you anyway, I'm not interested in you, I can take as many photographs as I like, I'm photographing the atomic-energy establishment, you're burying dead fish. How do you know I bury dead fish, he asks, this isn't the first time I've taken photographs here, I say, why do you bury dead fish? Taking photographs is forbidden, he says, he points to the notice-board, *Divieto di eseguire fotografie e rilievi anche a vista Art.250–250 oL.P.*, the murderer appeals to the law, the law protects murderers, murderers are part of the Establishment, it's forbidden to photograph murderers and atomic secrets, big murderers, little murderers, protected murderers, mutually protected murderers. Let's go to the police, I say, report me, denounce me for being a spy, I'll tell them you bury dead fish. Are you a spy, he asks, yes, I say, I am a spy. What's your name, he asks, I haven't asked you for your name, I say. He asks who I spy for, I don't spy for anyone, why does one have to spy for someone else, I say, I'm spying against nuclear energy, nuclear energy killed those fish, precisely, that's why I'm burying them, he says.

We start walking, the murderer and I start walking towards the town, we're anonymous, we don't have names, the murderer and I walk side by side, the wind whistles in our ears, there's no one on the main road, a couple of cars are on the main road, the sky is grey and empty as the main road. I won't report you, says the murderer, I won't report you for being a spy, I wouldn't even report you if you were a murderer, I say, if the bread's mouldy there's no point in looking for maggots, squirming maggots in mouldy bread. I understand the murderer, I hope the murderer understands me, why do you live in Foce Verde, I ask, Foce Verde is a mouldy dump, there's nothing in Foce Verde but soldiers guarding the secret, look at them marching around behind the barbed wire, they don't know why they're marching, they don't have an enemy, they're looking for an enemy, they march in circles looking for an enemy, the first will shoot the last, or they'll march against the beach-huts, better beach-huts than no enemy at all, enemy-seekers, soldiers. We might have understood one another, says the murderer, but it's too late, for me it's too late, for you it's too early, that's why we can't understand one another.

His hotel is near by, he comes to a standstill, give me that film, he says, his eyes glint behind his glasses, his face is dead, his eyes glint but he's dead, amputees think their legs are hurting but they don't have any legs. I need the film, I tell him, I can't give you the film, ME would give him the film. He doesn't know I have enough shots of him already, my father has locked the films up in his safe, my mother's jewellery is in the safe, lying alongside pictures of the murderer, dirty diamonds, dirty pictures, at Christmas my mother will bring out her diamonds, at Christmas Quest' Ora will bring out pictures of the murderer, my father has had a coronary, my father expects gratitude, it's his last request, I can't give the murderer the pictures.

I drive to Rome, people are coming out of church, religious blacklegs, on the right is a football ground, they chase after a ball, they wear convict uniform, black-and-red, white-and-blue, women push prams, fertile blacklegs, computers put saturation point at the year 2005, but they push prams, big-bellied women, big-bellied prams, I used to lie in a pram like that, two big wheels, two little wheels, Go to sleep, my little piccaninny, nothing ever changes, they go on pushing prams, nothing changes ever. LSD is like the football ground and the church and the prams, LSD was developed by old men, I didn't learn anything about myself, my mouth was salty, I only saw colours, like Pollock or Herbin, I could have gone to an exhibition, after six hours the psychedelic togetherness peters out and all that's left is a salty taste. Why bother to learn about ourselves, it's an old people's invention, a temptation, a great big spiritual confidence trick, we're back in our prams again, that's what they want, to see us back in our prams again, how can we turn this filthy world upside down if we're still wetting our nappies? I won't say the murderer caught me, I won't denounce the murderer, I won't denounce my father, if the murderer tries to escape let him, that's his business, I'll denounce the world, a world indictment, if they arrest the world the murderer can't escape, my father can't escape, the churches will burn, the football grounds turn into deserts, the children tumble out of their prams.

Visiting time. Go right on up, your father's better, says the nun behind the information desk, she looks like a man in drag, she has a heavy moustache, the whole building reeks of cleanliness, all the visitors smile apologetically: is your patient better, my patient's better.

The room is full of flowers, vases stand on the tables, vases stand on the floor, roses, carnations, chrysanthemums, potted

plants, I wonder if the Sacchi woman sent flowers, she probably
sent a whole shopful, she'll send a wreath, a big man gets flowers,
a big sick man gets flowers, two dozen means popularity, four
dozen fear, a potted plant opportunism, a single rose love, a
dozen take the place of a wreath. They've propped my father up
a little, he's shaved, I kiss him on the forehead, he smells of illness
and after-shave.

The Professor was here just now, he says, I'm a lot better, I'll
be home for Christmas, he says, the Professor is amazed at my
powers of recuperation. He's so ill he crows about his health, he
watches me to see if I'm pitying him, he checks whether I'm
grateful to him for not dying.

Come and sit here, he says, I'm glad you came, it's very important, I've got something to discuss with you. My constitution is
excellent, he crows, the Professor is absolutely delighted, but
three weeks' complete rest in bed and at least four weeks' recuperation at home, it will be March, possibly April, the next
few weeks are crucial. I take it he's talking about his illness,
about his heart, he's forgotten his illness and his heart, he's talking about Edizioni Vanetti, about *Quest' Ora*. No possibility of
altering our schedule now, millions of lire invested in the *Morelli
Story*, he whispers the name, Bossi has delivered the first instalments, I haven't had a chance to read them yet, he says, but it's
a great comfort, I got frightfully worked up about Bossi, it may
have been the excitement that did it, the Professor says I mustn't
overtax myself. We'll top one-and-a-half million with the *Morelli
Story*, you can bet your bottom dollar on that, he says, *Lui e Lei*
will be begging for mercy by Easter at latest, I've instructed
Janetti to put a brake on advertisement acceptances, putting out
ads at the old rates would be a dead loss with a circulation of
one-and-a-half million.

I get a sick feeling in my stomach, thinking of the circulation
figure, of the one-and-a-half million, my mouth tastes salty,
LSD-salty, my father is framed with flowers like a Bellini
Madonna, the chrysanthemums smell withered, I loathe chrysanthemums, they stink. ME wants to say it's nothing to do with
me, where do I come into it, ME wants to say, speak to Bossi,
speak to Janetti, speak to the editorial director, speak to the
advertising manager, speak to the Sacchi woman, she's your
mistress, speak to Beatrice, she's your pet, it's nothing to do with

me, I am a camera, I've met Morelli, ME is going to denounce the
world, ME has lain in my pram long enough. What does he
expect of me, I ask myself, but I say nothing, he'll find out sooner
or later, he gets frightfully worked up, he mustn't get worked up,
his cheeks are flushed, it wasn't Bossi who overtaxed him, he'd
just come back from the Sacchi woman, hot from her bed, why
am I sitting on his bed, where do I come into it?

No one has a clue about Morelli, he says, Bossi is gifted but
irresponsible, you're my son. He rambles, at first I think he's
rambling, he says he knows where I stand politically, he knows I
demonstrate, I have a perfect right to, young people have a right
to, unrest is useful, where would we get without unrest, the
older generation have been asleep, you're quite within your
rights, he says, the man who isn't a rebel in his youth never gets
anywhere, doesn't have any character, you can pick all sorts of
holes in the world, money isn't everything, the consumer society,
when you love you don't need cans, freedom is indivisible,
he understands me better than I think, he says—and what has
all that got to do with Morelli? He can't entrust *Quest' Ora*
to an outsider, he says, not at this stage, I must take over the
magazine until he recovers, I must prepare the *Morelli Story*,
Bossi will help me, he will help me himself, from his sick-bed, he
has an iron constitution, the Professor says so. He gets down to
details, he doesn't wait for me to say yes, I always say yes, he
decorates me with responsibility, he drapes responsibility round
my neck like the Grand Cross of the Légion d'Honneur, he
dumps responsibility on my shoulders, I'm Atlas the globe-
carrier, his globe is called *Quest' Ora*, he dumps *Quest' Ora* on
my shoulders. He talks about the cover, the cover is already in
production, Bellini's *Madonna*, the editorial board must be
informed nine days or so before Christmas, he lowers his voice,
Morelli's memoirs are a complete surprise to us, of course, the
murderer is a surprise, a bonanza, a stroke of luck, Bossi will
denounce the murderer shortly before Christmas, we can print
the placards at the last minute, lucky we have a printing works
of our own, lucky he built the new printing works.

I sit on his bed, his voice flows over me, the Fiume Astura, the
Fiume Astura is contaminated, the sea is big and the water is
clean, the river is contaminated, the sea is broad, no one sees the
boundaries of the sea, the forgotten sea, the river is narrow, the

river is visible, the v-i-s-i-b-l-e river, the river is contaminated, the fish are dead, when the dead fish drift out to sea they contaminate the live fish, the dead fish must be buried, my father's voice flows like the contaminated river. ME sees the sea, ME sees the clean sea, ME knows that the Fiume Astura can't contaminate ME. ME says no, ME says I can't accept the responsibility, I photographed the murderer, ME has nothing to do with the *Morelli Story*, thanks for the Grand Cross but leave me out of it.

My father goes pale, I ought to call the nuns, I ought to call the constitution-commending Professor, my father looks like a dead fish, he lies there in state, the flowers hang their heads, when someone's cremated the flowers are cremated, the flowers aren't cremated, they're sold, dead men's flowers are sold. He should have given me more responsibility sooner, he says, he bribes me with understanding, he bribes me with responsibility. He can't bribe me with an Alfa Romeo, I already have an Alfa Romeo, your very attitude proves you're the right man, he says, the magazine needs new blood, the whole chain needs new blood, he would prefer to confine his activities to *Quest' Ora* and the women's magazine and the economic journal and *Mickey Mouse*, when I've acquired enough experience I can take over *Positivismo*.

I'd kill *Quest' Ora* in a matter of weeks, I say, I hate every line in *Quest' Ora*, I hate the pictures, I hate my own pictures most of all, the pictures are faked, even the Vietnam pictures are faked, the pram didn't belong to Hertha Enzian, who's to know if the dead in Vietnam aren't faked, perhaps the prams in Vietnam are faked too, I hate spectators, I hate readers, Vietnamese children are dying because spectators are spectating and readers reading, new pictures aren't good enough, we need new spectators, you can't run a paper when you hate the readers, says ME.

My father says he hates the readers just as much as I do, but you've got to think logically, he says. He starts talking about abstract art, why does he talk about abstract art, he appreciates abstract art, he lies, but one can't think in abstractions, the world isn't a canvas, people don't consist of paint, people are three-dimensional, they have substance, they must be moulded. It's a good thing when youngsters rip up cobble-stones, cobble-stones are old but new streets have to be built in the end, streets made of new stones. I really must try to think logically, I have to start some time, aren't I interested in persuasion, why try to conquer what I already possess, millions of people listen to *Quest' Ora*, thousands of intellectuals listen to *Positivismo*, he reverts to Morelli. Morelli is a reflection, there couldn't be a finer reflection of society than Morelli, everything depends on presentation, I really must think logically, even the new society wouldn't tolerate Morelli, we're not glamourizing him, we're baring his soul, publicizing his confession, if the police had found him they'd never have publicized his confession.

I examine myself while he speaks, I examine myself while I speak, the ice beneath my feet is thin, Cellophane ice, the ice cracks, I put one foot in front of the other, anyone who walks, walks on thin ice, anyone who breathes is an accomplice, I walk, I breathe, I'm an accomplice. You're ambitious, I tell myself, he's left you his ambition, you're provided for in his *testamentum ambitiosum*, ME tells me that ME won't let ME be bribed, ME won't be bribed, not with a rattle, nor with a diphtheria injection, nor with a coronary, I tell myself that the *Ten Days* have arrived, I can wrest the enemy's weapon from him, I am twenty-three and can wrest the enemy's weapon from him, he hands it over voluntarily, all the better, no competition, no force, the enemy has managed himself out of existence, what matters is the means of production, says Marx, says Lenin, says Stalin, says Mao, *Quest' Ora* is a means of production. A lame excuse, says ME, you're an accomplice, you're a corrupt accomplice, the Establishment is cooing in your ear, the Establishment whispers like the Fiume Astura, the Establishment lolls against a white pillow framed with flowers like a Bellini Madonna, the Establishment has had a coronary and is cooing in your ear. I tell myself, ME tells myself, I or ME, I don't know who tells me, my father is alive, he's walking on thin ice, the ice cracks, he's trembling, he's afraid because of Morelli, because of Morelli he had to hand over the reins, it doesn't matter why the enemy hands over the reins, I grab the reins, I won't let the reins go again, I'll hoodwink the enemy, I'll hang on to the reins.

Take it easy, I say, I'll do my best, you've done too much talking, you've exerted yourself too much, you look tired, I'll come again tomorrow, we'll go over the details, I feel sorry for him, really sorry, a surprise, when I see him I'm sorry for him. Where's the key of the safe, I ask, I'd have got the keys of the safe even if he'd died at the Sacchi woman's flat, I'd have grabbed the reins, I took another dozen shots today, I tell him, telephoto lens, in the grounds of the atomic power station, he was burying dead fish. My father looks at me gratefully, Francesco, he says, his cheeks are flushed in spite of his cast-iron constitution, tomorrow I'll tell you who you can rely on, he says, we must get the *Morelli Story* moving for a start, everything will be simpler once the murderer has been brought to book, you know what I mean. In the bedside table, he says, because he's not allowed to move, even though he already has, in the bedside table, he says, Bossi has the manuscript, the pictures are in the safe, the key of the safe is in the bedside table, I pull open the drawer, I remove the key of the safe.

Oskar Enzian

I was feeling on top of the world Saturday, which is how I always feel when I can do the family a bit of good.

It was snowing for the first time, but that didn't bother yours truly. Just the opposite. There's nothing prettier than dear old Vienna when she puts her white frock on. We took the tram into town—we were going to take a cab back anyway, what with the parcels and all. Franziska and me, we sat by the window, but Hans had to stand. A proper lump came into my throat as I sat there looking out at the streets and the buildings and the churches, all with their white frocks on. "It's coming down in chunks," I pointed out to Franziska, although she hasn't got any feeling for Nature. Myself, I took the snow as a sign from heaven. There's only three weeks to go till Christmas, and snow is something out of the ordinary, especially when it comes down in chunks. Besides, snow puts people in the right mood for Christmas shopping. It all depends on your mood, that's the way I look at it.

We changed twice, once at the Liebenberg Memorial and once at the Bellaria. Old Stransky—that's another member of the Social Club—he'd recommended a furniture show-room in the Mariahilfer Strasse, so we headed straight for it. They call it the Furniture Paradise, and that's putting it mildly. You feel you're in Paradise, wading across those thick-pile carpets. It's more of a private mansion, really, a show-room like that, except that it's designed for the general public. I hadn't been inside a furniture store since I was a lad—I can't recollect the occasion. Well, you could have knocked me down with a feather. In the furniture shops down our way, in Hernals, the different items stand side by side, drawn up on parade, whereas here whole rooms are fitted out like a private mansion. There's no obligation to buy, though. You can purchase each item separately, and because it's a furniture paradise you can park yourself anywhere you like. I sat down in an arm-chair. The arm-chair was upholstered in a thick silky material and it had a pattern made up of nothing but roses, in plush, though you wouldn't have known unless you ran your fingers over them. I purposely didn't budge when Franziska and Hans went off on a tour of the three different floors because I wanted to see if either of them would take it into their heads to say, "Papa, that would make a nice new arm-chair for you." They didn't say anything of the kind, of course, because a bit of respect for the breadwinner is too much to hope for. I'd have to curl up and die first. Hertha, now—she'd have cottoned on right away. I don't know why, but the Christmas spirit took a hold of me after all, when I thought of Hertha. The people were crowding in as though beds were being distributed free of charge. Everyone likes to celebrate Christmas in a proper fashion. There'll be one chair empty at our festive board, but Hertha will look down on the family circle and the new couch and the television set, just as if she was saying, "At least there was some point in me passing on, Papa." But there won't be any point in it for me, because nothing can take the place of my little girl.

If there's one thing the Good Lord can't abide, it's a man who takes his money for granted, that's my theory. Well, I sat there in my arm-chair, and I could see Hans and Franziska through the swing doors, arguing over a red couch—the sort you can convert into a bed and vice versa, all very discreet. Franziska flopped down on it so you could hear the springs creak. If it wasn't for Hertha she'd have to be content with the old couch till her dying day, the one with the lions' heads that look like something off a bridge, but she never spared a thought for that. I got up with a sudden jerk and marched over to the sales-lady. "That's out for a start," I said, firm as a rock. She didn't half stare, because she saw straight off which of us wore the trousers. Franziska tried to talk me round, but there was nothing doing. I was choked because I knew she hadn't spared a thought for Hertha. A red couch is out in any case, because the old one was red. Besides, I don't fancy one of those convertibles. Hans is getting married soon, and I slept on a convertible till I got married. My old bones deserve something better than that. I put my foot down good and hard, which shows how the general situation has changed. Even the family are coming round to the idea that I've driven a hard bargain with both lots—Yids as well as Wops. We settled on a green corner-couch which'll go with the rest of the furniture like venison and red cabbage. Installation is included in the price. The Furniture Paradise is a reputable firm, Stransky was right there, and nobody does me in the eye. Not any more they don't.

There's a big radio shop across the way, and we spent a fair time looking in the window. They'd switched on a dozen or more TV sets, though they were all showing the same programme. Rapid were playing Sportklub. Being an old Hernalser, I naturally support Sportklub. The Black-and-Whites were leading two-one. Franziska would insist on going shopping on Saturday, even though it meant leaving a temporary in charge of the shop at a busy time and I'd have enjoyed watching Rapid versus Sportklub. No family feeling, my family haven't. Franziska only dawdled in front of the window because she'd got her eye on a new TV set. I'm too soft by half, and that's a fact. Instead of watching the Dornbach lads score from a penalty, I'd already picked out a Philips set on the quiet. The idea is to have it delivered when the joy-bells are ringing out, as a surprise for Franziska. You couldn't call the couch a surprise. What's more, I'm going to get the new set at Wotruba's in Hernals, because they'll give me a good trade-in price for our old gogglebox.

Mariahilfer Strasse was so crowded you'd have thought it was the last Sunday before Christmas, because people do their Christmas shopping early these days. There was a Santa Claus outside one of the stores, too, which I don't approve of because that came in with the Americans. I got bitten by the spending-bug all the same. The flesh is weak, as it says in the Good Book. That's why we're open to mass-suggestion. A fat wallet is a temptation, especially when you've been on short rations all your life—to use one of Major Schumpeter's favourite expressions. Even so, I didn't envy the people round me for being so carefree. Speaking for myself, I've never got anything out of life I didn't pay for.

The next item on the agenda was a visit to Gerngross's for some things for Franziska, Hans, and Mizzi. If I was honest, which I am, I'd have to admit I did a bit of window-shopping myself on the way there. I'm still set on giving Paula a gold bracelet. I've had my doubts, mind you, but there's no shaking me now. Paula's stuck by me through good times and bad. I don't fancy her as much as I did, but that's another story. She's too free with her "now-you're-a-rich-man"'s, that's all. Perhaps it's her little way of telling me I ought to show my appreciation. They always say it takes a crisis to sort the sheep from the goats. People flutter round money like moths round a candle—flies round rotten pork, some would say. Paula can have her bracelet, even if it isn't pure love with her any more. All the same, it needn't be eighteen carat—fourteen looks just as good. Another reason why I don't feel right about it is Hertha. Hertha wouldn't have approved of my goings-on with Paula. I'd better take the money for the bracelet out of the till. Hertha couldn't object to that because it isn't her money.

Franziska went into the fitting-room to try on a dress and winter coat. I spent the time staring out of the window. Hans didn't say a word to me. He'd been trailing around after us as dumb as Hexi, except that Hexi's more affectionate. Looking out at the crowds, I started reckoning up how much our shopping spree was going to set me back. Quite spoiled the sight of the Mariahilfer Strasse for me, it did, even though the snow was still coming down in chunks. That bastard of a Swiss lawyer refused to pay me anything on the side—not a groschen, the stuck-up sod. The Swiss don't know what it's like to be on their uppers because the War passed them by. That means Pospischil knows what I make down to the last schilling. He's like a vulture, the way he grabs his percentage. As for Dr Habichl, if I thought he was going to show a bit of consideration because we were both in the Party and belong to the same social club, it only shows what an optimist I am. He may be a first-class lawyer, but looking at his first bill I can't get away from the feeling that he's a bastard too, and a crooked one at that. I mean, he'd never have had the barefaced nerve to put in a bill like that if he didn't know what happened in Taborstrasse. If things carry on this way, with everyone thinking I'm made of money and ex-Party members lurking in the bushes with bills at the ready, there won't be a groschen left for my old age, and Hertha wouldn't have wanted that. It's enough to ruin anyone's Christmas spirit.

They called me into the fitting-room, where Franziska was waiting in the nude, or as good as. She'd picked out two dresses over and above the winter coat, claiming she was going to need them in Rome. I wouldn't consider exposing myself to the publicity, but she doesn't know that yet. Vanity never was one of my failings. Franziska still looks pretty good, I'll grant her that. It isn't her fault I don't feel up to doing my stuff. "Doesn't your wife look a treat?" the fitting-room lady whispered to me. I'll lay odds she says that to everyone, but Franziska was in love with her own reflection anyway. We marched out with three parcels, which made my wallet look pretty undernourished. And we weren't done yet, not by a long chalk. We looked like three loaded donkeys at the finish, even though they're sending the winter coat by post.

I couldn't help feeling cheered in spite of myself. Everybody wonders if he's done right by his family when Christmas comes round. I can't find anything to reproach myself with there. Thanks to working hard and putting a bit by, I can spend what Hertha left us on expanding the business. That red-haired Wop from Rome—Herr Bossi—he's welcome to go pumping the neighbours about me. They'll all tell him the same.

Afterwards I treated the family to a snack at one of those cafés in Ringstrasse, not just because Franziska never gets to see the inside of a café but because I had a nasty feeling. Franziska had gone and invited her mother to supper, so I knew I was in for a right old time later on.

It was warm in the café. The snow was still coming down outside, big flakes of it, and the opera-house was all dressed up in its white frock. "You can't beat dear old Vienna," I said, but I was wasting my breath on Hans. These modern youngsters haven't got a spark of patriotism.

I'd just asked the waitress for a magazine when somebody tapped me on the shoulder from behind and asked if I was Herr

Enzian. I went all cold, right the way down my spine, but when I turned round I saw it was only a married couple I'd never set eyes on before. The man mumbled his name, like you do when you're introducing yourself. He was a professor, that's all I caught—Professor Kretschmer or something similar. I knew straight away we hadn't served together in the Brownshirts because he belonged to an older age-group. His wife looked all shrivelled up too, more like a mummy.

"I thought so," the Professor said. "My wife recognized you from the newspaper photographs. 'Surely that's Herr Enzian', she said, and I said, 'I must shake him by the hand and express my sincere condolences'. To lose one's child is bad enough, my dear sir. To be smeared by the gutter Press through no fault of one's own is a disgrace."

I'd gone all red in the face. I was shaking like a leaf, too, but that was from before. The Professor spotted it straight off. Perhaps he was a doctor. "Calm yourself, my dear Herr Enzian," he said, but his wife tugged at his sleeve. "I told you not to trouble them," she said, but she shook hands with Franziska and Hans all the same. It was dead embarrassing, on account of the parcels. The chairs either side of Franziska were piled high with them— she was sitting there with parcels all round her, like the Santa Claus outside Gerngross's. "Be strong," the Professor said. "No man is master of his fate, no father can do more than his best. You did your duty, I'm sure. Decent people don't think like the gutter Press—I want you to know that." He took a squint at the parcels all the same, because they were level with Franziska's hat, at least on one side. What's more, she had a bloody great slice of *Sachertorte* and whipped cream in front of her, *Sachertorte* being her favourite cake.

The Professor and his wife didn't wish us a merry Christmas— too tactful to, probably. They'd only just left when Hans opened fire. "Serves you right," he said.

"What's that supposed to mean?" I asked.

"You would insist on getting yourself in the papers," he replied, all insolence.

"You know very well your father didn't have any choice," Franziska cut in, taking my part for once.

"You keep your remarks to yourself," I told him straight, but he kept right on.

"If you'd kicked that bunch of film people out," he said, "nobody would have said another word about Hertha."

"Perhaps you'd care to send your overcoat back," I remarked, very sarcastic.

"I'll pay for it myself," he snapped.

"That'll be the day, when you pay for something yourself," Franziska said, taking my part again. I must say I was surprised.

"I can get as many jobs as I like," the boy told his mother. "I don't need your charity."

"Then you won't be needing that flat," Franziska told him, quick as a flash. She'd been against the idea from the first.

"You're only ashamed because it was your sister," I said, trying to pour oil on troubled waters.

"It wasn't her fault," Hans replied. "You ought to have been more careful, you and Mother. It suited you very nicely, her sending Mizzi clothes. She was more sinned against than sinning, I reckon."

"You'll be telling us we sent her off to walk the streets, next," Franziska said. She was livid, and no wonder.

Hans raised his voice. "Girls'll walk the streets as long as there are streets to walk. This bourgeois state of yours is one big street-walker's paradise."

I didn't favour him with another word. "What did I tell you?" I said, turning to Franziska. "He's a Red, that boy, a nasty little Red."

"Better Red than Nazi," Hans said. "You can ride home by yourselves—I'll carry the parcels to the taxi. The overcoat's going back. I'm giving in my notice here and now."

That did it. Franziska left half her *Sachertorte* and started snivelling, even though she knows I can't abide the sight of tears. My father couldn't abide the sight of tears either, in spite of crying so easy himself. I could have given Hans a piece of my mind, but he'd only have started on about the Nazis again—at the top of his voice, what's more. Besides, it's a family man's duty to pour oil on troubled waters. "We're going," I said firmly.

Franziska went for me as soon as we were alone in the taxi. She'd lost a daughter, and now she was losing her son as well, she said, and it was all my doing. She also said she'd lost interest in her new clothes. I didn't argue, just stared out of the window. It had stopped snowing but the Burgtheater was all white, and I thought how nice life would be if only people showed a bit more understanding. I never thought our shopping expedition would end like that.

"Am I to be spared nothing?" old Emperor Franz Joseph said when he lost a child, meaning, if it isn't one thing it's another. That's what I thought myself when we got home and found the old woman—my beloved mother-in-law—waiting in front of the house. As a result, she saw all the parcels as I staggered up the steps with them. Sharp-eyed she may be, but she didn't notice that Franziska had been crying. Too interested in the parcels, she was.

Franziska went straight into the kitchen, and I turned the TV on because I wanted to find out if Sportklub had won. It was a draw, in spite of the penalty. I was hoping the TV would keep my beloved mother-in-law quiet, but you might as well try and plug Niagara Falls with a cork. She could see I was a rich man now—it showed, she said. That was a dig at us, of course. She'll be seventy-five come May, and then she goes into the old folks' home. It's all settled. Franziska's sister wants to get shot of her, which I can sympathize with. She was well away by the time Franziska brought supper in. Gertrude would keep her if we chipped in fifteen hundred schillings a month, she said, but then, you couldn't expect millionaires to look after their poor old parents. And so on.

"The old folks' home'll cost six hundred," I said.

"Yes, but Gerti's paying three hundred of that," she replied.

Once we were sitting at table—Hans's place was empty—she really got going. It was disgraceful, a famous man like me sticking his mother-in-law in an old folks' home. "They've had some quite well-known opera singers in there before now," I said. I read it in the *Kronen-Zeitung*, in black and white, but it was no good expecting Franziska to back me up this time. The blood rushed to my head, which is another thing connected with my lung trouble. "How I spend my money is my business," I said, thinking of my little Hertha and those sky-blue eyes of hers. "I'm getting Hertha's body transferred to Vienna as soon as it's released by the police," I said. "And that's more important than whether or not you go into an old folks' home." I shouted the last bit, in spite of being the type of man who likes his peace and quiet.

"Maybe," snapped the old woman, "but I'm Hertha's grandmother, don't forget. The neighbours are already talking, as it is.
You pack me off to an old folks' home and it'll get into the
papers."

"I'd never live down the disgrace," Franziska yowled. Blood's
thicker than water, and no mistake.

They didn't badger me into saying yes, for all that, because
I'm still master in my own home. The old woman's good for
another ten years at least, and fifteen hundred schillings a month
is eighteen thousand schillings a year—a hundred and eighty
thousand over ten years, because she hasn't even got diabetes.
I'm not going to be like that character in the fairy-tale who went
on swapping better for worse till he ended up with nothing at all.

I told Franziska so to her face, when we finally had the house
to ourselves again, but what answer did I get? She said I could
easily have spared her mother the disgrace of the old folks' home
if I hadn't gone shares with Pospischil to the tune of ten or
fifteen per cent.

That was when I lost my head, God forgive me. "If I hadn't
given Pospischil a cut," I said, "I'd be spending Christmas inside.
Not that my loving family would care a pinch of shit."

Franziska started yowling again at that. We didn't even open
the parcels, although we can't leave the things done up for three
weeks. They'd be all creased come Christmas.

Aurelio Morelli

All that distinguishes the man of action—to use an expression
whose shallowness derives from the impossibility of reducing
human character to a common denominator—from the thinker,
the quiet and contemplative soul, is the determination to convert
that which has been weighed and considered into actuality.
Every genius—even the artist who hugs his studio or the scientist who never leaves his laboratory—is a man of action, and
nothing could be more fallacious than the theory advanced by
the German dramatist Lessing, who asserted in his *Emilia Galotti*
that Raphael would still have been a colossus among painters
even if he had been born without hands. Himself an artist of
some stature, Lessing had unwittingly defined the nature of

dilettantism; for the gifted dilettante, though capable of evolving a grand design, is incapable of executing it in the grand manner —in other words, the dilettante is a handless painter, a designer without true executive ability, himself an unfinished *ébauche* from the hand of the Eternal Sculptor.

Eschewing dilettantism in any form, I had roughed out my plan of escape: a minor inducement was all that was needed to translate it into action. The last part of my manuscript I have retained on a variety of pretexts, being well aware that the inaptly named gentlemen of the Press will never risk publication until the last—the very last—line has been delivered, or rediscover their outraged sense of earthly justice prior to the appearance of their iniquitous periodical. The bearded youth who was aiming his devil's box at me from a place of concealment must have taken me for an utter nincompoop if he seriously supposed that I would give weight and credence to his trumpery tale of espionage. I need hardly add that I showed no emotion: the realization of betrayal would itself have sufficed to betray me.

Although austere in my habits and averse to extravagant expenditure, I did not undertake the journey to Rome by bus, my innate and ever-present intelligence having forbidden me to absent myself from my dismal place of exile for an undue length of time. Furthermore, I was in a hurry to return to the inhospitable scene of my banishment because it was Saturday, the third since my initial encounter with Agnese, and she had invited me —nay, begged me—to call upon her that evening in her parental mansion beside the green estuary. Accordingly I hired a taxi and had myself conveyed to Rome.

Città aperta, the open city, was the name given to Rome in the conflict popularly referred to as World War Two—how indicative that people have begun to number international conflicts with a view to their probable multiplication!—but for me it was a forbidden city, and I had to proceed with the utmost caution. Although I had not been able to secure payment of the expenses set aside for my air-fare, I was, on the other hand, in possession of the sums paid in respect of Mesdemoiselles Chiesa and Pisenti; and since banknotes afford no clue to their manner of acquisition—if it were otherwise the circulation of money would long ago have been discontinued from a sense of shame—I was, for perhaps the first time in my life, unencumbered by material considerations. I had brought my passport with me—it was fortunately valid for several years to come—but instead of going to one of the travel bureaux near the Via Veneto I chose a less frequented establishment in the Via Nazionale, where I stated my requirements—a visa for the Bolivian Republic and an air ticket to the capital, La Paz—with casual nonchalance. I had settled on December 24th as my date of departure, a Sunday, in the belief that few prospective travellers would choose that day of rejoicing to absent themselves from their dear ones and neglect the annually recurring opportunity to comport themselves in a semi-Christian fashion. There were no procedural difficulties: the desk-clerk, a courteous man of mature years, signified his willingness to complete the immigration formalities within the space of a few days. It says much for my quiet cunning that I abstained from any form of duplicity, for had I attempted to cover my tracks, here in the closed and forbidden city, I should only have rendered myself the more conspicuous. Once on the other side of the ocean I proposed to embark, calmly and in provisional anonymity, upon a second existence.

A second existence! Who has not retired to his restless couch many times in the course of his wretched span on earth, devoutly resolved to begin a new life on the morrow; and who has not—generally at the first morning glimpse of his own face in the mirror—capitulated to his own character, his own environment, his own past? Only in chess is it permitted to exchange a pawn which has attained the limits of enemy territory for a rook, bishop, cavorting knight, or other more valuable ivory piece: whatsoever he attains, man remains a pawn of inferior value. Besides, it is downright mendacity and self-deception to assert that one wishes to become a 'new man': man's hatred of his own life is matched only by his love of self; far from divesting himself of his personality, he wishes only to disguise it; his ambition is to put new wine in an old bottle; the new day is no more to him than an old masquerade.

Such were the thoughts that preoccupied me on the extended stroll from which nothing could deter me; neither circumspection, nor fear of being recognized as the murderer of the Via Sicilia, nor dread of falling into the hands of the young and evil Bossi. I lost myself in the indifferent crowds, obliged the odd tourist with items of information—indeed, lingered in wonder before the Fontana di Trevi, where, turning my back on Neptune, I superstitiously cast a coin into the fountain in order to propitiate the god and ensure a safe return to my beloved city. Looking up from the Piazza del Popolo, where I had commanded my taxi to await me, at the winding road which leads to the Borghese Gardens, I bethought myself of Lucia Chiesa and told myself, not without pride, that I had done my duty. My awed and affected gaze wandered over the obelisk which had withstood the passage of three-and-thirty centuries and the journey from Heliopolis; and I swore a sacred oath that, in my struggle against a younger generation which is girding itself to overthrow every obelisk in existence, I too would conquer time and space.

And what happened? The gods nodded their approval. There can in very truth be no other explanation of the fact that the motorized *carrozza* which was to convey me from the city to my craved-for assignation should have become embroiled in one of the youthful demonstrations which now, so I had read in the newspapers, formed part of the diurnal scene. I thought at first that it was merely the species of traffic disorder or congestion which is all too frequent in Rome, but my driver, a portly individual with the reassuring mien of a rustic wagoner, was quick to inform me that we had "of course" been balked by protesting students who claimed the streets as their exclusive preserve. The simple fellow blasphemed horribly and complained that, while he sat behind the wheel all day, the "young gentlemen" had nothing better to do than march up and down beneath red and black banners, thereby obstructing ordinary citizens in the peaceful execution of their duties. How, indeed, should my amiable Jehu have grasped that there was something symbolic in his situation—symbolic in his and mine both? Hundreds of automobiles stood motionless before and behind us, with the result that we were hopelessly hemmed in, frozen into immobility, unable to retreat without damaging or destroying our own or other vehicles, and equally unable to advance without putting ourselves, who were in the right, bloodily in the wrong.

I welcomed this opportunity to look upon the enemy face to face, and so, since my driver opined that we might well be "stuck" for a good hour, I abandoned our conveyance in order to mingle with the bystanders who were watching the vociferous triumphal procession with folded arms.

THE COMPROMISE

O my prophetic soul! That I should so early have diagnosed in the individual what has since become a general epidemic! They marched past me with arms linked, those young men and girls, wearing a jungle garb which enabled them to parade their private parts, exulting in a youthfulness for which they could scarcely claim credit themselves—in short, like a gigantic brothel on the march. And to think that there are still adults who give credence to the ideological trumpetings of young people, grown men who look upon pubescent parricides as the hotspurs and harbingers of a new society! The sole ideology of youth is youth, temporarily virulent, like syphilis, but all the more dangerous for that. Did not this demonstrator lay his grubby hand upon the budding breast of the girl beside him—did he not clasp her to him in an access of lewd exhibitionism? Did not that ugly lout with the non-existent forehead pose as a standard-bearer because his pretty companion might not later notice if he thrust his penis into her hand instead of a flag-pole? Did not the two youths with peroxided tresses march along in a close embrace because the Nietzschean *Umwertung aller Werte*, of which they were naturally in ignorance, permitted them to display their homosexual beastliness in public? Political anarchy is merely a consequence of the way in which we have sanctioned sexual anarchy among the young. Yet they reproach us with hypocrisy, the twice-tinctured hypocrites. Is it hypocrisy if one wishes to possess a woman for oneself, or hypocrisy if, in defiance of human nature, one shares her sex as if it were a public baths? Is it hypocrisy if, recognizing the dubious nature of man, we agree upon necessary restraints, or hypocrisy to speak of freedom and aspire to the freedom of the mongrel on the street-corner? Is it hypocrisy cautiously to define love as the place where Eros and Agape embrace, or hypocrisy to proclaim a love which has so far departed from the spiritual that man is encouraged to regard ejaculation and urination as one and the same thing? Is it hypocrisy to believe in the possibility of suppressing man's war-like instincts in an atmosphere of prosperity and justice—perhaps of eliminating the spirit of aggression altogether—or hypocrisy to assert that love is infectious and would halt the onrush of a tank? Is it hypocrisy if, timid and mistrustful, one speaks of a better future to come, or hypocrisy to claim that it is already here, conjured into being by an immature generation?

Is it hypocrisy to try, at least, to overcome hatred twixt class and race, or hypocrisy to deny its existence—abracadabra!—and substitute the far more catholic hatred of the juvenile for the redundant? Is unrest the prerogative of youth? War has a language of its own—in the vulgar but apposite phrase, our necks are at stake—yet we continue to prattle of peace.

The gods nodded their approval, as I said, for I returned to the car fortified in my resolve to make the very most of my distant exile by framing a manifesto. Since I cannot suppose and do not venture to hope that every man over forty will obey the law of self-preservation—philosophy subdivides the instinct for survival into the three categories of food, shelter, and defence, due prominence being accorded to the latter—and since I do not consider the intelligence and courage of the human race to be such that each man of my age will rid the world of three young creatures, I am planning not only to present parents and elders with a constitution but, more than that, to instruct them in its implementation.

Young people being interested not in a new ethos but solely in power, the first article of the manifesto or Code Morelli—it may equally be article eleven—will appeal to adults to bury or defer their differences, whether of a religious, racial, or ideological nature, and band themselves together in a holy alliance. Under the provisions of article seven, nine, or nineteen, all countries in which young people offer protracted resistance will ensure that procreation is halted by means of a sexual strike among adults, a Lysistrata rebellion in ultra-modern guise, since only a foolish general recruits new soldiers on his enemies' behalf; while, on the other hand, gratifyingly suicidal devices such as the 'Pill' render it unlikely that young people will augment their numbers to any dangerous degree.

The driver, beside whom I had sociably taken my seat, marvelled at my stoic calm: I could not tell the exasperated man that I was engaged in the formulation of a document whose thunderous diapason would make Karl Marx's *Communist Manifesto* seem mere chamber music by comparison.

In article seven, nine, or nineteen, I shall urge the older generation to punish youth, which has made an idol of ingratitude, by withdrawing all the privileges hitherto accorded it— which means, *in effecto*, that children shall be deprived of their pocket-money, adolescents of their allowances, and all young people of every form of luxurious indulgence, not excluding—if need be—the supply of food. In the first place, as I shall elaborate in my commentary, morality forbids that those who despise the acquisition and ownership of worldly goods be exposed to temptation by a lavish supply of the same; and, secondly, the basic rules of warfare dictate the cutting of enemy pipelines and logistical supply-routes. For example, all teachers, professors, scholars, and scientists shall withdraw their labour so as to prevent the further transmission of lightly esteemed knowledge—at least until the total subjugation of a youth-class which believes that it can dispense with experience; the abused guardians of an abused system of law and order, whom I had just seen mesmerized into immobility, shall decline to protect the persons and property of young people, and flatly ignore their potential pleas for assistance; and, finally, buyers and sellers of thirty-five and over shall exercise a ban on the purchase of goods from, and sale of goods to, members of the younger generation.

While I was striving to commit every last one of my brilliant ideas to memory there came a tooting from behind us, but no sooner had my driver started to manipulate his own horn than a behelmeted policeman strode up and sternly warned us to desist from any such manifestation of impatience. You would do better, I thought, to apprehend the murderer of Hertha Enzian or admonish the rioters. Had I only possessed, at that moment, a copy of the 'Code Morelli' which I could have pressed into the bewildered fellow's hand!

But to resume. An article of paramount importance—the first or eighth—will annul all rights peculiar to young people. In particular, steps must be taken to ensure that, even when perpetrated by young persons of student status, attacks on life, liberty, and property shall be subject to the same condemnation as other, equally reprehensible crimes; that youthful sex-offenders, if old enough to murder, rape, or merely indulge in obscene behaviour, shall be treated no more leniently than adult offenders; and that discrimination against parents, elders, and the aged shall be as little tolerated as, for example, is discrimination against religious minorities in civilized countries. In the new society to which I aspire, young persons shall once and for all be forbidden—article seven, fifteen, or three—to disport or exhibit themselves in such a way as to infringe the sense of decency and moral standards of the adult majority or arrogate a monopolistic position to the youth-class. The female population shall, by a majority vote, determine the length of skirts, the maximal depth of necklines, and the quality of underwear; deafening music, painting that offends the eye, and dance movements which flout the dictates of decorum shall be subject to the severest penalties. I consider it to be of supreme importance—perhaps this, after all, should constitute article one—that the frequency of sexual intercourse, if intercourse there must be, shall, as regards both general incidence and repetition on individual occasions, be reduced to a level which does not exceed the competitive capacity of men between forty and sixty years of age. In accordance with the higher principles of democracy, young persons shall be permitted to record their cares and complaints—even their demands—in writing, but justice requires that their manifestoes shall not be assessed by the older generation: instead, under article thirty or twenty-two (b), they shall be carefully preserved in the archives so that the young people of today, having once attained full maturity, can themselves pass judgment on the merits of their case.

A glance at my watch was enough to dispel even my superhuman forbearance. My Agnese awaited me, yet I was still seated in my motionless capsule, imprisoned by a canaille whose members disclaim membership thereof because—under our aegis —they are allegedly studying for university degrees. The lady in the small red automobile on my right had lowered her window and was unthinkingly flirting with a policeman, heedless of her imminent consignment to the sexual scrap-heap, while the grey-haired gentleman on my left had resignedly immersed himself in the *Corriere della Sera* behind the wheel of his limousine, never suspecting that some pretty young creature might spit in his face at any moment. I was tempted to inform them both in a stentorian voice that the extraordinary tolerance of the Code Morelli will not extend to traitors, renegades, or the Fifth Column within our own ranks.

Such tolerance would, indeed, be a luxury which no revolutionary movement could afford. Show-trials will be held, and, if necessary, criminal proceedings instituted—I have taken note of the unwitting reader and the lady in the red car—against all weaklings, turncoats, and deserters who establish contact with the foe and lend him succour. Indictment for treason, a term of not less than ten years' imprisonment, lifelong penal servitude, or even the death penalty—*vide* the provisions laid down under Roman "II"—shall be the lot of all persons aged between forty and ninety who, if of the male gender, cast lecherous *œillades* at the physical attributes of females under the age of thirty, or, if of the female gender, glance furtively at the genital zone of males under the age of thirty. Sexual considerations being of very secondary importance to me, however, similar penalties shall be applied to all adult persons who claim to comprehend the aspirations of the young or sanction the same, who call upon the old to surrender or simply abdicate, who are prompted by weariness or hypocrisy to suggest that young people be given 'a chance'—as if they had not always had that chance and squandered it—and who, finally, certify and acknowledge the superiority of the foe by imitation. Also numbered among these traitors shall be all adult persons between the ages of forty and ninety—*vide* my commentary on the law—who subscribe to the taste of the young in matters of art and culture, ape their intellectual, sexual, or modish excesses, and generally sap their contemporaries' will to resist by indulging in mimicry: of such traitors shall it be said that *accusatus esto quod senectutem corrumperet.*

Thus far advanced in my plans, I lost patience—or, more properly, was overcome with shame at having kept patience for so long: reaching for the steering-wheel across my driver's paunch, I pressed the horn-ring with might and main, not because I had lost my nerve—it would have taken something of far graver import to shake my composure—but because I was determined to sound a revolutionary call to arms. Chance alone prevented a car-borne assault on the *Bastille de la jeunesse*: the main road and side-streets emptied of demonstrators, and we were graciously permitted to continue on our way.

I cannot and will not gainsay that my homeward journey to Foce Verde—return, I should have said, not homeward journey —was given over to thoughts of a rather conflicting, dichotomous, and self-contradictory nature. My Agnese is not yet twenty years of age, so she blushingly confided to me, and it may well be that conventional historians will reproach me with inconsistency. Far be it from me to adduce in my defence that inconsistency is one of the inalienable rights of the genius—something without which he would be inhuman and remote from his fellow-men. Similarly, to state that the exception proves the rule would be a commonplace to which a man of my calibre could scarcely have recourse. No, truth to tell, I should greatly have overestimated the pernicious effects of treachery among the representatives of my own generation were I not to welcome treachery in the foe. My Agnese is the most enchanting of traitresses. After all, if there are black sheep among the white flock, why should there not be white sheep among the black?

The millions who will some day read my memoirs may be tempted to discover the smirking mask of the sex-devil behind my relations with Agnese di Doninelli. They have a bitter disappointment in store. Even were a certain erotic excitation to have possessed me during our encounters, I have nonetheless succeeded in preserving the absolute and unblemished purity of my affection. The proof is manifest. After each and every pleasurable weekend spent in her company, having switched out the light and plunged my lonely little room into darkness, I have, on becoming aware of my tumescent manhood and inflamed with sublime love of self, consistently and austerely refrained from conjuring up a picture of Agnese—indeed, valiantly eschewing her lovely image, I have disported myself sometimes with the skilful Madame Pompadour, sometimes with the bosomy waitress who attends me in my wretched *ristorante*, and once, even, with the ever-present sinner Vera Pisenti: never once have I permitted myself even to disrobe the enchanted and enchanting inmate of the mansion beside the sea.

The closer the hired conveyance drew to my place of exile—and a costly journey it was, for the driver refused to accept our delay as *vis major*—the more certain I became of my good fortune, and the more assured of the tender reciprocation of my love. Why should a lovely creature of not yet twenty summers, lovelier than all her sisters, or so it seemed to me, feminine as a high-born damsel of the *Quattrocento*, clever as a learned man, frolicsome as a filly, brave as a lion-cub, and timid as a deer— why, I asked myself, should this young aristocrat with the soft and silky raven locks of the Roman, the vivid blue eyes of the Irish colleen, and the curving lips of a Spanish dancer devote her leisure hours to an old man, roam the cold and barren country-side with him, share his singular sense of compassion, and, finally, invite him into her cloistered home, if it were not that she too wore the badge of love upon her brow? Fleeing from a younger generation to which she belonged in years alone, which offered her no security, and with which she had no desire to fraternize, Agnese had sought refuge with me.

Such were my thoughts. Quite how well-founded they were, I was unable to tell.

I had but a few minutes in which to refresh myself. With pounding heart, I hastened along the uneven path towards the headland. The sea had donned a dark silk mask and dark was the 'green estuary' of the Fosso Mascarello. The taverns on the far side of the little river, where at this hour cannibalistic fisherfolk were devouring their quarry to the accompaniment of red wine and tall stories, were but dimly illuminated. What a singular contrast! Lights were burning in only two of the mansion's windows—I ought by rights to speak of a castle, fortress, stout bulwark, or proud bastion—and I was reminded of an Advent calendar which a traveller from German parts once brought to Montefiascone in my childhood and presented to me: a piece of pasteboard which, I seem to recall, constituted my only Christmas present that year. This calendar depicted a castle complete with towers and battlements, rampart and ditch, and superimposed upon it were twenty-four little windows of which children were permitted to open no more than one each December morning, until, on Christmas Eve, in recompense for their frugal curiosity, all four-and-twenty stood open as if welcoming the Christ-child with arms flung wide. It could hardly have failed to impress me as a favourable omen that my paper castle had been transmuted into stone, that two windows were already open and warmly illuminated, and that the Advent calendar of my childhood had assumed vast proportions as though offering shelter and protection against the loathsomeness of Nature, the menacing rocks, and the cruelty of mankind. I was resolved to be a good child, patient and devout, neither did I intend to open any window before the appointed day.

The darkness of Foce Verde, the brightness of the Advent calendar—contrast enough, but naught compared with the shock that awaited me.

An elderly retainer opened the heavy door, a dignified man, though I could not see him clearly because the hall was lit by a solitary yellow lamp. I was, however, able to descry a lofty vaulted ceiling, a stone table of mythological dimensions, a threadbare tapestry, a few drooping banners of faded hue, and two or three suits of armour complete with helmet, greaves, cuisses, and gauntlets. How splendidly it all matched my picture of a high-born damsel, and how fearful the shock—I use the word advisedly—when I was at the very same instant assailed by the savage strains of jazz music! I say jazz, although a far more loathsome expression would be in order: the thing which impinged upon my ears was in fact—I can scarcely bring myself to write the word—'beat' music, that brutish din beloved of a rabble afflicted with St Vitus's dance, that sonorous invitation and musical accompaniment to the orgy, that melody- and music-spurning declaration of war upon the beautiful, that hysterical march-rhythm of anarchic sensuality and sensual anarchy. A nightmare, I told myself, a delusion or trick of acoustics, for what else could it have been, this cacophony which issued from the protective walls of the past, cascaded down stone stairways, reverberated among banners and suits of armour, and tore at precious tapestry?

No delusion! The servant preceded me along interminable passages and up flights of steps, but so far from fading, dispersing, or relapsing into silence, the piping, gurgling, groaning, and croaking hobgoblins of the future—eerier by far than the spirits of the dead—simply became more audible still: my horrified ear now identified the sick bellowing of one of those bands of long-haired Tarzans which have escaped from the jungle and invaded civilization, namely, the Beatles—yes, I admit that I know their name, recognize their voices, if voices be the word, and can distinguish their *yeah-yeahs* from other jungle noises, because, first, the dining-room of my hostelry boasts a 'juke-box', to give that instrument of musical torture its correct designation, and, secondly, the epidemic has become so widespread that performers of this type are as recognizable as the lepers of the medieval streets. As I followed the retainer through a number of handsome but somewhat neglected rooms the menacing noise grew in volume, drew nearer, embraced and engulfed me, and then, as the old man paused with his hand on the door-knob and announced with a certain gratifying formality: "The Signorina is expecting you, Dottore", abruptly ceased.

Although I was truly inclined to believe that my senses had played me a diabolical trick, it was borne in on me that, on a small table in the *petit salon* or boudoir of my high-born damsel, there reposed a record-player, gramophone, or personal 'juke-box'; that the sonorous Pandora's Box was still warm and had only been silenced at the last moment. As if that were not enough, I could not fail to be horrified by the attire of my fairy-tale fisher-girl, who came to meet me with hands out-stretched: in place of the billowing gown or elegant costume of my expectations, Agnese had donned a pair of garishly coloured close-fitting trousers which not only outlined the discreet curve of her hips and well-rounded plumpness of her young thighs but emphasized the mysterious mound which secretes itself between the legs in the form of a chaste triangle and rightly derives its name from the foam-born goddess Venus. In addition, she wore a blouse of reassuringly opaque material; not high-necked, however, but open between her dainty little breasts in the form of the obscene letter "V"; not provocative—not that, in God's name—yet betraying the inchoation of two small marmoreal spheres. Her throat was bare, and of the palest pink.

The natural and unconstrained manner of Agnese's greeting soothed my troubled senses but failed to allay my suspicions entirely. Her parents, she told me, had changed their plans at the eleventh hour and would not arrive until next morning, but she, reluctant to disappoint me and doubting her ability to warn me in time, had hurried on ahead to meet me as arranged. That, I could not but fear, was a half-truth, falsehood, or lie, for she was not to know that I had spent the day in Rome, and I could always have been reached at my hotel. I had scarcely recovered a modicum of composure when Agnese, in addition to plying me with some little tidbits, invited me with all the aplomb in the world to choose from a selection of alcoholic beverages which stood, shoulder to shoulder with glasses of every size, on a small circular table. Although saddened by the spectacle of these poison-bottles, I could not, being genuinely in need of medicinal invigoration, resist the lure of a glass of grappa.

I do not know how I should have disguised my bewilderment,

my horror—in short, the shock which I had just undergone—
had not Agnese miraculously and before my very eyes become
transformed or, more precisely, for the expression is inapt, re-
transformed into her original self.

The real reason why she had been so unwilling to postpone
our rendezvous was, she told me, this—and in a trice, miming
great effort and exertion with a series of delightfully grotesque
gestures reminiscent of that diverting mummer Charlie Chaplin,
she came over to me with seven books which had been lying on
the chimney-piece: the collected œuvre of Aurelio Morelli. How
could I have overlooked them, when the eye of the author—be he
ever so devoid of vanity, as I am—finds itself constantly and
magically attracted by his own works? She ordained that each
and every one of my books should be adorned with my handwriting and dedicated to her personally; it had cost her no small
pains to "track them down" or procure them, some from book-
sellers and antiquarians and one even from a well-intentioned
friend, but she now wished, having hitherto read only *Thou art
Alcibiades* and *The One-way Street*, to apply herself diligently to
the study of every work by her "favourite author". A pen was
quickly brought, and while I was endeavouring to inscribe the
fly-leaves with something cordial but not intimate, dignified yet
not banal, witty yet not frivolously ingenious, Agnese alarmed
me once again, this time by promising to reward my "hard
work" with a "present". I was all the more alarmed by her
promise because she had been standing behind me the whole
time, leaning over my shoulder so that her hot breath played
about my uncommonly sensitive neck. How touching it was that,
with the impatience of those who prefer to give rather than
receive, she could not wait for me to complete my "hard work";
that even before I could dedicate my *chef d'œuvre* to her she had
thrust her present over my shoulder—a bulky and extremely pre-
possessing volume magnificently printed on glossy paper and
entitled *Denizens of the Deep*: a profusely illustrated dictionary
of marine fish. Deeply disconcerted, I brushed her hands with
my lips, hands whose tomboyish yet dainty conformation had
impressed me during the burial of the luckless fish; and this,
together with my joy at receiving such a thoughtful and lovingly
chosen gift, probably the first that I had received since childhood,
put me in mind—oh, folly beyond measure!—of the words of

Romeo; in my old-fashioned but crystalline calligraphy, I inscribed *Alcibiades* with the lines:

> If I profane with my unworthiest hand
> This holy shrine, the gentle fine is this;
> My lips, two blushing pilgrims, ready stand
> To smooth that rough touch with a tender kiss.

Was she not bound to suppose that I was courting her thus, through the medium of Romeo, or was I courting her in actuality? Had I not hastened to her side, half in dread, half burning with expectancy, was not my heart abrim with new and undreamed-of sensations, and would I have fallen in love if she had not yearned for love in return? What was it, then, at the very instant when she rewarded me for my completed work and Romeo's ardent protestation by imprinting two swift but, so it seemed to me, far from childish kisses, one on either cheek—what was it that caused the cold sweat to break out on my brow? The December wind was rattling the narrow casements, which almost resembled arrow-slits, the mist had enshrouded the mansion's rugged walls, and the embers in the damp fireplace brought but scant warmth into the alien room. Long passages and darkened chambers separated us from the taciturn domestics, but that was the salient point: were Agnese as artless as I had imagined, how could she venture to remain alone with a stranger, honourable though his name might be; why had she received him in such coquettish attire; how came it that this ethereal being had taken pleasure in the ululating battle-cries of youth, incriminating evidence of which perfidy lay strewn about, brazenly unsheathed, in the shape of records by musical assassins and vandals? These and other questions plunged me headlong into a whirling maelstrom of doubt.

The night drew on, and still the clouds of doubt refused to lift. One topic of conversation reassured me, another alarmed me. With touching naïveté, Agnese inquired the source of my creative inspiration, whether I worked by day like Carducci or by night like Balzac, whether I used pen, pencil, or typewriter, what auspicious star had led me to Foce Verde, and what work I planned to accomplish there. Nevertheless, all this was said as she lay at my feet, embraced my legs, rested her head upon my knee. Why this physical proximity, this seductive warmth, this gentle provocation? Was it chance? It might have been no more than that, no more than a symptom of guileless innocence, for when she gazed up at me her resemblance to one of the white monumental figures surrounding the statue of some immortal artist was such that all thought of Vera Pisenti, Lucia Chiesa, and Hertha Enzian—I had thought of them, I must admit, as I laid my hand on her dark hair and my fingers inadvertently brushed her neck—all thought of that sinful trio immediately fled my mind. Conversation having turned to her studies, she spoke with some enthusiasm of her extensive preoccupation with the Greek tongue, but, when I tried to learn more about her life, displayed an extreme reticence, almost as if her life in Foce Verde were totally divorced from her life in Rome. Furthermore, when she mentioned that she would like to show me round the mansion at some sunnier hour, she expressed herself on the subject of her father's 'hobby' with a certain rebellious cynicism. Speedily reassured by her interest in my aquarium, of which I had told her, I was just as speedily startled when she expressed a wish to pay my aquatic friends a visit at the next favourable opportunity. She reinforced her strange request to visit me in my poor and provisional accommodation by stating that she would like to inspect a great author's place of work in person. As for my hurried objection that a visit by a young lady might infringe the rules of my hotel, and would certainly attract unwelcome attention, this she dismissed with the horrific remark that morals were "pretty lax" hereabouts—adding, nevertheless, that nobody would take exception to her visit because everyone in Foce Verde had known her since childhood. When I lightheartedly inquired if she were not afraid of me, her only response was a smile which, though doubtless innocent, haunted me throughout that night.

The last log had dwindled to ashes in the fireplace. After two hours alone in my beloved's company, I was aware how much she had learned about me and how little I knew of her. Not until she was conducting me downstairs through the slumbering house, switching on one dim light after the other, did I venture to ask whether I had not bored her or wasted her time, and what had inspired her to devote an evening to me. Down in the hall, beside the door, in the shadow of some knightly armour, she stood on tiptoe, and, in lieu of reply, kissed me swiftly on the mouth.

I crossed the bridge but left the road and continued by way of the beach. My feet sank into the sand, I stumbled over bushes, the wind drowned the waves and the waves the wind. If someone had loomed up beside me at that moment I should have confessed that Aurelio Morelli was a murderer, not because conscience admonished me so to do—my conscience is clear, and no one my judge—but because it seemed to me that my only salvation lay in prison, whose walls not only bar escape but deprive their inmates of knowledge. I, the omniscient, dreaded naught so much as knowledge.

Italo Canonica

Friday, 1st December. Contact with Christa Sonntag has paid off. How much does Bossi know? He's certainly on the same track. Roberto Pisenti informed me of a visit by a reporter from *Quest' Ora.* When I was told of a second visit I surprised Bossi in Lubriano. He couldn't conceal his embarrassment. I invited him to join me at the local inn for a glass of *Est est est*—the wine comes from the neighbouring township of Montefiascone and has a curious history. He followed me reluctantly. "Listen, Bossi," I said, "you're playing with fire. What do you know of the connection between the Pisenti and Enzian cases?" He smirked. "Nothing. I'm doing a series on unsolved crimes. There are plenty of them." "You're writing the *Enzian Story*," I said. "I'm even writing an Enzian film," he retorted. I didn't want to give Christa Sonntag away, but was forced to mention something I had heard from her. I trust that she isn't Bossi's only confidant. "Bossi," I said, "suppose *Quest' Ora* were to publish the memoirs of Enzian's murderer. I'm sure I could prevail on the Director of Public Prosecutions to issue a warrant for your arrest the moment they appeared." "Where did you get that half-baked idea from?" he demanded. "Are you writing the *Enzian Story* on your own?" I asked. He praised the wine, playing for time. "You always need collaborators on this kind of story," he said. "The research is too complicated—I don't need to tell you that." I produced my trump card. "I thought you might have secured the services of an author," I said. He wouldn't look me in the eye, as usual. "You'll only make a fool of yourself if you go bothering the Director of

Public Prosecutions," he said. "Editorial secrets are privileged. Besides, who says I've got a secret at all? You're conducting your investigations and I'm conducting mine. To be absolutely frank —yes, I'm satisfied that the Enzian and Pisenti murderers are one and the same person. You have the whole machinery of the law at your disposal, but instead of interrogating the murderer you grill me." "I'm not grilling you," I said. "I'm simply trying to make your position clear to you. If the murderer remains at large because you're withholding information, that's an offence. The Pisenti girl's father went to the police, which gives us an excellent reason for reviewing the Pisenti case. What inspired you to take an interest in the story?" He chuckled. "I'm a romantic soul," he said. "While I was doing research into unsolved cases I discovered that both these charming ladies were murdered on August 8th." We went our separate ways. On the one hand, Bossi has been alerted and will sever all contact with the murderer—if he knows him. On the other, the murderer is probably tucked away in Spain, and I couldn't have put Bossi under surveillance anyway. It's forbidden, and I can't afford any Press campaigns. At least Bossi realizes that I'll hit back immediately if he springs a 'surprise' on me. I can't imagine that he'd take such a gamble. I think he'll come forward before long.

. . . Inquiries in Lubriano have come to a full stop. They only corroborate Primavesi's 1965 findings. No one fitting the description of the Via Sicilia murderer was seen near the farm that night. Primavesi is combing the less immediate vicinity. I have a feeling that we shall learn more from Signora Chiesa—now Signora Manghera. She is scheduled to arrive in Paris from America at the end of next week. I shall probably fly to Paris myself.

. . . The wine I drank with Bossi has an amusing history. The tombstone of Bishop Johann Fugger of Augsburg, who was buried in Montefiascone, bears the strange inscription: *Est est est propter nimium et hic Joannes de Fugger dominus meus mortuus est.* This epitaph is said to have been composed by the bishop's manservant, whose practice it was to hurry on ahead of his high-living, wine-bibbing master and discover which hostelries had the best wine. He marked the door of any inn which served a decent drop of wine with the little word *est.* The faithful retainer was so struck by the excellence of Montefiascone's muscatelle that he chalked three *ests* on the inn door—a forerunner of the three little stars in the *Guide Michelin*. The bishop evidently shared his servant's opinion, because he drank so much Montefiascone that he dropped dead. I must get myself a few bottles of the historic beverage some time. I shall consume it in moderation.

Saturday, 2nd December. The first Saturday of the month. My friend Silvano Guerra and I always indulge in the same little game: we eat 'three' midday meals, and it isn't particularly hard on the pocket or the digestion. Having regaled ourselves with some pasta at one of the restaurants which serve unusually good spaghetti, we drive contentedly to a second restaurant which is noted, say, for its *Lombatine di vitello al cartoccio*, and, finally, our digestions functioning superbly, move on to third, where we consume a sweet—I like *Castagna al Marsala*, Silvano prefers *Budino di recotta*—and round off the meal with a capuccino. One really ought to take all one's meals out and eat them in three phases, because I can hardly think of a single restaurant which shines in the preparation of every course.

. . . Silvano and I always resolve not to talk shop, but inevitably succumb to *déformation professionnelle*. This time we reverted to the rising crime rate. Silvano attributes it to the decline of authority. He says the world resembles a room whose walls are covered with empty picture-frames. In the old days one frame was filled with a picture of God, others with pictures of heathen idols, princes, heroes, poets—even millionaires. All were father-figures, paragons, models of authority. In the long run any room occupied by empty frames becomes intolerable. Man itches to get rid of the irritating gaps in his décor, so he either fills the frames with new pictures or burns them. Silvano—he is only fifty, and more conservative than I am—does not believe that the conflict between generations stems from the older generation's wish to restore old pictures to their former place—only the young allege that. The old want to fill old frames with new pictures, whereas the young want to destroy the frames themselves. The iconoclasts have been succeeded by the 'frameoclasts'. That is how Silvano accounts for the spread of violence, also for the similarity between developments in East and West. Neither of the two systems which still dominate our world can find a suitable picture of authority, so both rooms are dotted with empty frames. Enthusiasm is reserved for pictures, not empty frames. A tempting analogy, I tell Silvano, but what created the void, and how can it be filled? We debate the causes. I submit that the root cause is not human misery but, paradoxically, the imminence of human prosperity. Nothing is new, neither the conflict between rich and poor, nor the cleavage between races, religions, and nations, nor oppression, nor the craving for freedom. On the other hand, technical, scientific, social, and economic progress (?) has brought the world so close to universal prosperity that all are snatching at it as though Utopia lay but a short distance away—almost within arm's reach. Thanks to the technical perfection of the mass media, misery and prosperity have been brought nearer—brought into the home, as it were. Slums and millionaires' villas, wartime atrocities and shell-shocked heroes, popular rejoicing and individual sorrow, mourning mothers and the agonies of the dying—proximity magnifies everything, the sense of common experience included: all men experience everything simultaneously, mass envy as well as mass compassion. And happiness? Happiness above all, I reply. Everything is on the doorstep, including freedom from war and coercion and misery. In the space age no one believes or is capable of believing in the insoluble. But because he soars into space with his everyday problems unsolved, man is becoming impatient. People like to call our age by a hundred different names: I would christen it the age of impatience. Open the papers, turn on the radio, watch television, and you constantly meet the word "Now!" Now, not a moment later, is the time to buy a car, drink coffee, put a wig on, annoint your armpits with a deodorant—now, not a moment later, must black and white become brothers, must the rich be humbled and poor 'participate', must the primitive become educated, the educated humane, the warlike peaceable, the peaceable victorious, adults tolerant, children adult, and all of us unadulteratedly angelic. Anyone who fails to grasp this necessity stands between mankind and its ultimate happiness, and is duly eliminated. Silvano sees the causes differently—more soberly, perhaps. The ignominious end of at least some of the dictators of the first half of this century has left the world in a traumatic state. Because people worshipped a false father-figure for decades, all fathers have fallen into disrepute. Totalitarian restraint is being replaced by totalitarian freedom, which is not only a paradox but a synonym for anarchy. Silvano finds it wrily amusing when the defence counsel who oppose him in court excuse their clients by pleading their 'social instability'. "Sometimes," Silvano says, "I'm tempted to say: 'My children are victims of social instability too—who isn't?'" What's to be done? Political and social revolution is no answer at all, Silvano thinks, because it's a contradiction in terms—a revolution within a revolution. At such an advanced stage of evolution, revolution becomes counter-revolutionary: it interrupts and retards—indeed, obstructs—a process which is already revolutionary. When revolutionaries speak of revolution they are quite as guilty of using obsolete terminology as any reactionary. A nostalgic desire to travel by stage-coach is no less outmoded than an attempted repetition of the storming of the Bastille. Silvano says that in reality the yearning for a father-figure is greater than ever, because man has no idea what to do with the products of his god-like creativity. This yearning for a father-figure resembles the feelings entertained by children of divorced parents, who only hate their absent father because they need him so desperately. Freud would have chuckled at the sight of modern man deserting him in favour of Marx, because that was precisely what he predicted: the sicker the patient, the greater his aversion to the psychoanalyst; the more he has to hide, the more unnecessary he deems its exploration to be. Man is afraid of being detected in his secret yearning for the lost picture of his father—consequently he sets fire to the empty frame. Yet he cannot root the father-figure out of his heart. Silvano, who likes to temper gravity with flippancy, says, "A lot of Marx's success stemmed from his resemblance to the Almighty. Freud ought to have grown a longer beard." In a more serious vein, he goes on to say that Freud analyses whereas Marx demonstrates. Freud summons man to self-examination, Marx to the examination of others. Prickly science and cosy philosophy could amplify one another, but we haven't reached that stage yet. Freud asks why a father-figure comes into existence, Marx delivers it to the door, ready-made. The one analytically calls the individual to account, the other absolves him of responsibility by demonstration. Silvano says that where the young people of the West are concerned—amazing how often they crop up in the course of conversation—it is unfair to reproach them with inconsistency if they demonstrate in the name of freedom on behalf of an ideology which has abolished the most elementary freedoms; unfair to accuse them of lying if they hoist red flags and simultaneously declare that they reject the political persuasions of the East; and, finally, unfair to ask what more young people who have 'everything' can possibly want. Orphans living in the lap of luxury are still orphans. Mao is a father-figure and Ho Chi Minh actually wears a long white beard. The Red Flag is nothing more than a symbol of authority. A fatherless child makes do with a step-father.

Sunday, 3rd December. After lunch, went to the Giardino Zoologico with all the grandchildren. On Sundays the caged monkeys probably think they're being shown a human zoo. It was a sunny day, and a few birds seemed to have mistaken December for spring. Erico, nine years old, said something which I can't resist jotting down. He said birds ought to be forbidden to fly over the Giardino Zoologico. When I looked surprised, and asked why, he replied that the poor animals in cages or behind bars must feel very sad to see other creatures flying around free. Like us, the birds were only visitors to the zoo. He also thought it was unfair to hunt and imprison animals just for the sake of their beauty. We become less humane as we grow older. I took the opportunity of visiting the spot where Lucia Chiesa was murdered. *Déformation professionnelle!*

... Came across the following in a Russian cookery-book full of amusing anecdotes. It came to the ears of Peter the Great that, according to current rumour, he was so crazy that he ate a minimum of one tallow candle per meal. The monarch invited his courtiers to a banquet at which thick candles were served for dessert. Etiquette demanded that the courtiers emulate their Tsar, who devoured every last morsel of his tallow candle with apparent relish. The delicacy agreed with nobody but the Tsar. He had got his confectioner to make him a perfect replica in marzipan.

Tuesday, 5th December. Great excitement at headquarters yesterday. Three members of the public, two women and a man, claim to have seen a passer-by fitting the description (?) of Hertha Enzian's murderer in Rome. Although I distrust 'informants' of this type, their triplicity is striking because no similar report has come in for over three weeks. The suspect swiftly vanished (?) into the crowd in all three cases. Ordered a comparative analysis of the witnesses' statements and called for increased vigilance by every precinct in the capital.

... Christa Sonntag, who obviously heard it from Bossi, reports that the proprietor of *Quest' Ora* is in hospital with a coronary and that his twenty-three-year-old (!) son Francesco has taken over the magazine. This has apparently caused great dissatisfaction among the editorial staff. Alfieri tells me that Francesco Vanetti is a known Communist and has taken part in almost all the recent demonstrations.

... Interpol reports that Lucia Chiesa's mother has left the United States with her husband and flown on to Rio de Janeiro.

... Invited Primavesi to a meal. My first attempt at a Hungarian recipe for chicken paprika. The birds should be young, but as plump as possible. After cleaning and washing, cut into eight or ten sections, wash once more, and place in a cloth to dry. Render down five or six ounces of smoked fat bacon. As soon as the fat is boiling, drop in some finely-chopped onion and sprinkle with a tablespoonful of sweet paprika. As soon as the fat begins to boil again and the onion is nicely browned, add the pieces of chicken, salt them, and fry for a minute or two, stirring carefully. Add a spoonful of stock, cover the saucepan well, and wait until the meat is tender. The individual pieces must be turned several times, of course. When they are nearly ready, add the prepared chicken livers and allow to cook for between fifteen and thirty minutes. Although I didn't have all the right ingredients, the result wasn't bad, at least for a first attempt.

Wednesday, 6th December. Went home early. Skimmed through diary. Re-read entries for 18th and 21st November. Breaded cucumber and philosophy. What was I really driving at? Probably just the truism that life goes on. It always has, obviously—people have philosophized and gorged themselves at the same time. The only new feature is that we all have a bad conscience—the average (?) citizen because he doesn't understand the intellectual, and the intellectual (?) because he is fundamentally uninterested in what constitutes daily life, even his own. The mass media, of which the most influential are in the hands of the intellectuals, have brought intellectuals and non-intellectuals so close together that they can plainly see how far apart they are. It can't be differences in education—these have grown smaller. The intellectual feels himself to be the man of the future and thus brands the non-intellectual as the man of the past. The deserted present—see above. I'm thinking of myself, of course. I don't exactly regard myself as uneducated, and in the old days I would have passed for an intellectual. However, now that the intellectuals form a new aristocracy—legitimized by the future instead of the past—I am as little part of them as I should have been of the landed aristocracy of a century ago. Lucky I'm not writing for publication, or I should now have to explain why I'm not an intellectual and what I understand by the term. I could only produce very indirect and random evidence. For instance, I don't 'belong' because I don't think sunsets are 'pretty-pretty'. I read Descartes, but I don't think sunsets are pretty-pretty. I mix with all kinds of people I can't conduct discussions with. Their lives interest me even though we can't 'converse'. The death of a passer-by in the street affects me more than the work of Heidegger, even if I have studied Vom Wesen der Wahrheit. I treasure experience even when it isn't speculative. I'm not a good Catholic, but I don't dismiss every churchgoer as a fool. I don't pray to a personal God, but I don't know for certain if He isn't up there, enthroned on a white cloud. There may be clouds we can't see. I don't know anything for certain—perhaps that's it. I know a bit, but nothing for certain, whereas intellectuals know a great deal, and all of it for certain. I raise my hat politely when I encounter intellect, but I'm on Christian-name terms with life. I don't appreciate modern music, or modern painting, or modern literary style. Because I concede that the fault may be mine, I'm not an intellectual. I don't close my mind to anything, but I feel excluded. I can't imagine it has anything to do with my intelligence, because I'm certainly a touch more intelligent than the average. If the intellectuals don't address themselves to me, to whom do they address themselves? Probably intellectuals are intelligent people whom intelligent people don't understand unless they're intellectuals themselves—I can't put it any better than that. All the same, I'm afraid that what is really involved is a subconscious (?) attempt by intellectuals to form a new caste which, though sprung from the intelligentsia, seeks to rise above it. Quite an understandable ambition, by the way. Mankind being unfitted for equality, its desire for exclusivity may well have been rekindled by the process of social decolorization. Throughout history the classes which fought most bitterly

have always been those who were socially underprivileged—
proletariat and *petit bourgeoisie,* for instance. There are relatively
few illiterates left in our civilization. The intelligentsia is no
longer exclusive. Could it be that intellectuals are possessed by
an arrogant desire to brand the non-intellectual intelligentsia as
illiterates? Why else do they blow up the bridges of communication and mine the paths of understanding? I speak of myself,
though the question isn't of great importance to me personally.
I am simply trying to apportion blame for the loss of the
present. Is the new aristocracy at fault? A claim to absolute
power—like that of the aristocracy, capitalism, or the proletariat?
The new aristocrats are always talking about the future, but the
picture they paint is that of a future for intellectuals. Everything
that was human in the French Revolution has survived the test
of time, whereas the *Être suprême* of Robespierre, the Incorrup-
tible, perished in a counter-revolutionary bloodbath. Robespierre,
another who thought he knew everything about the future,
knew nothing about human beings, human suffering, human
joy, envy, love, impulses, jealousy, and mortality. I am less
afraid of intellectual supremacy than of a revolt by the present
against the intellectual future. What forces will the 'supreme
being' unleash? Robespierre had already been mortally wounded
by the time he was guillotined.

Thursday, 7th December. Signora Chiesa, now Manghera,
could not be traced in Rio de Janeiro, but we have ascertained
that she will be booking in at the Hôtel Raffael in Paris at the
end of next week. I have contacted our friends in the Sûreté.

CHAPTER

4

The Alibi

Emilio Bossi

Francesco's installed in his father's chair. "Temporarily", but I wouldn't like to bet on it. I've half a mind to tell him to stew in his own juice. If the old man isn't back soon I'm quitting.

Vanetti I can work with. What if he was a Fascist in his salad-days? At least that gives me an edge on him. I was seven when the Mussolini bubble burst. Vanetti doesn't have much of a conscience and the little he does have is bad. What kind of Fascist was Vanetti, anyway? Opportunism is a party too, and I get on with opportunists. Opportunists keep the radio turned up all day long so they never miss a weather forecast. Like me, except that I don't have time to listen to the radio—I make my own forecasts. You have to know what tomorrow's weather is going to be like, at least roughly. There are days when an opportunist wouldn't dream of leaving the house without a raincoat, even when the sun's shining. I can identify my fellow-raincoat-wearers. People with convictions aren't identifiable. Sometimes they wear a raincoat in the rain, sometimes they wear an astrakhan collar when it's ninety in the shade. They change their convictions just as often as we of the opportunist fraternity change our opinions. Their motives are obscure, though. You can't rely on them.

Apart from anything else, I prefer working with older people. They're embarrassed about being old—the next best thing to having a bad conscience. They do their best to understand the young in case people think they're old. Vanetti feels slightly embarrassed with me, and I feel almost embarrassed with Francesco, although I know all about his non-existent past. It's ridiculous.

243

Vanetti's coronary happened at the worst possible moment. To think I have to put my faith in Francesco, of all people! Yesterday the bath-tub, today the boss's chair. Where will it end?

In the outer office, Elena, Vanetti's secretary, said, "Signor Francesco is in conference."

That's something else I have in common with Vanetti. We've both slept with Elena. She looks like a school-marm on vacation, pretty but prim. She isn't so prim in bed. She performs like a trapeze-artist. The neighbours swarm like bees when she gets passionate. I can't remember who slept with her first, Vanetti or me. Anyway, she's been going around swathed in black since his coronary. Discreet symbol of a nation in mourning.

"Who are you kidding?" I said. "The Crown Prince's conferences don't apply to me."

Francesco was sitting at the circular coffee-table with Ferrari, the publisher. Just like his father, who always condescends to join his more important visitors at the coffee-table.

"You know Signor Ferrari, of course," said Francesco.

I didn't have that pleasure. His name is the only thing I respect about him—must be the fast-car aura, I suppose. This Ferrari publishes books and we print them. Looks like a herring with a moustache. Reputed to have the finest collection of Gothic Madonnas in Italy, two or three palazzi, and the odd Rolls. Makes his money by publishing the whole of the avant-garde. Flies to South America to take part in demonstrations. In his private jet, probably.

"Emilio Bossi is our ace reporter," said Francesco. A pat on the back from Francesco was all I needed.

"I have to speak to you right away," I cut in, deliberately ignoring Ferrari and his print order.

After he'd gone Francesco offered me a drink. He opened up the neon-lit bar and handed me a Scotch on the rocks. Then he joined me at the coffee-table with his Coca-Cola. At least he didn't sit in the old man's chair.

"Things are hotting up," I said, and told him about Canonica. "I can't pay any more visits to Foce Verde," I said. "The gnome is having me watched, you can bet on that."

"What were you doing in Lubriano?" asked Francesco.

I slapped a copy of the manuscript in front of him. "Morelli has disposed of three girls," I said. Then I gave him a verbal synopsis of the MS. I'm an expert at synopses. I don't know if publishers can read. You always have to sing them your stories with guitar accompaniment. I feel like a troubadour sometimes.

"Does my father know all this?" asked Francesco.

"I didn't know myself till I read the manuscript," I said.

"A nice mess," said Francesco.

We observed a minute's silence.

"Well," asked the budding genius, "what are we going to do?"

A fair question. A little funny, though, coming from Francesco. After all, he'd wanted to shop Morelli for the sake of one measly little murder. Fools come in two categories. One sort park their bare bottoms on red-hot stoves. The others are sane.

Francesco was beginning to amuse me. I said discreetly, "I could 'phone Morelli and tell him to send the balance by post."

"Wouldn't that be too risky?" asked Francesco.

I, patronizingly: "Most spies get caught because they hide their reports in tubes of toothpaste and hand them to black-masked men under railway carriages in deserted sidings at dead of night. If they sent them by post they'd still be at liberty. There's nothing the matter with the post. Of course I need the last instalment. I could send him the money in a fiendishly clever way. By postal order." I knew it was a crazy idea, but I wanted to see if my new boss would come up with one of his own.

"They'd be able to prove we sent him the money," said Francesco. A prodigy, that boy. No red-hot stove for him.

"We've bought the memoirs of Aurelio Morelli, novelist, and we're not disputing it," I said. "That isn't the problem."

"What is?" asked Francesco.

"If I don't send Morelli his last instalment, we won't get ours," I said. "He's even more hooked on money than he is on girls. If I do send him the money he'll decamp."

Francesco looked so thin there was nothing left of him except nose and beard. I almost gave in, but my heart of gold refused to melt. It worries me when a saint discards his halo like an old hat.

"We must stop him escaping at all costs," he said.

"Who are you telling?" I said. "If he gets away no one'll believe in our lily-white intentions. We'll be in the soup, like a couple of drowned flies. We must turn him over to the police at least twenty-four hours before publication. For the sake of the publicity, among other things."

I hope Francesco grasped that, but I'm doubtful, even if he is a prodigy. A sensation has to mature. Earthquakes pay bigger dividends on the second day than the first. To have the murderer and start with his memoirs would be too much of a good thing. First, the dailies must report that Quest' Ora has brought Hertha Enzian's murderer to justice. Then the memoirs. Free publicity is the best kind.

Francesco walked up and down with one hand on his chest. Like Napoleon on Elba. Let's hope it doesn't turn out to be St Helena.

"I can't ask my father," he said.

"What won't occur to us won't occur to him either," I said.

"We must put a guard on him," he said, helplessly.

"We can't initiate anyone else," I said.

"Then we must turn him in!" said the late Che Guevara. That was the extent of his originality.

"Sacrifice the Enzian killing and we throw money down the drain," I said. "The Enzian murder is our banker."

He brooded. "Our solitaire, you mean."

Something had rubbed off on him after all. Vanetti's diamond-ring theory: a big solitaire in the middle of a ring makes the less valuable stones round it shine too. You can sell a load of dross as long as there's a big story to go with it. Take away the solitaire and everyone notices. The dumb peasant-girl and the dim school-girl won't shine unless there's a call-girl in the middle. Hertha Enzian is our solitaire.

"Can't you think of something?" asked Francesco.

He was already visualizing himself in striped pyjamas with a tin plate in his hand. Revolutionaries can contemplate martyr-dom but they're scared stiff of gaol.

I'd thought of a solution long ago, of course. I poured myself another Scotch and said, "Does Beatrice know anything about this?"

"Why do you ask?" he said suspiciously.

"Because it's a family matter," I said. "If I can count myself as one of the family."

Francesco nodded. "I told her."

"Bravo!" I said. "I'll call Morelli and notify him that Signorina Vanetti will be bringing the money in exchange for the completed manuscript. Cash on delivery. As soon as she has Enzian tucked away in her bag she calls me—even before she leaves Foce Verde. Ten minutes later I'm with Canonica."

"I've had an idea," said Francesco.

"Like what?" I said, all agog.

"I'm told it's Canonica's last case," he said. "Couldn't we offer to buy his memoirs?"

"Not all policemen take bribes," I said.

"The Beatrice idea is out," he said. "It's bad enough me being mixed up in this mess without dragging her into it."

I acted as if I'd been born yesterday: "I don't have to mention her name," I said. "I'll simply tell Morelli: 'A young woman wearing a carnation will bring you the money.' What's a bit of Simenon between friends?"

He shook his head. "I can't discuss it with Beatrice," he said.

A pity. He probably gave his sister the full treatment—moral indignation, plutocratic contamination, social decadence, and so on. *Nations, obey the call. Up, guards, and at 'em*, my likely lad. I was tempted to leave him floating in the soup. Unfortunately, that would have made two of us.

"Suit yourself," I said. "I'll speak to her."

"She's getting married in January," he said, rather inconsequently.

"Congratulations," I said.

He kept up the hear-no-evil act for a while longer. Hypocrites ought to be put in withdrawal centres, like morphine addicts. It's inhuman to cut off their hypocrisy from one day to the next. In the end he surrendered, chanting the *Marseillaise* like the French at Dien Bien Phu.

I made a date with Elena for that evening. The discreet symbol of national mourning needs consolation, and my sexual exchequer is as broke as the Bank of England. I've been spending too much time on Morelli's sex-life. Work and love are like oil and water.

Then I called Beatrice and asked her to meet me at the office, urgently. I didn't want to drive out to Vanetti's and we couldn't speak in a public place.

I don't know if I ought to envy her ski-instructor, but Beatrice makes my antennae vibrate. She's twenty-five or six, to the best of my knowledge. Looks twenty-two and will look like forty when she's thirty. Eyes like a double bed with the covers off. Her father's intelligence, but you don't find that out until you clear away the educational garbage. Two kinds of women intimidate me. The athletes shake you well before use, the blue-stockings read the *Kama Sutra* over your shoulder. Not my style at all.

I knew she was fond of Vanetti—someone had to be—so I played a trill on the *vox humana*. Vanetti wouldn't survive a scandal, I said. I even defended Francesco. After all, the thing did drop into his lap. Revolutions are more in his line.

"Morelli's insane, of course," I said. "Not so you'd notice, but he is."

"I'd notice," she said.

"Anyway," I said, "wear a fur and keep your collar buttoned up." I eyed her legs. Her legs are magnetic.

"Leave it to me," she said.

"The forensic psychiatrists will have a ball with Morelli," I said. "Pity we can't have him examined in advance. I'll have to rewrite the original manuscript from A to Z, but as soon as it's ready I'll submit it to a couple of experts. One expert covers a multitude of sins. We can make an extra instalment out of the psychiatrists' reports." I felt like Vanetti. "He's an extremely complex character," I said. "Don't be misled by his high I.Q. He haggles like a horse-coper."

"Don't worry," she said.

Forewarned is forearmed. "The *dottore* has started his story at the year dot, and I'm sure it's deliberate. He knows we have to kick off with the Enzian killing. He's taking everything in chronological order so we can't turn him in before he's extracted the last centesimo. Once Enzian's been delivered we'll have a couple of hours at most."

"The man intrigues me," said Beatrice.

"All the better," I said, feeling relieved. "The main thing is to have a quick glance through the manuscript before you buy."

"I don't do anything in a hurry," she said, crossing her magnetic legs.

If Vanetti finds out I've sent Beatrice to Foce Verde he'll have another coronary. An infatuated man thinks everyone lusts after his woman. A doting father thinks everyone wants to kill his daughter. Vanetti's daughter the fourth victim... What a frightful thought! Crime doesn't pay? Not even the readers of *Quest' Ora* will buy that. Moral endings went out with the horse-drawn tram.

"Don't go up to his room whatever you do," I said. "The dining-room is usually empty."

"You must think I'm an idiot," she said. "Did you ever hear of a sex-maniac murdering an intelligent woman?"

She had a point. I said, "The manuscript must contain the *Enzian Story* complete. Morelli's quite capable of palming off a chunk of the *Divina Commedia*."

"Not on me." Beatrice gave a full-blooded smile. "I studied psychology, in case you didn't know."

"I did," I lied politely.

"I could write a report on him myself," she said.

"Great," I said. Psychologist-cum-ski-instructor's-girl-friend—I liked that. However, all that concerned me was whether she was prepared to drive to Foce Verde.

After she'd gone, confident of her ability to cut the murderer down to size, I sat down at my typewriter and set to work on the manuscript.

A hell of a job. I'll have to leave Hertha Enzian out and start on the fifth or sixth instalment. The reader mustn't notice that we've put the cart before the horse. I'll only have one or two days at most for the first instalment, and I wanted to go to Cortina before Christmas, for the skiing.

The diatribes against modern youth must go, of course. Subscribers to *Quest' Ora, the Magazine for the Discerning Reader* would never understand them. There's a Morelli lurking in every man over forty. My father didn't envy the young. They were forbidden to do everything and couldn't afford to do anything. We're allowed to do everything and can afford it too, so we're envied. There's no point in growing old these days. Age means a bit more money but less freedom. The old don't want to be young again, they want to be young now, with the emphasis on now—says Morelli. They make a dash for the Y-train and fall under the wheels. Stormy times ahead for the old, icy winds, torrential rain, snow on high ground. Anyone who keeps his ears pinned back and his radio on knows better than to go out into the street with an old man. Our younger readers mightn't have anything against Morelli—he's living proof that the old are potential murderers—but eighty per cent of our readers are over thirty. Vanetti bases all his decisions on market research. The oldies won't want to identify with Morelli, in my humble submission. The rest is up to the trick-cyclists. Or to Beatrice Vanetti, girl-psychologist. Readers are quite as happy with one interpretation as another. They want sex-maniacs, anyway, not revolutionaries. Only ten per cent of readers dream of revolution, ninety per cent of orgies—although the market research boys haven't verified that yet. *Quest' Ora* readers sleep with their wives and take part in paper orgies.

Although I generally whip through my work like a man with twenty fingers, I only typed ten pages. Must be a moral hangover. Not because of Morelli, nor because he'll hardly recognize his memoirs. He'll never get to see them. Prisoners aren't allowed to read anything that concerns them personally—it's clipped out of the papers.

No, I've got the hangover Francesco ought to have. He wanted to kill his father; instead, he's sitting behind his desk. A heavy fine in lieu of the death penalty. Vanetti thinks Francesco is only keeping his seat warm. He may be wrong. Canonica, who's a wine-connoisseur, told me that wines mature while travelling. Francesco has matured en route for power. I don't find him any more likeable. Who wants to belong to a club which anyone can join? Vanetti and I belong to the same club. We ought to introduce the blackball system: one black ball, no admittance. Vanetti has smuggled sonny-boy on to the membership list.

Why should I worry? If all goes well with Morelli I'll be world-famous. After the Enzian film I'm going to pack this lousy job in. Maybe I'll write a book. The Morelli case has been too much of a headache. Too many tarts patrolling the same patch knock the bottom out of prostitution. Francesco planned to shop Morelli in order to save his own skin. I shall shop him because he murdered three girls. I can hardly wait. Once I've handed him over to Canonica I'll take a bath. It isn't advisable to get to know heroes personally—I learned that on one of my first assignments. Murderers are no better.

I'm glad I made that date with Elena for this evening. She'll take my mind off things. Must remember to ask her some time what Vanetti's like in bed.

THE ALIBI

Carlo Vanetti

The doctors propose to discharge me on December 23rd, which means that I shall be able to celebrate Christmas in the bosom of my family.

I'm not sure if doctors are wise to insulate their patients against every form of excitement. The more one avoids excitement the more one dwells on oneself, which is far more upsetting than any *Morelli Story*. Even a man like me, who has never been guilty of self-deception, catches himself out in the occasional falsehood. When I made my will I not only decreed a large-scale funeral but actually specified who was to deliver the last addresses —I couldn't bear to let go the reins. Then, when I was actually afraid of dying, I had a sudden vision of a simple burial. I shall amend my will. That isn't enough, though. I ought to mend my ways as well—a pretty hopeless undertaking at the age of fifty-four. Besides, death whispers some fairly incomprehensible things in your ear, as they say in our serials. It urges you to act differently, but you're not told what to do differently or how to do it.

There are going to be a lot of changes. I shall have to conserve my energies. If everyone had a coronary, everyone would work less—it might solve the unemployment problem. There'll be a change in my relationship with other people—or, rather, in their relationship with me. Perhaps it's the same thing. *Few are so bold as not to have lived the life expected of them.* They say one rarely recovers from a second coronary and almost never survives a third. From then on one lives in a leasehold apartment, and there's little point in looking for a new one. Other people know this. The first question a prospective buyer asks about a used car is: "Has it ever been involved in an accident?" I've been patched up and resprayed, but I shan't be able to disguise my accident.

My attitude towards the ageing process underwent a change while I was wrestling with death—another cliché: I should have said "making friends with death". I've always feared old age, mainly for reasons of virility. What saddens me now is not the little that lies ahead of me but the little I have to look back on. *Old age is the sum of our missed opportunities.* I thought that only death was irreparable, but the same applies to old age. We ought to repair our youth, but youth is like the poison recently distributed by a pharmaceutical firm in place of medicine. They issued warnings over the radio, but it was too late—the poison could not be retrieved. *Man dies, not of old age, but of irretrievable youth.* Since my illness, old age seems only slightly preferable to death.

I'm grateful to God, for all that. My thoughts have turned to God more often in recent days than ever they did in all the years since my childhood. Not that I have suddenly started to believe in heaven and hell. It's simply that I feel a need to occupy my mind with something beyond my comprehension. *God will retain His popularity for as long as men feel the need to pray. People have forgotten who they're afraid of, but it doesn't make them any less afraid than they were. Technology is evolving in the direction of metaphysics. Faster aircraft and electronic brains are merely by-products. Even the exploration of outer space is a by-product. Radio was the first key to the mystery of the waves. Another few decades, and man will be transmitting thoughts like a TV show. Instead of writing with a typewriter, he will use a thought-machine. Likes and dislikes will be regulated by waves. A man who wants to conquer a woman will tune in on her wavelength. There won't be room for God in the world of waves. The first Pope to speak into a microphone was capitulating on God's behalf. Now, Vatican Radio broadcasts beat music and people clap in St Peter's like a football crowd. If Mother Church can't salvage God, she can at least preserve prayer.*

I have prayed. What is more, I have extolled God's goodness by promising to give Claretta her marching orders. Less out of fear or piety, I admit, than because death reigns in a hierarchical fashion: it brings an awareness of priorities. My thoughts have turned more often to my deserted desk than to my abandoned bed. I should have gone straight home after that scene with Bossi. However intimate my relationship with Claretta, I shall have to devote my remaining energies to my work. If I am to be summoned, I intend to put my house in order for the family's sake.

I have spoken to Claretta daily, ever since I was permitted to use the telephone. I wouldn't want to give her the *coup de grâce* before Christmas. She suspects nothing, and sends me flowers every day, anonymously. I get the nurses to distribute them

THE ALIBI

among the second-class patients. After the holiday I shall write her a farewell letter. *"Epistola non erubescit" as Cicero says. Most affairs drag on painfully because men and women dread the final five minutes. Women think farewell letters are cowardly. Feminine logic! A farewell handshake would leave them just as lonely. What it really boils down to is indignation at being robbed of a chance to revoke the irrevocable. Their idea of a farewell conversation is to appeal, physically or emotionally, to old memories. Men often renounce what they love; women cannot even renounce what they have long been indifferent to. That is more cowardly than any farewell letter. I once read that "one does not write at undue length when saying farewell". Even so, a detailed letter of farewell is more honestly meant than a farewell visit which ends with a period of probation. It is inhuman to leave an affair languishing in a death-cell.*

I find myself in something of a dilemma, nevertheless. I have more in common with Claretta than with any of my former mistresses. In the course of three years, I have confided to her my low opinion of most people. That is a bond in itself. Nor was it her sexual demands upon me that led to my coronary. Claretta is blameless. Anything I gave her I took from Maria. When a man like me suffers a coronary the world blames his mistress. I don't wish to be unfair. The mistress of the older man competes, not with his wife, but with his work. He can cope with a wife and a mistress, but not with a mistress and his work. It will be some time before I can afford any more peccadilloes. *Marriage retains its popularity because it combines maximal opportunity with minimal excitement.* On the other hand, the hurt that I shall inflict on Claretta will not be pleasing in the sight of God. I can only pray that she will soon find consolation. It was easier in Luisa's case. *It is always wiser to engage in extra-marital relationships with young, beautiful, and desirable women. Most women suffer from a dearth of affection, most men from a surfeit. A man ought to beware of women who are totally dependent on him. It is distressing to leave more than one widow behind.*

The Professor must, incidentally, be justified in praising my cast-iron constitution, or I should never have survived the shock of reading Morelli's memoirs. I cannot stifle the suspicion that Bossi deferred delivery of the manuscript because he knew the full story long ago.

253

When a man hears the rustle of Death's wings he examines his conscience. *"Wings of Death" is an oft-recurring phrase in our magazines. Like it or not, clichés are still the best medium of communication.* Oddly enough, I have been far more oppressed in recent days by my unfaithfulness to Maria than by the Morelli case. The conscience of a public figure is like a barometer. A barometer doesn't create the weather, it merely registers it. It would be presumptuous of me to suppose myself the conscience of the public. The public is the weather.

I am justified by events. My first newspaper, the *Corriere della Sera*, was brought to me by Birgitte, the delightful Swedish auxiliary nurse—a good omen that my interest in the opposite sex should have been rekindled by a woman who is not dependent upon me. In the paper I found a remarkable little news item. The dailies always print the most important items in the smallest possible type-face. The report spoke of an offer by the Algerian Government to sell film of the kidnapping of Moise Tshombe, the Congolese ex-Premier, to an American TV company for two hundred thousand dollars. It was published without a word of comment. The Algerian authorities claim that they had nothing to do with the kidnapping of the African politician—that he dropped into their mouths like manna from heaven, as it were. If he had, think what the TV cameras in Tshombe's 'plane would have missed! How did his 'unexpected' arrival at the Algerian airport come to be filmed? Did the television people know about the kidnapping in advance? In fact, the Americans turned down the Algerian offer because they wanted the full story, complete with trial and any subsequent execution. For his part, Tshombe is busy writing his memoirs in prison. He plans to retain France's most expensive lawyer with the proceeds. How can an accused man defend himself if he doesn't even write his memoirs? Accused men's memoirs are part of a humane legal system. I called Beroglio and instructed him to splash the story in *Positivismo*. The Algerian episode may prove useful. After all, who would have the gall to reproach me for giving a sex-maniac a temporary reprieve when a genuine kidnapping is filmed like a Hollywood production? Must private initiative lag behind public enterprise? It's very fashionable nowadays to inveigh against the evils of the mass media. Being a student of history, I am reminded, for instance, of the Prague Massacres of the fifteenth and seventeenth centuries. They treated people just as brutally in those days, but they didn't film them. It may be that no further atrocities would have occurred if the massacre had been transmitted via Early Bird. I disapprove of the Tshombe kidnapping, with or without cameras. Especially after my bout of self-examination. However, I can't swim against the stream in *Quest' Ora.* I leave that to *Positivismo.*

Bossi visited me shortly before lunch. Nurse Birgitte, who was on duty, announced him. Unlike the nuns—"You really mustn't excite yourself, Signor Vanetti!"—she doesn't issue warnings the whole time. She doesn't treat me like a used car, either, even if she is in the trade. A man who has had a coronary could do far worse than take a mistress with medical qualifications.

Bossi brought some flowers—an uncharacteristic gesture. He plunked them down on the table like a briefcase. His awkwardness made the act almost touching. I'm sure it was pure coincidence that the flowers came from Claretta's shop. Bossi has been behaving with the utmost consideration since my illness, almost like a son. *Only a man who has looked death in the eye sees people as they really are.*

Bossi assured me that we shall get the *Enzian Story* from Morelli in good time. "He won't give us the slip—I've made sure of that," he said. He made no mention of the three murders, not wishing to over-excite me. He simply mentioned, in passing, that he had obtained some superb photographic copy on Chiesa and Pisenti—a reassuring thought.

We talked about his research in Vienna. I glanced through the material yesterday.

"The family don't appeal to me," I said.

"Nor me," he replied.

I don't think he knew what I meant. I said, "What we needed was an unsuspecting family of solid citizens, shattered by the turn of events. Or the opposite—a broken home, the father a drunkard, the mother a prostitute. In the first case people could have sympathized with a family, in the second with the victim."

"I can paint the family any way I like," said Bossi. "The old man will be happy to get off without a roasting. What do you say about his having been a storm-trooper?"

A good thing Bossi reminded me. "We won't print the Brownshirt picture," I announced.

"Why not?" he asked. "We include a couple of former Fascists in every number. Mostly in uniform."

"The Italians like hearing about their own history," I enlightened him. "People get sentimental over Mussolini. With Hitler they don't. There's enough politics in the magazine as it is —more than enough, since the Arab-Israeli war."

"We made the most of the Arab-Israeli war," said Bossi. "The number with the girl-soldiers on the cover sold like hot cakes."

"The *Enzian Story* is directed principally at the woman reader," I said. "Sixty-one per cent of our readers are women. Of the thirty-nine per cent of male readers, seventy-two per cent buy the magazine to please their wives. People need a rest from politics once in a while."

"Francesco is very keen on the Brownshirt picture," Bossi said.

There followed an exhaustive discussion about Francesco. To my surprise, Bossi spoke of him as an elder brother might: with a mixture of disapproval and affection. "Francesco's no Communist," he said. "He doesn't know what he wants, that's all. He'd like to turn the *Enzian Story* into a sociological treatise."

"Sociologists are the bane of our existence," I said. "They see the world as it should be, not as it is. Take the sociology students —they've got too much time on their hands. Medical students and budding lawyers don't demonstrate, they're too busy working for their examinations. Sociologists get degrees too easily, that's why they flock to the barricades."

"I think the barricades will have to manage without Francesco," Bossi assured me. "The Brownshirt picture is only a rearguard action. He even had the idea of offering Canonica an advance on his memoirs."

"Not bad at all," I said with paternal pride.

Bossi shook his head. "We'd burn our fingers on Canonica. Francesco thinks everyone over thirty is corrupt."

"I had no choice, Bossi," I said, "you know that. I had to leave Francesco in charge of the shop."

"You'll be back in no time," said Bossi.

I felt genuinely touched. I asked about the film.

"I've already sent the treatment to Berlin," Bossi told me. "Another few days and we'll be able to insert the real names."

We went on to speak about the first instalment. Bossi wants to juxtapose the three childhood pictures of Enzian, Chiesa, and Pisenti. "Don't worry," he said, "we'll pull it off. Nobody's going to get worked up or shed tears over the Enzian family, but the fact remains that most readers will identify with them—and there's something to be said for identification."

I had to smile. It does a man good to hear his own words from another's lips. In Bossi's case my seeds of wisdom have not fallen upon stony ground.

He was clearly bent on giving me a treat, because he said, "We developed the last of the Vienna pictures yesterday. Francesco shot the police superintendent brother-in-law going into church. We've also got another picture of the superintendent—a first-class action shot of him grabbing me by the collar and chucking me down the steps. I staged the incident so Francesco could photograph it. Francesco wants to put the church-goer and the bouncer side by side."

"If it amuses him," I said, not being permitted any over-excitement.

"Rest easy," Bossi said, getting up, "I won't let him do anything stupid."

"I shan't forget this," I said. "I've got something in the pipeline for you which will put even the *Morelli Story* in the shade. How would you fancy a trip to Australia?"

"I wanted to go to Cortina, actually," said Bossi, but I could see his nostrils twitch.

I wasn't going to tell him any more because it would have taken his mind off the *Enzian Story*. All I said was: "Get yourself fitted for a nurse's uniform." Then I sank back on my pillows.

After lunch—if hospital fare merits such a description—I failed to get off to sleep for the first time, even though the Professor claims that every little afternoon nap prolongs a man's life-span by a week.

Bossi's remark—"Francesco's no Communist, he doesn't know what he wants, that's all"—went round and round in my head.

So my instinct was as sound as ever when I entrusted Francesco with a big assignment. My original intention was to concentrate entirely on politics, but that's impossible. I shall reassume control of *Quest' Ora* very soon—there's too much at stake. Francesco is gaining experience, though, and I shall be able to put him in charge of *Positivismo*. We'll build the paper up, change its format, and turn it into a news-magazine. L'Exprès tried the experiment successfully in Paris. What *Positivismo* needs is new blood. The paper has never been a success because Beroglio is an optimist at heart. I shall put him out to grass on full salary. Papers are living organisms. You can't corrupt anyone but an utter narcissist by telling him how good he looks. Tell someone he has warts and he'll believe it implicitly. Francesco will produce a thoroughly distasteful paper with complete conviction, and people will lap it up. The fact that he doesn't know what he wants qualifies him perfectly to become editor-in-chief of a news-magazine.

This is not a cynical thought—I never think cynically. It's just that we're entering an era of honest journalism. Once upon a time popular newspapers were produced by highly educated people. That was cynicism. These days there is a growing approximation between the journalist's intellectual level and that of the reader. The senior editor of a tabloid genuinely believes that a story about a pigeon-poisoner is more important than a report on a Common Market conference. Sartori, my layout man, is sex-mad. Only a sex-mad layout man like Sartori can display bosoms to full advantage. With Francesco, people will sense that he understands the world as little and condemns it as utterly as his readers do. A news-magazine edited by Francesco will be just as honest as a tabloid edited by an illiterate.

We won't have any trouble with our advertisers. On the contrary. *Industry is convinced that the best way to combat Communism is to take the wind out of its sails with intellectualism. The modern intellectual is a harmless Communist. The West enthuses over Eastern intellectuals, the East over Western intellectuals. The masses want "panem et circenses", as they always have done, but modern adults cannot be amused and diverted by trapeze-artists and lion-tamers. The place of the trapeze-artist, lion-tamer, and circus clown—especially the latter—has been taken by the intellectual. What he shares with the clown is an ability to entertain the public by turning a series of neat somersaults, and still command applause even when rolled up in a carpet and borne struggling from the arena. He affords the world genuine pleasure and malicious amusement. There's a glut of clowns at the moment. Civilization has made such strides that people can at last earn money by intellectualizing. Intellectuals* flirt with Communism, but intellectualism is merely the social excuse for capitalism. Industry prefers to advertise in left-wing papers. Advertisements used to promote sales; now, more often than not, they serve as full-page alibis. A mere fifteen years ago, "Positivismo" would have had to pander to capitalistic interests. A short-sighted policy! The Press has finally taken over the job of self-criticism. Everyone knows that self-criticism changes nothing. Paradoxical as it may seem, the more the Press saws at the branch it sits on, the safer its perch. The public thinks: What a stout branch it must be if they can saw away at it so blithely! Or, to be more precise, the reader rejoices to see the branch being sawn and the advertiser knows that we won't saw it right through. Sawing and violin-playing entail roughly the same movements. The musical saw and the sawing violin-bow are the instruments of modern journalism.

I've devoted an increasing amount of thought to Francesco since my illness. I'm lucky to have a son. Who cares if Francesco doesn't know what he wants? Bossi put it crudely because he belongs to an age-group which no longer understands the younger generation and has yet to reach an understanding with it. In my young days, the young thought they knew what they wanted. They really knew as little as they do now, so they felt insecure. Now they know for a fact that they don't want anything, which gives them a warm glow of security. The successes of the younger generation may look new, but this is an illusion. The young have always won battles and lost the war. They both are, and are not, the future. The old always constitute the majority under every system. They are reinforced by the ageing young, whereas the young only receive weak batches of child reinforcements. Moreover, the young tend to be swallowed up by the even younger, and are thus caught between two fires. This time, the defeat of youth will be particularly swift and devastating. It has only itself to blame. The under-thirties suspect the over-thirties of treachery—Bossi is right in that respect—so they boost the majority of the old. Only a poor strategist swells the ranks opposing him. Youth is a disease which has never yet killed anyone, not even the old. Workers, for example, are dangerous because they remain workers. An old worker's interests are essentially the same as those of a young worker. Because the young don't remain young, they turn against youth in the *fullness of time. Every twenty-year-old is a potential Fifth Columnist. Social problems aren't subject to the laws of Nature, unfortunately. Problems of generation are. I was Francesco's age once, so I know precisely how the enemy feels. Francesco has never been my age, so he lacks all idea of my aims and intentions. My intelligence service is better than his—consequently, I shall defeat him. He will be victorious himself some day, but only when he has children of his own to defeat.*

Is it blind of me to let Francesco experiment with *Positivismo*? Not at all. Bossi was quite right to advise against any attempt to bribe Canonica, but Francesco's plan to bribe him shows that the boy is on the road to recovery. I must tread carefully, of course. The Communists exploit the anarchy of love, which enjoys such popularity with the young, for their own ends. Given the opportunity, they would brutally suppress it. We must exploit it in our society too, but without brutality. The British make sixty million pounds annually out of the hippie industry. Every worker who helps to manufacture hippie buttons is a potential opponent of anarchy, firstly because he earns money and secondly because victorious anarchists don't need any buttons. We must ensure that the so-called flower children join *Interflora*—it would be wonderful business for Claretta. *The newspapers are right to sneer at affluence. Only criticism can render a materialistic world tolerable. There is no danger that the majority will ever waive their claim to affluence. Affluence will only nauseate them if they are denied the satisfaction of condemning it. Continuous revolution is our finest alibi. It inhibits revolution proper, creates unrest, and dispels boredom. Bored masses reach for their guns. From the publisher's angle, continuous revolution is a pearl beyond price. Earthquakes are a fortunate quirk of Nature and not to be banked on, whereas continuous revolution has the predictability of a royal wedding.* What a gamble I took with Morelli! If Francesco makes the most of continuous revolution in *Positivismo*, *Quest' Ora* will be able to dispense with investments of such a speculative nature.

I endeavoured to keep my thoughts within bounds. It would be better for my cardiac condition not to think of Morelli. I shall feel happier when he's safely behind bars.

Nurse Birgitte opened the door gingerly because she thought I was taking my afternoon nap. She wanted to say au revoir before going off duty. I shall have to do without her for twenty-four hours. She stroked my hair. Her hands smelt of almond soap.

Aurelio Morelli

Since I do not lay claim to an expert knowledge of the cosmetic tricks and subterfuges employed in this berouged and bedizened age by womenfolk, young and old, I am unable to say whether the doll-like Hertha Enzian bleached the hair of her head, or whether, by contrast, she was a natural blonde who did no more than trace the line of her eyebrows with some dark-hued chemical substance. A judicial inquiry—held in camera, of course—would very soon establish the facts of the matter. Judges like to be left alone in intimate conclave with the perpetrators of so-called sex-crimes, so that they can, by addressing the most obscene questions to the accused, derive secret titillation from their replies. My learned judges, not to mention that sworn band of conspirators known as jurymen, would no doubt distrust my nescience of Hertha Enzian's hair-colouring because, women being reputed not to dye their pubic hair, a 'sex-maniac' would logically possess the most authentic knowledge of his victim's natural pigmentation. It so happens that I never saw her naked, nor did I ever crave to ascertain the colour of her pubic hair: whether she was blonde, raven-locked, brunette, or auburn is a question best left to the hundreds of libertines who paid to share her venal couch. The predilection for a contrast between coiffure and eyebrows—an unaccountable idiosyncrasy, but wholly devoid of sinister purport—is one which I have cherished since childhood. That is why, of all the strumpets—to use an archaism—who saunter along the Via Veneto, I focused my attention upon Hertha Enzian and none other.

It must have been towards the end of March when I resolved to embark on the composition of a new novel, choosing as my subject the life of a call-girl, or glorified prostitute. The bitter blow which I had suffered in respect of my immortal *Signora Angelotti* had left me reluctant to commit another line to paper, and determined to inflict condign punishment upon a sottish world by means of literary abstinence. Nevertheless, circumstances are such that the writer—and I say this without depreciatory intent—practises masturbation for professional reasons, as it were. He gratifies himself before the mirror, so that his abstinence penalizes no one but himself. On the other hand, his illusions about the indispensability of his work increase in proportion as the memory of his most recent disappointment fades.

Still stranger is the fact that I, who have always been animated by the loftiest of moral principles, should have selected a call-girl, at first an imaginary one, to be my protagonist. I did so out of a certain wayward opportunism: no contradiction, that, for there are times when only compliance with the laws of society can reduce them *ad absurdum*.

The custom whereby announcements of forthcoming novels make mention of the number of pages seems to me to be outmoded: the publisher would do better to list the number of sexual acts, since the success of a book, as of an Olympic competition, depends solely upon championship performances of this kind. Obscene booklets available to all comers are arrayed on station bookstalls like whores in the dockyard quarter of Marseilles. I, needless to say, was thinking of something original, of a contribution to *belles-lettres* whose very quality would consign the modernists to the cribbed and cabined enclave where they rightfully belong. There is no future in erotic literature, as understood by that gargoyle of an editorial director Paolo Canova, because, while describing the pleasures of the flesh, it fails to clothe the copulators in flesh and blood. It would be otherwise if obscene passages were incorporated in works such as *Anna Karenina*, *Le Rouge et le Noir*, or *Signora Angelotti*. It would, within a masterpiece whose characters become incarnate and genuinely exercise our minds, be quite pleasing if, for example, Vronsky were to thrust his hand beneath the austere Anna's skirts in the railway carriage, if Julien went through the perverted motions of the *soixante-neuf* with his Mathilde, or if my own chaste heroine, Agnese Angelotti, occasionally employed her riding-crop for other than equestrian purposes. And yet, even as it is understood by the dilettante, erotic literature cannot be denied a certain validity: increased life-expectancy has prolonged the period of pubescence by several decades, with the result that modern man, as he conceitedly likes to call himself, leap-frogs manhood in a direct transition from puberty to senility—both of them states in which one is regrettably prone to *cochonnerie*.

THE ALIBI

Every evening of last summer the authorities closed a portion of the Via Veneto to traffic, doubtless so as to render it more accessible to those in quest of sexual intercourse. Where once people had promenaded on either pavement, the chattering youth of Rome now kept tryst on the broad roadway between the Café Doney and the Café de Paris. In former times young and old alike had met on the terraces of coffee-houses, but now an invisible barrier had suddenly sprung up here too: the middle-aged and elderly kept to themselves, chatting quietly or sitting in solitary state behind glasses of orangeade or goblets of vanilla ice-cream; ensconced in the little iron chairs which formed their *loges*, as it were, they watched the comings and goings, the shameless dalliance and badinage, the kissing, cuddling, and embracing which took place in the roadway. Call-girls, prostitutes, girls of good family—how to distinguish between them? The girls whom I observed from my old man's box were young without exception, half children, provocative to behold in the transparent little summer dresses which exposed so much, both above and below, the whores among them scarcely recognizable as merchandise or contraband.

However fleeting my references to dates hitherto, I remember with certainty that it was on July 21st, a Friday, that I first spoke to Hertha Enzian, the girl who was destined to gain world-renown by my agency. It was she who addressed me, not I who accosted her, although I had for some considerable time harboured the intention—motivated, of course, by scientific and literary considerations—of making the personal acquaintance of one of these dark butterflies.

Of all the girls of the Via Veneto—I had given them names which I proposed to use in my novel—"the Innocent", as I christened her, seemed by far the youngest. I should be guilty of false romanticism were I to assert that she looked unhappy, and yet mirrored in her bright blue eyes—or so I, in my genuine innocence, believed—was a yearning for far-off places; they were the sort of eyes which reflect the object of their yearning: an expanse of countryside, a playground, a soaring bird, a man's hand, a garden amid chimneypots, a hat in a shop-window. She looked like a character from one of those ballets in which a toy-shop comes alive: the doll skipped, described jerky movements with both arms, lowered its eyes, fluttered its eyelashes, wagged its head, shook its curls, and behaved with specious innocence. Sometimes another girl would join the young charmer at her table, an elegantly attired creature with freckles and red hair; sometimes, too, a man, but she generally rose after only a short while, sauntered slowly past the voracious entrance of the Excelsior, crossed the street, lingered beside the overladen news-stand, glanced absently at the covers of the illustrated papers which hang there side by side like brassières on a clothes-line, and vanished into the Via Lombardi. I could not resist the urge to follow her once or twice, unobtrusively and at an appropriate distance, but she accosted no one, and if she herself was accosted it was usually by young people who stopped their sports-cars or ludicrous little motorized beetles to banter with her. The girl would then proceed on her way, shoes tap-tapping ahead of me on the asphalt, divinely spherical buttocks balanced atop long, slender legs like balls on the end of a juggler's rod. She would pause in front of the window displays, although she must have seen all the *calzature* a hundred times over, then return to the Via Veneto or vanish in the direction of the Via Sicilia.

It so happened, at about half-past ten on the night of Friday, July 21st, that I made my way into the interior of the aforesaid Café Doney in a highly irascible frame of mind. Despite my urgent and repeated pleas, no waiter had deigned to bestow so much as a casual glance upon me for a considerable time, so I betook myself to the cash-desk, there to lodge a complaint and pay for what I had consumed—one glass of grappa and half a bottle of San Pellegrino. Scarcely had I addressed my protest to the deaf-mute cashier when I heard someone address me: Hertha Enzian had taken up her station beside me and was lamenting, in execrable Italian, that I had "already paid". "Why, Signorina," I demanded, "should you object to that?" Following me to the door, she replied that we could have taken a glass of my "favourite tipple" together. "My favourite tipple?" I asked in surprise. "How would you know what it is?" Her over-small but remarkably merry mouth curved in a mischievous smile as she replied that she had been watching the silent amateur of his country's native *schnapps* for some weeks, but was bound to assume that my surprise was feigned, because I too had been keeping her under more than cursory observation for a considerable period of time, there being no other explanation of the fact that I had "regularly" followed her down the Via Sicilia and as far as her front door. This, of course, was an exaggeration, since the future celebrity's address was still unknown to me, but I could hardly dispute that I had followed her from time to time.

We sat down at a table on the pavement—it happened more from weakness on my part than personal volition—and she modestly ordered a glass of grappa, thereby affording me a renewed opportunity of correcting her obvious misapprehension. With the suicidal honesty which is peculiar to me, I enlightened her on her misunderstanding: I could not afford to indulge in any amatory adventure, even were I so inclined; I was, I told her, a writer, but not one whose hack-work lent itself to filming, and, had I observed her in an unseemly fashion, it was only in the course of research which I was conducting for my new novel.

Now, when I think back on Hertha Enzian and contrast her, as well I may, with Lucia Chiesa and Vera Pisenti, I bow my head in shame and acknowledge that both of them, the teenager of the Giardino Zoologico and the girl from my native countryside, seem pure angels by comparison.

This has little to do with Hertha Enzian's sluttish profession. In the age of Lucia Chiesa and Vera Pisenti, even the middle and upper ranges of society regard the sexual act as a *Ding an sich*, to use a Kantian term freely adapted from Malebranche, so that the call-girl is at liberty to regard herself as the representative, though not by any means the precursor, of the successful isolation of things sexual. Just as that which has long been offensive becomes beautiful, so *ancienneté* renders immortality socially acceptable.

I had no intention of converting my blonde, dark-eyebrowed object of study, of conducting her along the path of righteousness, or of chastising her. Why should I have? I cherish the most tender recollection of the woman who long ago initiated me into the art of love, yet that woman was one of the prostitutes who in my time—as if every time were not communal property, and thus mine—haunted the Piazza del Popolo at night. Thither came the student Aurelio Morelli, who shared his airless lodgings with an evil-smelling Sicilian, and there, to his chaste consternation, he was one evening accosted by an elderly prostitute. No one could have mistaken her for anything else. In those days—in "my time"—all such women were recognizable by their at once conspicuous and wretched attire, by their painted cheeks and swelling hips, and by the size of their dangling handbags, which traditionally contained a clyster or syringe. They spoke a vulgar *patois* compounded of wheedling clichés such as "How about it, sonny?" and the like, sauntered in the shadow of buildings, loitered in doorways, and took care not to offend the virtuous gaze of any passer-by. There was something motherly about each and every one of them, something affecting about the way in which they tutored bashful youths, warmed the hearts of husbands weighed down by family life, bestowed morsels of youth upon the elderly, sat with the lonely at coffee-house table, applying the balm of their worldly wisdom, and gave nocturnal sanctuary to the homeless poet. Had I but revisited the woman who so sympathetically disabused me of the notion that I had made love to her seventeen times in succession—an innocent conceit based on my assumption that each individual thrust of the body constituted a separate act of love—and who sent me on my way with a jar of home-preserved fruit—apricots, to be precise—I should have been spared much tribulation. Instead, I felt inspired to practise my new-found skill upon a vivacious cousin—a willing creature, but also an envenomed repository of gonorrhœal infection, and thus, to state the obvious, totally miscast in the rôle of 'first love'. Although doomed, therefore, to live in a society which, unlike that of my confrère Zola, has sunk to the level of the prostitute instead of raising her to its own, I feel myself unfettered by bourgeois prejudices. I rid the world of a young creature, true, but the fact of her dissolute existence cannot be described as other than coincidental: he who would extol me on that account does me too much honour.

It ought to have occurred to me, on the occasion of my very first encounter with Hertha Enzian, that the little *poule de luxe* not only failed to understand my searching questions but was clearly ignorant of the significance of the term 'author'. Uninvited, she informed me that she had not in any case intended to "take me along" to her place of residence because it was Friday, and, as on every other Friday, she had already entertained a disagreeable visitor. A wealthy old industrialist—she stressed the words *ricco* and *vecchio* with relish and disgust respectively —made a habit of visiting her twice a month with his catamite. The old man apparently lived in constant dread that the youth, who was of a wholly normal disposition, might deceive or desert him; consequently, he deemed it better to escort him to a hired woman under his own paternal aegis. The catamite was a pleasant youth with skin as smooth as marble, she pursued, handsome in appearance and easily aroused, whereas nothing could have been more repulsive than the withered old man, who profited abundantly by his own beneficence: instead of leaving the boy alone with her, he insisted that they copulate in his presence while he, cross-legged and clad in formal attire, observed their sexual exertions from the comfort of an arm-chair—nay, more, plied them with directions which were calculated to reduce her, Hertha Enzian, to the status of an inanimate object, while simultaneously enhancing the boy's physical attributes in the most agreeable manner.

Perplexed but as yet unsuspecting, I returned to my modest lodgings. The warning which fell to my lot that night I left unheeded—the warning, I said, for in that same night there came a knock at my door: I opened it to reveal none other than Hertha Enzian—I had given her neither name nor address— leading by the hand a naked youth whom she introduced as her protégé. Her excuse that she had mistaken the door in her quest for the old man was threadbare in the extreme, nor had she any explanation for the nakedness of the young man: brushing aside my request that she leave, she impudently declared that one old man was as good as another, and that what she had done for the one she would not scruple to do for the other. The young man, whose excitement was plain to see, used my bed in order to assuage his outrageous sexual appetite no less than three times in succession, whereupon, ignoring my presence altogether, the two of them drained my one and only bottle of grappa to the dregs. The sober-minded reader will need no further proof that there was something uncanny about the entire proceedings if I state that next morning my bottle was full: my unwelcome visitors had evidently replaced it before slinking out of the apartment under cover of darkness.

I had arranged to meet the girl on Monday at a small restaurant near the Via Veneto. The restaurant was of her own choosing, but I had already on Sunday familiarized myself with the menu posted on the door, because tutorial work was hard to obtain in the summer season and I feared that my resources would not run to a costly repast. As luck would have it, I waited for the blonde with the dark eyebrows in the street, and was thus spared unnecessary expenditure.

Hertha Enzian neglected to honour me with her presence, nor did she deem it necessary to apologize for her gross breach of manners. Next evening, when I encountered her in front of the Café de Paris, she summarily announced that she now "had time" to dine with me. Never craven, I at once carried out my intention of the preceding day. How came it, I demanded, that she had trespassed upon my premises with the marble-skinned youth, used my bed, and consumed my grappa? Instead of denying it, the shameless wretch declared that she was delighted to have "made a hit", and hoped that I had had "a rare old time"; elderly dreamers of my type were always welcome, and—here she stroked my hand—she was sure that I would show my appreciation in due course.

The two hours which I spent with Hertha Enzian that evening should have been enough to acquaint me with the abject character of the girl on whom uninformed organs of the Press are still squandering their maudlin sympathy. I was nonetheless robbed of my cool objectivity—I cannot disavow it—because the girl had behaved quite divertingly in my quiet retreat, and because I have always had a weakness for blonde hair and dark eyebrows, especially when, as in the case of Hertha Enzian, the hair is upswept to reveal a slender neck streaked with down at the nape. Because "Unto the pure all things are pure", as St Paul says, though Nietzsche's parody—"Unto swine all things are swinish"—may be nearer the mark, I did not persist in reproaching her for her discourteous and unheralded intrusion; instead, I endeavoured to explain to her why a man of my importance should be taking any interest in her whatsoever. In so doing I deliberately expressed myself in an idiom appropriate to her humble standing. I did not mention that I was planning to write a sociological study of the call-girl, but confined myself to inquiring, tactfully, how she had gone astray, why she had sold her soul to the devil, and whether she were still capable of love or had become insusceptible of finer feelings.

She listened to me at first with eyes dilated and a foolish smile on her lips—no smile could be more imbecile than hers, God rest her soul—but then, from one moment to the next, demonstrated the most vulgar aspect of her character. She warned me against assuming the rôle of those candidates for the Salvation Army who wasted a professional charmer's time: "Clients who ask me 'how I came to sink so low' get charged double," she said. "I don't need their sympathy, and besides they're impotent." On being pressed further, however, she spoke with affection of her father, a respectable Viennese butcher, though she did refer to him as a "poor devil" who had "worked his hands to the bone" and grown old before his time. Her memories of her parental home were anything but nostalgic; on the contrary, she seemed to cherish little but pity for her worthy family —her brother-in-law, she mendaciously informed me, was a senior police officer. The "poor devils"—her stock phrase—knew nothing of "the beauties of life", had seen nothing of "the big wide world", made a great fuss about love, which did not exist anyway, and took a childish delight in the crumbs that fell from her, Hertha's, table. If she regretted anything it was not that she had become a *putain* but at most that her abnormal exertions were inadequately rewarded. Like so many people of little intellect, she had an excellent understanding of money, price, and relative value; indeed, had she been granted the gift of clairvoyance she would doubtless have inquired the cost of her own funeral. When, having been offered *Il Messagero* by a newspaper-seller, I fleetingly mentioned the war in the Near East she said that she had sympathized with the Israelis until she learned that they were Jews, whereupon she had revised her opinion. Glossing over this almost incredible display of ignorance with a doll-like smile, she at once reverted to material questions.

On the subject of her prices, which she candidly enumerated for my benefit, our views differed: judged by my modest standards, they seemed exorbitant. Being a shoe-fetishist, as I had already surmised, she converted the wages of sin into footwear currency: the price of copulation amounted to no more than two pairs of shoes, she explained, participation in an orgy to approximately four or five, and she had once, but only once, earned a hundred and twenty thousand lire—the price of ten pairs of shoes—for a weekend spent in the home of a flagellant. I, who had never in my life expended more than four thousand lire on a pair of shoes, could have stocked my cupboard with a lifetime's supply of footwear from the proceeds of one such weekend. I converted fornication and *calzatura* currency into tutorials and publisher's fees, and, being adept at mental arithmetic, readily calculated that the brilliant author of *Thou art Alcibiades* could scarcely earn the heels of a single pair of shoes with one tutorial, and that the cheapest bout of copulation carried a higher market-value than four tutorials or four hundred lines of manuscript.

Ah, yes, I should have discerned the nefarious creature's hidden designs even then. Before she took her leave, she said, she must contribute still further to—and here she inserted some acoustic inverted commas—my "novel". How, asked the self-appointed Scheherazade of the Via Veneto, could she be expected to take pleasure in the antics of an American ice-box salesman who always came armed with a Polaroid camera, placed it on a table, carefully set the automatic shutter release, and trained the lens on the bed? No uncommon perversion, this, she emphasized, save that the conceited ape was always at pains to display himself at his best—at peak performance, so to speak—which was difficult to effect in the fifteen seconds during which the self-timer purred out its allotted span; and so he dodged back and forth 'twixt bed and camera, swiftly developing the film, furiously destroying such prints as did not show him at his best, resetting lens and self-timer, hopping back into bed, and rebuking her savagely if she failed to transform him into a peak-performance photographic model within fifteen seconds.

Two days before her abrupt demise we met at an establishment known simply as the *Night-Club*, which is situated in the courtyard behind Hertha Enzian's former abode—the "House of Death", in gutter-press parlance. It was the only occasion on which she induced me to disburse a substantial, though not outrageous, sum of money. Hot from her bed, as it were, my iniquitous Scheherazade of the Backyards recounted the story of a Belgian couple who had given her a handsome gold piece, roughly equivalent in value to four pairs of shoes, for a comparatively modest expenditure of effort. She had been required, she said, to watch while the wife, a robust person with enormous breasts, forced her husband, a little man of clerkish aspect, to disrobe in the presence of the two ladies, then chained him to the bed-post and thrashed him mercilessly with a whip of the sort employed by ring-masters. While Hertha Enzian described the whole performance in full and unmentionable detail, she eyed me askance with an expression whose horrific purport and significance did not become clear to me until our final meeting.

Only a kindly Providence dissuaded me from carrying out sentence of death upon Hertha Enzian that selfsame night. The truth is that the word *vecchio* had begun to assume a supremely irritating prominence in the girl's largely monosyllabic vocabulary: she described the hapless Belgian as an "old" fool who had not even been permitted to settle the bill—that, too, to Hertha's annoyance, had been dealt with by the wife. Although she of all people must have known that in general only grizzled veterans of daily toil can afford to pay bed-artistes in hard shoe-currency, and that it would be grotesque, in view of the extent of unpaid competition, if young people squandered their pocket-money on venal love, she bemoaned the age of her clientèle and the trouble which she was compelled to bestow on its extinct and withered representatives. Of the striptease dancer who was performing in front of us she remarked contemptuously that she ought to have her breasts "lifted" and that it was "cheek" to put "shop-soiled goods"—the dancer could not have been more than thirty—on public display. I bethought myself of the good woman who had instructed me in physical love, if such there be: in 'my day' prostitution, too, demanded a certain maturity; prostitutes were paid for their hard-won experience and enjoyed the respect of their younger, though never unduly young, colleagues, whereas the Hertha Enzians speak of their worthier *consœurs* no whit differently than do the Paolo Canovas of older writers. Senescence is as impermissible in a dishonourable profession as it is in an honourable one. Once the *ne plus ultra* of degradation, the gutter has now become a pathway to success.

Evening descends on Foce Verde as I sit in the twilight and musingly regard my illuminated aquarium. Reluctance to reach the end of his labours prompts a man to defer the evil hour, and I must have risen a dozen times to console myself with the spectacle of my Zebra Danios (*Brachydanio rerio*), my Angel Fish (*Pterophyllum scalare*), and my Paradise Fish (*Macropodus opercularis*).

Events might have taken a different turn—who knows?—if only the fat Belgian woman so graphically described by Hertha Enzian had not been awaiting me outside the entrance to the *Night-Club*. Scarcely had I parted from my 'professional adviser' when the corpulent creature began to dog my footsteps, whispering that she was about to subject me to the same treatment as that which she had accorded her spouse. She pressed her exuberant breasts against my arm, grabbed me by the neck, pursued me, when I managed to break free, across the crowded Via Veneto, cracked her circus whip, caught me up, croaked, "Down with your trousers! Down with your trousers!" and promised me obscene delights for which, God knows, I hankered not at all. Only when I had leapt, utterly exhausted, on to the steps of a departing bus did I manage to elude her—or so I fondly imagined, for shortly thereafter she reappeared in my apartment, seated herself in my arm-chair with legs splayed, then rose with smiling menace and chastised me in a way which I had not experienced since childhood. It is not impossible, for justice enjoins such an interpretation, that the apparition in my lodgings may have been a chimera, nightmare, or figment of a fevered imagination, yet what could have accounted for the ghostly vision save the humiliating scene in the public thoroughfare?

You must forgo my company, beloved little fish, mute companions of my solitude. Switching on the light, I bend over the paper: it is time to recount the end of Hertha Enzian.

"We can have a quiet chat at my place," the imbecile Scheherazade had said. On the stroke of half-past five, on Tuesday, the eighth day of August, I entered her apartment. It was my fifty-eighth birthday, not that I am entitled to congratulate myself on any grand design; regrettable as it would have been, Hertha Enzian might well have survived this anniversary. A good hour previously, however, I had undertaken a sentimental journey to the place where Lucia Chiesa's brief but disreputable earthly career had ended four years earlier. I remembered her with a certain devotion.

To translate the rent of the three-roomed apartment whose bell I now rang into shoe-currency à la Enzian would have been a fruitless labour of love unless one had requisitioned the entire stock of a footwear store for purposes of comparison. The greatest writer of our age had naught left but a few items of garden furniture, whereas the apartment of this youthful tiro of an age-old profession was decked out with genuine Empire pieces such as are not infrequently found in furnished apartments; for the pomp associated with the Corsican lawyer's son—specious charm, mock Egyptian, pseudo-classicism, fake caryatids, sham aristocracy, in short, the Empire style—is typical of apartments which are let to foreigners. At all events, the sinful abode was luxurious enough. This is not to say that Hertha Enzian's quarters lacked the personal touch: in one or other of the Empire arm-chairs sprawled rag-dolls and woolly dogs of the sort peddled in restaurants by itinerant vendors; stuck into the frame of a gold mirror were favours won at some fair; the tea-trolley would have looked at home in a provincial tourist haunt; the roses and tulips were of wax; and there was a panopticon garden and many another feature more reminiscent of the living accommodation of a Viennese butcher than of the palaces of the Emperor of the French.

To my relief, Hertha Enzian was attired quite decently, though in a dressing-gown of garish pink. She conducted me politely into the drawing-room and bade me be seated, uttering a raucous laugh when I inadvertently subsided on to a violet dog. She herself stretched out on a broad sofa—a professional adjunct which naturally conflicted with the rest of the décor and was covered with a Turkish bazaar rug—coquettishly clasping a huge stuffed bear to her breast as she did so. It did not escape me that pinned to the somewhat worn fur of the bear was a medal—of American origin, as I was soon to discover: the bear's "daddy", a colonel in the American Air Force, had bequeathed my hostess one of his medals in addition to the whimsical gift—pretext enough for her to tell me about the sexual prowess, if hurried habits, of her aeronautical client.

She had, she said, procured a bottle of grappa, my favourite drink, but I declined because the afternoon was insufferably close and I had already fortified myself with a glass at the near-by Café Doney. The windows were closed, the air was heavy, the room wreathed in shadow by the building opposite—even the ears of the shaggy little toy dogs seemed to droop with exhaustion. *And Scheherazade, perceiving the approach of day, paused in her permitted discourse*, to quote one of the concluding tales from *A Thousand and One Nights*; but Hertha Enzian, so far from

273

"pausing in her permitted discourse", embarked on a new tale, this time of a "funny old man" from Turin whose custom it was to rouse her at seven o'clock in the morning because "love comes easiest to old people in the mornings—but I don't have to tell you that".

Why indeed was she telling me such things, I demanded, controlling my crescent impatience with supreme self-restraint; why indeed should she imagine that I was interested in the impetuous *colonello* and his toy bear, in the camera-conscious American, in the matutinal weakling, or even the whip-wielding Amazon from Belgium? My novel, though wholly modern in tone and written without prudishness, had no room for sick minds, pathological phenomena, and unnatural aberrations, nor had I ever misled her about the nature of my scientific, literary, or, if she preferred it, psychological research.

If I say that the infamous creature thereupon yielded to a paroxysm of laughter, I do not exaggerate in the very least: she smote the bear's bemedalled breast, clapped her hands, and rolled about on the divan with tears trickling from her round, doll-like eyes and down her rosy, doll-like cheeks. That her dressing-gown fell open in the process may not have occurred by design, yet it did not escape my eye that one of her suspenders was undone, exposing the naked flesh above the stocking: suspender-belts are a diabolical device because they frame the seductive flesh and thus redouble its allurements.

What was it that she found so amusing, I inquired, averting my gaze. Her response was to inform me that, of all perverted clients, I was by far the most perverse; furthermore, I was a miserable old hypocrite because I refused to admit that I "drooled" over her stories—yes, that was the word she used. The only thing I had in common with an author was a lively imagination which enabled me to derive satisfaction from "listening" rather than "watching". My only motive in denying all this, she pursued, was to avoid settling my bill, evade payment, defraud her of time and money. Her face, no longer smiling, had undergone a transformation reminiscent of the many Japanese netsukes which display two contrasting faces rotating on a single axis: the merry little mouth, now immobile, had dwindled to a pair of hard, thin lips; two vertical lines etched themselves into the skin between her nostrils and the corners of her mouth; as if turned to stone, her features seemed to have aged a good ten years.

Had I strangled the trollop at that moment no court in the world could hold it against me, but I was too *bouleversé* to serve the cause of justice. To my shame, I must admit that I sought to justify myself: having hitherto concealed my name, I now uttered it aloud. Had she never heard of Aurelio Morelli, I asked the illiterate girl, of Dottore Aurelio Morelli, immortal author of *Alcibiades*, was she not sensible that it was an honour to be allowed to contribute her humble mite to a masterpiece?

Ill boded the silence in which Hertha Enzian received this, and my foreboding was justified. She sat up and fumbled with the drawer of a dainty little Empire table on which, in apt proximity to her harlot's couch, there stood that incongruous emblem of her profession, the white telephone. While opening the drawer she declared that she had never heard of a Signor Alcibiades—she confused the name of the author with the title of the book—and had no wish to make his closer acquaintance; whether I was really a "pen-pusher" or merely a *vecchio porco*, a "dirty old man", was a matter of supreme indifference to her; she had written out her bill, *il conto*, neatly and without overcharging, and as soon as it was settled I could "toddle off" quietly —the sooner the better, in fact.

A devil must have possessed me at that moment, for, taking the proffered sheet of paper with an involuntary gesture, I numbly read what the whore had written in her clumsy hand. To be more precise, the letters were clumsy but the figures were not—Hertha Enzian was well versed in simple arithmetic. First the date, then: *Queer with boy-friend, dot-dot-dot, ten thousand lire; American with camera, dot-dot-dot, ten thousand lire; Belgian couple, dot-dot-dot, ten thousand lire; Personal visit, dot-dot-dot, fifteen thousand lire*—the total would have been forty-five thousand lire had not a further ten thousand lire been added beneath the line, making fifty-five thousand in all. "I rounded off the total," said my erotic book-keeper, "because the old pansy and his bum-boy ought to be worth double to you. After all, you did dream about me and the boy as well."

It was this brazen lie, or so I am inclined to believe, which exhausted my last reserves of patience. That the impudent jade could suppose me to have felt aught but abhorrence at her stories, that she could think—for even this lay within the bounds of possibility—that I required her graphic accounts in order to find a fulfilment which my own imagination regularly bestows on me in far greater measure—all this I might have stomached. However, the insinuation that I had merely dreamed of her and the youth whom she had, in a sense, delivered to my door unsolicited, proved too much even for my temperate disposition.

This is not by any means to say that I lost my head or acted imprudently. On the contrary. Seating myself beside the girl— who had meanwhile sunk back against a frightful cushion of the kind sold in provincial markets—I discreetly laid my hand on the white telephone and, gazing steadfastly at the grotesque 'bill' as if reading its contents aloud, enunciated the death sentence which I had carefully formulated in my mind.

Were she of the Roman Catholic persuasion, I told her, this would be the moment to confess: although it was too late to summon a priest, I myself felt empowered to hear her last confession and speed her on her way to the realm of everlasting peace with a *te absolvo*.

Had the dark-browed blonde but taken me seriously, had she but believed my words, it may be that I should have yielded to the promptings of my all too humane temperament.

But no. I was not to run away with the idea, she said, raising her voice, that I could "blind her with science"; I was a bilker of the worst sort, a confidence trickster whose only intention was to cheat her out of her hard-earned money—twice-earned, she added, for, if I must know, the story of the Belgian couple was not based on first-hand experience but culled for my benefit from the personal reminiscences of a friend. "You don't honestly believe I'd have wasted my precious time with you, over a miserable little glass of your disgusting pig-swill, if I hadn't known what category"—category, she said—"you and your sort belong to." Besides, she went on, the price was fair enough, a *prix d'ami*, so to speak, unworthy of a call-girl of her standing, a mere trifle earned "on the side". "Sometimes even I have to walk the streets, with business the way it is."

"The Belgian couple a fabrication!" I exclaimed with a triumphant laugh. In that case, could she explain why the lady with the enormous bosom had pursued me the entire length of the Via Veneto, and why I had managed to elude her only by leaping boldly on to a bus?

Another change came over Hertha Enzian. The netsuke rotated, to display a second grimacing mask. With eyes which reflected terror with the clarity of a mirror-cabinet, she started up, groped for the telephone, and cried, "*Ein Irrer! Ein Irrer!*"

My command of the German language, as of English, French, and, needless to add, Latin and Greek, proved the harlot's undoing: she had voiced an outrageous aspersion upon my sanity in her native tongue—had, indeed, called me a madman.

Providence, gracious as well as vengeful, once more absolved me from all need for sordid violence. Although the Neapolitan pugilist alleges that the impress of my fingers was found upon the doll-like creature's slender neck, this is a patent attempt to humbug, bluff, and deceive me: my slim but powerful hands could only have left their mark, if anywhere, on the white telephone. It so happened that the white flex of the telephone, a woven plait not unreminiscent of the pigtails worn by soldiers in the service of Frederick the Great, began to writhe in a mysterious way—or not so mysterious after all, since the inarticulate vibrations which pass through the telephone cables of sinful cities become condensed into the human voice and transformed into inhuman words by the telephone's white pigtail. What things the innocent contrivance must have heard, what shameful assignations it must have served to arrange, how abject the pander's rôle to which it had been relegated, how vile the traffic to which it must have lent itself, what hideous worms must have wriggled from the docile mouthpiece, what foul toads become enmeshed in the smooth and shiny pigtail! Now, as I watched, some supernatural power breathed life into the inanimate victim of a conspiracy between the willing strumpet and her lecherous clientèle: released from servitude, the pigtail wound itself about the throat of its depraved mistress and turned into an ever-tightening noose. There was a single cry, then silence: the cord left the throat from which no mating-call, no pert invitation, no vile promise, would ever again come forth. The girl lay still, the cord relaxed its grip.

A murderer would have hastened to leave the scene of his outrage and cover his tracks. For my part, I bent over the girl at leisure, reluctant to depart without carrying away a mental image of the sort which, where the silent forms of Lucia Chiesa and Vera Pisenti were concerned, had helped me to beguile many a dark hour. The foolish organs of the Press, in their supposed omniscience, reported next day that Hertha Enzian's mouth was "smeared" with lipstick, and naturally inferred that she had been smothered with passionate kisses such as might have been designed to titillate the obscene imagination of the public. Hertha Enzian's mouth was indeed 'smeared', but I had liefer have nuzzled a mangy beast than kiss my vile detractor: if I did not remove the traces of lipstick from mouth and chin it was merely because the cosmetic had traced a seeming rivulet of blood 'twixt corner of mouth and dimpled chin, and I hoped to re-discover this delightful feature in photographs published by the morrow's avid Press. Again, my motive in pocketing the bill presented me by my dead Scheherazade was not to aggravate the task of an imbecile police force; I did so because I had unfortunately omitted to take any such mementoes from Lucia Chiesa and Vera Pisenti. Heedless of the 'incriminating evidence' by which the police set so much store, I have preserved Hertha Enzian's death warrant to this day: it will accompany me to Bolivia, and no price which Quest' Ora might be willing to pay for such a souvenir will ever persuade me to part with it.

Undismayed by my encounter with a bucket-laden, broom-wielding slattern outside on the landing, I answered her challenge with a haughty inclination of the head. I left the premises by the side-door leading into the Via Sicilia, true, but was speedily engulfed by the evening bustle of the Via Veneto.

Ah, Rome, my divine and glorious city! It was nigh on seven o'clock, but the days were long. One sensed rather than saw the approach of evening. The air was positively visible, an obedient page spreading a velvet carpet before his master's feet. The bells rang out, miraculously drowning the din of the metropolis like celestial voices rising above the sound of things transitory to proclaim some great and eternal truth. The sky was pale as a Michelangelo marble—pale, full, and threaded with the veins of creation. A little breeze had sprung up, and the scent of the Borghese Gardens mysteriously superimposed itself upon the stench of humanity—Nature gently triumphing over the brute unnaturalness of man. The breeze stirred the skirts of the girls who were beginning to assemble in the roadway and outside the

THE ALIBI

cafés, but I regarded the young creatures with pleasurable contentment. My hatred was spent, my freedom gained, my work accomplished. No whip-brandishing Belgian pursued me, no naked American lurked in ambush with his camera, no catamite spread his limbs in lustful abandon: for one fleeting moment, I felt tempted to look round in quest of Hertha Enzian's bobbing buttocks, but quickly told myself that the little whore would never more saunter past the Café Doney, never more pause before the clothes-line with its array of brassières, never more give ear to the tooting sports-cars, never more survey the windows of the footwear bank. I should have laid the *colonello's* bear upon her breast before departing—she deserved a medal and a military salute.

It had, after all, turned out to be a pleasant birthday—a blessed birthday. As befits a son on such an anniversary, my thoughts turned to my worthy mother, and nothing affected me more painfully than the realization that I could not embrace the beloved woman who had borne me in sorrow, and say: The score is settled, *Mamma*, take pride in your son. For proud I was— I say it without vainglory—proud because I knew at that moment that I had vanquished my misgivings and done my duty. I had not acted with malice aforethought: instinct had guided my hand. Quite instinctively, I had selected a young creature who had exalted herself above her elders, male and female, who had poured scorn on ageing men, robbed my erstwhile instructress of a living, impugned my own virility and that of my entire generation, and, finally, passed sentence of death upon herself with the word "madman".

I was standing outside the Hotel Flora, but a few doors distant from the scene of my final victory, when sirens rent the air and a police car vomited its cargo of uniformed monkeys on to the pavement. I bade farewell to Aurelio Morelli, the murderer, who had fulfilled his task and was destined to spend the evening of his days with conscience assuaged. How ends the tale of the *Thousand and One Nights*, to which my thoughts had so often reverted in recent days? "*Extolled be the perfection of Him whom the vicissitudes of time do not destroy, and to whom no change happeneth, whom no circumstance diverteth from another circumstance, and who is alone distinguished by the attributes of perfection.*" Rest in peace, Scheherazade!

Oskar Enzian

The minute Pospischil told me the Italians were going to fork out I took a trip to Simmering, to the Central Cemetery. I'd been wondering whether to pay my parents a visit, that being where they're laid to rest, second class. The snow had left off but the slush was something chronic, because they never clear away the snow properly. They're keen enough on raking in taxes, but clearing away snow's different. Proper funereal, the atmosphere was.

I had my eye on the headstones even before I got out of the tram—drawn up on the left, they are, for sale. They look sadder there than they do in a cemetery, really, because they're waiting for customers. A monumental mason's looks like a terminus where everyone has to get out. A lot of people buy their headstones in advance, which is safer but morbid. All the same, it's just as morbid buying a headstone for the dear departed. Putting up a headstone is like sealing a letter. There's something final about it.

I only had one idea in mind, though, and that was a headstone for my Hertha. I didn't fancy any of them, not from the tram. I was set on it being the poshest stone in the whole of Simmering. There's only one thing wrong with posh-looking stones—the ones in black marble, say. They don't really suit a youngster—they're more for old people, millionaires and Cabinet Ministers and the like. I favoured a pink stone with a picture on it, in enamel. I could have used my favourite snap of her, the one she sent us from Capri, but only with the head enlarged, of course. My idea was to have Lechleitner do a proper portrait of her. He paints from photographs, true to life but even better.

I never thought Stangl would help me to give Hertha a decent burial, not when he turned up out of the blue like that. I was just shutting up shop, which used to be Hans's job in the old days. Franziska was upstairs already, in the flat. If he hadn't said it was about Hertha straight off I wouldn't have spoken to him. He looks a proper beatnik, Stangl does, with sideburns like bell-ropes and hair long enough to plait.

I looked out at the headstones with the snow draped all over them like a dirty tablecloth. It was Hertha who sent Stangl—it didn't strike me till that moment.

He talked about himself, to begin with. How he plays the piano in a café where the lonely hearts meet, but it'll be closing soon, the café, because there aren't any lonely hearts left these days. He said he was planning to take up singing, which is probably why he's letting his hair grow. Then he told me they were sweethearts, him and Hertha. He pulled a bundle of letters out of his coat-pocket as he said that. I saw it was Hertha's writing straight off—she was a great one for letter-writing, no denying that. I went all cold, from head to foot. Like chilled pork I went, because I thought he wanted to blackmail me like Pospischil and Dr Habichl and my beloved mother-in-law.

I had to squeeze right into the corner in the tram, because an old lady with a wreath came and sat down next to me. She shoved the wreath half into my lap. It never occurred to her that I mightn't fancy having a wreath marked *In Undying Memory* jogging up and down on my knee.

Never jump to conclusions, though—that's what I told myself, because I was too quick to judge Stangl. "It was a big thing between us," Stangl told me. "She went on writing to me long after it was over—even from Rome. The profession didn't suit her. She ought to have stayed at home, Hertha ought." He talked about her proper respectful, as if he meant every word. He wasn't shooting a line, either, because she gave him her diary before she left for Rome. "I won't be keeping a diary any more," she told him. "That's all behind me now." But she wanted to keep her girlhood memories, and she didn't want to leave them lying around at home—which is understandable, because up until a few years back Franziska even used to rummage through my pockets. It's only since I got my lung trouble she thinks I don't have any little secrets from her. Which is just where she's wrong, but still.

I felt a bit ashamed, thinking of a thing like that with the wreath on my knee and the headstones standing there waiting for customers, live or dead. Money's no object, not where Hertha's concerned. Best of all I'd buy her a mausoleum, a proper family vault, but the truth is it would be a waste of good money, because the family doesn't rate a vault. Besides, the money belongs to Hertha and nobody else. I'll never forget that.

To cut a long story short, Stangl—Christian name Richard—
he'd read in the paper that Hertha's career was going to be made
into a film, and that the Wops were publishing her life-story. He
could have offered them the diary and the letters direct, but I
was "a man with connections"—that's what he called me, and
dead respectful he sounded too. "If you offer them the letters
and the diary," he said, "they're bound to snap them up." He
suggested we went fifty-fifty.

It started to drizzle as soon as I got out of the tram. They
hadn't carted away the piles of snow—us poor old ratepayers'd
have to die of pneumonia first—and the drips were making holes
in them, like revolver shots. I wasn't worried about the weather,
though, even if it does go straight to my lungs.

I went into the office building, where they shuttled me around
from one department to the other, just like the Tax Office. I
couldn't have Hertha buried with my parents because they're in
the second-class section. I told them to show me the best plot
they had, in the first class. The man took me out to the cemetery.
Looked like a weasel he did, scuttling around between the graves.
Didn't show any respect for the dead, just took bloody good care
not to get his shoes wet.

I've had better men than him for breakfast before now, so
I couldn't have cared less if his shoes did get wet, and I wasn't
bothered about my lungs either. There was a plot left next to the
family vault of the Edler von Loebengraetz family. The Edler
von Loebengraetzes' family vault has a proper door—bricked in,
naturally, because doors are no good to the dead, and the living
wouldn't want to go down there anyway. There were two weeping women on either side of the door, made of stone but dead
lifelike. They were hiding their faces in sorrow. It was them
that gave me the idea of putting a weeping woman on Hertha's
grave—smaller, of course, because it isn't going to be a family
vault. The grave won't be smaller on account of our not being
titled, because titles have been done away with, and my Hertha
was just as much of a lady as any of the von Loebengraetzes.

We got forty-nine thousand nine hundred and eighty-two
schillings. I won't keep a groschen of it—that's to say, only
what's left after the funeral expenses. I'd never have taken the
money if I hadn't been thinking of my little Hertha's mortal
remains, and how they ought to be given a proper burial.

Stangl is a pretty tactful sort of chap. He saw straight off I didn't want to set eyes on my poor little girl's letters, nor the diary. Just put him in touch with the right people, he said, and he'd show them everything he had to offer. "Nobody buys sight unseen," he said. Very smart of him, I thought.

I went and saw Pospischil right away. His wife's in hospital— on her last legs, poor soul. It won't be long before Pospischil pays for a funeral himself. I'd promised not to do anything without consulting him first, and my word's my bond. I did say I was a bit worried, though, because the letters were addressed to Stangl, and Stangl says there are sexy bits in the diary. "Don't be a fool, Oskar," Pospischil said. "Some people are even more famous than Hertha," he said, "and their letters and diaries get auctioned off almost before they're cold." There was something in that, I had to admit. The *Kronen-Zeitung* had the nerve to publish the correspondence between Emperor Franz Joseph and Kathi Schratt, and His Majesty was married, which doesn't apply in Hertha's case.

Next, Pospischil outlined his plan of campaign—he's bright, Pospischil, no two ways about that. He suggested asking the Wops for a hundred thousand and paying Stangl twenty thousand in full settlement of all claims. I didn't say yes just like that—after all, the letters and the diary really belonged to Stangl —but Pospischil soon put my mind at rest. "That diary's family property," he said. "You're acting as if we were planning to cheat Stangl," he said. "I ask you, that would make every middleman a swindler!" I really pinned my ears back, because Pospischil's got brains—there's no denying that. "Are you going to tell me you buy your Hungarian salami at the same price you sell it for?" he asked me. "You don't give the Hungarian Government a percentage, do you? You buy a given amount of salami, which is a gamble from your point of view, and then you resell it at a profit. After all, you mightn't shift the stuff." He's got the gift of the gab, Pospischil has, but I didn't give my consent right away.

I didn't inquire about the price of the grave to begin with. I don't know if weasel-face thought I couldn't afford it, but I had him show me a couple more plots just in case, even though I'd already settled on the one next to the Edler von Loebengraetzes. I waited till the rain was trickling down inside his collar before I told him I wanted to speak to his boss. Never deal with under-lings if you can go to the top, that's what I always say.

The boss gave me quite a different reception. Proper respectful, he was. I told him I was ready to make a down payment. When was the funeral going to be, he asked, but I steered him off the subject because I don't know myself, not yet.

I wrote the Italian authorities a letter which they won't put up on the mantelpiece in a hurry. For a start, they'd dissected the remains of my deceased daughter without parental consent, so I reserved the right to take legal action. I demanded the release of the body, because even the Wops know they haven't got a hope of finding the murderer. While I was on the subject, I told them to forward all personal effects rightly due to the family, as well as the ready cash discovered on the premises, by return of post—otherwise I'd complain to the Austrian Consulate. That was just bullshit, of course, because the last thing I want to do is get mixed up with the authorities, but there's no need for the Wops to know that. I'm not bothered about the money anyway, and Mizzi's the only one who's keen on having the clothes. The body's the main thing. They've got to transfer it to Vienna because Hertha won't rest easy till she's safely tucked up in her native soil. I just put my name at the bottom: *Oskar Enzian, father of Hertha Enzian*—and left it at that. No Yours Faith-fully.

The boss confirmed receipt of my deposit, which is to say, he made out a slip for the cashier. He didn't half open his eyes when I said my name. "Are you a relative of . . . ?" he asked—he didn't come out with Hertha's name, almost as if it was Hertha who'd murdered someone and not the other way round. People seem to think it's a disgrace, being murdered. "That's right, I'm the father of Hertha Enzian," I said, staring him in the eye till his glasses misted over. "Terrible, terrible," he said, which is what everyone says when they can't think of anything better.

Outside the offices I stopped and looked across the cemetery, but there wasn't a headstone in sight to compare with the one my Hertha's going to have, even though they were all in the first-class section. And as I stood there all by myself in the rain I knew my girl was looking down at me with those sky-blue eyes of hers, smiling. Your mother doesn't know anything about the money, I said. She doesn't know anything about the letters either, and it's nothing to do with her if I order a weeping woman. The plot's big enough, I said. Maybe there'll be a bit of ground left over for your poor old father. What's more, I'm going to see Hans comes to your funeral, even if he is a rotten little Communist. And just so you don't think I want to line my own pockets, I said, I'm going straight off and order that head-stone.

I'd sooner have spent the whole of the forty-nine thousand nine hundred and eighty-two schillings on Hertha. Stangl asked for twenty-five thousand, which was all right with me. Now he can get himself trained as a singer. The Italians coughed up ninety thousand, so that left sixty-five thousand. Pospischil had to make a good thing out of it again, of course—twenty per cent, though it wasn't part of our bargain. Subtract thirteen thousand, leaves fifty-two thousand. He also deducted expenses, to cover the cost of 'phone-calls to Rome and photocopies. He had to make photocopies of the letters and the diary. A schilling the page, it cost.

They only had finished stones at the first monumental masons, opposite the main entrance. Half of them were too big and the rest too small—bloody awful, they looked. Concentrate on the personal touch, I always say, in business as well. The stone-mason next door knew what I had in mind. We settled on a little pyramid with a weeping woman on it, but that'll have to be carved special. A blind door too, of course, just with *Hertha Enzian, 1944–1967* on it, and a plain cross. I had to do without the picture, worse luck.

The stone's going to cost in the region of six thousand five hundred schillings—he couldn't say to the nearest hundred. The plot and a first-class funeral will set me back another six thousand at least, which leaves thirty-seven thousand. I'll put that towards the butchery—that's to say, the exension. Hans'll come back like a shot if I open a proper butcher's shop—he's dreamt about a butcher's shop since he was a nipper, and I'm not keen to lose my son even if he is a Bolshie, the silly young sod. Hertha would have wanted the family to stick together.

The tram was nigh-on empty for the return journey, as though everybody had stayed out there with the dear departed.

Time was when I thought rich people only pretended to have

their worries. It isn't all beer and skittles, though, being rich.
The higher you climb the dizzier you get. If your income goes up
your expenses get bigger—it's a law of nature. Stangl was a
stroke of luck, seeing I hadn't reckoned with the expenses—Dr
Habichl and Pospischil, for instance, and my beloved mother-in-
law. She'll never see the inside of an old folks' home, that's a dead
cert. At least I'm getting the forty-nine thousand nine hundred
and eighty-two free of tax—Pospischil saw to that. Stangl took
his share under the counter, and the Wops are charging the
whole fee to general expenses. I don't have any scruples, not
about the tax. The Government are a bunch of chisellers anyway. They don't even clear away the snow.

I couldn't help feeling nervous, though, on account of the
diary. Stangl says it mentions at least three company directors
by name. You can never tell what Pospischil's got up his sleeve,
even if he did say, "Not to worry, Oskar, you know my moral
principles." He always talks big, Pospischil does—can't help
himself. "Two things are sacred," he said, "tax avoidance and a
man's sex-life. Anybody who makes trouble for someone else on
account of tax or women is an unscrupulous bastard."

It's true. Except that if there are sexy bits in the diary people'll
lay the blame at my door just the same, because I released it for
publication. No one'll think twice about Pospischil and Dr
Habichl and Stangl—all they do is cash in. Envy is a bad coun-
sellor, as the saying goes. The more people envy me, the more
they poke their noses into my private life. I'd sooner be older by
a couple of months and have the whole shooting-match behind
me. All the same, Hertha must have known what she was doing
when she sent Stangl to see me. The dead watch over the living,
no doubt about it.

I told Franziska I'd been to the Tax Office because that was
the best excuse I could think of. She'd think I was off my rocker,
ordering a headstone when the Wops haven't even favoured me
with a reply. It all went off easy enough, though, even if I did
get a nice fruity cough on account of the weather. Hertha, I said
to myself, you're going to have a slap-up funeral come what
may. I'll walk behind your coffin with my head held high, no
matter what people say. It doesn't concern anyone bar me and
my little girl.

Francesco Vanetti

At night I get into my car, it's late, I'm the last to leave the office, only the printing works is lit, I roar down the autostrada, sometimes it's wet, at Orte I leave the autostrada and head for Amelia, twelve kilometres, then I see the palazzo; the palazzo stands on a hill, there are lights in the windows, I turn off into the grounds, Giulietta is waiting for me, I know Giulietta's waiting for me. Her father's in Rome, maybe her father isn't in Rome, who cares where her father is, her father is Ferrari, Enrico Ferrari, they call him "Red Ferrari", he's Red Ferrari, she came to the office with him, he introduced me, "Francesco's in sole charge now that his father's ill," he said, she nodded, I nodded, we were in love, we are in love, I'm in sole charge.

Giulietta's mother is dead, she died when Giulietta was two, nobody brought Giulietta up, she brought herself up, her father is her friend, he didn't bring her up. She's two years older than me, she's older than her father, she brought him up. She wears her hair combed back, parted in the middle, she looks like a Madonna, not like a Raphael Madonna, all innocent and surprised by the Holy Ghost, she looks like a Gothic Madonna, nothing could surprise her. Ferrari wouldn't have got where he is without her, everyone says, maybe it's an exaggeration, she's the power behind the throne, maybe it isn't an exaggeration.

Ferrari doesn't bother me, he's my friend, my father, I've never had a friend, I've never had a father, the guest-room is next to Giulietta's room, we talk till midnight, when Ferrari's there we talk till two, I go to Giulietta's room, Giulietta comes to the guest-room, she wears a transparent nightdress, every night a different one, the bed in the guest-room is narrow, Renaissance, the bed in Giulietta's room is wide, baroque, a Venetian gondola, we go boating in the gondola. When her father spends the night at the palazzo she drives to Rome with him in the morning, they drive in the Rolls, I drive ahead of the Rolls, the chauffeur drives slowly, then I let the Rolls overtake, on purpose, I wave, she waves, she doesn't know she's sitting in the Rolls, she's sitting in a gondola, she goes boating in the Rolls, I'm Marco Polo, she's Princess Cokachin, I call her Princess Cokachin.

I'm going to marry her, she doesn't know yet, marriage is a bourgeois institution ripe for dissolution, a tradition due for demolition. I'm going to marry Giulietta, I won't tell anyone, I'll keep it a secret from my father, we'll live in sin, marriage is dull, we'll have five children, three boys, two girls, illegitimate children, secret children, we won't educate them, we'll feed them, not educate them, mothers have birth-pangs, children ought to have birth-pangs, they ought to give birth to themselves, with birth-pangs. Giulietta doesn't know we're getting married, she wanted to marry an actor, she didn't marry him because he went to the provinces, he was content to be a provincial Hamlet, a summer-season Hamlet, she wanted to marry a Member of Parliament, she didn't marry him because he was beaten at the last elections, "It was his own fault," she says, "he only worried about me, a man who only worries about me is a failure. I hate failures."

Ferrari and I don't talk about the marriage, I won't ask for Giulietta's hand, Ferrari would laugh at me, we don't need his consent, we love each other in the gondola, Marco Polo and Princess Cokachin. We talk about *Positivismo*, we agree about *Positivismo*, Ferrari will buy *Positivismo*, my father will sell *Positivismo*, *Positivismo* is losing money. We'll turn *Positivismo* into a news-magazine, more views than news, news is all lies, all manipulated, we'll fight the Establishment, "They call me Red Ferrari," says Ferrari, "but all colours are Establishment colours, the rebellion is only a mini-revolution, we can't use a mini-skirt revolution, we need a naked revolution, the classless society is humbug, we need a society-less society." We'll change the format of *Positivismo*, tabloid, coloured cover, not like *Time*, *Time* is reactionary, we're going to create a revolutionary *Time*, without news. My father can keep the printing contract, we'll let him make money out of the printing contract, all that interests him is making money, in return he must undertake to distribute *Positivismo*, that's the proviso, we'll put it in the contract, Ferrari's publishing house doesn't handle distribution, there'll be no point if we don't sell the paper, we won't be helping the revolution without distribution, we need distribution. Every young author in Italy works for Ferrari, every young author in Italy will work for *Positivismo*, twenty pages of text, say I, fifteen, says Ferrari, twenty if we pull in enough advertising.

Ferrari understands me, "Once upon a time writers sang the praises of revolution," he says, "now they make revolution, the editorial section is the most important, the French Revolution is past history, now it's the Literary Revolution, it's good enough if five per cent of our readers read the literary section, the masses don't read, the masses only eat." Writers are writing revolution, poetry instead of slogans, brothers instead of blood, friends instead of flags, flowers instead of bread, *Positivismo* will replace the barricades. "We won't plug all your books," I say to Ferrari, "Francesco must remain independent," says Giulietta; if I remain independent she'll marry me, I'm no summer-season Hamlet, I'm an election-winner. "On the contrary," says Ferrari, "you've no need to review my books at all, my authors will review other books, that's more important," perhaps we oughtn't to discuss any books at all, we ought to discuss the authors, authors don't owe their fame to books, authors are more important.

"You're terrific," says Giulietta, she's proud of me, of my conversation with Ferrari, she lies on my bare chest, I ought to ask for a share of the equity, she says, "my father makes enough money," she does want to marry me after all. She loves her father, you can't help loving Ferrari, he makes money but money is unimportant to him, he never wears a tie, he rides in the Rolls in an open-necked shirt, he buys Gothic Madonnas, in the society-less society the Madonnas will go into a museum, the Rolls will go into a museum, the palazzi will turn into museums. "I'm spoilt," says Giulietta, she won't consign her father to a museum, she says, lots of publishers think like Ferrari, they only think, unsuccessfully, thinking isn't enough, there's only one Ferrari. "My father's schizophrenic," she says, I'm not sure I understand her, she loves her father because he's schizophrenic, in spring and autumn she has her clothes made in Paris, in Rome she shops at Mila Schön and Valentino, *alta moda*, she says, her father's *alta moda* too, he's schizophrenic, I mustn't do everything he says, I'm not sure I understand her.

I'm not one of those editors who pander to the proprietor, I tell Ferrari next evening, there are too many editors who don't write, rotary-coolies, galley-slaves, His Master's Voice; "A leader every week," says Ferrari. He has an idea, he's full of ideas, but not like my father, who buys sex-maniacs' memoirs, Ferrari's ideas are political. Ferrari is independent, he published a novel which was smuggled out of the Soviet Union, the novel was reprinted all over the world, fourteen million copies, twenty-one languages, the Soviet Union was furious, Ferrari didn't care, he publishes Russian authors, the Soviet Union doesn't care. Ferrari has an idea, I ought to write my memoirs, he says, "People shouldn't write their memoirs when they're old, nobody's interested in the memories of unmemorable old men." I'll record my memories of the demonstrations, I haven't forgotten a thing. Old men's memories are sweet, even the bitter ones, old men's memories are a sugar-coated pill, memories are birthday cakes, birthday cakes with stale icing and burnt-out candles. I shall only recall what everyone still recalls. *I protest* would make a good title, says Ferrari, I say no, I won't be dictated to by my father-in-law; "You're right," Giulietta says in the gondola, "the title is off-putting, and you can't dispense with the general reader," her father's a dreamer, she says, but he can't stand failure, he has a schizophrenic allergy to failure, if his dreams don't come true he blames his advisers, sacks staff, *Positivismo* has got to be a success, anyone can lose an election, anyone can play Hamlet on tour. I'll write my memoirs, I don't have to do everything Giulietta says, anyone would do as she says, Ferrari will publish the memoirs in book-form, twenty-one languages, we won't review them, it would be corrupt to review a book by the editor, we don't have to review what we print in *Positivismo*.

I won't mention Sofia in my book, I won't mention any names, the human being is anonymous, when he suffers he's anonymous, he's only human if he suffers and has no name, I won't mention Sofia. "My father's a worker" is just as old-fashioned as "My father's a millionaire", all fathers are in league, workers and millionaires, Ferrari's an exception, he's forty-six but he's an exception. I find it hard to oppose Ferrari, sometimes I only oppose him because Giulietta's looking at me; "You don't need any father," she says, "I've got a father, that's good enough." Sofia is a hypocrite, she's a virgin, she mans the barricades but she's waiting for her wedding-night, what do you lose when you lose your virginity, if I'd married her she wouldn't have thrown any stones, she throws stones and keeps her virginity. What makes this night different? Nothing makes this night different, Giulietta and I make love all night, sometimes we get up in the middle of the night and change beds, we go to sleep baroque, we wake up Renaissance; maybe Giulietta does have more experience than I do, but I don't let on, I stay independent. We're going to travel, we talk about travelling but we don't talk about a honeymoon trip, honeymoon trips are trips in a stage-coach, we'll travel to the moon, we'll travel to Iran, Marco Polo escorted Princess Cokachin to Persia, the Khan gave his consent, we don't need the Khan's consent, I'll tell Ferrari he must cut me in on *Positivismo*, an editor must be independent, Ferrari will buy *Positivismo* and cut me in.

We talk about *Quest' Ora*, Ferrari and Giulietta and I talk about *Quest' Ora*, we sit round the fireplace, the fire in the fireplace dies slowly, the Gothic Madonnas cast long shadows, they become long and lean like tall figures or invisible objects by Giacometti, the Madonnas are six hundred years old, the shadows are new, Giacometti Madonnas. I can't tell them why I took charge of the key to the safe, why I've taken charge of *Quest' Ora*, I can't tell them that I'm waiting for Morelli's last instalment, for the first, that I won't feel easy until the Christmas number is in print, that the cover is already printed, that I'll only feel easy if we report Morelli, if Morelli's arrested, if people believe we didn't know anything. Ferrari fulminates against *Quest' Ora*, he wears a polo-necked shirt, he paces up and down, he fulminates against *Quest' Ora*, "Your father owns too many magazines," he says, monopoly capitalism, his magazines ought to be taken away, first *Positivismo*, then *Quest' Ora*, monopoly capitalism is manipulative capitalism, the woman's magazine ought to be taken away too, and *Mickey Mouse*, "You can't imagine the harm Mickey Mouse has done," says Ferrari, a book publisher can't influence public opinion, one has to become a newspaper publisher to influence people. I try to excuse myself, Lenin went to Petrograd with the Kaiser's blessing, I said, *Quest' Ora* is the train for Petrograd, I had my reasons for taking over. "You're doing an excellent job," says Ferrari, it's strange, he says it disapprovingly, if the circulation increases my father will ask a higher price, why should he sell *Positivismo* if *Quest' Ora* is booming, he sets *Positivismo*'s losses against tax, what makes me think my father will sell a successful paper, asks Ferrari, I say nothing, I can't give anything away, say something, say Giulietta's eyes, she has a headache, she says, when I get upstairs she's asleep, I don't sleep, I think about the actor and the Member of Parliament.

I go to our general manager, I raise my salary: "You're going to pay me as much as Beroglio gets," I say, "I shall have to consult Signor Vanetti," he says, "No need to consult him," I say, I'd be crazy to work for a news-photographer's salary, "As much as Beroglio," I say, I work three times as hard as Beroglio, I slam the door. I'm looking for a flat, I won't marry Giulietta from the parental home, my father's coming home from hospital, I can't bring Princess Cokachin to our house, the house is full of fake pictures and fake furniture and fake antiques, twelve rooms, a twelve-roomed bourgeois home, a feast of fitted carpets; Ferrari sneers at the bourgeoisie and fake antiques. My mother won't hear of my leaving the nursery, rock-a-bye baby, my mother starts wailing, Papa mustn't be told, she wails, when I was little I used to be asked: "Who do you love best, Papa or Mama?"—"I love them both the same," I lied, anyone who hates his father has an Oedipus complex, I don't have an Oedipus complex, parents are parents, you call them parents because you can't distinguish between them, I can't distinguish my mother from my father, she goes on wailing, I shall take a flat, snap the umbilical cord.

Giulietta is staying in Rome, in the town house, six rooms, genuine antiques. I fetch her, we drive to Trastevere, it's raining, I park in front of Santa Maria in Trastevere, half a dozen hippies prance round the car, I put up my umbrella, they ought to invent something that looks less ridiculous than an umbrella, less ridiculous, less counter-revolutionary, we run across to Sabatino's. "I'd like to see what you look like without a beard," says Giulietta, it's probably because of the hippies; "The beard stays," I say, she isn't going to marry a man who shaves for her sake. I told Elena to book a table, the best table in the best room; "Signor Vanetti?" asks the waiter, he probably expected my father and his mistress, "That's right—Vanetti," I say, we get the best table in the best room, against the wall. Giulietta is wearing a plain costume under her fur coat, Yves Saint-Laurent, she says, I ask about her scent, Yves Saint-Laurent, she says, it goes with her costume, there isn't a good scent for furs, she says, it's best to use bath-essence.

I order lobster, lobster goes by weight, I order white wine,

I drink too much, I talk too much, the wine goes to my head, I've always drunk Coca-Cola till now, I've swallowed LSD, Coca-Cola tastes of mothballs, LSD tastes of salt, I drink wine, I talk too much.

I talk too much because Giulietta is untalkative; Giulietta misunderstood my silence when her father was fulminating against *Quest' Ora*. "We sold twenty thousand more copies of the last number than the one before," I say; "Well, then," says Giulietta. That irritates me, what does she mean by "Well, then", what's that supposed to mean, I ask. "Why didn't you tell my father?" she asks, her father would just love it if *Quest' Ora* lost ground, my father would just love it if I ruined *Quest' Ora*; "My father has spoiled me," she says, "my husband will have to spoil me too or he won't be a proper husband." I'd sooner she'd waited for me to ask her to marry me, she speaks as if I don't have any choice, but it doesn't matter, I order champagne, we don't talk about magazines any more, we stop talking about Ferrari and my father, I'm Marco Polo, she's Princess Cokachin, I shall spend Christmas at the palazzo, Giulietta is giving a party, she has to give a party because her father wants to give one but doesn't want to admit that Christmas is a Christian festival, Christmas has done even more harm than Mickey Mouse. We walk through the rain, we kiss in the rain, we kiss in the car, I drive her home, she says goodnight at the door, I'm disappointed, she says her father's at home, I don't understand what that's got to do with it, her father being at home.

Editorial conference is at nine o'clock, my father always held it at ten, even later on Wednesdays, he spent every Tuesday night with the Sacchi woman.

"We're putting the Capri picture of Enzian on the cover," I say, Bossi turns pale, the others protest, they gabble at each other, everyone has a different opinion, they all have the same opinion, none of them shares my opinion, they had an opinion when my father was there, his opinion. "Why raise Enzian now?" says Belotti, "We're launching the *Enzian Story* in the Christmas number," they're furious enough as it is, not having seen the manuscript, "We can't kill off Enzian," Ida Gottardi says: "Another nude girl? I thought this was a magazine for the discerning reader; we've got a splendid picture of an American airman shot down in Vietnam, he looks like a child-murderer in

293

Sing-Sing pyjamas"; it's nothing to do with Gottardi, she ought to stick to her fashions; "The Enzian girl isn't Christmassy enough," says Castellani, he specializes in religion and animal stories, if he had his way no cover would ever carry anything but saints and poodles, Giudicelli suggests Loren, very original, Rusconi asks what's got into me, it's December, he says, "Bikinis in December? One look at Enzian in a bikini and the readers'll catch tonsillitis."

I think of Princess Cokachin, I let them talk, they're only talking to themselves now, I'm not there, Francesco Vanetti isn't there, the Son isn't there, I close my agenda file, slowly; I say: "The Capri picture of Enzian goes on the cover."

I stand up, I go to my office, I sit down at my desk, I summon Bossi, Bossi doubles up with laughter, they're still sitting round the table, he says, Gottardi will resign, Gottardi will withdraw her resignation, she always does.

"We must peg the cover somehow," I say, "write a short piece, like *Are the Police Asleep?*"

"The cover's O.K.," says Bossi, "why do we have to needle the police?"

"So people see we've nothing to hide," I say. "We must bring Enzian to the boil again; naturally, we won't say anything about publishing the *Enzian Story*." Bossi is still laughing, he's thinking of the editorial conference. Bossi is surprised, he didn't expect me to bang the table, I didn't bang the table, I simply said: "The Capri picture of Enzian goes on the cover", I'm going to fight for democracy, no readers no democracy, Ferrari suffers from a failure-allergy, Bossi doesn't understand that, nobody can fight for democracy with democratic methods, how far would Lenin have got if he'd fought with democratic methods, there can't be any democracy in a publishing house, how far would you get if every member of an orchestra played whatever came into his head, one would play *Lohengrin*, another *Santa Lucia*, no conductor no orchestra.

I send for Sartori, he didn't say anything at the conference, he's a silent sort of person, he speaks in pictures.

"We'll only make it half-length," I say, "her legs are nothing special."

"It's an amateur shot," says Sartori.

"All the more authentic," say I.

THE ALIBI

"We've got a Bellini Madonna on the cover of our next number," says Sartori.

"I know," say I. "That's life."

Sartori goes off with Hertha Enzian under his arm, Bossi says, "You're following in your father's footsteps." I don't contradict him, there's no point, Bossi wouldn't understand, footsteps, what are footsteps, it's a stupid analogy, if you follow in someone else's footsteps you obliterate them, I'm following in my father's footsteps, I'm obliterating my father's footsteps.

I don't go and see Giulietta, I'm still in the office at midnight, I'm the last one in the office, I read Bossi's Morelli manuscript, it's the best thing Bossi has ever done, Bossi's a dumb genius. Elena's still fidgeting around in the outer office, she's probably waiting for me to drive her home, I'm the only person in the building who hasn't slept with Elena, I shall go on being the only person who's never slept with Elena. I ask for Giulietta's number, Elena puts on a pitying expression: the poor boy, sleeping with someone else. "You can go home," I say.

I've told Giulietta about my volume of poetry, enough poems for a slim volume, Ferrari will publish the poems; "Haven't I ever inspired you to write a poem?" Giulietta asked, I feel inspired, I write:

> When I through you of life had learned so much,
> My erstwhile thoughts stood grieving at the gate.
> I asked myself what I had felt of late,
> And early harvest withered at my touch.
>
> When from today, through you, my face I turned,
> Lost, in that moment, what I'd been of yore
> And put our shameful bliss all else before,
> I felt regret for everything unlearned.
>
> Old ecstasies can ne'er return again.
> Is life not that which man must needs resign
> Or wine from grapes ungathered on the vine?
>
> Has not our bliss the others' bliss deceived,
> Am I not weakly hiding from their pain,
> Mourns not my love achievements unachieved?

I look out of the window, it's raining, the lights are burning in the printing works, the keyboard operators are sitting at their keyboards, you can see the compositors through the dancing window-panes, neon lighting, I read the poem, the lines rhyme, it's almost a sonnet, I didn't mean to write a sonnet, anything that rhymes is dangerous, nothing rhymes, why should a poem rhyme, I doesn't rhyme with ME, ME rhymes with me, it's a lie, it isn't a lie, I won't show the poem to Giulietta, I tear the poem up.

Antonio Zempach

Yvette and I flew to Rome. I had something to do in Milan first, a probate case. Yvette refuses to fly on principle—just nervousness, not air-sickness, but she made an exception. She betrays her principles once in a while, like all clever women. The stewardesses concentrated exclusively on Yvette—they make a great show of devoting themselves to your wife when you're flying *à deux*. Chattering girls in a Lausanne boarding-school.

It was a trying flight. Something always goes wrong when Yvette flies, as if to demonstrate the perils of air travel. I bought a couple of papers in Milan. They were full of the latest air disaster, a passenger 'plane which had crashed with a football team on board. No survivors. I buckled myself in and stuffed the papers down between our seats. A stewardess promptly offered us some new ones. "It's true," said Yvette, "football teams put a jinx on aeroplanes." At that moment the Milan team trooped on board, all in tremendous form. With a bit of encouragement, they'd have practised shooting goals through the door to the pilot's cabin. South of Florence we ran into dense fog. "That comes of flying with a football team," said Yvette. We circled Rome and landed thirty minutes late—on instruments, I suspect.

In the afternoon I drove to Vanetti's office. "Signor Vanetti is expecting you," the secretary said, but it turned out to be Signor Francesco Vanetti. He was sitting at his father's desk. I didn't recognize him at first. Flannel suit, striped shirt, blue tie, no beard. Hadn't I heard about his father's coronary, he asked, he was better already, God be praised, my journey wouldn't be wasted, his father had discussed everything with him.

I submitted the documents relating to the Liechtenstein holding company. It was obvious that he didn't know much about it, but he asked some intelligent questions. A beginner eager to learn. We went across to the administrative offices and he introduced me to the general manager, a solid-looking citizen with a conciliatory manner. Young Vanetti puzzled me. He handled his new-found wisdom like an old pro. When we were outside again he said he had something to discuss with me, urgently. He cancelled all calls and ordered coffee.

It was about the sale of the *Morelli Story*, he said. His father wanted him to raise the matter with me and put me to work on the contracts.

"What's the *Morelli Story*?" I asked.

"We commissioned a well-known author to write his memoirs," he said, "Aurelio Morelli."

"Never heard of him," I said. I don't regard myself as a vulture for culture, but if I haven't heard of an author's name it won't be Dante or Pirandello. Only the ill-read are so unsure of themselves that they pretend to know every name in the book, even the Nobel Prize-winners.

"We almost fell flat when he submitted his manuscript," said Vanetti junior. "It turned out to be the confessions of a sex-maniac."

"Don't tell me," I said, as sarcastically as I could, "he strangled Hertha Enzian."

"And two other women," said Francesco Vanetti.

I went cold. A lump of granite materialized in my stomach, and I suddenly knew where my heart was. A painful realization —no man should locate his heart under the age of fifty. The young man might at least have apologized for his new face: Sorry, my old face was a mask, or, my new face is a mask— something like that. I was riled by the sheer blatancy of the lie. An author who turns out to be a murderer and makes a voluntary confession to *Quest' Ora*? They might have done me the compliment of dreaming up something a little more plausible than that. The young man must have thought me a dim-wit if he hoped I'd forgotten our conversation in the car. All that talk about memoirs and accomplices!

"You've turned him in, of course," I said.

"We hope to do so within the next few days," he replied.

"Why only in the next few days?" I asked.

"We don't want to make fools of ourselves," he replied. He was well-rehearsed. "A confession isn't proof. We're making inquiries. Apart from that, we don't know Morelli's present whereabouts. He's left his flat, and we're trying to trace him."

"Isn't that a job for the police?" I asked.

"We'd prefer to hand him to the police on a plate," said Francesco Vanetti.

I could have said: You spoke about memoirs in the car, you knew about Morelli's confession even at that stage. But perhaps Francesco Vanetti really had taken me for one of his father's accomplices that time in the car, when he drove me back to my hotel. The old, old story of the three wise monkeys: you know it and I know it but there's no need to talk about it. Perhaps he still thought I was an accomplice. He didn't say so, just left the channels of communication open.

"You wanted to discuss something with me," I said.

"My father would like to negotiate the foreign contracts via Switzerland," he said, "or Liechtenstein, as the case may be. Speaking strictly in confidence, Dr Zempach, we're launching the *Morelli Story* in our Christmas number."

"Without knowing whether the confession is authentic?" I asked.

"Only if it is authentic," he said. He shoved a bunch of files under my nose. More stage management. "We have draft contracts with Paris, London, New York, Buenos Aires—thirteen in all. They refer to the *Enzian Story*. That would have to be amended. Also, the purchase prices don't meet our requirements any longer. My father has noted the revised figures in the margin in red ink."

"And my job?" I asked.

"Liechtenstein regulations apply," he said. "My father wants you to check the contracts' validity under Swiss law. He told me he'd already discussed it with you."

That was about the sixth time he's enlisted his absent father's support, and there was a note of uncertainty in his voice. I couldn't help it, I felt sorry for him. He's riding the escalator, I reflected. Some people are escalator show-offs who stand in the middle of the step without holding on: I'm an expert—look, no hands. A lot of others start walking—why use an escalator if you want to climb stairs?—because they aim to beat the escalator to the top. That's how I saw Francesco Vanetti, escalator underfoot but climbing steadily, bound for the exalted heights of the ready-to-wear department. I felt compassion for him, the uniquely genuine compassion that subsists between people suffering from related diseases.

"You mentioned the word memoirs ten minutes after we first met," I said. "You knew who the murderer was, even then."

He was afraid now, I could see it in his face. Was he afraid that the police would question me, that I'd emerge as a prosecution witness—not a colleague, not a wise monkey, a prosecution witness? Or was he afraid of his father because he'd gone about things the wrong way? It wasn't his fault, it was his father's fault. He'd probably instructed him to be quite frank with me: the man is bound by professional secrecy, we'll be publishing the confession in a few days anyway, the Swiss will pocket his *Fränkli* and vanish. Just after I joined the firm the managing director of an insurance company—one of Dr von Helis's clients—went down with mastoid trouble. His other trouble was that he'd transferred the company's legal reserves from one country to another—a Peter-and-Paul operation. They were still there when the next audit was held. He couldn't confide in anyone. The fraud was discovered in his absence, and the insurance company collapsed. If you play crooked games you shouldn't get mastoid trouble. Or a coronary.

"I wasn't talking about the Morelli memoirs," said Francesco Vanetti. "Surely you don't think . . . I was talking about Enzian senior, you'd just come from Vienna, you remember. . . . It's only a matter of days now," he assured me.

Liars have it easy—you can't tell them what they are. It's an insult to call someone a liar. Thief, extortioner, murderer, yes, but you can't call a liar a liar.

Young Vanetti asked me to pay him another visit next morning. His beardlessness and flannel suit made him look more vulnerable than the beard and checked shirt of a few weeks earlier. He looked fifteen. Any minute, Papa would come in and yank him out of his chair—a fine mess you've made of things, my lad.

I told the taxi-driver "Hotel Hassler" but wondered whether

to go straight to the police instead. It would have been the only way of proving to Yvette that I was fed up, bilious with ambition, ready to diet. If not, I'd have to suppress the whole thing, my entire conversation with Francesco Vanetti. The branch had snapped—I was lying at the foot of the tree. Whether or not I concealed the conversation from Yvette, I couldn't continue to represent Edizioni Vanetti. The publishing business had gone to the dogs, so back to my home-grown property speculators.

Yvette was still in bed. It takes her at least twelve hours to recover from a flight. I sat down beside her and said, "Know something? I've been acting for Murder Inc." Then I told her about my talk with Vanetti junior, every last detail.

She listened patiently, as usual. She didn't interrupt, but eyes as expressive as Yvette's influence the telling of a story and sometimes change its course.

"What are you going to do?" she asked.

"What am I going to do?" I said. "I'm going to call the police and tell them that Hertha Enzian was murdered by an author named Aurelio Morelli."

"Anonymously?" she asked.

"No, not anonymously," I said. "Nobody takes any notice of anonymous informants."

"They're offering a reward for the discovery of the murderer," she said. "I read it somewhere."

"Damn the reward," I said.

She said, "You'll get it anyway."

"Does that mean I shouldn't report Morelli?" I asked.

"You can't report Morelli without reporting Vanetti," she said. "They'll ask you where you got Morelli's name from. Vanetti is your client."

"Francesco Vanetti isn't," I said.

She slipped into her mules—I always wonder how someone so small manages to have such big feet—and put on her housecoat. Then she sat down at the dressing-table.

"That's a legal quibble," she said.

"Anyway," I said, "my client didn't entrust me with any secrets. Francesco Vanetti gave himself away inadvertently."

We talked about Vanetti junior for several minutes. I got hot under the collar because Yvette misunderstood me. She said I felt smug about the young man's conversion. "If we corrupt the young," she said, "we get the same kick as a parent who's told his children take after him." Then she said, "Your name will be in all the papers tomorrow morning. Photographs, interviews, reward—the full treatment."

"All right," I said, "we'll let the murderer go."

Yvette shook her head. "You're going to report him, but not until a few days after Christmas."

"Peace on earth, goodwill to men," I said. "He'll be somewhere over the rainbow by then."

"He is already," Yvette said. "So far, though, nobody knows you're acting for Edizioni Vanetti."

She said it as if I'd caught an unmentionable disease, not to be discussed in polite society. It suddenly dawned on me why Yvette was so chary of my going to the police. As usual, she was playing pig-in-the-middle between me and her father, as if she wanted to protect us from each other. I wasn't so sure, though. Perhaps she was just protecting her father. How to explain to the public at large that Dr von Helis's firm had no connection with *Quest' Ora*, that Dr Zempach was acting for Vanetti on his own, that he'd bought the life of a dead call-girl on the side, an extramural activity, a young lawyer, somewhat rash and over-enthusiastic, coincidentally the boss's son-in-law? Then, aglow with moral indignation, he had denounced his client. A brand-new hero for the illustrated magazines, but back on the Dolder Yvette would bite her lip. It isn't done to get into the papers on the Dolder, not unless you're appointed Commander-in-Chief or celebrating your eightieth birthday, short on hair and long on respectability, which means never getting into the papers. I wasn't to report Aurelio Morelli, author and murderer, because there are only two sorts of citizens: the ones who want to avoid getting into the papers at all costs, regardless of circumstances, and the ones who don't want to be mentioned at any price, except possibly in a nice obituary: his memory will endure for ever. . . .

"The firm will survive," I said.

"I'm not thinking of the scandal," said Yvette.

I said, "It isn't scandalous to witness a murder, even if the newspapers do publish your picture. A witness can't help it if people confuse his picture with the murderer's."

"It's too late," Yvette said, without reproach. "You acted for

Vanetti *in re* Enzian and you set up the holding company in Liechtenstein."

"The firm acts for fraudulent bankers," I retorted. "As for holding companies, we churn them out like sausages. I had no idea—"

Yvette cut me short. She didn't say anything, but the look in her eye cut me short. Of course I had an idea—I didn't know for sure, that was all. You get penalized for lack of instinct, not lack of knowledge. The right instinct is as indispensable as the right adviser. Rashness is a crime in Switzerland. Thought precedes action with us; the converse is high treason.

"They won't believe you," said Yvette. "They'll say you denounced the murderer for the sake of the publicity."

"Quite possibly," I said. "I can't help that, though. If someone discovered a cancer serum tomorrow they'd say he was trying to upstage the Beatles."

The conversation would never lead anywhere unless I admitted that the whole thing had been a mistake, the Vienna trip, Enzian, the holding company. Yvette would never say it herself. "I told you so" isn't part of her vocabulary.

"I realize I've made a lot of mistakes," I said, "but there's a limit—a frontier you can't cross." That was a banality, a throwaway line: there's a limit to everything, but maybe that's the whole point. "Lines of demarcation are very widely drawn these days," I said, "but you come to them in the end. For instance, when you fail to report a murderer."

"If you report him today," Yvette said, "the result will be exactly the same as if Vanetti reports him tomorrow. Have you received your fee yet?"

"Yes," I said, "that's to say, for Enzian and expenses. I was going to send a bill from Zürich for the rest."

"Suppose you make them a present of the money," said Yvette. "Why not give up acting for them?"

"Just what I meant to do," I said. "After our night out with Vorneweg. You were against it. You wanted to know the whole story. Well, now you do."

That was unfair, and I knew it. Yvette had never been convinced that I meant to give up. When Yvette shelves something it stays shelved. When I shelve something I keep on taking it down, like a child peeping at a dirty book.

She rose, came and sat beside me on the bed, and stroked my hair. "Everyone makes mistakes," she said. "Our mistake"—she said "our"—"was to get involved with Chichikov. Ambition in your case, curiosity in mine. We'll fly back tomorrow. . . ."

"Back to our snug little world," I cut in.

"Our comparatively snug little world," she said. "Don't be ashamed of it. You said there was a limit. We can't do more than stop when we reach it."

She mightn't have convinced me if she hadn't started to talk about her father. I don't think she'd ever spoken as freely before. Naturally, the firm would survive the scandal, but it would mean a break between me and Dr von Helis. "The only thing we can do is keep quiet," she said, "otherwise one thing will lead to another." She seemed to know more about me than I did myself. I wanted to denounce the murderer to show her that, having compromised a hundred times, I refused to compromise any more. "Let's wait till Christmas," she said. "If Chichikov hasn't made a move by then, we can still think it over."

"The last chapter of *Dead Souls* was never written," I said.

"Who ever does write the last chapter?" said Yvette.

Aurelio Morelli

Albeit that activity does not accord with my contemplative disposition, I well understand what my colleague, Johann Wolfgang von Goethe, meant when he wrote: *The allotted sphere and heritage of the human mind is the realm of conduct and action. It will seldom err if active.* I had been roused to exceptional activity in recent days; I can assert, with every justification, that I did not err.

First and foremost, I had to compose the letter which I intend to hand to Agnese at our next encounter—a singular undertaking, since we are already pledged to a tryst in the grounds of the atomic power station, that murderous spot which our meetings have so gloriously transfigured. I could thus communicate to her by word of mouth what I have bashfully committed to paper, yet one should not, I feel, lightly dismiss the Thucydidean definition of the writer as a man "who cannot speak". During the long, neon-lit nights in my gastronomic dungeon there has matured in me the resolve to confront Agnese with a decision, to present her with a gentle ultimatum—in short, to persuade her to share my Bolivian exile. The prospect of having to part from her for ever, or at least until the victory of the revolution and my triumphal homecoming, the prospect of never more being privileged to wait, atremble with impatience, for the hours to pass until our next meeting, the prospect of forfeiting her physical presence—for what is love, if not the craving for physical presence?—all these thoughts have become unbearable to me. We could, paradoxically, survive the end of the world because, dying, we leave naught behind; yet how to take individual leave of a world which will continue to stew in its sour and acerbic juice without us? Our fear of death amounts, fundamentally, to a reluctance to slough off responsibility, however onerous it may have become; we are attached to the burden we bear, and this is especially true of me and Agnese, for I know the baneful influences to which she is exposed, know what temptations so menacingly surround her, know that her path must lead down into the abyss unless I, a friend in the direst need, take her hand in my own sure grasp and preserve her from calamity. I am as little in doubt that she is the sole exception among the hosts of youth as I was on that blessed day when a being from another world bent over me and my murdered fish; I doubt not that she is Homunculus and Pygmalion both, that I can alchemize and mould her into an exemplary being: into all that youth could be, but is not.

The desire to live persists for as long as there is life within us, yet we are at fault if we suppose—as I myself have done—that life-expectancy, to employ the clumsy jargon of the insurance world, has become greater or longer; it has diminished, because youth identifies age with death, and believes that a forty-year-old is already dead, on the grounds that life is limited to fifteen or twenty years at most. He who has but fifteen or twenty years to live, lives with a truly diabolical intensity, is incapable of practising the fine art of hoping, waiting, and reflecting, offers stubborn resistance to the process of maturation, and locks himself up in the incubation chamber like some demented chicken; he leaps from the first rung of the ladder to the last; should something fail to happen the same day, the same night, he fears that it never will; he yearns to have arrived before ever setting eyes on his destination; to him faster aeroplanes and automobiles are merely symbols of instant knowledge, instant profit, instant fulfilment, instant marriage, instant love; quickly replete, he looks about him for epicurean delicacies with which to tempt or glut his already sated appetite: and if word goes round that the Almighty is, by way of natural compensation, inflicting new diseases upon the world of antibiotics, foolhardy operations, and frustrated wars, no one dares to call the new plague by name. *Gioventú*, youth, *Jugend*, *jeunesse*—such is the name of the new divine scourge, a curtailer of life in an age dedicated to its prolongation.

It has been borne in on me that not even my Agnese is free from this pernicious bacillus, which being so, her only hope of preservation or cure is to entrust herself to me, the knowledge-able physician. That my letter avowed the love of an ageing man is momentous enough; still more importantly, it also, in the most decorous terms, offered her sanctuary. Although I was unable to confide the true reasons for my sudden departure and transoceanic journey in my letter, which comprises six closely written pages, the sweet conspiracy of elopement is no novelty: *Die Entführung aus dem Serail* has its happy ending—Belmont sails for distant shores with Konstanze, Blöndchen, and Perillo. Generously, my letter—which I shall, with pounding heart, hand to Agnese in person, hoping that look and gesture will eloquently stand surrogate for the words I cannot utter— generously, my letter offers to defray the cost of our joint voyage. I shall arrive in my new home bereft of financial resources, yet what is that beside my unerring certainty that we two, Agnese and I, are inflamed with love for the first time in our lives?

Much else remaining to be done, I set to work with steadfast determination. I refer to the giant fish *Carcharias glaucus* which mine hosts have exposed to the scorn and contumely of the hoi polloi who frequent the dining-room of their hotel—an excrucia-ting spectacle which has repeatedly caused my blood to boil and intensified the bitterness of my wretched exile. I had long been tormented by the thought that, although the scene of my last sojourn upon the soil of Beldam Europe will doubtless boast a commemorative plaque in marble, and although hordes of admirers will make pilgrimage to Foce Verde just as they do to Beethoven's former home, the tomb of Garibaldi, or Stratford-on-Avon, the visitor will here—here, of all places—be confronted by a manifestation of the basest human instincts, a monument to murder most foul.

Being in no hurry to complete my letter to Agnese, I waited patiently until midnight was two hours old, so that I could execute my plan safely and at leisure.

For more than a week I had been the sole patron of my inhospitable hostelry, the commercial travellers who alight there in the winter-time—and not infrequently pay court to Grazia, waitress and holder of the local record for mammary development—having long since hastened home to spend the Christmas holiday in the bosom of their families.

In stockinged feet—I had removed my shoes and was carrying them in my hand—I gingerly opened my door, which for once deigned not to creak, almost as if it were privy to my enterprise, and went out into the perpetual gloom of the corridor, whose lights never burn even when they should. It filled me with mocking satisfaction to behave like a thief, housebreaker or cat-burglar, for never had I been more keenly aware of the laughable stupidity of circumstantial evidence: at that moment many people might have thought me a hotel thief, whereas they would in reality have been looking at a man who was setting forth to perform a noble deed.

I groped my way along the wall, following the familiar route to the lavatory, until I came to the downward-leading staircase; never stumbling, cautiously setting one foot before the other, I attained the dining-room without incident. Being a far-sighted man, I had long since ascertained that the room would not be in total darkness: the provocative legend on the façade, *Specialità marinari sempre vive*, remains illuminated all night long—idiotically, for what benighted traveller would pause here and request live fish to eat? The green neon glow penetrates the green curtains of the dining-room. Without making the smallest noise, I placed a chair beneath the cadaver of my friend, slanderously described as a "man-eating" shark but privately christened "Alfonso" by me, and set to work to detach the victim of treachery from the strip of wall to which it had so humiliatingly and barbarously been nailed.

The operation was not altogether as successful as I could have wished: I had no tools at my disposal, and my mute companion weighed far more than I had supposed, having seemingly been intended as a permanent *mene tekel* of man's inhumanity. My physical strength was, however, augmented by a fury born of brooding anger and an agonizing sense of solidarity. Although I did not manage to release my martyr among fish from its pillory intact, I was nonetheless able to detach pieces of the victim with my bare hands, thereby destroying the spectacle of humiliation in its entirety. Quite half a dozen times I descended from the chair, a fragment of my guiltless Alfonso in either hand, then clambered up again, twice upsetting the wooden quadruped with a clatter which, though considerable, failed to prevent the hotel's murderous proprietors or their bosomy domestic from continuing to sleep the sleep of the unjust. Shreds of the luckless creature lodged beneath my finger-nails, my suit became smeared with preservative grease, and my back pained me, but I remained undeterred.

I could very well have left the ruined spectacle of shame *in situ*, beyond the capacity of any expert hand to reconstruct, but my motives were primarily of a devotional nature. I therefore left the hotel by the glass door, which was easily opened from the interior, taking with me as many relics of the long-suffering martyr as I was able to carry. The moonlit sky was serene and glassy as only a winter's night can be. The tide was out—or, rather, the sea had fled in loathing from the shore. I came within an ace, as I was crossing the road, of being captured by the harsh beam of light from a south-bound lorry, but I nimbly evaded this threat and, threading my way through a wilderness of bathing-huts, reached the net-strewn shore. Here I entrusted Alfonso, the *Carcharias glaucus* or blue-green shark, to the blue-green element; and, as I did so, the waves began to sing a hymn of thanksgiving, ballerinas in silvery tutus danced across the foaming stage, and the fishes of the sea—or so I fancied—welcomed the dead martyr and, to a murmurous accompaniment of water music, conducted him to his cool sepulchre beneath the waves.

Next morning—I mention this quite by way of digression, for there are things of greater import to relate—my hotel, ingloriously renowned for its cannibalistic bill of fare, was plunged into a turmoil which could not have been more clamorous had some crown jewels been stolen from one of the rooms overnight. The "inexplicable" act—and how could it have been aught but inexplicable to the plebeian herd?—formed a topic of conversation not only in the Hotel Palma but also, as I learned on my visit to the stationer and newsagent, throughout Foce Verde. Not only did no suspicion fall on the respected hotel guest—respected as are all who pay their bills with promptitude—but he was, ironically enough, enlisted as an expert: an author who travelled with his own aquarium was deemed incapable of such destruction. I was hard put to it to conceal my amusement when it was generally agreed that an act of vandalism was involved: legalized murder regarded as a civilized necessity; its victim's liberation an act of vandalism! What could be more compulsively hilarious?

My preparations for departure, which entail, first and foremost, the safe bestowal of the more important parts of my manuscript—to wit, those that I have not yet relinquished to *Quest' Ora*—and the making of my will—I call it that, though it consists merely of a simple letter in which I ordain that my aquarium shall be transferred, intact, to the Institute of Oceanography—my precautionary measures, in short, were interrupted by a highly distasteful visit.

At about three o'clock on that sunny December afternoon I was informed of the arrival of a lady. Had Agnese, spurred on by irresistible longing, hastened to me, unannounced, from Rome—had she, in defiance of my express prohibition, penetrated my place of residence? I was swiftly disillusioned. The female intruder who awaited me in the deserted dining-room, indeed, directly beneath the lingering traces of piscine martyrdom, in no wise resembled my Agnese: a young lady conspicuous for her elegant attire, if that be not a *contradictio in adjecto*, she summarily introduced herself as Beatrice Vanetti, daughter of the proprietor of *Quest' Ora*. Signor Bossi had been stricken with a sudden indisposition, she told me, and, in view of the confidential nature of the transaction, she had been entrusted with the task of collecting the residue, concluding chapter, or *dénouement* of my work, and of delivering the last instalment of my agreed remuneration.

I have often wondered, during my span of sentient existence, whether the height of human folly may not consist in supposing one's fellow-mortals—what hypocritical familiarity in that word!—to be still more foolish than they are. Even before

the creature with the remarkably long and slender neck had
finished her preamble, I realized that, once possessed of the
Enzian chapter, she would immediately hasten to the myrmidons
of the law and set them on my trail. I found it vexatious in the
extreme to be taken for a fool, and I can only describe it as a
masterpiece of deception that I avoided showing the fact—first,
because I should greatly have welcomed the final payment, and,
secondly, because I succeeded in suppressing symptoms of panic
only by a supreme exercise of the self-control which is my
birthright. So the evil witch judged me ripe for slaughter even
earlier than I had supposed! I had grazed the lush pastures long
enough, she thought, and there was no time to be lost. Even as
our conversation proceeded, I debated whether it would not be
better to change my abode prematurely, and, air-ticket and visa
in pocket, to tarry elsewhere until the expiry of the few days
that remain before my aeroplane wings its way to the promised
land.

I was on the verge of finishing the last chapter, I told her, but
one or two more corrections were indispensable. While apologizing, on the one hand, for its belated completion, I did not, on
the other, scruple to extol my own work in general and the
Enzian chapter in particular, stressing its vital importance and
promising a multitude of unexpected tidbits still to come. In so
doing I played the part of the unworldly artist who knows no
goal but perfection, is uninterested in financial reward, and
would rather be defrauded of his fee than of one well-chosen
word. The young woman was so stubbornly insistent that she
reinforced my suspicions still further—indeed, she had the
effrontery to declare that my manuscript would in any case be
"edited"; and that minutiae such as stylistic refinement and
phraseological subtlety were unimportant.

As if that were not enough, the sorcerer's lovely daughter
assumed a nonchalantly conversational tone, and, in an un-
successful attempt to convince me that she had abandoned her
designs, began to chat about my memoirs, which she appeared
to have read with relish. She complained that my otherwise
admirable manuscript embodied no details of my childhood, and
asked if I would permit her to pose some questions on the subject.
I vigorously repudiated her suggestion that I might have suffered
as a result of being born out of wedlock: illegitimate children

were so frequent a phenomenon in our district that whole dynasties bore the maternal name—and why not, when the Catholic Church showed itself exceedingly indulgent towards unmarried mothers provided they reared their children in the one true faith? Even so, she said, I could not have failed to hate the man who had so vilely deserted my mother. On the contrary, I replied. As a young boy I had entertained the most romantic illusions about my vanished sire, whom I thought of as a fairy-tale prince of the sea. Quite understandable, she said with a nod, clearly understanding nothing at all; I had probably laid all blame at my mother's door, and my hatred for women and desire for revenge presumably stemmed from shame at my mother's immoral behaviour. "You attribute the sad loss of your father to her," she stated categorically. "To you, she is a murderess who has deprived her child of a father."

I should scarcely have been able to repress my overpowering urge to interrupt the brazen creature in her abominable discourse, chastise her in the name of my worthy mother, or at least show her the door, had I not swiftly grasped her underlying motives. Psychoanalysis, whose philosophical significance I would not wish to underrate, resembles a medical technique capable of application only, say, to persons with red hair: it can only avail those of a certain intelligence, yets its application is limited in their case, too, because even an imperfect knowledge of the technique permits the patient to delude and mislead his analyst.

I told her that my relations with my mother—on which the Neapolitan pugilist had already cast doubt—might justly be described as ideal: I had enjoyed the warmest affection from her in my childhood, had been nurtured and cherished by her, and still entertained the most dutiful feelings towards her. I was free from the sort of misogyny associated with Schopenhauer or Strindberg: my admiration for beautiful women—here I bowed slightly—was wholly in accord with my aesthetic sense; woman, the daughter of Nature, interested me far more than man, with his tangled web of instincts; and, finally, the execution of Mesdemoiselles Chiesa, Pisenti, and Enzian being a simple act of justice, I bore no animosity towards the three girls who had passed over in so tragic a fashion.

Ah yes, the would-be psychiatrist broke in, eyeing me as if I were a madman, that explained a great deal. Apparently—she smiled—I cherished exaggerated ideas about the purity of women, hence—she lowered her voice—my predilection for ridding the world of prostitutes or those women whom I regarded as such. But no, I replied, the worst charge I had to bring against women corresponded precisely with that which my shrewd *confrère* Mark Twain described as the worst attribute of the Negro—namely, his equal claim to humanity. I expected no great thing of human beings, whether male or female; consequently, I could never be disillusioned by them.

A lecherous creature, this Signorina Vanetti, and the longer I observed her—her jumper was so taut as clearly to reveal, not only her breasts, but also her pointed nipples; she several times ran her fingers provocatively through her soft and lustrous hair; she crossed her legs with the unmistakable intention of baring the flesh framed by stocking-top and suspender—in short, the longer Signorina Vanetti subjected me to inquisition, the more I commended her good fortune in not having made my acquaintance earlier and under other circumstances. The lewd hussy not only presumed to explore the 'sexual motives' for my behaviour, but offered me a choice of several such motives, after the fashion of 'quiz' programmes intended for the feeble-minded: I could have chosen between impotence, physical deformity, persistent childhood or venereal diseases, homosexual tendencies, traumata of the most diverse kinds, or downright sadism. If ever there were a time when I detected sadistic instincts in myself, that time was now: it gave me amusement, pleasure, nay, a heathenish delight, to plunge Miss Inquisition 1967 into utter confusion by painting myself the happiest of mortals; on the one hand, I asserted—a pure fabrication—that my many and enjoyable sexual experiences had included several of a homosexual nature, and, on the other, I told her that I had defended my mother's lovable cats against rough boys in my childhood. It drove the insidious deep-sea diver to despair when, questioned about my most vivid childhood memory, I promptly began to speak of our village priest, who had one day led his young charges up a hill and there, in a truly biblical setting, declaimed the Sermon on the Mount. It was, I said, the same clerical gentleman who had later enabled me to attend university. "My memories, Signorina," I continued, "are thronged with the

kindliest folk imaginable. The man most favoured by fortune is
he who attracts the better members of his species. How pleasant
to have met you—on that note, *salute!*"

Just as I had expected, the sorcerer's ambassadress refused to
be cut short: keeping her gaze fixed on the ruins of Alfonso and
rudely cavorting from one topic of conversation to the next, she
reverted to that part of my manuscript which dealt with the
Enzian episode.

My "no" was final. Only that which the Neapolitan pugilist
chooses to describe as the *Enzian Story* stands between me and
imprisonment, or, more properly, death, for I would rather cur-
tail a most worthy and worthwhile existence than permit a
brutal horde of policemen to lead Aurelio Morelli away in handcuffs. My "no" was final, but I was obliged to resort to a white
lie. I named a specific day, the day after my mutually agreed
rendezvous with Agnese: I should, I said, have pleasure in
waiting upon her on that day with the final chapter of my
revelations.

Like the daughter of Herodias, the little minx seemed eager to
serve up my head on a platter. Edging towards the door for
safety's sake, she warned me against any fraudulent breach of
contract or attempt at flight: upon delivery of the last chapter
the good Signor Bossi would do all in his power to help me across
the frontier, whereas if I tried to deceive him he would have no
recourse but to take my fragmentary chronicle, my eighth
symphony, the *Unfinished*—she did not, of course, refer to my
work as such herself—and go to the authorities. To reassure her
I feigned stupidity, began to speak about the cost of my air-trip,
and enjoined her to attend our next meeting armed with the
sum outstanding in respect of travel and surgical expenses.

Adieu, Salome, you will have to perform your hysterical dance
of death with an empty platter! I have taken your admonitions
to heart—yes, but I have construed them otherwise than you
intended. The many-coloured, zebra-striped posteriors of the
bathing-huts evanesce into the evening mist; like empty hoods
newly removed from the heads of hanged men, the nets dangle
from the hideous gallows at either end of the deserted basket-ball
pitch; the arid dunes along the wintry shore are veiled in flurries
of sand; a murderous fisherman, bent on mischief, trudges with
bowed head towards the mouth of the Fosso Mascarello; in the

entrance to the empty hotel, Grazia of the vaccine udders squirms and bridles as each lorry rattles by. Like my sinful *confrère* Oscar Wilde, as he took leave of Reading Gaol, I am seized with an unaccountable sense of melancholy. Foce Verde must bid me farewell.

Christa Sonntag

It put me in mind of the Turk. That's a sort of saying in our family. When I was at school in Munich we had a classmate called Hanna Heftner. Stinking rich, she was—her father had a clothing store right beside the Town Hall, which was why the Heftners always gave a children's dance every Carnival-time. Fancy dress, naturally, or it wouldn't have been Carnival. One year I went as a mermaid. I must have looked pretty cute even then, with my red hair, which is my best feature. Another time I went as Helen of Troy, because I always did have a thing about ancient history. Well, the year before I reached school-leaving age and left school, Hanna's grandfather—old man Heftner— upped and died, which meant cancelling the party at the last minute, worse luck. They put everyone off except Johann Ertl, who they forgot about. Hanna told us the whole story at school, and we laughed ourselves sick, because children are like that— death leaves them cold, so to speak. It's too far away, and they don't know anything about infant mortality. Anyway, just as the Heftners were off to the cemetery, all black crêpe and faces a mile long, Johann Ertl barged into the room dressed up as a Turk, wearing baggy trousers and waving a curved sword over his head. It must have been a proper scream, really, a Turk at a funeral party. Ever since then we've always called someone who turns up at the wrong moment a Turk.

This time Bossi was the Turk, except that it wasn't a laughing matter because he barged in in the middle of an orgy.

The thing is, I've got a regular customer who orders himself a repeat of the last days of Pompeii two or three times a year. I supply the girls, which puts up my overheads because they get a percentage. Mostly I limit myself to three because I don't want to fork out too much in percentages—I'm not as green as I'm cabbage-looking. He insists on a minimum of three, though, and pays all expenses. He supplies the men's team himself, three or four of them. Eolo—that's his Christian name. They say his father produces so much cooking-oil the chefs in the Excelsior could keep going on it for a thousand years. He can't be more than thirty but he hasn't got a hair on his head, which always makes me think—not about his bald head, of course, but his age. When I came into the business nearly all the clients were men of a certain age, specially the ones who went in for orgies. Then the picture changed, as they say. I mean, if a lad like that takes regular trips up and down Mount Venus at the age of fourteen, he'll find a woman's breasts about as exciting as a camel's hump by the time he's thirty. That's why he needs orgies.

Eolo spends most of the last days of Pompeii in the kitchen, fixing drinks and sandwiches with stuff he brings along himself. The rest of us have a good time in the lounge. Mostly, I avoid letting the good time develop into a proper orgy because Eolo pays a flat rate however many clients you oblige, so you don't get anything extra for piece-work. Eolo doesn't care. He trots out in the middle of the last days of Pompeii, naked as the day he was born and very interested in what's going on, to judge by the state he gets into. There's nothing more to it than that, though. He wears a laurel-wreath round his bald egg, even though he's meant to be a Roman slave. You can tell he's a slave by the way he goes round the various couples, bowing and offering them vodka Martinis or caviare sandwiches. We have to shout at him or kick him, as the case may be. I don't care for that bit, myself, being a friendly soul, but it's all part and parcel of the last days of Pompeii, and besides, you only have to look at his physical condition to see he enjoys being treated like dirt. Sometimes he really asks for it because he forces sandwiches on you when you haven't got a free hand. Then he disappears into the kitchen again. He leaves the place in a hopeless mess, which is just like a man, but clearing up is reckoned as part of my working-hours. I don't give the other girls a percentage on that, which is only right and fair because they don't help me clear up. What's more, any silly cow of a charwoman gets six hundred lire an hour these days.

This time the last days of Pompeii were interrupted half-way through. I was just trying to introduce little Roberto, a friend of Eolo's, to the French technique—cheeky of the French to call it that, because it's an international habit—and Eolo was crawling like a worm and begging Françoise's pardon because he'd just spilt a vodka Martini over her tummy—on purpose, naturally, because of the punishment—when there was a ring at the door and I had to get up off my knees, which isn't a very comfortable position anyway. I pulled my dressing-gown on quick as a flash because I was afraid it was the law. They don't hold with communal sex, the law. Bossi was standing outside—a grown-up Turk in this case. That wasn't all, though. He'd brought the whole of his general staff along, three photographers and enough equipment to shoot *Cleopatra* all over again. I saw red, of course, because if there's one thing I can't abide it's gate-crashers who won't have the courtesy to let you know in advance. I kept my temper all the same. "I've got company," I said, in my best Contessa voice. "Kindly do me the favour of shoving off." At which Bossi, being the sort of swine he is, passed some filthy remarks—"We wouldn't mind photographing what's going on in there, Contessa" and the like. Firm as a rock, that's me. I told him to come back next day, by himself, and said there wasn't anything in our àgreement about photographs. "It's tonight or nothing," he said. Well, I couldn't very well leave my guests in the lurch—I know what being a hostess means—so I said yes. I didn't blink an eyelid when I went back into the lounge, either. As it turned out, there was a good side to me leaving the room. La Napolitana had taken over where I left off. Little Roberto probably didn't even notice, being too young to worry about variations in style, and Eolo had disappeared into the kitchen again.

Bossi must have waited downstairs till the party broke up, because just before midnight I caught sight of his ugly mug through the spy-hole. On its own.

He blew up almost before he was inside the apartment. Started by asking me, all sarcastic, if I thought *Quest' Ora* was paying me for the sake of my baby-blue eyes. Come Christmas, he said, they'd be starting on the life-story of my "best friend"— which Hertha wasn't, of course. That's why they needed the photographs of me and my premises. "You'll be on the cover," he said, in a dictatorial sort of voice. "You'd better start looking out your scantiest bikinis."

"You never said anything about a cover picture," I said. "It wasn't me that was murdered. I'm still alive and kicking so far, more's the pity from your point of view."

"We can't serve up Enzian week in week out," he said, hard as nails. "When people have had enough of her, you're next in line. You'll get paid for it."

"Not a chance," I snapped. "It'd be bad for business, and if you think I'm going to be deported for the sake of your stupid magazine, you want your head examining."

But that was just what he'd been waiting for. He went for me like a tiger. Said I'd given him away to Canonica, and that I was a dirty little police informer. Canonica would pay for it, he said, because senior police officers weren't allowed to sleep with call-girls, let alone foreign ones.

And that was where Bossi got an earful himself. It's years since I walked the streets back in Munich, and even then I only kept to the better-class districts. What's more, although I speak Italian *perfettamente* I have trouble finding the right words, specially when I'm feeling hard done by, but I told Bossi a few home truths which never soiled any contessa's lips. I'm famous for my refined manners, but anyone who takes them for granted is taking a diabolical liberty. I won't let anything happen to Canonica, either—he's a perfect gentleman, which is more than you can say for some of these traffic cops—and nobody could call me an informer, because who ever heard of an informer who never gets paid?

"You're a rotten bastard, that's what you are," I said, keeping a careful check on my tongue. "If you want to know, a fellow called Aldo Fontana from *Lui e Lei* offered me half a million for my memoirs, but because I'd made an agreement with you, exclusive, I turned him down flat. Aldo looks like a Greek god, too, and you look like an appendix—a pickled one."

That shut him up, the little worm, but not for long. Then he started on at me again in that common way of his—if Bossi comes from a decent family, my name's Lucrezia Borgia. It all came out in a rush—how the police couldn't protect me because the Press carried more guns, and how I hadn't heard a thing when Hertha was done in, and only a fool like Canonica would believe me, and the story about the writer occurred to me a bit late in the day, and before I started accusing him I ought to bear in mind that he was a respectable Italian citizen and I was only a call-girl, and a foreign one at that.

I didn't know what he was driving at. It wasn't on account of the cover picture because he'd have been more likely to get his way by talking nicely and offering an extra fee. To be vulgar, I had the feeling he was shit-scared. Anyway, I said, "You're not only a pig, you'd win first prize at any agricultural show in Bavaria. Compared to you, Aldo Fontana's a knight in shining armour. Now say what you came to say and get out. Closing time's in fifteen minutes."

He turned gentle as a lamb at that, on the outside at least. "I don't know why you're yelling at me," he said, "when the only reason I came was to hand you a million lire."

That brought me up short, I must admit.

"A reward of one million lire," he said, "has been offered for information leading to the arrest of the murderer. Could you use a million lire?"

You bet I could use a million lire, specially now that real estate has gone up again. What did it mean, though—information? Not wanting to commit myself, I told him I didn't have any information, which was true.

"You told me the Enzian girl was going with a writer," said Bossi.

"Big deal," I said. "So what?"

"So you put me on the right track," he said.

"Do you know who the murderer is, then?" I asked.

"I'm almost sure," he said. "Not sure enough to turn him in, but almost. Go to a little trouble and you'll get your million."

"Go to the police, you mean," I said, quick as a flash. I may not have read as many books as a university professor, but my mind works faster.

"I'm a reporter," he said. "I don't take money from the police. If I say you put me on the right track, you'll get your million."

"You're not doing this for the sake of my baby-blue eyes, I'll warrant," I retorted, because it stung me, what he'd said earlier about my baby-blue eyes.

"No," he said, "but maybe you remember that Hertha told you she needed the bottle of grappa because it was her visitor's birthday."

I didn't remember anything of the kind, but he wanted me to

say so, and a million lire isn't to be sneezed at. That's why I didn't tell him either yes or no, because I had to think it over first. You see too much in the papers about people who do things without thinking, specially on the crime pages.

"Another two or three days," Bossi said, getting up, "and you'll be able to sleep easier at nights. I'm only sorry it has to be Canonica I hand the murderer over to. Well, at least you'll have earned your million—that's to say, if my suspicions are correct."

It was half-past one by the time he left. I wondered whether to call Canonica there and then, but the old boy needs his sleep —he works too hard as it is. Besides, a girl ought to think before she opens her mouth. You've got to get your priorities straight.

So I went into the kitchen, which looked like the remains of the battle of Waterloo. I washed up—in the dish-washer, of course —because it's one of my principles that you can tell a lot about people from a dirty kitchen. Anyone who starts the day in a dirty kitchen must be dirty by nature. Actually, it's been more of a superstition than a principle with me since Hertha died. It was past describing, the state they found her kitchen in. She didn't have a decent upbringing, that girl, not that I blame her for that.

Then I sat down on the stool and spooned out the rest of the caviare. I can't abide the stuff, myself, but it's a sin to throw away good caviare when the kiddies in Vietnam aren't getting enough to eat. In the meantime, I put my thinking-cap on. If Bossi thinks I'm a police informer he's bound to reckon on me telling Canonica all about his friendly little visit. Perhaps he thinks I want to cash in on the reward, come hell or high water. He didn't turn up for the sake of a cover picture, that's certain. When Canonica was here the first time he told me I could tell Bossi anything I liked—all that interested him was what Bossi wanted to know. Well, I can tell him what Bossi wants to know and still keep my promise.

I decided not to make up my mind till next morning because I wouldn't have been able to sleep. What's more, things look quite different in daylight. I often think of Hertha—in fact I light a candle for the good of her soul every time I go to church. All the same, I can't spend the rest of my life brooding about the girl.

Italo Canonica

Thursday, 14th December. Have been giving some thought to Christa Sonntag's 'phone-call. She sounded confused. Writer, grappa, birthday. In spite of my searching questions, hard to tell exactly what he said to her or she to him. Bossi knows as much about the murderer as I do. Or more? His methods remind me of an instructional game which I used to play with young detectives. We started out with a fictitious unsolved murder. Every detail of the crime that could possibly be known to the criminal was jotted down on a slip of paper. The paper was then folded and placed in a hat with several blank slips. The 'murderer' was the one who drew the slip with writing on. I sat back while the others interrogated each other. The 'murderer' usually gave himself away pretty soon because he alone had a detailed knowledge of the crime. Knowledge implies guilt. Presumably Bossi has initiated Christa Sonntag into certain details so as to be able to claim later on that he got them from her. Alternatively, Bossi expects the Contessa to tell me all—among other things, that he still needs 'two or three days' (?) in which to run the murderer to earth, and that he isn't 'absolutely sure' yet. Alibi. I fly to Paris on Saturday.

. . . An embarrassing interlude, my talk with Giannini, but it's behind me now. I couldn't conceal the reason for my trip to Paris, nor could I keep him in the dark about the results of my investigations. The first of the two hours I spent in his office passed off remarkably smoothly. He jumped up from his desk when I came in, as usual, but we then sat down informally at the conference table. Needless to say, I didn't hide anything from him. He concurred with my deductions, also with the idea that Signora Manghera, formerly Chiesa, holds the key to the whole problem. The Enzian and Pisenti cases have led us down a blind alley, but careful scrutiny reveals some gaps in the Chiesa case which might be filled in. Investigations were discontinued prematurely because it was thought that the 'culprit' had been found. If Signora Manghera also remembers a writer who had something to do with her daughter we shall very probably be on target. Nobody ever asked her that—why should they have? I soothed Giannini by remarking that there were good reasons for discontinuing inquiries: he conducted the Chiesa investigation himself. He praised my discernment (?)—not an expensive thing to do in private. If all three cases—three blots on the police escutcheon—are cleared up simultaneously, Giannini will be well on his way to the commissionership. Well, why shouldn't I give Rome's next police chief a helping hand? I shall read, cook, and possibly work on my memoirs. It's fortunate that I'm not ten years younger or they'd have appointed another chief of Homicide over my head. Ten years ago it would have hurt. Everything happens too late in life, they claim. One could phrase it less depressingly—for instance: the later in life things happen too late, the less they hurt. It's impossible to determine whether what we deemed important in our youth was really important, or as unimportant as we later deem it to have been. Because the fox never reached the dangling grapes, we assume that they were sweet, when they may have been sour all the time. Not everything unattainable is sweet. Many an old fox mourns for sour grapes without realizing it. When I mentioned my suspicion that *Quest' Ora* had known the murderer's identity for a long time, and might even have commissioned him to write his memoirs, conversation took an unwelcome tack. Giannini turned pale. "Quite impossible," he said. "I know Vanetti personally—he's a man of principle." I confined myself to enumerating the facts. I went easy on Vanetti and concentrated my fire on Bossi. I said, "If *Quest' Ora* publishes the murderer's memoirs our only recourse will be to call in the Director of Public Prosecutions."—"Circumstantial evidence, *caro amico*," said Giannini. "Don't you think we have enough trouble with the Press as it is? Newspapermen are one big happy family: they may scratch each other's eyes out, but they always gang up on outsiders." I tried an appeal to his vanity. It might well be, I said, that *Quest' Ora* would steal a march on us. "Then we'd have been caught napping," said Giannini. He naturally meant that I would have been caught napping, but his reluctance to fall out with me made him gloss over the implication quickly. He launched into a ponderous dissertation on the value of the Press: "After all, the main thing is to bring the killer to book. Why should we complain if the Press make our job easier?"—"If a dangerous criminal wanders around loose by courtesy of a magazine," I said, "the magazine is culpable." Culpability and non-culpability, replied Giannini, are interpreted differently these days. He might just as well have called me an old cretin. "Of course," he added quickly, "the whole thing does sound rather suspicious. I'm glad you drew my attention to it. On the other hand, you base your information on statements made by a known call-girl. You can't call that conclusive evidence." "Publication of the memoirs would be evidence," I said. "Only if *Quest' Ora* springs them on us," Giannini replied. He laid his hands on my shoulders, metaphorically speaking. "How we're going to miss you! I know you'll solve the Enzian, Pisenti, and Chiesa cases with your customary brilliance—then you can rest on your laurels." He meant that he was going to rest on my laurels, possibly with Vanetti as a bedmate. I let it pass. As long as the murderer is at large, my position remains shaky. I shall adopt quite a different tone when I'm back from Paris.

...Postscript to Sunday. It being Pia's birthday, the family gathered at her house for a ceremonial lunch. There was *Minestra di spinaci* made in the Florentine manner, *Maccheroni con ragú alla bolognese, Arrosto di cinghiale romano,* and a chestnut flan which I contributed myself. Pia and Eugenio, Alfredo and Bianca, Flaminio and Elisa, and the seven grandchildren. I presented Pia with nineteen different cooking utensils which I'd collected over the years. Each item was separately wrapped, making nineteen separate presents. Pia crooned over them like a child, although Eugenio can buy her anything she wants—his pharmacy is flourishing, and he's planning to open branches in the provinces. Flaminio has at last bought himself a new car, a handsome Fiat, which he proudly showed off for our benefit. "Isn't it remarkable how well we all get on together?" Alfredo whispered to me when we reluctantly said goodbye at six that evening. Perhaps it is remarkable. There's a lot to be said against us. Although we're all very different—Pia resembles Adele and has my temperament, Flaminio resembles me and has Adele's temperament, and Alfredo bears no resemblance to either of us—not even my son- and daughters-in-law suffer from nervous debility. We do have our problems but they're all pretty commonplace, as far as I can judge; none of us gets bored, though we probably bore everyone else. Illness is the favourite modern hobby and 'healthy' a term of abuse. There's no denying the fact that we're contented (?)—in other words, we make no contribution to progress. Another incriminating factor: we aren't even ashamed of our contentment. The seven cardinal virtues of Christianity have become sins. *Prudence* conflicts with radicalism. *Fortitude* is disreputable because of its military connotations. *Temperance* is regarded as bourgeois. *Justice* is suspect because it disregards the glorified individual on the one hand and the interests of glorified collectivism on the other. *Charity* extends only to those who share one's intellectual prejudices. *Hope* militates against modish pessimism, and *Faith* may degenerate into religion if unchecked. The seven deadly sins, by contrast, have become virtues. *Pride* is the watchword of selective intellectual society. *Avarice* is the mainspring of capitalism and the hidden lure of Socialism. *Lust* is promoted by every available means, even when it is not a natural impulse. *Ire* is evidence of youthfulness and progressive sentiments. *Intemperance, see Lust.* *Envy* is the prerequisite of the competitive system and an advertisement for the classless society. *Sloth* prevents a relapse into Christianity. This reversal of morality is made possible only by a ceaseless flow of propaganda ridiculing private life. The man who loves his family runs the risk of loving his fellow-men; hence, it is essential to brand family life as "middle-class". Well-ordered affluence not only diminishes Avarice, Ire, and Envy, but conflicts with the Lust and Intemperance of an 'élite' minority, so it must be condemned as stultifying and insipid. Improved living conditions diminish revolutionary ardour, although one might suppose a better life to be the aim of revolution. Nobody dares to investigate the new terms of abuse— majority, bourgeois, materialism, automation, morality—that is to say, to ascertain whether they really do describe something reprehensible and are identical with truly derogatory words such as stupidity, laziness, greed, ruthlessness, and hypocrisy. We instinctively resist what we are and defend ourselves by imitation. Must we really attribute all this to mechanization? Modern philosophers—sociologists in disguise—claim that we must, and plausibly so. But what do they suggest? When I was a boy, parents used to say: "Eat up your spinach—think of all the poor children who would enjoy it." I was suspicious of the injunction even then. I wondered how the poor children were supposed to benefit if I ate up my spinach. It would only leave less for them. Alternatively, was I meant to wolf my spinach with extra gusto because I knew other people were starving? Finally, spinach tastes no better because somebody else covets it—which remains to be proved, anyway. Modern philosophers evade the danger of solutions, an evasion which would be permissible in pure or 'superseded' philosophy but is impermissible in sociological philosophy. They are spinach-philosophers. Like most of us, they complain that technological progress is turning man into an automaton. They have a justifiable fear that automation will render man easier to manipulate, but they summon him to resist manipulation without tackling the mechanistic evil that underlies it. They lack the courage of the Silesian weavers who smashed the power-looms of the mid-nineteenth century—because that, again, would be 'unprogressive'. Besides, not everyone who smashes machines is a revolutionary, unless, of course, he reveals what he wants to put in their place. The Silesian weavers may have been underprivileged but they were rabidly bourgeois as well, and their aims were reactionary. We know perfectly well—even the sociological philosophers know it—that the machine remains intact. So what do we do—respect the individual? Another spinach-phrase, unless we equate it with respect for private life. This, however, is equally suspect because everyone knows that only the bourgeois have private lives. If washing-machines and space-ships are endangering individual coexistence—a superficial synonym for morality—the only answer is to reinforce morality. A difficult task, now that the Ten Commandments have been abolished. Philosophy disguises itself as sociology but fails to keep step with social exigencies. Capitalism (?) may be *démodé*, but Socialism is yesterday's Utopia. In bourgeois society it has led to bourgeoisification (?), in Socialist society to bankruptcy. It may be that capitalism and Socialism both overlook the majority's simple yearning for private life, or, rather, for the present. When Marx talked about the dictatorship of the proletariat he was talking about democracy, because the downtrodden and exploited proletarians of his day were in the majority. There is not a single piece of evidence to show that the machine devours people with any less relish in Socialist society than in bourgeois: the machine is a *gourmand*, not a *gourmet*. The Establishment, a vogue-word, exists wherever there are machines: no assault on the machine, no assault on the Establishment. In its passivity, modern anarchism would offer no resistance to automation even if it were attractive to the majority.

... Asked Pia how she prepared her excellent *Arrosto di cinghiale romano*. Basic recipe: marinate approximately three pounds of saddle of wild boar over-night. The marinade consists of two to three tablespoonfuls of olive-oil, three tablespoonfuls of finely-chopped rosemary, two cloves of garlic, salt, pepper, and one tablespoonful of wine vinegar. Fry in one-and-a-half ounces of oil, sprinkle with salt, and cover with stock. The braising should be done over a medium flame. After half an hour, add one glass of red wine, one tablespoonful of vinegar, and one tablespoonful each of raisins, pine-kernels, and currants, and allow to simmer together. Finally, season the gravy with about a teaspoonful of ground pepper, and preferably sprinkle a few more pine-kernels over the top. Polenta makes the best accompaniment.

Friday, 15th December. Air-ticket ready and waiting. Signora Manghera arrives in Paris today. Appointment fixed for tomorrow. Looking forward to the trip.

Giannini received a surprise visit from Bossi. I'm not in the least worried about having been by-passed. Bossi is apprehensive. He handed Giannini a diary belonging to Hertha Enzian— *Quest' Ora* bought it in Vienna with a view to publication. It contains no leads. He also announced that he was on the murderer's track and thought he could "deliver" him in a few (?) days' time. Giannini was naturally obliged to question the man, but was impressed by his "good intentions". Bossi claimed to have a "sound basis" for his suspicions, but didn't want to make a fool of himself or "mislead" the police. He also said it was "a nuisance" that, although he could certainly (?) put us on to the killer of Lucia Chiesa and Vera Pisenti, the tie-up with Hertha Enzian was still "uncertain"—hence his reluctance to come forward. I asked Giannini if he had drawn Bossi's attention to the consequences of withholding information. Evasive answer. Bossi apparently replied that he was a crime reporter, and couldn't afford to denounce anyone on the strength of unsupported conjecture. "Let's be diplomatic," said Giannini. "A couple of days don't matter. After all, we'd sooner be able to say we traced the murderer without help from the Press."

... Had supper with Silvano Guerra. We discussed every aspect of the case until 1 A.M. Silvano is an outstanding authority

THE ALIBI

on criminal law. I enlightened him about the machinations of
Vanetti, Bossi & Co. The case may come within his jurisdiction.
I'm afraid he shares Giannini's view that an indictment based
predominantly on a call-girl's evidence doesn't stand much
chance. "I'm sure Vanetti has an alibi," said Silvano. Which
brought us to his pet subject. Silvano gives lectures on the alibi
concept, and advocates a new interpretation of the word. "It's
extremely confusing," he said. "Juridically speaking, an alibi is
construed as evidence that someone was absent from the scene of
a crime, whereas in everyday speech alibi is a synonym for justification. Innocence by virtue of absence—very convenient! The
biggest criminals of the century were absent from the scene of
the crime."—"For all that," I objected, "people also recognize
the concept of murder by rubber stamp."—"Yes," replied
Silvano, "but bureaucrats are carefully provided with a political
justification, a second alibi. Forget your criminal for a moment.
Is absence any justification at all? The whole of mankind is
searching for an alibi." The citizen who doesn't vote is seeking
an alibi, he went on. What happens happens without him, in
his absence. Bad Governments—dictatorships, for instance—are
another form of alibi: people are absent from, or not party to,
their decisions. Governments in their turn like to stress that they
don't meddle in the affairs of other Governments: they too are
absent from the scene of the crime. Time, said Silvano, is the
cheapest, most convenient and popular alibi of all. "Especially,"
I said, "if we live in the past or the future. Absence from the
present is our alibi." I tried to steer conversation back to Vanetti.
Perhaps it's my wounded vanity, but I'm spending more time on
the Vanetti case than the Enzian case. Silvano said that Vanetti
was no exception. Just as technology enables man to commit
remote-controlled crimes so intellectual cogitation turns out
mass-produced alibis. Only the law, with its physical notions of
presence and absence, remains hopelessly retarded. Modern man
is no less violent than his jungle ancestors, but he is 'absent' or
remote from his actions: the factors which are 'present' and
therefore responsible for them are social environment, parental
blunders, youthful complexes, and the aberrations of society.
The alibi of youth is youth, Silvano went on—the most rudimentary and convincing of all alibis. We all accept it because,
although we may not love the young, we want to be just to

them. What was that supposed to mean? "Two ideals have alternated throughout history," said Silvano, "the ideal of love and the ideal of justice. More precisely, human history consists of epochs which aspired either to love or to justice. At the moment we're living in an age which aspires to justice." I said that was all right with me. What possible objection could one have to a younger generation which strove for justice? Silvano's idea was new to me. I must think it over. Perhaps he has put his finger on it—perhaps the very reason why young people talk so much about love is that they really mean justice. "It's an ice-age," said Silvano, "because it mistakes the inferior for the superior. Even if we attained the goal of justice, which is highly unlikely, we should freeze. Christ on the Cross believed in the love of God, but he would have despaired of His justice. Justice is selective, love is not. We shan't throw off the wretchedness of this age until we've emerged from the hypnosis of justice and entered the reality of love." A peculiar gem of wisdom to fall from the lips of a public prosecutor. Fortunately, Silvano still has a sense of humour. "Of course," he said, "you and I are no exceptions either—we take care to leave a well-prepared alibi behind at the scene of the crime."

... I have only noted the bare bones of our conversation—it's late enough as it is. Silvano failed to convince me entirely. I suspect sentences that don't end with a question mark.

Saturday, 16th December. A sunny winter's day, very agreeable flight to Paris. Read the papers. Reports of fighting in Asia, Africa, the Near and Far East. Fears of a Third World War —they ought to call it the fourth, considering how long ago the third began. The two super-powers have been waging war for years, but on foreign soil. War by instalments—very appropriate in the age of hire-purchase. What is taking place in Vietnam or the Near East isn't a war but a series of battles—constituent battles of the Third World War. You can't pick your battlefields once war is in progress. Where will the next battlefield be? The most frightening aspect of war is the corruption it lures us into. We no longer ask ourselves what is right, merely what our rights are. We support Negroes and suddenly feel conscious of our white skins. Communism has made us aware of our wallets. Is "My country right or wrong" to become a moral axiom?

... Amused myself by dipping into a *Philology of Cooking*.

Found an explanation of the old Italian saying: "He needs some of Sixtus V's salad". Pope Sixtus was an interesting man—he made up his mind to die in conclave, but reigned for five years. One day he sent a basket of lettuce-leaves to a friend who was seriously ill and in wretched material circumstances. The Holy Father's niggardly gift was greeted with some dismay at first, but the old man's striking and speedy recovery gave rise to a legend concerning the salad's miraculous properties. In reality the Pope had hidden a purseful of sequins under the lettuce-leaves. Anyone who is more likely to benefit from money than kind words "needs some of Sixtus V's salad". Not that salad isn't good for you too.

. . . Drove straight from Orly to the Hotel Raffael. Refined atmosphere, quiet and old-fashioned, handsome tapestries. The ex-widow of the lavatory-seat manufacturer has risen in the world. Signora Manghera's present spouse manufactures paper handkerchiefs. She greeted me in a large suite whose murals recalled the stage of an amateur theatre. Still quite a young woman, with no need to pretend to be younger than her years, which she does. Her dress, as she casually injected into the mainstream of conversation, was a Courrèges model which had been "waiting" for her in Paris. Her exaggeratedly warm reception betrayed social insecurity. It wasn't easy to manœuvre her towards the subject of her murdered daughter. A Freudian block, or was the topic unwelcome to Signor Manghera? He was also in attendance—an elderly little man, clearly one of those businessmen who are completely at sea outside their special field. Cautiously, I steered us in the direction of Lucia's friends and acquaintances. Signora Manghera avoided any mention of her daughter's pregnancy, but insisted that the acquitted boy-friend was guilty. She tried to incriminate him during the trial, and what woman doesn't cling to her mistakes? I put a direct question: Did her daughter's circle include any authors or poets? No, she couldn't remember any. A lot of young people used to breeze in and out of the house, self-styled artists—"You know what I mean"—who may have included a writer or two. Rather disheartening. "I'm talking about a man who would have been just on fifty at the time," I said. "Impossible," she replied. Lucia had shunned the society of older men. And her own circle of friends? "Personally, I've always preferred older

men," she said, eyeing me and Manghera as if to say: From my
angle, even you two aren't quite ripe for the cemetery. But a
poet or author—no, she had spent nearly all her time in industrial circles, among her late husband's friends. "That was how I
met Stefano, actually." My heart sank. I thought of Giannini
and Bossi. Why had I imagined that Signora Manghera, formerly
Chiesa, must have been acquainted with her daughter's murderer? I opened my briefcase and brought out a police artist's
impression of the killer, based on descriptions supplied by the
housekeeper and the assistant in the shoe-shop. "Does that remind you of anyone you knew in those days?" Her face grew
serious, reminding me of those modern dolls which still have
dolls' faces but don't smile any longer. "Well," she said, "perhaps. . ." She massaged her brow. "Of course, the eyebrows! But
the mouth and nose are different." I enlightened her on the
notorious inaccuracy of police artists' impressions. "He wasn't
an author, though," she said. "Also, he was with me at the time
of the murder. My poor little Lucia. . ." She had tears in her eyes
now. Manghera cleared his throat impatiently, perhaps because
he was jealous. Elderly men do feel jealous of the past—they're
afraid of comparison. "We only have a rough indication of the
time of death," I said. "Lucia's tutor," she mused. "But that's
out of the question!" She plunged into a laborious account
of why Lucia had needed special tuition—she had probably
told her second husband that Lucia was a model pupil. "Why
should it be out of the question?" I asked. She reverted to the
alibi: the murder occurred early in the evening, while she and
the tutor were sitting on the terrace of the Café de Paris. She
described him as a rather nervous, mild-mannered, unobtru-
sive man in late middle age—"I put him at sixty, but when
you're young . . ." She had engaged him on the strength of an
advertisement. "He certainly wasn't an author." Did she remember his name? A tension-laden pause. I couldn't help smiling at
myself—I was behaving like a novice who thinks his career
depends on the solution of one particular case and no other. A
pretty ludicrous attitude to adopt after more than five hundred
murder investigations. She stared at the picture. "Of course,"
she said, "a very ordinary name—ordinary names are the easiest
to forget. Morelli. Augusto or Aurelio Morelli—Aurelio, I
think." The name meant nothing to me. "The eyebrows," she

said, "my poor little girl made fun of them." I asked her to describe her daughter's relationship with Morelli as fully as possible. She misunderstood me: "There was no question of a relationship." Then she described him: pedantic, humourless, irascible, punctilious in the extreme, nineteenth-century morals, obviously very poor—"he looked disappointed if he didn't get given a coffee, and slunk off with his tail between his legs"—and prone to constant complaints about Lucia. Always wore the same suit, very clean, but all the poorer-looking for that. Had she ever made inquiries about him? No, she hadn't thought it necessary—the man made such a respectable impression. "My poor, poor Lucia!" She was now as certain that Morelli was the murderer as she had earlier been convinced of his innocence. I questioned her about their conversation in the café in the Via Veneto. He had suggested the meeting, probably with a view to making more complaints about Lucia. She couldn't remember what they had talked about. "Did you never mention him to the police?" I asked. "Nobody asked about him. He was such a grey person—a nobody." A twinge of malicious pleasure: I shall mention to Giannini that nobody made inquiries about the tutor, "nobody" meaning Giannini. "Did you ever see Signor Morelli again?" She thought he had written her a letter of condolence, but wasn't sure. "He came to the funeral, I know that." I remembered the funeral myself—Giannini asked me to stand in for him. One up to Giannini, though I don't know why I should have been expected to recognize the tutor or identify him as the murderer. I told Signora Manghera that I would get in touch with her—she flies to Rome tomorrow. I checked the address of the Italian Library at the porter's desk and drove there straight away. Looked up the name Aurelio Morelli in the general index. There were seven books listed, of which only one, *Thou art Alcibiades*, was still in print. Asked for a *Who's Who* of Italian authors, but couldn't find the name. It occurred to me that Morelli's last book appeared in 1954. We unearthed a year-book for 1953. *Morelli, Aurelio, novelist, b. Montefiascone, 8th August 1909*. I didn't read on. Wondered whether to 'phone headquarters, but there was another 'plane for Rome in an hour. I wanted to catch it at all costs.

... Always the same feeling—victory sans triumph. It wouldn't be a triumph even if the murderer were already behind bars. Faith in the ultimate victory of justice—a resounding phrase, but my life would have been a farce if I didn't believe in it—is mingled with wry astonishment at the difficulties which attend such a victory. What are you pitting yourself against when you tackle a murderer? Or is it that a man-hunt remains a man-hunt even when the man in question is inhuman? Or is it the hopelessness of the whole thing? We say we're fighting crime when all we do is fight criminals. One man murders while another is being sentenced. Who is next in line? It's a continuous process, except that it won't concern me for much longer. When I come to think of it, tears would be inappropriate in a superannuated head-hunter. I shall find Morelli even if he's hiding in Spain. I could go out to grass on the first of January. I hope they don't give me a gold watch, but perhaps I'm being premature. I certainly wouldn't like to clear my desk before verifying Morelli's links with *Quest' Ora*. Is he the "collaborator" Bossi was referring to when he told me that he had secured the services of a writer? Alibi. Isn't the fight against the Vanettis of this world even more hopeless than the fight against the Morellis? And even if Vanetti's guilt could be proved, how would it affect all the other Vanettis? Don't they fulfil a need, just as murderers and policemen do? People make a great fuss about the manipulation of public opinion. Hasn't intellect kept pace with technology? Isn't it an aspersion on the human mind to believe it incapable of seeing manipulation for what it is? Technology isn't as glorious and mankind as stupid as the high priests of manipulation allege. Supply is determined by demand, regardless of whether the consumer's needs are served by private enterprise or the State. Perhaps Silvano is right: as long as man has a conscience which he would rather be rid of, he grubs around for an alibi. Every newspaper kiosk is an Aladdin's cave heaped with alibis. The alibi-seller isn't a cunning devil acting on behalf of some mysterious power, nor does it require sorcery to dispose of a popular commodity like the alibi. Of course, the alibi-seller needs an alibi himself—after all, bakers eat bread and cobblers wear shoes. Vanetti supplies the masses with their alibis, and the masses, always glad to return a favour, supply him with his. I'd do better to concentrate on Morelli. He's an easier proposition—all he did was murder three women.

. . . Landed Rome 9.10 P.M. Alerted Primavesi by 'phone. Records traced Morelli's address even before I reached town.

CHAPTER

5

Silent Night

Aurelio Morelli

I have ordered a taxi. Although my destination remains uncertain, and it is not at all inconceivable that I shall change cars
as coachmen once changed post-horses, I intend to strike southward because my enemies doubtless assume that their fugitive
quarry will make for Rome. I shall instruct the driver to steer his
conveyance along the coast, farther and ever farther from Foce
Verde, miserable but memorable scene of my first exile. I shall
also instruct him never to let the sea out of his sight, familiar
objects being our only shield and buckler: only where the
denizens of the deep feel at home do I too feel at home; only
where I feel at home do I feel myself secure, and never did I
stand in greater need of security than I do at this moment.

Man, in his irrationality, at times refers to water as a hostile
element, although no element could be more hostile than the
inhabited earth: only the earth harbours man, the foe of man;
every ship, every fishing-boat, and wheresoever man sets foot, is
an extension of hostile terra firma. I, however, en route for freedom, shall hail the boundless habitat of my mute friends, who
erect no cramped buildings and sterile enclosures as human
beings do, nor any secret lairs and refuges as do the beasts of the
field; free from fear and mistrust, unable and unwilling to barri-
cade themselves against the envious, the curious, and the predatory, fish are the first and last creatures to enjoy unbounded
liberty.

The sight of the sea, that eternal mirror of eternity, will soothe
my troubled soul—yes, troubled, for even the hand of the
conscientious executioner cannot but tremble at the knowledge
that he has put his guilty love to death. Before anyone can discover the corpse of my lovely Agnese—for I set about the burial

of the girl and her three or four youthful companions with the utmost care—I shall betake myself to Rome so as to arrive no earlier than the prescribed hour in advance of my flight to freedom. I am travelling with the lightest of luggage.

My letter to the witch, who will find the cage beside the green estuary empty, is already penned. I have more than one motive for wishing to gain time, and even if my life means nothing— less than nothing, now that I have accomplished my mission— I am conscious that the battle has still to be fought to a finish, that victory is imminent but not yet won: we live for as long as we have enemies. I wrote the letter to outwit my foe, promising her a Christmas present in the shape of Hertha Enzian's murder: I would, I said, commit the manuscript to a post-box once I had reached safety—a distasteful lie, but wholly unavoidable. In actuality, the closely written pages are safely bestowed among my poor effects.

As to the young traitress Agnese, I cannot say for certain if I acted with premeditation when I reduced her three or four confederates to eternal silence at a single stroke—the myrmidons of the law will say so, because they habitually confuse retrospection, or careful deliberation after the event, with murderous intent and malice aforethought—but it would not surprise me if my redeeming act owed its inspiration to despair, for my hopes had long subsided when the girl with the flowing tresses, in her turn, subsided to the ground before me.

Ah, guilty mirror, no doubt of your complicity in my act! Not many minutes before I set out to keep my yearned-for but ill-fated tryst, my eye lighted upon the looking-glass affixed to the wall above the wretched wash-basin in my prison cell of a hotel room. I felt, in truth, as if I had not seen my face for many a long year: it was the face of a stranger, or, worse still, of a man whom one vaguely recollects but cannot 'place'. Where was it, and when? Is the recollection pleasant or unpleasant? If pleasant, the transformation wrought by time seems the more bitter. Of course! The face is familiar beyond doubt, but it belongs to another man, similar enough to be mistaken for the beholder, but so dissimilar as to strike terror into his soul. The word ruin has a dual significance which renders it applicable both to the miraculous relics of Greece and Rome and to the architectural skeletons left by war: we can, for instance, admire the Forum

Romanum and the ruins of Egypt because no personal recollection is associated with them, because we never saw their columns rent asunder. Ancient churches, residences, and places of public assembly did not fall to dust before our eyes; dead they are, but not of our kin; young they once were, but we never knew them in their youth; ruined they stand, but we did not witness their decay. The ageing man is an embryonic ruin.

To me, as I gazed into the mirror early that afternoon, my hope that the maid of the mansion would follow me into exile seemed as derisory as my missive to her now appeared a token of unconditional surrender. Age had wrought insensate devastation in my face, and time ravaged it like a madman who destroys all that is beautiful, noble, and sacred. How had I transgressed, that the integument of chin and jaw should have become so flaccid, the throat a yellowed parchment scribed with indecipherable hieroglyphs, the Adam's apple a pointed stone; how came it that I had failed to resist the decay which afflicts all living men, genius and bungler, kindly and cunning alike? My pores were enlarged, the hairs of my head sparse, my eyes milky, my lachrymatory sacs heavy with unshed tears, my lips drawn into parentheses enclosing naught of consequence, my wrinkles deep and empty as the trenches of a long-deserted battlefield. A tree discloses its annual rings only when it has been felled; man alone carries his tale of years in his face. Who dares to speak of justice? Of liberty and fraternity, perhaps, but not of equality, when no state of parity can exist between those with life before them and those for whom it is already over, when certain defeat awaits all who are not destined to die an early death, when the enemy knows and exploits their weaknesses, and when they are not permitted even to hide their dishonourable scars in shame. "Old in years, young in heart..." What cynical irony, what footling self-deception! "A man is as old as he feels...." What vain consolation, what senile conceit, when, alone with his mirror, a man can descry no trace of higher intelligence and feels older than his years warrant! It was an old man who stared back at me from the mirror, a mimic who had transformed himself into the object of his derision, a conjurer whose tricks had been exposed. Just as in childhood days, I grimaced and stuck my tongue out, but, otherwise than in my childhood, the face in the mirror remained unchanged.... And, indeed, what change could a grimace have wrought upon the gargoyle grimace of old age?

Although it was still early, too early for my assignation at the tomb of the murdered fish, I dreaded to linger in the departure-haunted gloom of my hotel room, with its tankful of unsuspecting but—or so it seemed to me—reproachful friends.

The first mists of afternoon were scudding along the shore, and it was as if the shore itself were scudding southward while the road which overlooked it hobbled, stonily indifferent, to meet the long embrace of night. It so happened that as I made my way towards the precincts of the atomic power station, my attention was drawn to a band of children at play—three boys and a girl whose ages ranged, so far as I could judge, between eight and ten. They were romping in circles and hopping over some ritual pattern of chalk-marks, yet they seemed to take little real pleasure in their game: what with the cold and the way in which their scanty and unsuitable attire exposed them to the elements, they blew into their minuscule fists and hugged the lee of the houses.

I must categorically reject any imputation of tenderness, sorrow, or sentimentality on my part, also any suggestion that I felt pity for the little monsters: children are the most human of human beings, and, hence, doubly malevolent. Ever intent upon defiling the beautiful and destroying the weak, stupid but self-assured, pert but plaintive, clinging but insensitive, they are, in short, fitting candidates for enlistment in the murderous ranks of youth. I must with equal vehemence deny that I ever deliberately sought affection, that I ever yielded to the inane hope of leaving behind a favourable impression in Foce Verde: a revolutionary who does good individually instead of concerning himself with the general weal is a traitor to the revolution he serves. On the contrary, the sight of the unmannerly little band had inspired me with an exquisitely amusing idea. The flimsy periodical had not only blackmailed me in the most brazen manner but cheated me of a substantial proportion of my hard-earned revenues. How to avenge myself—worthily, if not in due measure?

To be brief, I accosted the frolicking, shivering quartet and asked if they would care for some sweetmeats. This they affirmed, but only after a whispered council of war. Their parents had evidently warned them against 'kindly strangers', but no doubt reflecting that there were four of them, and that the baker's shop, whose stock included all manner of pastries, candied fruits, and alluring confectionery, was situated on the next corner, they demurred no longer and accepted my invitation.

While the little ones were noisily smacking their lips, I addressed myself to the proprietress of the shop, a lady who appeared to have partaken too freely of her calorific riches, and asked her if, in the case of a sizeable order, she would be prepared to extend me credit and forward the bill to the magazine *Quest' Ora*. My trustworthy appearance, coupled with the fact that the corpulent creature had often observed me on my lonely promenades, prompted her to accede to my request, with the result that I acquired four vast and outrageously overpriced bonbon boxes which I distributed to the children, charging them to deliver them to their parents.

Followed, like the legendary Pied Piper of Hamelin, by my troop of children, I then repaired to the neighbouring department store—or what passes for one in this dismal little town—confidently summoned the *gerente*, or manager, made reference to a charitable venture sponsored by the at once illustrious and illustrated magazine, and elicited the man's obsequious consent. The children gave their names and addresses. In pursuance of my order, as commercial jargon has it, little Piero will duly be supplied with a winter coat and an electric train. Ugo with a new suit, a droll little cap, and various party games, Renato with a checked coat and a magnificent box of bricks, and, finally, Margherita with a warm wrap, three little frocks, and a doll's house. I emphasized that responsibility for the order rested with a certain Signor Bossi, chief reporter to the aforesaid magazine, and that queries should be promptly addressed to him in the event of difficulties regarding payment. Although the male children were too overwhelmed by this cornucopian deluge of gifts to make any additional demands, Margherita, as might have been expected in a child of the female gender, picked out an exceedingly repulsive doll clad in pink tulle and insisted on bearing it off forthwith; and, when I succeeded in fulfilling her importunate request, rewarded me with a swift and spontaneous embrace.

337

True though it is that the sole motive for my charitable undertaking was a wish to embarrass the Neapolitan pugilist and his employers, the fleeting episode did put me in a milder frame of mind. I can attest that at 4.30 on that fateful afternoon I regarded my revolutionary mission as complete, at least in respect of personal involvement, and that had not Agnese di Doninelli's friends, cronies, and fellow-conspirators trespassed upon our assignation I should have borne my disappointment with characteristic temperance.

The car is long in coming. The green gloom of the green estuary enshrouds the man bent over the bare little table at which he has toiled this many a night. Writing, so my few honest *confrères* would corroborate, is a nervous reflex. The admiration which posterity will accord me on the grounds that I was able, even at this oppressive hour, of artistic discipline and superhuman concentration—genius, I was once told, consists of talent, industry, discipline, and will-power, every last one of which assets I possess—the admiration of posterity, I say, will not by any means be merited. I am ever and again impelled to lay my pen aside and bid farewell to the inmates of the iridescent aquarium. Little you know, my friends, what fate awaits you at my hand, but you must understand that I cannot, upon mature consideration, confide you to the custody of strangers, of bureaucrats and institutes. It was in truth something more than a mere dream which last night caused God to manifest himself to me in the guise of *Neopilina galatheae*, the vast fish which ruled the universe long before the God of Man—even if the inquisitive Swedes confuse late emergence with early existence and allege that it first appeared five hundred million years ago. The Great God *Neopilina* approved my plan and promised my companions a place in heaven, which is, after all, naught but a boundless sea: fish, who vegetate beneath us during their lifetime, swim above us after their death—indeed, I have only to scan the heavens to see them soaring through the ether, cradled in the immeasurable *piscina* of the dead. I am writing because, for the very first time, I dare not devote myself to my fish. One writes as a means of extruding something sad but inescapable. Even I am tainted with the cowardice of the writer.

Yet am I really so craven? Any attempt to describe the ensuing hours will, in its very daring, be a tribute to my courage.

SILENT NIGHT

Contrary to my habit of strict punctuality, I arrived at our prearranged rendezvous in the atomic wilderness six minutes late. The ear being quicker to hear than the eye to see, I had yet to catch sight of Agnese when I was assailed by the sound of lovesick singing: a mawkish voice, devoid of masculinity and patently that of a Sicilian hermaphrodite, was lisping something about *amore*; so far as I could tell, the boy-singer was promising his beloved the kingdom of heaven and eternal bliss—little doubt of what he meant by either—if only she would yield to his entreaties.

Following the voice to its source, I soon discovered Agnese at the appointed spot beside the fishes' cemetery. Her hair fell ungirt to her shoulders, as always, her cheeks were flushed, she wore a short fur jacket over a dress of provocatively knee-revealing cut, and in her hand she held a small black box with a gleaming silver rod protruding therefrom, a so-called aerial which at once identified the apparatus as that Devil's megaphone the radio or wireless set. Far from hiding her magician's box, casting it aside, or at least enjoining it to silence, she manipulated a small wheel and amplified the voice of the treacly troubadour still further.

Overcome for the first time by a feeling of irritation, I angrily bade her silence the blockhead; but, instead of complying, she eyed me with astonishment, for all the world as if my request were unreasonable, and confined herself to subduing the singer's erotic warblings by a renewed manipulation of the controls. She did, nevertheless, deny all intention of offending my ear, declared that her only thought had been to beguile the time—she had already roamed the fields for half an hour—and claimed that she had supposed it would please me to converse with her to the strains of music.

For the nonce—and I stress this most emphatically—I continued to find excuses for the unworthy object of my affections. She could not, after all, have known that the greatest hour in her life had struck, that Aurelio Morelli, author and revolutionary, the intellectual colossus of his age, had chosen that precise juncture to transmit his lover's ultimatum. Unwilling to retract but reluctant to give further offence, I handed her my proposal in silence, pulled on my rubber gloves, and proceeded to kneel by the banks of the Fiume Astura. I did so not merely in reverence—not a single corpse was drifting seaward along the poisoned stream, as it happened—but because I had no wish to watch Agnese at her reading. Though free from the trivial superstitions that afflict the imbecile canaille, I have nonetheless learned in the course of my luckless sojourn on earth that no good thing can happen in my presence—indeed, the rare pieces of good fortune that have befallen me have done so without my assistance and in my absence: thus, being unable to don a cloak of invisibility, I wished at least to avert my gaze from the beloved creature as she read. Let her read the letter in peace, I told myself, reflecting—not without a certain grim amusement—that if she found my declaration grotesque, if my presumption enraged her, if she declined my proposal, she would at least be left with a memento and personal tribute in the shape of a small work, a *parvum opus*, of the man whom she herself had called her favourite author. There I crouched upon my knees, gazing into the turbid waters, a frustrated salvager of corpses, a burier of the dead without dead to bury. From time to time I thrust my hand into the icy stream, my rubber-encased fingers squeaking gently as I withdrew them. Behind me, on the embankment, stood my beloved, letter in hand; listening to the rustle of pages, I could readily guess what passage in my epistle she had just skimmed through—and that despite the strident tones of the radio announcer or fairground barker who had temporarily usurped the place of the Sicilian lecher.

What occurred thereafter was a beatific interlude, and because I am not one of those who, when viewing a tragedy in retrospect, see every contributory factor in a sombre light, I do not hesitate to describe it now. Still standing behind me, Agnese laid her hand on my head as if blessing me tenderly, as if sealing our lover's pact with a benediction. Then as I crouched there at her feet, savouring my bliss, a metamorphosis took place in her—or, more properly, in her hands, which underwent a gradual change: little by little the hand that had rested on me began to describe gentle, stroking movements, ceasing to be the hand of a mistress and becoming that of a nurse or attendant. Regret, indulgence, concern, even pity—all found expression in those loveless caresses, and because I did not perceive this vile transformation with sufficient speed, nor rise swiftly enough to my feet, the hand changed yet again: the nurse's touch became transmuted

into that of a lion-tamer who fondles a wild beast merely to keep
it docile.

I was shocked to the core by what greeted me when I rose,
turned, and faced her, yet I know not which horrified me more:
the expression of the lion-tamer who smiles for the public's
benefit, hiding her fear beneath a mask of jollity, but never for
an instant taking her eye off the savage beast; or the sight of the
noisy, diabolical contraption which she had chosen to place—no
court of law would believe this, nor accept it as an extenuating
circumstance—on the very stone beneath which reposed the
piscine victims of nuclear assassination.

She now responded to my letter in words besmeared with a
hypocrisy which could not fail to affront me twice over because
of her probable conviction that she could lead me, a feeble-
minded dotard, by the nose. Her fault it was and hers alone, she
said, if she had not with due clarity defined the boundary between her admiration for the writer and other sentiments of
quite a different complexion—those which she entertained for
the man, she meant; her fault alone if she had not put a rampart
and ditch between that which was genuinely present and that
which in no wise existed. I was, she pursued, fully justified in
having mistaken her tender but childish emotions for "something else"—she was naturally referring to the pleasurable
excitation of her privy parts—and it was wholly "understandable" that I should have fallen prey to illusion, misapprehension,
or confusion. In this context she used a revolting staple of the
pubescent vocabulary, originally adopted from American usage
but since become rooted in the civilized world: she was, she said,
my "fan", and it was a shame that "fans" lionized the great
but were in reality content with the inferior, because their hero-
worship could easily be mistaken for "something other" than a
symbolic emotion.

"So your answer is no?" I said, holding myself tightly in
check and keeping one eye on the clamorous youth who had just
recommenced to warble some chanson, 'hit', 'number', or other
species of mating-call above the last resting-place of my aquatic
friends.

What woman would not have deemed herself fortunate to have
aroused so ardent a passion, so eloquent a love, and such noble
sentiments in a great man and immortal artist? She flattered

me, true, but her flattery was merely a prelude to the most unbelievable jibes. After reading the first few lines of the letter, she said, she had supposed it to be one of those fictitious effusions which occur not infrequently in world literature—indeed, she did not scruple to quote *Modeste Mignon*, by my *confrère* Balzac: however, she could not but question my common sense, if not soundness of mind, if I genuinely supposed that she would be willing to depart for distant shores with a man whom she revered greatly but knew only slightly. It was, she said, high time for her to open my eyes: no high-born damsel she, for all that I, her "dear, dear romantic" had characterized her as such, nor was she a saint and angel; only my creative imagination— "oh, you poets!"—had endowed her with such attributes. She had the liveliest sympathy with my "eccentricities"—here she glanced at the burial-mound—but this was quite understandable in someone of her tender years. "We hate everything conformist," she declared. "We love unusual, grotesque, individualistic behaviour, and what could be more bizarre and endearing than an author who buries poisoned fish?" The news of my departure had saddened her, she went on. She was heartbroken that I should have chosen to make my new home in a far-off land, and would tell her grandchildren—she did not jib at the word— about the *Don Quichote delle pesce*, but she was no different from other young girls of her age: like them, she loved practical jokes and merry pranks, roamed aimlessly about with her contemporaries, whiled the nights away in frivolous company, liked to adorn herself with pretty baubles, and, in short, enjoyed her youth to the full.

I did not interrupt her, for only a society which denies man jurisdiction over himself prevents the suicide from casting aside a burdensome life, and, of all absurd laws, that which prohibits self-destruction is by far the most presumptuous. I did, however, venture to ask what she had meant by inviting me to attend her in her unprotected home, by her provocative request to visit me in my hotel room, by the kiss at the door of the benighted *castello*, by her seductive behaviour.

She walked to the tombstone, laid a hand on her Devil's box, and seemed about to turn and go. In so doing she displayed witch's cunning coupled with a gaucherie which I could not fail to note. Beneath her dainty hands the silver rod, shaft, or aerial became transmuted into a gargantuan penis, and, fearing lest I should remark her sorcery, she reached for the spherical knob and thrust the phallus back into its sheath, presumably intending to reduce the singing youth to silence. The male sex-symbol, recognizable by virtue of its very size as an attribute of the God Priapus, who was often and with justification erected as a scarecrow, vanished into the black vagina, but the arrogant youth only croaked the more lasciviously.

As if unconscious of her own manipulations, Agnese—or the girl I had so called—began to speak in an altered tone of voice: let me not make myself look ridiculous, she said; let me not wantonly destroy the image she had formed of me; a casual invitation signified little; her request to see my aquarium had been intended as a harmless indulgence; a goodnight kiss meant no more to her than a handshake, and I was grossly mistaken if I thought it conferred any special rights; I was old enough to be her father, possibly even her grandfather; she intended to revel in her youthful existence for years to come; besides, she was in love, and content with her young man; she had told him about me, and he would have been genuinely delighted to meet me. We must speak of the matter no more, she continued; further discussion would only embitter our parting—she felt certain that I would understand. Why should we not remain friends, I a great writer, she a young girl, I preoccupied with things eternal, she unappalled by the voice of a sentimental singer?

The funeral flags of eventide fluttered above the forbidden fields. Gloom had engulfed the building which housed the atomic centre, and the site of that poison-brewery was now occupied by a stony nothingness. As happens in the all-devouring dusk, trees and bushes had assumed that most hideous of guises, the human form. The river-bank was scarcely to be seen: concealed from my prophetic eye, the river flowed, pellucid and untouched, into the handiwork of man, to emerge polluted and gravid with death.

There she stood before me, the adored exception who had seduced me from my exalted aims, the person for whose sake I might have been prepared to grant youth my forgiveness, the human clay which I had resolved to mould in my own image. Who was she? None of the three whores already redeemed by me had needed to unmask, as at the close of a carnival ball, for

their harlot's guise had concealed naught but harlotry, whereas
the carnival queen of Foce Verde—the most perfidious of all—
had masked her whoredom in virginity. The exception had
proved to be no more than an object-lesson. She was youth incarnate—an arsonist who kindled fire only to quench it, and
quenched it only to kindle it anew, terrible and imbecile, a
disciple prepared to listen to higher things in the afternoon, at
night a sultry paramour, decorous to the bed's edge, in bed a
semen-sucking viper, sexless in the presence of an old man yet
baring herself gladly before a ravenous youth, not averse to
conducting discussions on Roman mythology with the same old
man yet simultaneously yearning for the young swan which
would turn itself into a lecherous Jupiter; a mourner who shed
crocodile tears over a fish's grave, and at the same time a wanton
who, once in the arms of her lover, laughed her ageing fellow-
mourner to scorn.

I now saw clearly that she was afraid of me, that she planned
to flee our lonely trysting-place and escape me.

Her terror filled me with celestial lust. I avow it without
shame, for there can be no finer proof that I did not err in denying the same when I described the final minutes of the three girls
Enzian, Chiesa, and Pisenti. I do not gainsay that in this instance
my *membrum virile* rose as if it had been the aerial which the
girl had fondled and metamorphosed into its true shape; that I
was eager to take the reluctant creature by main force—reluctant,
because she would without doubt have resisted her lustful old
suitor; that I craved to bury the personification of arrogance
beneath me, fight my way into her palpitating body, elicit
groans of pleasure and humiliation. A man of superhuman
clemency, I had ever found it more shameful to instil fear than to
experience it, but the girl's terror whipped my desire into painful
ecstasy—ah, yes, into an ecstasy which ebbed before I had truly
savoured it; before I could carry my beautiful, bestial plan into
effect, wetness flooded my loins, my strength subsided, and I was
vanquished. For the very first time, a fellow-being—no dream-
figure—had raised me to man's estate, but it had been no more
than a fleeting illusion: the hero had proved incapable of violence,
and, thus, no hero at all.

"Liar!" I cried. "Miserable liar!" But Agnese, wrapped in the
irresistible embrace of fear, vouchsafed no reply. Unable even to

obey her undoubted impulse to flee, she began to walk with dragging steps towards the nearest site of human habitation.

She might yet have escaped her doom, but as I came up with her, as I pursued her and grasped her hand, she did what only a madwoman could have devised and executed: she summoned her minions. Although I did not see it, I am sure that, just as a priest repels the Devil with his cross, so she held the Devil's resounding emblem before my face: conjured by her from the hellish contrivance came three or four of her bastard bodyguards. The air was filled with jungle voices, the hullooing of Tarzan, the howl of mating monkeys, raucous invitations to the orgy, the tom-toms of approaching savages, the war-chants or "Beat" songs of long-haired bogymen in gleaming silk waistcoats, challenges to the duel, sounds of mortal combat with the unsheathed penis, grunts of satisfaction, youth's ringing call to arms, its battle-din and final paean of triumph.

What would it matter if I preened myself on having strangled her who had betrayed my love? Yet why should I have assailed one lone weak woman when I had at last been granted the un-hoped-for, unexpected—nay, blessed—opportunity to rid the world of several young males—three or four, I cannot be precise. With the unerring hand of the executioner, I reached for the clamorous chimpanzees and squeezed with superhuman strength. My loins were weak, my hands all the stronger: a brief struggle, and the voices died.

Only then did I become aware that I was still wearing the rubber gloves recommended by the Neapolitan boxer. Their squeaking was the only sound to be heard! Another and more important realization smote me: I had no need to conceal or bury the three or four cadavers, for, prior to her own death, the sorceress had laid her aides and victims to eternal rest within the small black coffin which now lay silent at my feet. A third and final flash of enlightenment: my motive for retaining the gloves with which it was my custom to rescue poisoned fish from the stream was to retrieve the poisoned girl who had scorned my fish and bury her in a fitting manner. For that reason, and not as a means of covering my tracks, I dragged the lifeless body back to the river. I stumbled over stones, fell, scrambled to my feet again, towed the girl first by her hair, then by her ankles, was detained by a bush but pressed on in the direction of the stream until, with

345

unwavering instinct, I discovered the path bounded by the stones beneath which my precious friends lay buried. I wished to accord Agnese the posthumous honour of interment beside my fish.

Meanwhile, roused by the voices from the ether, the revolutionary had reawakened within me. I acted with cool deliberation. This time a sex-murder was to be simulated: for that reason, and that reason alone, I proceeded to divest Agnese of her clothing. First came the fur jacket, then the smart little dress—she had worn no brassière, and my hands glided momentarily across her still warm breasts; then a pair of silken knickers trimmed with lace; then the suspender-belt, which stubbornly resisted my fingers, together with the stockings attached thereto. Finally, to assure myself that I had forgotten no item of apparel, I passed my begloved hand across her belly, thighs, and pubic hair. None of this afforded me the least sensual gratification, gentlemen of the jury, although I cannot pretend that, in kissing the two little breasts and the dainty orifice between the thighs, I did not relish recollection in advance, as it were, nor bear away some provender of memory to sustain me in my future hours of solitude. My spoils were not purely abstract, however. After I had concealed Agnese among the bushes beside the tombstone and covered her, too, with a scattering of sand and pebbles, I took possession of the warm fur jacket with the coquettish collar, and also of my letter, testimony to my shame, together with the frilly knickers which now repose uppermost in my suitcase and will accompany me to a better world. The fur jacket I steeped in the envenomed stream until it grew heavy in my hand and finally sank. Then, skirting the barbed-wire entanglement, I set off on my return journey towards the guiding star formed by the lights on the distant bridge.

Outside the road is hushed. A car approaches, slows, halts outside the entrance. I shall now go to my night-table and remove the tiny receptacle in which I plan to bury my remaining friends. Two long nights of carpentry have produced a fine coffin, rich in material and fair of form. Before I embark upon my life's most grievous step, and before the light in the aquarium is dimmed for ever, the hand of the master shall inscribe the coffin with the words: *Requiescant in pace.* Fish alone rest in peace.

Oskar Enzian

It was dead decent of Mader to pull his finger out and deliver the
new sign before Christmas, no two ways about that. We put it
up straight away. It's the old sign, really, because I was set on
the new one being decorated with gentians like the old one.
Mader dreamed up a few saveloys to go with them, because
artists never can resist gilding the lily. They aren't showy,
though, the saveloys—it's a job to see them for all the greenstuff
painted over the top of my name. One reason why I didn't
change anything is because I'm superstitious. The other is, I'm
against change on principle. It only gives people the twitch.

Just the same, I wasn't all that happy about the new board
because—as the poet says—there's no such thing as pure happiness. What I really wanted to put was *Oskar Enzian & Son,
Sausage and Cured Meats*. In the first place, my father never
put my name on the board, God rest his soul, and I didn't want
my son to suffer on account of me being petty-minded like my
father was; and in the second place, that sort of firm's name
shows it's an old-established family business. Hans has gone and
got himself a job in Linz, though, thanks to the economic
miracle. It isn't all milk and honey, the economic miracle. Life's
like a slice of sausage—there's always two sides to it. No wonder
young people lose their respect for everything, with vacancies
going begging all over the place. It's just propaganda, what they
say about there being more Reds when people are down on their
luck—that's what Pospischil told me the other day. A revolutionary movement needs time, he said, and the Reds have got
plenty of time these days, plus a guaranteed income into the
bargain. It hurts all the same, when it's your own son. I tried to
talk Hans round when he came to collect his things—without
losing my dignity, of course—but he told me he wasn't interested
in expanding the business at Hertha's expense, which is plain
bloody stupid, because Hertha wouldn't have wanted me to
chuck the inheritance away. Well, I've bought the shop next
door and be damned to him. Franziska always was dead against
me buying Hans and Hermi a flat, so now I can put the money
to better use—productive investment, Pospischil calls it. I'm
going to take on an assistant. I'll have to pay him more than

347

THE POISONED STREAM

Hans because of the union, which is chock-full of Reds, but I'm
not up to butchering myself, what with my lung and all. People
won't half sit up and take notice when I open a multiple. My
father never needed an assistant. I was happy to work for my
food and keep, but that was before the Reds took over. Still, a
multiple does have its advantages. Franziska can watch the till
for both shops so nothing gets nicked.

No rose without a thorn is what I always say, but it works
both ways. Mizzi's police superintendent is waving the olive-
branch, in a manner of speaking. He's invited himself and Mizzi
to spend Christmas Eve with us. He only did it on account of
Mizzi getting a fur coat from me—a short one, of course. Added
to that, he was shitting himself because I gave Mizzi a tactful
hint—on advice from Pospischil—that I was thinking of cutting
her out of my will for what they call filial ingratitude. The
Superintendent announced that taking it out on a person's family
the way the Nazis were supposed to have—which is just something dreamed up by the Yids and niggers—doesn't fit in with
the Christian faith, so it wouldn't be fair of him to hold his wife
and her esteemed relatives responsible for Hertha's way of life.
None of which alters the fact that he's a pain in the neck. I go
all soft inside when we have a sing-song at Christmas as a rule,
but the carols'll stick in my throat if I've got to look at his ugly
mug all evening. My beloved mother-in-law will be there as well.

I went to wish Dr Habichl the compliments of the season
yesterday. Took him a genuine leather wallet which cost all of
three hundred and twenty schillings, though old Dvoryak made
me a special price because I always knock a bit off his Frank-
furters. I'm disappointed enough in Dr Habichl as it is, but he's
that thick-skinned he never even noticed what I was getting at
with my present, which was meant as a bit of tit for tat. It was
supposed to signify that he'd filled his wallet with the proceeds
of blackmail, which isn't what you'd expect from an old Party
member. After all, Hertha couldn't have wanted anything to go
to him.

I'm glad I wished Dr Habichl a happy Christmas, just the
same, because I'm still not easy in my mind. That's on account of
Matzleinsdorfer, the reporter who came along with the Wop
that time. He's nosing round the neighbourhood, the fat sod.
What's more, he's been down the Social Club. I got that straight

348

from the horse's mouth—that's to say, from Paula. Taking an interest in my previous history, he is, and going on and on about the Brownshirts. The Jew-boy business shouldn't come up again because I can always say the witnesses made a mistake. They're still looking for the lads who cleaned out Pollack's villa, though. Pollack's son escaped to America, and everybody knows a Jew goes on worrying about his property even when he's six feet under. What's more, young Pollack struck it rich over there, whereas I had to sacrifice my last saveloy to get a bottle of milk for my little Hertha.

Dr Habichl did calm me down a bit all the same. He knows his stuff, that man, and no mistake.

"Listen, Herr Enzian," he said, "I'm going to tell you a story. In the First World War Professor Wagner-Jauregg, the famous neurologist"—he needn't have bothered to explain who the Professor was, because they've got his picture on the fifty-schilling note—"had a madman in his hospital who kept on yelling, 'Something must be done! Something must be done!' One day the Professor went up to his cot and asked what had got to be done, whereupon the madman said, 'Either you lick my arse or I shit the bed.' To which the Professor replied, 'In that case, my dear chap, I suppose you'd better adopt the second course of action.' "

The point is, Dr Habichl went on, nobody knows if the man really shit his bed because madmen never do anything except yell that something's got to be done, and nothing ever is. They may threaten to shit the bed but they never do, because they'd have to lie in it if they did. And nobody's arse gets licked, neither, which means everything stays the way it was. Some people are scared to go out in the sun, but other people's hides are just as tender, and nobody risks a dose of sunburn if they don't have to. People talk and write a lot of hot air, but it never comes to anything. For instance, Dr Habichl says that if the Wops make out I'm guilty of political theft—which would be daft, because political theft isn't theft—we can always ask what Vanetti—who's the owner of the magazine—was doing when the Duce was in charge; and besides, nobody's likely to get mixed up between the Good Book and a magazine which makes money out of unfortunate call-girls. "Your notions of morality are out-dated," Dr Habichl told me—very approving, he sounded—and

349

then he produced a few examples from experience. Take crime, for instance. Criminals still get locked up these days, but as soon as they're let out it doesn't matter about them having been inside. Then again, people are warned not to drive too fast, but there are fifty road casualties every Sunday because there are ten new cars that do two hundred kilometres an hour to every road safety appeal they put out. "The laws are down there in black and white but nobody cares to enforce them," Dr Habichl said. "The statute books are collector's items—you can only obtain them on a lending-library basis. Actually, I was against your taking money from the magazine and the Jewish film people," he said, "but it won't harm your turnover. It doesn't matter whether you took it or not—either way." He might have thought of that earlier on, before he started bleeding me white because I needed him in case something came up. Well, live and let live, that's what I always say. After all, it's as good as a Christmas present, knowing nothing can come up.

I stopped off at Paula's on the way home because I can't spend Christmas Eve with her. I gave her the gold bracelet, which led to intercourse. I've still got what it takes, thank God, even if I did think the tragedy had made me old before my time. That's why I haven't got a bad conscience, because it's a well-known fact that you can do your duty by your business and family better if you work off your sexual urges. Besides, I won't see Paula any more this year. A bloody awful year it's been, too.

Christmas is on the doorstep, like it or not. Franziska's doing her Christmas baking—star-cakes and coconut kisses and rum babas, which puts me in mind of my sainted mother, except that her stuff beat Franziska's into a cocked hat. There's a Christmassy smell drifting round the house, which is enough to give anyone a lump in the throat. I've stowed my presents in the parlour chest. The couch is installed already. I bet the Superintendent never saw one like that in all his born days—far too good for his backside, it is. The TV set won't be delivered till Christmas Eve. The Austrian Broadcasting Service is putting out a top-class programme, which will save me having to listen to the Superintendent talking la-di-da and my beloved mother-in-law griping. One thing, though: Franziska's going to have to see to the tree decorations herself, because the sight of all those shiny balls and candles and the angel with the silver hair being taken out of their boxes would be bound to put me in mind of my little girl. She always used to peep through the keyhole Christmas Eve, Hertha did, and now she's buried in foreign soil. When the bells start chiming my Hertha will come floating through the room dressed up as an angel—not that anyone except me will notice.

Still, I did spare Franziska the job of decorating the shop. Old Joseph Birner, who I bought the Christmas tree from, he let me have a bloody great mountain of fir-branches free of charge, which was dead decent of him. I draped some over the hooks on the wall, so the hams and salami and Krakauer look like Babes in the Wood. I also put some sprigs round the dish of assorted cold cuts. The two boars' heads make a fine show. I've stuck fir-cones in their mouths, being a born window-dresser. Hexi's sniffing around all over the place because she knows she always gets a saveloy at Christmas. She'll get two this year, on account of her having been my Hertha's pet.

Antonio Zempach

It was the usual scene in St Moritz, pre-Christmassy bustle beneath a gracious sky, which here means gracious to skiers. Not that I grew up on the Cresta Run. We never went to St Moritz when I was a child—a family hotel in Lenzerheide was our limit. Blasé implies satiated, but sometimes one isn't satiated, just unhungry. Socially speaking, I'm unhungry as opposed to satiated. I don't have anything against snobbery—I'm not even an anti-snob, like most snobs. It's simply that snobs are beyond my ken, hence irritating. Some of them want to 'belong' in order to get somewhere, others want to get somewhere in order to 'belong'—too fine a distinction for an amateur snob to draw. I don't have anything against people who want to 'get on' in society—I can't fathom their motives, that's all, just as I never understand why mountaineers want to reach the top. The Swiss team which climbed Mount Everest stayed up there for two hours. Two hours of freezing solitude. *Tant de bruit pour une montagne.*

We stayed at the Suvretta-Haus—more staid than the Palace, but no cheaper. Dr von Helis always puts up there. This time

351

he was in the States, so we stayed at the Suvretta-Haus instead of him. I deputize for Dr von Helis more and more often in court; now I deputize for him with hall porters.

We meet on the Cresta, lie motionless in the sun like oily mummies, barbecued human steaks, *bien saignant, s'il vous plaît*, perhaps even *bleu*, he who peels gets more out of life. We have an *après-ski* date at the Palace. The proprietor sometimes joins a more favoured guest at his table, but you have to have known the proprietor's father to qualify for the hotel aristocracy. Or we squeeze into Hanselmann's and Yvette sends my mother chocolates and I send her mother chocolates. We could just as easily send chocolates to our respective mothers, but that wouldn't be so considerate. We take sleigh-rides from the Palace to the Suvretta-Haus, to Samaden or Pontresina, hailing people like long-lost friends—too bad we don't even know them. It's like a cruise liner, where you become bosom pals with people you never see again. It may be eccentric of me, but I'm not interested in knowing who's just broken a leg.

Not being the holiday type—something inside me says I've no real right to a holiday—I off-load my bad conscience on to society. What society? St Moritz society, for instance. I tell my-self that its members ought to have a bad conscience, but my contempt for socialites isn't genuine or it would be aggressive. In reality, it's protective: I'm afraid the rest of the world will rumble them. I confuse society with the system, a common blunder. This sleigh-riding, bob-racing, jewel-laden, caviare-hogging set is no more representative of our system than the stench of lagoons is representative of Venetian Baroque. It's the fashion these days to regard everything as typical. Everything is a sign of the times and every doltish playboy representative of his age. Anything which lacks symbolic significance has no significance whatsoever, commentary precedes the event, and people mistake the dog that cocks its leg against the corner-stone for the corner-stone itself. Is Vanetti representative? Probably, though it isn't clear what he represents. Crude conversationalists base their assertions on an isolated example—we only under-stand things if they're illustrated by means of examples. There weren't any Vanettis a century ago; on the other hand, nobody cared if a child lay dying unless it was the Tsarevitch. Both facts are symptomatic, but of what?

I bought a copy of *Quest' Ora*—not a regular habit of mine—and broke it down into its constituents. Nude girls... So what? I occasionally leaf through old copies of *Vie Parisienne*: women only showed their ankles then, but the intention was the same. The old-fashioned sensualist has gone modern, which simply means that he becomes impotent earlier. People confuse tastelessness with freedom, though it may not be a confusion at all: lack of taste being a characteristic of the majority, democracy entails that freedom be tasteless. Several pages devoted to society scandals... Very reassuring. If society were scandalous they wouldn't be scandals. The link between the French Revolution and Marie Antoinette's necklace is arbitrary. A contented nation would merely have laughed at the affair. Nobody ever regards Countess X as a class-representative until she shoots her lover—she only becomes one after she pulls the trigger. A third constituent: murder and violence... Do people get worked up because they occur or because the Vanettis of this world report their occurrence? Doctors identify symptoms and pass on quickly to the question of treatment; we become infatuated with symptoms and let treatment go hang. *Quest' Ora*'s admixture of politics struck me as a new departure—young Vanetti's influence, probably.

I was back on the subject of Vanetti. I said to Yvette, twice a day: "I'm going to call Rome now." Her standard response: "We agreed to wait till Christmas." My standard rejoinder: "What if the murderer doesn't wait till Christmas and strikes again?"

I chewed over the problem of complicity while skiing. Silence equals connivance, he who profits is an accessary—we ought to be experts at that in Switzerland. Then some people came and asked if we knew who'd won the slalom. I ordered a Bourbon sour. It's hard, working overtime on your conscience, especially at the Palace.

I said to Yvette: "I'm an accomplice—not of the murderer, but of his accomplice." If Vanetti hadn't been my client I'd have turned him in. I don't think Vanetti conspired with the murderer. The murderer is merely his client, so to speak. Equally, I didn't conspire with Vanetti—accomplices have no need to conspire. I can think of a dozen people who are protecting me, who am protecting Vanetti, who is protecting Morelli. Everybody has a client and is one, simultaneously.

"You don't have to torpedo a ship just because you abandon it," said Yvette.

"No," I said, "you row ashore."

"Why not?" she said. "It isn't your ship, anyway."

Of course not. We leave our bags in the station yard and pick them up next day. Nobody pinches them and if someone did it would be a foreigner, which doesn't count. Why shouldn't I enjoy my skiing holiday? We're all going to watch the figure-skating tomorrow.

"I'm a paragon of virtue," I said. "I've given up acting for Edizioni Vanetti. It cost me twenty thousand francs, not to mention the hundreds of thousands I might have earned."

Yvette said, "You abandoned ship—that's good enough."

There was a Christmas tree in the hotel foyer. Hotel Christmas trees are a democratic institution. They do their best to look no less frightful than the Christmas trees erected in public squares for the delectation of the poor. It would be interesting to know if the freezing firs on the snow-covered slopes envy the decorated tree in the warm hotel foyer or despise it, or both.

I went out on to the balcony in my dinner jacket. The cold was biting, but you never catch cold when you think you're catching cold—I must ask a doctor the reason some time. Moonlight, the Corviglia violet, not a breath of wind, no snow falling, the trees weighed down like pastrycooks carrying iced birthday cakes, the sky a guarantee of first-class skiing weather next day, no extra charge. I could see lights twinkling in the little houses in the valley. It would be nice to be behind one of those twinkling windows, I thought. If I had been I should probably have envied the dinner-jacketed man on the balcony of the brightly lit hotel. It's quite simple—I don't know why the same principle shouldn't apply to fir-trees.

I went back inside. Yvette was installed at her dressing-table, my ex-writing-table, wearing her third-best evening dress. The second-best is earmarked for Christmas Eve and the best for New Year's Eve at the Palace. I found her just as lovely in her third-best as in her best. Stupid of her to marry me, really.

I walked over to the 'phone and picked up the receiver.

Yvette said, "Good idea. We'll have our Martinis up here instead."

"I'm calling Rome," I said.

"High time too," she said.

"What do you mean?" I asked. What I wanted to say was, I love you.

"You won't have to sneak off and buy the Italian papers any more," she said. "You've been deceiving me with the *Corriere della Sera* for days now."

"But it isn't Christmas yet," I said.

"So?" she said, like someone getting up without a murmur even though the alarm clock has gone off too soon.

The operator said it would take about half an hour. I tried to impress on her that it was urgent. I had asked for police headquarters, after all, but she didn't understand. If somebody had stolen my wife's jewels—which was unlikely anyway, in our snug little Swiss world—I would have called the house detective. Why should anyone be in a hurry to speak to foreign policemen?

"What do you mean, high time?" I repeated.

"It's high time because it's high time for you," she said. "If it had been high time for you yesterday you'd have 'phoned yesterday."

"It's too late, probably," I said.

"If anything had happened it would have been in the papers," said Yvette.

"I'm sure nothing's happened," I said. "All the same, I've known what I know for too long."

"You just called Rome," Yvette said.

For the first time it dawned on me how pretty the room was. There was a passable Segantini copy above the beds. I didn't call room service. I didn't want to be disturbed.

"You skied like a goddess today," I said.

I kissed her. We glanced in the mirror and laughed because we looked like a pair of clowns. I'd forgotten about her lipstick.

It took nearly an hour, of course, but headquarters came through at last. I asked for the head of Homicide. The man at the other end refused to understand. He made difficulties—obviously it isn't done to report murders or denounce murderers by 'phone, from St Moritz. Eventually the word *avvocato* sank in. I was calling from Switzerland, land of the precision-built, eighteen-jewel reputation. Not even the Almighty would refuse to take a call from a Swiss lawyer.

I was put through to someone called Giannini, Chief of

355

Homicide. I had learned my speech by heart like a bad barrister; like a good barrister, I forgot it. It was all rather confused, I'm afraid. A lawyer, calling from St Moritz, recently engaged to act for *Quest' Ora*, *Quest' Ora* had paid the Viennese butcher Oskar Enzian for the life-story of his murdered daughter, Hertha Enzian, I had discovered in the course of my inquiries that the girl had been murdered by one Aurelio Morelli, novelist, of Rome, yes, that was right, Aurelio Morelli, I therefore deemed it my duty... Who was going to understand all that?

The man named Giannini understood perfectly.

"My heartfelt thanks, *Avvocato*," he said. "Unfortunately, none of this is new to us. A warrant has already been issued for the arrest of Aurelio Morelli." Why unfortunately? He probably thought I was staking a claim to the reward.

Yvette was standing facing me. I cupped my hand over the mouthpiece. "They know already," I said.

"What did you say?" asked Giannini.

"I was just telling my wife that you already knew," I said.

"If you feel you have a claim of any kind," he began, "please submit it in writing to—"

I interrupted for fear he would hang up. "*Quest' Ora* has known the murderer's identity for a long time," I stammered. "He actually wrote his memoirs for them." I felt like a stool-pigeon.

Giannini said soothingly, "Of course. Information was laid against him by the magazine itself." He paused, perhaps because he was afraid I might be playing along with *Quest' Ora* for the sake of the reward. Quickly he added, "The police knew the suspect's name prior to that, I may say."

"Everything's fine, then," I said.

"Everything's fine," Giannini confirmed. "May I have your name again?"

"Dr Antonio Zempach," I said, "Suvretta-Haus, St Moritz." That was stupid—a typical blunder, the Suvretta-Haus bit. I should have given the firm's address. I was shielding Dr von Helis's firm.

"Very good of you to call, *Dottore*," said Giannini. "How's the weather in the Engadine?"

The weather in the Engadine is excellent, thank you. Powder snow.

"Happy Christmas," said Giannini.
"They reported him," I said.
"It's too late for Martinis," said Yvette.

Christa Sonntag

I've never been a sun-worshipper myself, but sunshine at Christmas is a proper insult. Christmas isn't Christmas at all unless it's a white one. I go all homesick at Christmas, in spite of having had such a rotten time of it in Munich as a kiddy.

Which was one of the reasons why I invited Peter to Rome. They've let him out, thank God. I'm against punishing homosexuals, even if they are unfair competition.

I felt a bit nervous, to be honest, standing at the station waiting for him, because he's the kind of queer you spot right off. Flutters around like a love-sick butterfly, he does. I got a pleasant surprise, though, as it turned out. He'd cut his hair short, and he was wearing a blue suit that would have done credit to a Cabinet Minister. There's a protest movement on these days among the queers, because all the other youngsters look like queers too.

We drove straight out to *Pace*, because I'd shut up shop early so as to be able to concentrate on Christmas. The Italians are a nice enough crowd but they don't have the first idea about a German Christmas, which is the only kind, so I had a bit of a job getting hold of a tree. It was a stroke of luck Peter being there, from that point of view. He spent the whole day carting the tree from one part of the garden to another, wherever the shade was. The thing is, Christmas trees die off quickly in the south. Peter brought a water-container with him—a new gadget specially for putting Christmas trees in so they don't go withered. Except that he hadn't reckoned on the size of my Christmas tree. It's so big it wouldn't fit in the container. I mean, a Christmas tree isn't a potted azalea.

I didn't invite any men to the Christmas hand-out, unless you count Peter, because I see plenty of them all year round. I'd have liked to invite Françoise, but Christmas is just another binge to the French, being the way they are—no sense of intimacy, the French. As for Rosa, who's in the same line of business and comes from Munich like me, she can't make it because she has to spend

357

Christmas Eve with her pimp, the sentimental bitch. I have got some guests, all the same. There's Rita, who comes from Salzburg, and Anneliese, who comes from Passau, and Karin, even if she is a Berliner—i.e., a dirty Prussian, not that that matters at Christmas. Rita and Anneliese are here already. They're bed-and-breakfasting at Anzio, because Peter's sleeping in the spare room. The house isn't perfect yet—for instance, I can't do without my model kitchen in the Via Sicilia—but it's lovely just the same.

For dinner Christmas Eve there's carp, which was just as much of a job to get hold of as the tree. On Christmas Day, goose with red cabbage and roast potatoes. The recipe's a winner, but I didn't keep it to myself. I had to send Canonica a Christmas-box anyway—nothing valuable, because that would be bribery, but something to show the poor old soul a bit of womanly warmth. I bought the prettiest Christmas card I could find and wrote the recipe down in my own handwriting, which is educated-looking but easy to read. It goes: *Clean goose well, also remove last bits of plumage. Wash in cold water. Salt inside and out. Stuff with two apples and an onion. Skewer the goose together again, then put into the baking pan with a little cold water. Set oven at two hundred and roast. When one side is done, turn over of course.* You never know what a man needs to be told. *Very important—baste all the time! When the bird has made a lot of fat, ladle off well so that it only lies in a little fat.* And then I added my secret tip, because I've got a soft spot for Canonica. I gave Françoise the same recipe, but I left out the end. *When the outside is good and crisp, baste with beer for another five minutes.* I put three exclamation marks after that.

My hard-earned haven of rest is really starting to smell like Christmas now. I stand over the stove all day long in a white smock which makes me look like Professor Sauerbruch doing a surgical operation. While Peter was humping the Christmas tree backwards and forwards I made a start on the Christmas cake. I'm an artist at that, though I do say it myself. There's more to a Christmas cake than almonds and raisins—good taste comes into it too. For instance, the gingerbread angels look like real angels. Comets are my speciality. The stars of Bethlehem are pink, but that's a bit of artistic licence. I got Peter to put a little silver loop on each of them so they can dangle from the tree.

It's no wonder Canonica enjoys cooking. You need to be

intelligent to cook, and besides, your brain never works better than when you're bending over your own stove.

I can't get Hertha out of my head, firstly because I just can't, and secondly because it was last Christmas she moved into the Via Sicilia. I still recall the way she cried on account of being alone Christmas Eve. I don't know what she expected, because any fool knows trade slumps at Christmas. Christmas is the time when clients decide to turn over a new leaf and concentrate on making their wives happy. They keep it up till about Twelfth Night, which is when the Christmas tree gets slung out as well. It's more sensible to take a break, really, because clients are down the pan financially, due to their families. I mean to say, there aren't many businesses which don't have their ups and downs, so it isn't fair to grouse. Winter resorts are dead in summer, and Christmas is a family season of the year. Hertha never hoisted that in, not that she was such an exception; most of my so-called colleagues think sex is a spare-time occupation, which is about the same as a hotel proprietor thinking he can take a holiday in his own hotel. Any girl who regards her sex-life as part of her private life is in for a thin time. Girls like Hertha don't spare a thought for their private lives the whole year round and treat the profession as if it was a hobby. Then, when Christmas comes along, the poor bitches find they're on their lonesome, and that makes them feel as lost as a kiddy looking for its mummy in a big store.

I'll spare a kind thought for Hertha this Christmas, all the same. I told Canonica the truth and I didn't sour things completely with Bossi, either. They're putting me on the cover, but Bossi is having to pay extra for that. As a result, I've been able to make a down payment on that plot next door. Come summer, I'll sit there and listen to the murmur of the sea. It's making me nervous just at present, the murmur of the sea, because somehow it doesn't go with the Christmas atmosphere.

In the afternoon we sat in the living-room, me and Peter and Rita and Anneliese, seeing to the final preparations. I supervised the whole thing, like a general. I painted the nuts, some in silver, some in gold. Rita painted the fir-cones—not that she didn't mess up the table while she was at it. Peter cut up different-coloured sheets of tissue paper for Anneliese to wrap the special bonbons in. He's on his very best behaviour, Peter, except that his style

359

of dress is a bit off. He insists on lounging around in one of my nighties, which the girls think is a scream. Peter's going to give each of us a hair-do tomorrow morning—it's all fixed. My theory is, a woman who only makes herself beautiful for the sake of the menfolk gets old before her time, because beauty is a habit like everything else, and you can't get used to it if you're not looking tip-top the whole time. Besides, only Onassis keeps a private hairdresser, and even that may be just a rumour.

While we were in the middle of wrapping parcels, which everyone was doing in separate corners to keep it a surprise— Rita turned quite hysterical if anyone took a peek over her shoulder—little Luigi came across from the villa next door and said I was wanted down at the post-office straight away. There was an express registered packet for me, but they couldn't spare anyone to deliver it because of the Christmas rush. They'd rung the neighbours, because I don't have a 'phone yet, and I won't ever have. I've done enough 'phoning to last me a lifetime.

I hared down to the post because I thought it was a Christmas present, which it was, even if it didn't look like one. Far from it. It was just a grey envelope, and it came from the Aliens Department in Rome. They'd forwarded it to me from the Via Sicilia. I wondered whether to open it, because nasty surprises can keep till after Christmas as far as I'm concerned. It's cowardly, though, not opening a letter, so I took my courage in both hands, and— bingo!—inside the envelope was my resident's permit, which had been extended for another year. I got quite a lump in my throat when I saw it, because it was a Christmas-box from Canonica, sure as eggs, not that there was anything else inside. I'd asked for an extension, which you always have to do in December, but extensions are only for six months, normally, and there isn't another girl in the whole of the Via Veneto who can boast of having a year's permit. It's like getting a medal. I'd sooner have the permit than a diamond ring—that I could buy myself. I'm glad I sent Canonica the roast goose recipe. My woman's instinct didn't let me down after all. At least there's one policeman who isn't rotten. Being decent pays off. It's nice to know that, specially at Christmas.

Francesco Vanetti

There's a copy of the Christmas number in my bag, tomorrow we start distributing, Bellini's *Madonna* on the front cover, one hundred and eighty-two pages, the fattest number ever, one hundred and four pages of adverts, page nine carries the opening of *The Enzian Story by Aurelio Morelli: How I murdered Hertha Enzian*, subtitle: *Confessions of the August Murderer, a Quest' Ora exclusive, Copyright by Edizioni Vanetti*. The presses are still turning, newsagents' placards, lucky we handle our own printing, half a million placards, an edition of one million six hundred and fifty thousand, by mid-week we'll be sold out, better under-run than leave yourself with returns, *Lui e Lei* are launching *The Kennedy Plot*, Kennedy is old hat, laughable.

Before I drive out to the palazzo I tour the building, I shake everyone's hand, the whole editorial staff is drinking champagne, I had champagne sent up, my father never had any champagne sent up, he economizes in the wrong place, he's old-fashioned. Everyone congratulates me, they all beam at me suddenly, nobody dares to say so, but most of them hope my father never comes back, "There's a new wind blowing at last," says Castellani, it dawned on him a bit late. I tour the administrative offices, I tour the accounts department, I tour the printing works, I tour the dispatch department, old crones are bundling up the magazine, I pause beside each old crone, I shake them all by the hand, *Buona festa*, I say, *Auguri*, I climb up on to the rotary press, I shake the machine-room overseer's hand, *Auguri*, my father economized on expenses, my father economized on handshakes, he never heard about worker-participation, he never understood people, he was old-fashioned.

I leave the building, the lights are still blazing, the glass box looks like a huge aquarium, fish are swimming in the Vanetti aquarium, no more fish are swimming in the Morelli aquarium.

Bossi escorts me to the car, he's resentful because he has to fly off the day after tomorrow, to Sydney, he'd sooner have celebrated Christmas with his mother and Fiorella, I sent Fiorella some flowers, not from the Sacchi woman's shop, of course, we really owe everything to Fiorella. "Give Fiorella my regards," I say. "Why did Morelli try to strangle her, anyway?"—a question I'd been meaning to ask for ages, Morelli always acted with premeditation, always on the 8th of August; "He was probably under the spell of the happening," says Bossi, you can't rely on murderers, "Morelli is unpredictable," says Bossi. As I drive off he smiles and says, "By the way, thanks." It's a struggle but he does say thanks, I gave him two hundred thousand lire, a bonus, a Christmas-box, I don't care how many advances we give him, if Bossi goes to *Lui e Lei* they'll pay him double, we mustn't lose Bossi.

I don't know if Morelli's unpredictable, unaccountable, who is accountable, who is predictable, why should we tot people up like accounts, twice two is five, Morelli's a cheat, he's vanished, he got into a taxi and vanished. He's cheated us out of the *Enzian Story*, Bossi wrote the first five instalments in the murderer's name, *How I murdered Hertha Enzian*, it can't be helped, the *Chiesa Story* or the *Pisenti Story* would be worthless, the Enzian girl is our banker, Bossi's stuff is so authentic it might have been written by Morelli, we had to rewrite Morelli in any case. We know everything about the Enzian girl, her family told us everything, Christa Sonntag told us everything, the girl next door, we know Morelli better than he knows himself, he murdered Hertha Enzian in exactly the same way as he murdered Lucia Chiesa and Vera Pisenti, Bossi is a stickler for detail, Morelli isn't going to cheat us and get away with it. Bossi went to Giannini, he denounced Morelli, "You have no claim to the reward," Giannini told him, Canonica arrived from Paris a few hours earlier, there's a warrant out for Morelli, Morelli knew we weren't his accomplices, he knew we'd denounce him, Morelli has vanished. "It would be better if they never found him," says Bossi, Morelli's unpredictable, he'll say we received the memoirs in instalments, we'll say we received them all at once and reported him on the spot. "Canonica can work out for himself that we didn't lay information immediately," says Bossi, it's technically impossible, the machines were already running, we'll say we doubted the story until the last moment, we took a gamble but we were doubtful, nobody will believe it. "It doesn't matter if they believe it or not," says Bossi, "they want to believe it, they want to be the first, they won't want to tangle with us." But they'll ask why we were interested in Aurelio Morelli's memoirs at all, Canonica is an enemy of ours, the files are still open; nobody can stop us taking an interest in Morelli the novelist, says Bossi, we thought he was a crackpot, we had to check whether he was a murderer. It would be better if Canonica had retired already, it's better for Bossi to be in Sydney if they come asking questions, Giannini won't ask any questions, he can't stand Canonica and he's a friend of my father's, we won't claim the reward.

The party is in full swing when I get there, I have to change, Giulietta escorts me to my room, she says the party can wait. She's wearing a long evening dress, pale blue, hair piled up, flowers in her hair, she looks like one of the two sisters in *Gabrielle d'Estrées and Her Sister in the Bath*, the sisters' breasts are bare, Giulietta's dress is only cut low on one side, Yves Saint-Laurent, she says, her right breast is almost bare, best of all I'd like to go to bed with her, the party can wait. I stand naked in the bathroom, I shave, the door is ajar, I've never spoken to a woman through the bathroom door, naked, from room to room, it's as if we were married, we're getting married in February. "There's a copy of the Christmas number in my bag," I say, I lather my face, I tell her to take a look at the Christmas number, it's a surprise. I want to tell her that we knew the murderer's identity all the time, I struggle for the right words, I want to tell her the truth, the murderer supplied the murders in instalments, he delivered the way he murdered, Bossi knew who the murderer was, my father knew who the murderer was, I inherited the murderer, I struggle for the right words.

> And the words are liars,
> flowers, graves, love, freedom, the gate,
> you open your heart,
> you dissect yourself,
> when you state you misstate,
> your tongue tripped,
> you lied.
>
> Speak without words!
> Words are in league,
> leagued lies,
> words are soldiers,
> commas are soldiers,
> stops, they march, they kill,

the lie is the general,
be incomprehensible,
you die for the general,
you speak.

Brother, hands, fences, death.
From syllables, words, from words, phrases,
on and on,
you are captured,
you wear uniform,
steel helmet, medals,
hush!
Only the dumb speak true.

I wrote it a year ago, *Opus* VII, I know it by heart, I could recite it, I don't recite it, everything I've written I know by heart, I won't recite it, I'll forget it, Giulietta wouldn't understand it, I don't understand it; nothing is harder to understand than that one used to be a child, the same person but a child, one can understand other children, other children were never me.

"Why didn't you tell me?" asks Giulietta; "I had to promise my father," I say, "it's no surprise to me, I spoke to the murderer, I photographed him." Giulietta doesn't ask why we let the murderer go, why he wrote for us in instalments, she dives into the magazine, why should we have reported the murderer, I don't need to find any words. "Where are your photographs?" asks Giulietta, "We're bringing out the childhood photographs first," I say, a single picture of the murderer in the Christmas number, with his mother, the victims, childhood photographs of the murderer, childhood photographs of the victims. "Have you disposed of the book rights?" asks Giulietta, no, I say, we haven't disposed of them, I scrape my chin, the book rights aren't disposed of. Giulietta hands me the dinner jacket, it's lying underneath the fresh copies, I hope the shirt stayed clean, I hope the dinner jacket doesn't smell of printer's ink, I slip my shirt on, Giulietta knots my tie, "You have a word with Father about those book rights," she says.

The hall is dark, the servants are lighting candles, candles in the big drawing-room, candelabra, candles in every room, warm light, ghostly light, All Saints' Christmas. Ferrari carries a long candle in his hand, he stares over the sea of heads, he looks around for guttering candles, looks for candles like a sea-captain sighting land, they're changed, new candles for old, he beckons to the butler, he lights them. Ferrari is wearing an open-necked shirt, most of the men are in evening dress, lace shirts, some of them wear open-necked shirts or polo-necks, women in evening gowns or jeans, low necklines, silk culottes, one girl completely encased in leather.

I don't know a soul, I know two or three of the men, they back away, glass in hand, I don't know a soul, a woman walks over to the fireplace, the candles flicker, she vanishes into the fireplace, she gets scorched. They're all young, Ferrari is old, nobody minds him, he lights candles, only the servants are old, I've never seen them before, one of the lady's-maids is old, I know her, I'm glad I know the lady's-maid.

Nearly all the guests are Ferrari authors, says Giulietta, her father says the future belongs to them, nobody knows where the future begins but it's important for the future to belong to you, you live on advances, down payments on the future; I ask myself if the future belongs to me, my poems aren't published, I don't know if the future belongs to me, I am the Unknown Poet, my poem's name is *Quest' Ora*. "Very nice," a poet says to me, he has blond hair, dyed, "but why the candles, has something fused?" Ferrari doesn't hear, luckily, two candles go out at once, fused candles, Ferrari calls the butler, he lights new candles. I drink champagne, two glasses, quickly. A woman with heavy horn-rimmed spectacles and small breasts, you can see her navel, says, "Do you write too? I'm married to Ennio Regazzi." I've never heard of Ennio Regazzi, I'm ashamed of never having heard of Ennio Regazzi, no, I don't write, I can't tell her I wrote the leader in *Quest' Ora. A Happy Christmas to All Our Readers.* The Gothic Madonnas have been cleared away. "Last time somebody poured champagne over the Sacro Bambino's head," the lady's-maid whispers to me, I'm her confidant, the Sacro Bambino had to be restored, Sacri Bambini don't take kindly to champagne. "The aggressors can't win the war in Vietnam, the Americans will bleed to death," says a man in dinner jacket and sandals, "Ferrari's getting old," says the girl in the leather dress. "I spoke to your father," says Ferrari, but he doesn't look at me, he has tiny candles in his eyes. "Your father," he says, with angry candle-eyes, "won't sell *Positivismo*, he's asking an exorbitant price, he's making a monkey out of me." He turns away, he'll disinherit me, your father won't sell *Positivismo* so you can't marry my daughter. Giulietta's dress has slipped off her shoulder, she twitches it into place, that dress burns in February, Yves Saint-Laurent goes to the stake, my wife isn't Gabrielle d'Estrées or her sister, school of Fontainebleau, I go up to Giulietta, she's talking to a raccoon. "The Vatican and the C.I.A. are in cahoots," he says, "we must get to the root of the evil, the Pope is a neo-imperialist warmonger." Three women are sitting on the long table where the Madonnas usually stand, two of them are pretty, I think I'll annoy Giulietta, I bring them some champagne, they don't say thank you, I listen to them, they don't look at me, it's funny, they speak Italian but I don't understand them.

I stumble into a room, someone has forgotten to switch off the light, I blink in the electric glare, the Madonnas are standing on the floor, in file, like garden gnomes for sale, a film projector stands against the wall, spools of film beyond the Madonnas, aluminium wagon-wheels, Ferrari plans to show a film later on, in the cellar, an avant-garde film, Czech; in Rome the machines are still turning, the machine-room in neon, the machines are spewing out the *Enzian Story*, the machine-room overseer shook my hand, *Auguri*, I should have stayed in Rome, I forgot to 'phone my father, I'll 'phone my father.

"Where were you?" says Giulietta, "I spoke to my father, my father's looking for you." We go into the big drawing-room, a girl in jeans emerges from the fireplace, a blue wax doll emerges from the fireplace, the girl laughs, they laugh in chorus, I don't know why they laugh. Ferrari takes me by the arm, he isn't angry any more, he doesn't speak about *Positivismo*; "I'm buying the book rights of the *Morelli Story*," he says; "You can't publish that," I say, I look him in the eye, his eyes have fused. I say Bossi rewrote the manuscript, journalism, sensationalism, primitivism, food for morons, realistic kitsch, Establishment kitsch, the murderer is old-fashioned. "Bossi converted literature into sensationalism," says Ferrari, "my editorial director can convert sensationalism into literature, Zanolini is a good man," he says, "have a word with Zanolini, he's sitting over there, the one with the pipe." I say it's a murder story, a detective story with real names. "Substance is nothing," says Ferrari, "form is everything," he lights a candle, "Victims of society," he says, "you could write the introduction, they're victims of society." He wants to bribe me, my father bribed me, Ferrari dangles the introduction under my nose like a child's rattle, a diphtheria jab or an Alfa Romeo, I say, "We'll see, the Italian rights maybe, the foreign rights we hang on to at all costs." I'll develop *Positivismo* myself, I don't need Ferrari, I don't need my father, the idea's mine, there's no time for poetry, no time for candles, no time for fathers, I shall build up *Positivismo* myself. "Spoken like a man," says Giulietta, she strokes my hair, "my father will have to make do with the Italian rights, you won't hand over *Quest' Ora.*" I say, "Princess Cokachin, what say I carry you off to Persia, or, failing that, Rome?" Three days in the palazzo, unbearable, Christmas, I think of Rome, the old crones are bundling up magazines, Bossi flies to Sydney, my father mustn't get over-excited, Canonica will ask questions, the files are still open. "My father's driving to Cortina tomorrow," says Giulietta, "he's meeting his mistress there, we'll stay on by ourselves."

The servants put out the candles, it's almost dark, nobody notices how dark it is, "My piece on Vietnam is nearly finished," a skinny man says in French, "My volume of poetry is coming out in Russia soon," says a woman in a yellow evening dress, "Do you write too?" asks the wife of the famous poet whose name I don't know, she already asked me if I write, it's so dark you wouldn't recognize a poet if you saw one, the electric light comes on, I must 'phone my father; "Realism is a betrayal of the people," says Zanolini, knocking his pipe out. "Of course," says the girl in the leather dress, "You'll soon see where it leads," says Zanolini, he leads the way to the cellar, the servants lug the aluminium wagon-wheels downstairs to the cellar, we watch the avant-garde film.

Emilio Bossi

I had to come face to face with Canonica sooner or later, so why not in Foce Verde? I told Giannini the murderer had been lying low in Foce Verde the whole time, and that he'd made a run for it after delivering the manuscript. I had to show my face in Foce Verde or the Sydney trip would have looked like a moonlight flit.

I didn't take the coast road—it's quicker not to. A dismal afternoon with a sun like a hibernating bear. On the left, Moorish castles, half a mosque, a medieval tilt-yard complete with grandstands. All made of papiermâché—they shot a film here, I *figli dei Moschettieri*. I ought to tell the Kronos people. Maybe they could use some of it. Not the buildings, of course— Moorish wouldn't fit into the *Enzian Story*. The soil is red. Let's hope they shoot the film in colour.

I have a friend who writes novels. His theory is, you never finish a novel, you leave it in the lurch. The same goes for reporting. I lived with Morelli, now I'm abandoning him. He's as non-existent now as if I'd invented him. Maybe I did invent him. The public will swallow my story whole—me, I'll just flick through it. Misprints are all that interests writers once they've abandoned their work. I'd like to have wished Morelli *bon voyage* at least. He appealed to me more than I appealed to him, which is funny, considering he's a three-time killer. I hope they don't make him too odious in the film—he deserves decent casting. I'm even prepared to forgive him for leaving me to kill off Hertha Enzian by myself.

The first policemen stopped me on the bridge over the Fosso Mascarello, in spite of the Press badge on my car. They checked my papers. Then one of them grinned: "Ah, *Quest' Ora!*" Big deal, as Christa Sonntag would say.

Too many policemen around for a murderer, even one of the three-time variety. The place was swarming with flat-footed four-minute-milers. Radio cars, two black saloons from Homicide, walkie-talkies, lots of plain-clothes men—the sort any criminal could recognize blindfold. Foce Verde was in festive mood, shop windows decorated, the whole town decked out like a fancy cake. Things couldn't have been livelier at the height of the summer season. Almost all the locals were clutching copies of *Quest' Ora*—the sight of them would have made Vanetti take up his bed and walk. Everyone will be talking about the murderer over Christmas dinner. Foce Verde will rate a bigger dot on the map—maybe even a star in the tourist guide. The hotels will be booked solid next summer. I shouldn't wonder if they don't give the bathing-huts a lick of paint. They look like tired old zebras.

Trentini came up to me outside the hotel. He's my favourite

member of the Homicide Squad. When I was a cub reporter we used to spend hours in the trattoria opposite Headquarters. I must have bought him a barrel of rum in my time. Trentini's addicted to rum.

"We've found her," he said.

"Who?" I asked.

"The Doninelli girl," he said.

"Really?" I said. He might have been talking Greek.

"That'll give you something fresh to write about," he said.

I'm not all that slow on the uptake. "Did he strangle her?" I asked.

"What do you think?" he said. He rubbed his hands. Not with delight but because he was cold. He ought to get himself transferred to Palermo—he looks like a gloomy barometer for six months of the year.

"Any details?" I asked cautiously.

"Nineteen," he said, "father a millionaire. She was often seen with Morelli. They went fishing together, apparently."

"Sounds improbable," I said.

"Sex-murder," he amplified.

"How do you know?" I asked.

"She was stripped," he said.

"Where did they find her?" I asked.

"Out near the atomic energy place," he said. "Her father didn't report her disappearance till early this morning. He'd just arrived for the holiday. Thought she was waiting for him at the house. The servants thought she'd driven to Rome." He waved a mottled hand in the direction of the big house. "The *castello* belongs to her father," he said. It was hidden by Wagnerian clouds of sea-mist. "Filthy swine," he said, masticating the words. "He likes his meat young and tender."

"Of course," I said, nodding. "Is Canonica around?"

"It's Ascension Day for the *Professore*," he said. A missing persons report from Foce Verde, and five minutes later Canonica knew that it could only have been Morelli.

"You look like death warmed up," said Trentini.

"How about a rum?" I suggested.

We had a rum. The dining-room was seething with people—not to be facetious, it was murder in there. The fringed curtains were drawn and the lights blazing, far too early in the day.

Plastic flowers on the tables—I recalled that Morelli had complained about them.

I felt sick, and considerably more in need of rum than Trentini. I should have reported Morelli forty-eight hours earlier; Vanetti urged me to, but I still had hopes of getting the authentic *Enzian Story*. Elaborateness deputizes for completeness, and detail for authenticity—one of Vanetti's basic principles. Me, I only invent a story when I have to. It never occurred to me that Morelli might kill someone else. I thought he'd retired, but then, murder isn't pensionable.

"Can I see his room?" I asked.

"It's locked," said Trentini. He made an exception, though. For old rum's sake.

The room was no different apart from the floor. There were patches of wet, fragments and splinters of glass. No one had swept them up.

"He smashed his aquarium," said Trentini. "Putting on an insanity act, I suppose."

"Maybe it wasn't an act," I said.

"He must have cut his hand," said Trentini, brilliantly. "The towel was soaked with blood." He meditated. "You might be able to help me."

He left me alone in the room, but reappeared almost at once with a remarkable object in his hand. A tiny coffin fashioned out of cigar-boxes, hexagonal, first-class workmanship. Affixed to it, a cross cut from shiny black paper. Inscription: *Requiescant in pace*.

"Can you explain that?" asked Trentini.

There were dead fish in the coffin. Angel Fish, Paradise Fish, Swordtails—he'd shown them to me in the aquarium but I'm still no expert. Now they were packed on top of each other like canned sardines. The stench was deplorable.

"He couldn't take it with him," I said.

Trentini didn't understand.

I thought of driving back to Rome and going to ground until take-off time. I dismissed the idea at once. Always choose the boldest of two alternatives and the other takes care of itself. Vanetti was sick and Francesco with his light of love. Meanwhile I stood there holding a box of dead fish. End of an aquarium.

I almost knocked Canonica over beside the porter's desk. A victorious general surrounded by his staff, red-cheeked with triumph and cold. A modern painting: *Pickled Gherkin in Red.* He behaved as if I didn't exist. At least twenty reporters, all *paparazzi* from Rome. I stole half Canonica's limelight, which was some consolation. A few of the brethren actually brought themselves to congratulate me. My stomach heaved and the rum came up. I asked for details without giving away how little I knew. Her name was Agnese.

Suddenly Canonica said, "I want a word with you, Bossi." No Signor.

We went outside, across the road.

"You've got a brand-new murder on your conscience," he said.

"How do you figure that out?" I said.

"You shielded the murderer for weeks," he said.

"You flatter me," I said. "If you didn't know, how was I to?"

He said, "You plied him with money. You visited him four times, here in Foce Verde."

"He was working for us," I said.

"How did you meet him?" he asked.

"He volunteered to write his memoirs for us," I said.

"Since when has *Quest' Ora* been a literary review?" he asked, sarcastically.

"He told us he was a multiple killer," I said.

Canonica hadn't expected that. He paused beside the fence enclosing the basket-ball pitch.

"You didn't believe him, of course," he said.

I said, "I hoped he was telling the truth, but I thought he was conning us." I couldn't resist saying it. "With you, people deny that they're murderers; with us, they try and sell themselves as such. There are three self-confessed killers to every unsolved murder. Con-men copy their confessions from newspaper reports."

"You investigated the Pisenti case," he said.

"Quite so," I said. "All the evidence was against him—or for him, whichever you prefer. I don't have to tell you that. After all, you didn't unearth anything yourself."

"I didn't have the benefit of the murderer's confession," he said.

It isn't wise to volunteer anything to the authorities, but I said, "The only story which could have been checked easily, he never gave us." I was on firm ground with Hertha Enzian.

"That time in Lubriano," Canonica said. "You mentioned a collaborator. Was Morelli under contract to you?"

"Of course," I said. "You can inspect his signature if you like."

Canonica went over to the hotel to speak to his sidekicks. A match had started on the basket-ball pitch. I pretended to watch with extreme interest.

When Canonica came back I said, "Why did you issue the warrant so late? You might have been able to prevent the murder."

His face became more naturalistic: the pickled gherkin turned green. He said, "You don't know when I issued the warrant, nor when Agnese di Doninelli was murdered. It wouldn't surprise me to hear that you'd helped him to escape."

"That's slander," I said. "Why make trouble for yourself unnecessarily?"

"You seem to take it for granted that he's out of reach," he said. "His arrest can only be a matter of hours."

"I'll give you a tip," I said. "Comb the coast."

He asked what had given me that idea. I told him it would take a lot to separate Morelli from his fish. "According to him, water is the only thing that makes dry land tolerable. He wrote a long chapter on the subject. I cut it. You can see the original manuscript."

He acted as if my tip meant nothing to him. "You called on his mother," he said.

I repeated that I'd been looking for evidence. "His mother says he's a genius. You can read it for yourself in the eighth instalment."

We crossed the road. The other reporters watched us hungrily, frightened that I was going to hog every last scrap of information Canonica had to offer. Envious people don't stop to wonder what they're envious of.

"You printed the series before you denounced him," said Canonica.

"At our own risk," I said. "There's news value in a man who claims responsibility for three murders, even if he isn't the murderer."

"You could have touted his photograph round the Via Sicilia," said Canonica.

"The sooner you find Morelli the better for me," I said. "He's my star defence witness. He hated me more than he feared you." That was the unvarnished truth. "He never confessed to the Enzian murder," I went on. "Why should I have shown his picture round the Via Sicilia, anyway? You can be responsible for the next murder. You're just as familiar with the killer's identity as I am, now. Know something, Canonica?" It was my turn to leave out the Signor. "You're a great detective and you've proved it—which reminds me, when you write your memoirs don't go giving them to *Lui e Lei*. On the other hand, you don't know the first thing about the Press. You've got a complex, that's your trouble. One murderer in two writes his memoirs, either before he's locked up or afterwards."

"The law doesn't recognize prescriptive rights," he said.

I didn't feel like explaining that prescriptive rights are an integral part of the law. Canonica will have to get used to the idea. Or he might prefer to stick to his principles—in retirement. Morality is designed for old-age pensioners.

"Just between the two of us," I said, "where would you be without the Press? I've done half your work for you. There's more in this week's *Quest' Ora* than you'd have found out in a month of Sundays. A confession, carriage paid. The police can extort confessions but they can't buy them. Extortion is obsolete. I promised Giannini the whole manuscript before publication." I mentioned Giannini deliberately.

"Don't rely on prescriptive rights," he said, with the obstinacy of all old men. "You told Christa Sonntag you knew who the murderer was. You said he was working for you in Madrid."

"You're contradicting yourself," I said. "Why should I have hit on Madrid? It was me who dropped you the first hint that your man might be an author, remember? We were too slow, both of us. I told the Contessa I was groping in the dark only a few days back."

"That was your alibi," he said.

I said, "How was I to know you were using a foreign call-girl as an informer?"

A uniformed police officer came over to us from one of the

patrol cars. He whispered to Canonica, who came to life with a sudden jerk. All he said was:

"*To be continued*—isn't that what you put at the end of your serials? There'll be a sequel to this affair, I promise you that."

"Sounds exciting," I said.

Canonica's threat was only a rearguard action. I climbed into my car. I'd had enough. What's more, I wanted to spend the evening in Rome. I'm leaving the Doninelli case to the dailies. We've got time—the Doninelli girl comes last, after all. I shall groom young Maspoli to step into my shoes. Canonica's too old to be a superintendent, I'm too old to be a crime reporter. It's time to start on something else. Vanetti says I have an unerring instinct. There's no such thing as unerring instinct, nor unerring judgment. Reason has to be given a hearing too, sometimes—reason and instinct, whichever applies. Maspoli can cut his teeth on the Doninelli case. I'll rewrite his material if necessary, otherwise the readers may notice the switch in style. They know nothing and notice everything. All instinct and no judgment.

The fourth murder was superfluous. It would have been smarter to help Morelli escape—then he wouldn't have done it. Canonica doesn't understand. I do have a conscience but it isn't a police-type conscience. Perhaps he'll develop a new conscience too, once he gets his gold watch. I hope he stops prefacing his remarks with "In the old days..." There were conventions in the old days, granted, but they weren't the same conventions. The current convention is that you don't shop a murderer until he's delivered his memoirs. Canonica gets a free subscription to *Quest' Ora* from January first.

It started to rain just before Rome. My mother and Fiorella will have to eat the Christmas goose without me, but I'm glad I'll be installed in the 'plane on Christmas Day. I'll make a good nurse. It's high time people were given new hearts. Their old ones are a dead loss.

Italo Canonica

Saturday, 23rd December. At 1.30 P.M. came the first report that Morelli had been seen in the vicinity of Salerno. The distance factor made it seem unlikely at first. The usual spate of false alarms from all over the country. All that seemed certain was the direction of Morelli's flight: southward. Sifted the probable from the improbable at the carabiniere post in Foce Verde. Growing conviction that Salerno might be correct. Drew in escape route (?) on map. Anzio-Labina-Gaeta, then a zigzag course, partly along the coast, partly inland as far as Caserta. Peasants, taxi-drivers, inn-keepers. A doctor bandaged his (?) hand. He spent the night (?) in Torre del Greco, or, alternatively, moved on during the small hours. We theorized: being in possession of an air ticket from Rome to La Paz, he was heading for Naples with the intention of flying from there to Rome, thus leap-frogging his pursuers as they bore down on him from the opposite direction. Methodical insanity. Alerted police in Naples and district. Returned to Rome by quickest route, radioed instructions to clear road to Fiumicino and hold police 'plane in readiness at Leonardo da Vinci Airport. Landed at Capodichino, Naples Airport, at 4 P.M. Prefect of police reported that suspect had very probably left Salerno. Had apparently been seen on a farm cart near Battipaglia. Puzzling, because it would have meant a retreat from Naples. Obeyed a hunch: left instructions in Naples and drove to Salerno in person. Arrived there at 6 P.M. Report from Battipaglia confirmed, so drove on. Stopped by patrol car five kilometres short of Battipaglia. Carabinieri reported that a man matching Morelli's description had committed suicide at Paestum. No details. Was met on the outskirts of Paestum. Morelli dead. It was 7.22 P.M.

. . . Local police report, Paestum: *Suspect had persuaded Renzo Icardi, 61, farmer, to give him a lift in his cart from Battipaglia. Requested Icardi to stop outside an inn three-and-a-half kilometres south of Battipaglia, on the road to Paestum. Entered the inn and spoke to trainee mechanic Mario Rodoni, 19. "Urgently" requested lift on the latter's motor-cycle. Rodoni was struck by the suspect's unkempt appearance, torn clothing and incoherent speech. Suspect produced a number of large-denomination banknotes. Rodoni declared himself unable to transport suspect's suitcase. Suspect then requested the proprietress, Luigina Calabrigo, 58, to keep his case for him, first removing a large quantity of papers together with what the proprietress took to be an article of woman's underwear. Suspect mounted pillion-seat of motorcycle. Proceedings observed through open window by three* young customers, who laughed because the "old man" looked "funny" on the pillion-seat. Suspect turned and shook his fist. Motor-cycle travelled southward along Route 18 at an average speed of forty-five kilometres per hour. Just after 3 P.M. suspect asked to be dropped on the outskirts of Paestum. Gave Rodoni a ten-thousand-lira note. Situated immediately beside road is a turnstile giving access to enclosed area containing Roman ruins. Suspect approached turnstile and bought ticket, watched by Rodoni. At 3.16 P.M., Battipaglia police station notified us that Luigina Calabrigo's suspicions had been aroused and that she had supplied the registration number of the motor-cycle. The vehicle was halted eight kilometres south of Paestum. The driver stated that he had dropped his passenger at the ruins. Corporal Ricardo Rezzonico, 29, and Carabiniere Eligio Malfanti, 24, drove to the ruins immediately. A number of week-end sight-seers were visiting the site, among them a party of eleven American war veterans who had landed there during the 1943 invasion. Rezzonico and Malfanti discovered the suspect among the ruins of the Temple of Neptune. He had knelt down and was kissing one of the columns, which caused the tourists some amusement. According to subsequent statements, they thought he was rehearsing a film sequence. Suspect then left the Temple of Neptune and walked briskly, though without breaking into a run, towards the low railings that separate the site from the beach, Rezzonico and Malfanti hurried after him but did not call on him to stop, (a) because the warrant stated that he was dangerous and might be armed, and (b) because they assumed that he would in any case be stopped by the railings. They endeavoured to approach the suspect unobserved, concealing themselves behind the temple's thirty-six columns and working their way forward by dodging from one to the other. Both men had removed their safety-catches. The suspect evidently spotted them because he started to run, (a) taking advantage of his lead and (b) trying to seek cover behind the American tourists. He did not react to the carabinieri's challenge. Rezzonico fired two shots into the air but could not aim at the suspect because of the risk to the tourists. Additionally, the suspect described movements with both arms which Rezzonico and Malfanti interpreted as a sign that he wished to surrender. It was later ascertained that he was only scattering papers. With the exception of those which the suspect scattered in the sea, these have since been recovered. The tourists not only failed to heed official instructions but laughed and tried to take photographs of the suspect and his pursuers. This wasted valuable time. Moreover, the suspect negotiated the railings with "surprising agility"—so Carabiniere Malfanti reports—and ran straight into the sea, fully-clothed. He took less than a minute to traverse the beach. Rezzonico challenged him again and fired two more shots, both of which missed. Rezzonico, Malfanti and the tourists are unanimous in stating that the suspect never looked back. As soon as the water was up to his knees he halted, spread his arms wide, and waded slowly out to sea. Since a moderate sea was running, he disappeared almost immediately. He made no visible attempt to save himself, possibly because he was unable to swim. According to a statement made by the American tourist Lowell T. Whittaker, 54, the suspect shouted something just before he disappeared from view, but Whittaker could not distinguish the words. The suspect's head reappeared only once. A search was promptly instituted, but all efforts to recover the body have so far failed.

... Like most police reports, this one does its clumsy and laborious best to whitewash official ineptitude. To be fair, one of the battlefield tourists—what would become of the tourist trade without battlefields and war cemeteries?—did confirm to me that he had not taken the incident seriously. "A criminal marching solemnly into the sea with his head held high? It never happens outside Hollywood!" Another tourist told me that for one moment he had thought the "suspect" was conjuring white doves from his pockets. Pages of the Morelli memoirs, not doves.

... The sheets of manuscript found on the beach effectively demolish my case against Quest' Ora. They include pages carrying a description of Hertha Enzian's murder. There would be no point in demonstrating to the public that the Enzian Story as told by Quest' Ora is completely bogus. Vanetti had to invent the very story he bought, but the irony of that would be lost on everyone. The public would only seize upon the magazine more avidly. In this day and age, a bad reputation is better than none. The dupe is to blame, not those who dupe him. Bossi would claim that "in the one case that mattered" he remained unconvinced of Morelli's guilt until the very last.

377

Sunday, 24th December. Although it was Sunday and Christmas Eve, I spent the entire day at Headquarters. Giannini insisted on holding a press conference at which he buried me in laurels. I had apparently written finis to the "last glorious chapter" in a long career. Human vanity survives the death of others—speak no ill of the dead because the dead have ceased to be dangerous. The papers are hailing me as if I'd discovered radium. My photograph dominates the front pages, usually the preserve of murderers and politicians, and the telephone has never stopped ringing. If only I knew what everyone is congratulating me on! I was too slow—I failed to prevent the murder of Agnese di Doninelli. I even failed to bring her lunatic killer to justice—earthly justice, that is. The most I did was help him on his way to divine justice. I remained a deputy to the very end. We abolished the death penalty; Morelli reintroduced it over my head. "So crime really doesn't pay, eh, Dr Canonica?" How is a policeman supposed to react to such arrant nonsense? Who wants to be told that for every crime solved there are ten which never come to light at all? Or that we must define the people for whom crime doesn't pay? A criminal may punish himself, but what about all those who profit by his crime? The journalists wanted to know what I thought of *Quest' Ora's* "Morelli Story". Giannini replied that the magazine's editorial staff had made a "very creditable" contribution towards solving the multiple murders. I said nothing: the alibi of silence. Schoolboys plan to beat up their teachers after matriculating, but if they don't beat them up before matriculating they never will. I ought to have headed an investigation into Vanetti, not Morelli. Instead of an inglorious success I should have been a glorious failure. Clearly, one only discovers society's Achilles' heel so as to know exactly where not to aim one's spear.

... Late that afternoon I finally found time to start clearing my desk. It was the right day for it—no danger of sentimentality. A man who seals his career with a success excites less pity, so he pities himself a little less too. Desk drawers are treasure-chests of triviality. I found a diploma from a wine-tasters' club. I was very proud when they awarded it to me, but forgot to attend the presentation ceremony when the time came. In one drawer lay a ticket that had belonged to Lorenzetti, the train murderer. It must have fallen out of his file. I concentrated on the case for six

long months, just as whole-heartedly as I did on the Morelli
case. That was three years ago now—I doubt if Morelli will
mean much more to me three years hence. A picture postcard
from Switzerland, from the only other woman I might have
married, some years after Adele's death. I don't know what
became of her. Right at the back of the centre drawer I even
found a cigarette with half the tobacco missing—and I gave up
smoking six years ago. A disgraceful mess, considering my
finicky reputation. Morelli smashed his aquarium because he
didn't want to entrust his fish to strangers. For my part, I'm
satisfied that even the underworld will manage to get on without
me.

...I drove home through the deserted streets. Did myself
some chicken livers in Armagnac, using a recipe in *From the
Parisian Court Kitchen of Catherine de Médicis*. I know the
recipe by heart, of course. Then I got down to wrapping
Christmas presents. They'd been lying there for weeks but I'd
never found the time. I wanted to go to midnight Mass but was
too tired. The bells rang out over the Piazza Navona. I thought
of Adele. She would be overjoyed at my retirement. I feel as if I
were on the threshold of a new home which she furnished for us
long ago.

Monday, 25th December. We had arranged to celebrate
Christmas at Flaminio and Elisa's—or, rather, I had engineered it
by means of discreet blackmail. In the first place, Flaminio and
Elisa are the only ones who haven't produced any children so far.
If we'd celebrated at Pia's, Alfredo's children would have been at
a disadvantage; if we'd celebrated at Alfredo's, the same would
have applied to Pia's. Secondly, Flaminio's ménage is more modest
than the rest, so entertaining us was a feather in his cap. I dealt
Elisa a trump card by passing on the recipe for goose *à la Christa
Sonntag* in strict confidence. The naughty girl was so overwhelmed by her success that she gave the game away. Her
indiscretion had its good side, actually, because the grown-ups
laughed their heads off at the story of my bosom friendship with
a call-girl. The banquet was not without its ghost, however. The
older children had noticed the journalistic encomiums on their
grandfather—the dailies are naturally playing me off against
Quest' Ora—and had thus learned of my retirement. I was
obliged to tell a brazen lie—on Christmas Day of all days: I told

379

them that I was going to become a private detective, and that private detectives were far more efficient anyway, as witness Sherlock Holmes and Hercule Poirot. If it comes to the pinch I shall simply have to invent imaginary cases in future. The children had made a big *presepio*, which I duly admired. The crib had been on display since early that morning, complete with Holy Family, shepherds, and Three Kings—touching old figures which Pia had saved from her childhood. The distribution of presents lasted until nearly lunch-time, and lunch-time until well into the afternoon. Alfredo drove me home and helped me to carry my presents into the flat. If I thought I had earned even a fraction of the love which my children and grandchildren heap me with, my Christian humility would be in bad shape. I had some difficulty in pretending to be equally delighted with every one of my presents. Pia had surpassed herself with an original edition of *Isabella Gonzaga di Mantua's Cookery Book*, published in 1494.

. . . The strangest Christmas present of all was waiting for me outside the door on my return. *With best wishes from Edizioni Vanetti*. A bribe, I thought. It was probably meant as such, but I don't mind bribes of that sort. Xerox copies of Morelli's manuscript, just as he handed it to *Quest' Ora*—probably only part of his entire draft, and fragmentary at that, but what reading! Justification. The desire for self-justification is common to all, even the buffoons of this world. One man justifies himself for his acts, another for his omissions, the first publicly and the second privately. The forensic psychiatrists would have explained Morelli's sexual motives. Hatred of women induced by a first experience of love (?) which left him with a venereal disease? One can't use enough question marks. Crude tools for precision work. Morelli built a rampart of justifications round his sexual-pathological propensities. A complex of motives deputizing for what was really one simple (?) motive. It could be that young people, as seen by Morelli, activated his latent insanity. Equally, of course, he may only have been seeking an alibi for the acts which his insanity forced him to commit. I'm ashamed at how little I knew. A murderer goes about his business, possibly a sex-maniac, possibly unaccountable for his actions. He has to be stopped. He is hunted down and killed: *è finita la commedia*. One's thoughts turn to other things—cribs, children, recipes, family happiness, chiming bells. And then, in the literary remains of Aurelio Morelli, murderer, I found sentences, passages —whole pages, even—which I might have written myself, I, Dr Italo Canonica, Deputy Chief of Homicide, widower, pater-familias, grandfather, custodian of morality, guardian of the State, maintainer of law and order. Calm down, I told myself, you haven't murdered anyone. But is it the accomplished act that matters? Aurelio Morelli may have had a syphilitic father, whereas my father was healthy—is that the only difference? A shiver ran down my spine at the thought that I should have had to appear as a witness if Morelli had been brought to trial. A sex-maniac? Certainly, gentlemen of the jury. But what if the murderer had cross-examined me? What if he had asked me what an ageing man feels when, sound of mind and body, he finds himself thrown on the scrapheap? What if he had asked me if I thought it fair to pillory people as soon as the first wrinkles show? What if he had asked me if the malaise which is enlisted to excuse the sins of youth does not afflict the old as well—if it is really harder to inherit an ailing world than to leave that world without hope of witnessing its recovery? What if he had asked me why rebellion should be the prerogative of youth, when elderly rebels are laughed to scorn? What if he had submitted that the old merit as much pity as the young? You're a sex-maniac, I should have replied. What have my feelings to do with you, a man who has murdered four young people? I confessed all that long ago, he would have retorted. Why am I not being tried by a senile court? If there are juvenile courts there ought to be senile courts. The young are allowed to cite their youth as an extenuating factor. Why shouldn't the grand malady of old age be accepted as a plea in mitigation too? The bells rang out and still I read on, well into the small hours. We shall never cross swords in court, Morelli and I. The guardian of the law will be spared the need to disclose his resemblance to a murderer. By tomorrow I shall have forgotten all about our common features. But I shall never believe that I have put finis to "a last and glorious chapter", neither tomorrow, nor the day after, nor throughout all eternity. Morelli is dead; I am clearing out my desk. According to the reporters, Vanetti is much better. He has great plans afoot, Quest' Ora is unbeatable now, Vanetti is going to invest millions of lire in Positivismo, he's thinking of launching a daily paper. If I were younger I might blame it on the society in which we live, but I don't delude myself: every law is subordinate to another law and every society to another society. Laws are human pyramids, societies are human pyramids, and right at the top, at the apex of the pyramid, precarious but triumphant, trembling and immutable, stands human nature. The Vanettis are always on top.

Carlo Vanetti

To give Maria pleasure, I rose early on Christmas morning, just as I used to in the old days, when Beatrice and Francesco were still children.

Maria had set up the Crib with the help of the household staff and arranged the presents round it. My Christmas present to Maria, a seven-carat solitaire, was a fortunate acquisition made during my Spanish trip. One should always buy jewellery in Spain. *The law of supply and demand dictates a steady appreciation in the value of jewellery, because in troubled times people like to acquire easily portable assets which they can "take with them"*—though I don't know where they would "take them" if they had to. The ring is an excellent investment, not that I am indifferent to its sentimental value. Maria's jubilation proved that I had struck just the right note. *Jewellery retains its popularity because men find a rational excuse for their folly in buying it, while women show off their trophies just as head-hunters' wives flaunt enemy heads severed in their honour. A diamond ring is as much a sex-symbol as a severed head.*

I naturally sent Claretta a handsome present too—as a prelude to farewell, so to speak. Not so cheap as to seem paltry, but not so lavish as to revive her hopes. *Yet another demonstration that mistresses always get the worst of it, which serves them right for becoming involved with married men. The Latin peoples—and they are not alone—like to poke fun at cuckolds and deceived wives; it would be far more realistic, as well as more amusing, if they mocked the deceivers. When I remember the number of times I was forced to disappoint Claretta because I had to take Maria with me on a business trip at the last moment! Maria's bout of pneumonia prevented me from seeing Claretta for three*

SILENT NIGHT

whole weeks; the reverse could never have happened. Who cuts a more ridiculous figure, the man who catches his wife in bed with her lover, or the naked Lothario who has to scuttle out on to the freezing balcony? Most mistresses are dependent upon a woman who is a complete stranger to them. And as for false hopes! A man deserts his wife either in the first six months of a new affair or not at all. The deceived mistress gets a mink stole for Christmas instead of a solitaire. Mistresses are for giving treats to; when it comes to capital investment, they're non-starters.

It was a radiant morning, and the December sun was strewing gold ducats over the wall-to-wall carpet. After taking a childish delight in her ring, Maria abruptly donned a funereal expression. Unfair it may be, but men can't endure sick people and sad women. I found it easy enough to fathom her thoughts: a middle-aged couple whose fledgelings had flown the nest. However, I found her remark over breakfast—"We're alone together for the first time, Carlo, do you realize that?"—utterly uncalled for, in the first place because she knows I mustn't get over-excited, and in the second place because Nature ordains that young birds abandon the nest as soon as they're fledged.

Being consistently honest with myself, however, I have to admit that I was deeply affected by Beatrice's absence. She had to drive her snow-brained swain to St Moritz because that is where he instructs rich American women in the ridiculous art of tottering uncertainly on two strips of wood instead of standing four-square on their two flat feet. The Swiss are overdoing it when they import fashionable foreign labour as well as the menial variety. Maria ascribes it all to modern standards of up-bringing, of course, and claims that in the old days it would have been unthinkable for a girl of good family to spend her holidays alone with a strange man. Perhaps, but it's too late to stop the rot now. *Hypocrisy frightens us more than immorality, although hypocrisy is not so much amoral as a clumsy obeisance before morality. My generation granted its children every freedom, heedless of the fact that children are not guinea-pigs, with the result that they grew up into a younger generation which is quite as much of a disaster as most experiments. Our children are punishing us for the freedom we granted them, one manifestation of this being early marriage. In the old days, the young married man was a fool who assumed financial responsibility for the daughter of a stranger; now, the father is an old fool who looks after a stranger's child as well as his own. It probably makes no difference. Whether you bottle-feed baby lions in your own home or imprison them in a cage from birth, their predatory nature asserts itself sooner or later. Adolescent lions belong in the wild or in a zoo, not at home. No lion ever looked back on its cubhood with a sigh of gratitude.*

I am once again reminded how little we know about our off-spring. I was convinced that Beatrice would marry a prince or a millionaire—preferably a combination of the two—whereas Francesco would end up with some grubby flower-child. And now Francesco has just informed me on the telephone that he plans to marry Ferrari's daughter in February. She occupies such a prominent position in the *jeunesse dorée* that we once published a full-page picture of her—though that was before high society lost its entertainment value.

Not that Ferrari's publishing house would interest me. I know precisely what I make out of Ferrari's print orders, and there can't be much in it for him. Ferrari is a conceited intellectual who doesn't know what to do with his success. *Some people are ennobled by success, like me; others become deformed. No one remains unaffected by it.* Ferrari is exceedingly proud of his firm's 'slant', which is a guaranteed symptom of future bank-ruptcy. *Slant implies angle, and anyone who imagines that he can get by on one angle is blind to the rigours of competition. Only the wide-angle publisher has any chance of weathering the storm these days.*

One revelation deserves another, so I rewarded Francesco by telling him that I planned to found a book-publishing house of my own. I really could, because it wouldn't be hard to set off any losses on book-publishing against tax—losses only make sense when you can afford them. I didn't mean the idea too seriously, even so. All I want is a bargaining counter. If Ferrari refrains from invading the periodical market I shall refrain from found-ing a book-publishing house which I never intended to found anyway. I told Francesco that I wouldn't consider selling *Positivismo*. He took the news surprisingly well. I linked my refusal with a Christmas present. I plan not only to appoint Francesco editor-in-chief of *Positivismo* but also to give him an interest—say twenty-five per cent, initially. *A newspaper with leftist tendencies can only succeed if the man who edits it shares in the profits. Ill-paid employees fall prey to capitalist ambition, a fact which cannot escape the public's notice in the long run. The only thing which renders Socialism credible is affluence.* I can't help feeling afraid that if Francesco marries the Ferrari girl he will lose touch with progressive youth. If I hadn't wanted to create something revolutionary I could have hung on to Beroglio. Of course, I shall keep a discreet check on Francesco for some time to come. *New ideas can only stem from old men— more so today than ever. The young reproach us for having done everything wrong, but they're too lazy to do things better—or even to specify what they consider to be wrong. You don't clear away muck by squatting on it. Passive resistance isn't revolutionary, it's just an excuse for inactivity. Young people of today treat their elders as critics treat the creative artist.*

The house is empty and the Crib stands in the drawing-room as if it had been left there and forgotten one Christmas morning when the children were still children. Francesco telephoned last night and again this morning—independence makes the heart grow fonder, apparently. Beatrice also promised to ring again, but she must have forgotten. My relationship with Beatrice was almost lover-like, which is why it took no more than a ski instructor to oust me. Francesco never loved me, which is why he's learning to respect me.

I got dressed after my afternoon nap, for the first time since my illness. It was like a new lease of life, because even the most virile man feels old in dressing-gown and slippers. I drank a cup of coffee with Maria, but nothing could dispel my boredom and impatience. *The institution of marriage does not stand condemned by the bad marriage, which is merely an unfortunate accident. What really condemns the institution of marriage is the good marriage. The good marriage resembles a chronic disease which you neglect to treat because its symptoms are too mild to cause alarm.* I wandered through the house, which struck me for the first time as too big. I wondered whether a childless couple—all elderly couples are childless—really needed such a large house. The larger the house, the less one partner respects the privacy of the other. I'm afraid that I shall keep on bumping into poor Maria, now the place is so empty. It was growing dark outside, and Beatrice still hadn't telephoned. Above all, though, I was upset at not having heard from Bossi. He ought to have remembered that anxiety is prejudicial to my cardiac condition.

I sat down by the fireplace and leafed through the Christmas number for the hundredth time. It ought to be headlined *He was Hertha Enzian's Murderer* instead of *How I Murdered Hertha Enzian*, but the placards are already printed. Inconsiderate of Morelli to do what he did.

An old fisherman in Portofino once said to me: "I've had a lot of troubles in my life, but most of them never happened." I know what he meant. If it hadn't been for the Morelli affair I should never have had a coronary—and there were no grounds for apprehension in the first place.

From the authorities' point of view, it is far more beneficial for murderers to record their memoirs in writing before being arrested rather than afterwards. Even if one fails to catch a murderer, one should at least be able to profit by his recorded experiences. The recollections of murderers who have confessed, on the other hand, are quite uninteresting. Men of the latter category do not possess the requisite objectivity. Ideally, of course, criminals should be able to sell their crimes before committing them. A potential murderer-for-gain who sold his memoirs might never get round to enriching himself by violent means at all. Again, if politicians, revolutionaries, and generals were given an opportunity to write about their diplomatic campaigns, subversive schemes, and sanguinary battles before they were launched, executed, or waged it would be possible to eliminate political miscalculation, civil disorder—even war itself. There is nothing absurd in this idea. Everyone knows that predicted revolutions never take place. How much less likely a revolution that has already been described in detail! Where murderers are concerned, the publication of their memoirs is a public service of the first magnitude. Their despicable acts are fully publicized in court as it is, so there can be no talk of discretion. On the contrary, court-room reports are not subject to any form of censorship, whereas organs of the Press are at liberty to pass statements exclusively commissioned and paid for by themselves through the filter of morality. Take Morelli, for instance. As presented by "Quest' Ora", his actions are simply murders committed by a sex-maniac, and cannot fail to revolt any normal reader. On the other hand, his motives might commend themselves to an impressionable mind. Ergo, we have suppressed them.

It was only my over-sensitive conscience which alerted me to the possibility that our motives might be impugned and an attempt made to turn the Morelli memoirs into a trap. Agnese di Doninelli's murder was deplorable, of course—her father is a respected figure—but at least the crime has been solved. Without our co-operation it might have remained unsolved, thereby undermining authority and encouraging further crimes of violence. The police are fully aware how much they owe us, even if we do have to forgo public recognition. Moralists, so-called, are old-fashioned people who refuse to grasp that increased freedom goes hand in hand with a more liberal interpretation of morality. They indulge their middle-class ethics by remarking, spitefully, that little fish hang while big fish go free. This inflammatory pandering to the prejudices of the average citizen dates from an undemocratic era when the complaint still held good. It has fortunately been superseded. Democratic justice now prevails—nobody hangs these days, big fish or little.

Despite such soothing reflections, I still find it impossible to insulate myself against all forms of mental excitement. I paced up and down, gripped by a mounting anxiety that the pressure of events might have given Bossi cold feet. What Bossi lacks is Francesco's revolutionary background. He tries to compensate for his inhibitions—I've noticed it before.

My nerves are still on edge, that's what it is. I shall spend three weeks on the Riviera in January, which ought to strengthen Francesco's self-confidence as well as my own constitution. I have managed to secure Nurse Birgitte's services in a private capacity, a fact which should not only reassure my family but facilitate my return to a normal mode of existence. Accustoming oneself to the unusual may be easier than returning to normality. I naturally sent Birgitte a crocodile handbag for Christmas. When a man enjoys my social status, nothing can pave the way for an affair better than a crocodile handbag, which is expensive enough to rate as a generous gift but not so expensive that it cannot be improved on—if necessary.

It was nearly six, and I was just about to retire uneasily to bed when a call from Bossi set an agreeable seal on what had otherwise been a rather depressing Christmas Day.

Bossi appreciates my having entrusted him with the Australian assignment—that much is obvious. However, he won't be able to bank on a percentage this time. It's unhealthy to spoil employees by giving them a personal interest and lulling them into an illusion of independence. What's more, Bossi earned more from the *Enzian Story* than he deserved. Above all, though, the Australian story is my very own project, and one which not even illness could prevent me from organizing with my customary care.

A splendid scheme, this, and it gives me great satisfaction to be associated with such a progressive venture, however indirectly. Professor Stephen Conning, the Australian surgeon, proposes to transplant a human heart—in other words, to replace the failing heart of a doomed patient with a sound heart taken from a dead man. This is not only a heroic scientific feat which will open up entirely new perspectives; it is also an experiment which like all experiments—and most heroic feats—requires a considerable financial outlay. Professor Conning, a forward-looking young man who recognizes the value of publicity, intends to found a private clinic complete with its own heart-bank. It is only natural, therefore, that he has accepted tenders from a number of international magazines for the publication of his memoirs. A few weeks ago the Italian rights might have been offered to *Lui e Lei*, but we have finally routed that bungling rag with the *Morelli Story*. Gone are the days when I was satisfied with a good story that carried an American copyright. As I've demonstrated to the younger members of my staff yet again, exclusiveness is what counts. I have secured permission for our man—the tried and trusty Bossi—to be the only journalist present at the operation. To eliminate unnecessary fuss, which might harm the patient and alert our competitors, Bossi will observe the sensational proceedings in the guise of a nurse. This was tricky to arrange because I had to secure the patient's consent. I have bought his memoirs too. If he dies, his wife will write them.

Francesco produced some really admirable pictures of the murderer—the New Year number will carry a shot of Morelli beside the Fiume Astura, a temporary departure from my usual principle, which is to reserve the front cover for feminine pulchritude. A great shame Francesco couldn't have gone to Sydney—I'd have preferred him to take on this important assignment too—but young Spagnoli must win his spurs. I've instructed him to photograph Bossi as well as the operation. The public will find the spectacle of a stocky little reporter in nurse's uniform quite as intriguing as the operation itself. The Americans have taught us that human interest is of paramount importance, and pictures of Bossi will be the best way of proving that *Quest' Ora* was on the spot. Ever since the triumph of television, virtually nothing has happened without the public being on the spot. Our heart-transplant story will beat everyone to the draw —television, competitors, and public.

There's a certain disadvantage in being deprived of the faithful Bossi for a spell, but I shall have to make the best of it. The trouble is, no one can tell when a heart suitable for transplantation will turn up. Birth can be forecast, but death remains as unpredictable as ever. When—thanks in no small measure to my help—medical science makes still further strides and hearts are stored in the same way as blood plasma is today, the element of chance will have been eliminated.

Bossi telephoned as late as he did because his 'plane to Sydney had been delayed five-and-a-half hours. The poor boy spent the whole of Christmas Day at the airport. He was very upset, but I assured him that they would never start the operation before his arrival. Mankind has been waiting for this *tour de force* from Adam and Eve onwards, so a couple of hours either way can hardly matter.

I retired to bed in a calmer frame of mind. The anxiety which had been crippling me since the early days of the Morelli affair subsided. I face the future with a clear conscience and unalloyed optimism. Most heart cases suffer a second coronary, but it isn't inevitable.